WHISPERED KISS

Chase gazed down at her, drawing her close to his chest. "I need you, Maggie," he said.

Maggie. Margaret smiled at the nickname. No one had called her that since she was a little girl. "Why did you call me that?" she asked.

"Margaret's too formal—too staid. You've got depths within you, Maggie. Depths that haven't been tapped yet."

Suddenly, his smile faded. Margaret knew he was going to kiss her; she also knew that she wouldn't protest when he did.

When he lowered his head, capturing her lips with his own, her knees weakened. The touch of his lips, the musky scent of his skin, mingling with the taste of tobacco that lingered, the feel of his mustache, much softer than she could have imagined, sent her senses soaring.

Her heart pounded. When he kissed the pulsing hollow at the base of her throat, her cheeks, her forehead, the embers of desire banked dormant within her flared into a raging inferno of passion. . . .

MILLIE CRISWELL
TEMPTATION'S FIRE

Best Wishes
Millie Criswell

ZEBRA BOOKS
KENSINGTON PUBLISHING CORP.

To the memory of my mother,
Nicky,
a strong and courageous woman
who epitomized what a true heroine is all about.
I will miss you.

ZEBRA BOOKS

are published by

Kensington Publishing Corp.
475 Park Avenue South
New York, NY 10016

First printing: June, 1992

Printed in the United States of America

Chapter One

The tall man shifted wearily in the saddle; the well-worn leather creaked in response to the sudden movement. Removing the red bandanna from around his neck, he wiped the sweat staining his brow while leaning forward to survey the town from his position atop the rise.

Overhead, the relentless orange sun beat down mercilessly on the parched, shimmering Arizona desert. The arms of the tall saguaro cactus thrust upward toward the heavens, as if to beg for mercy from the unrelenting heat.

In the distance for as far as the eye could see, the desert blazed with May color. The yellow-gold blooms of the paloverde trees mixed harmoniously with the white, waxy flowers of the saguaro. Pink-hued mountains jutted forth against a palette of azure blue sky.

It was a beautiful and breathtaking vision, but one that Chase Gallagher chose to ignore. Taking a sip of water from his canteen, he wiped his mouth with the back of his hand, then soaked the neckerchief, mopping his face with the warm, wet rag.

The squat, white-washed adobe and ramshackle wooden buildings he observed in the distance gave credence to the name so fittingly bestowed upon the town: Purgatory—a living hell if ever he'd seen one.

Drawing a ragged breath, Chase wondered how he'd ever let Tom Fraser talk him into filling the vacant marshal's job left by Tom's upcoming retirement. He and Tom had been friends for years, but even as close as they were, he wasn't sure their friendship warranted this kind of sacrifice. To end his career in a two-bit town like Purgatory, after Abilene, Dodge City, Omaha and a slew of others whose names blurred in his memory, seemed a mockery of his life's work.

Purgatory. The end of the line. The last vestige of the Wild West that, in the year 1887, was wild no more.

There would be few challenges to face—few outlaws to contend with for a United States marshal whose only job was to keep the peace among poor Mexican peasants and white Christian town folk. Even Geronimo, chief of the Chiricahua Apaches, had surrendered a year ago, putting an end to the Apache wars.

Why couldn't it have been Tucson, which sat only twenty miles to the southeast, or Phoenix, farther north? Why did it have to be Purgatory? He shook his head, his lips twisting into a sneer.

With a click of his tongue and a nudge of his knees, he urged the big black stallion into a trot, descending the rocky, sand-covered trail that would bring him to his new home.

6

* * *

With her teeth clenched in concentrated study, Margaret Parker examined the angry gash on Wooley Burnett's right forearm. Satisfied that the neatly wrought stitches would hold, she applied the salve and white gauze dressing, tying the ends of the bandage together to bind the wound.

Stepping back to admire her handiwork, she smiled in satisfaction at the bewhiskered deputy. "That should do it, Wooley." She brushed back the stray wisps of chocolate brown hair that had escaped from her bun. "And next time, stay out of Concita's way when she's angry. You know she can wield a mean knife when she's a mind to."

Smiling to display teeth yellowed by years of neglect and chewing tobacco, Wooley nodded, spitting a stream of foul-smelling tobacco juice into the brass spittoon near Doc Watson's examining table.

"That woman's been a thorn in my side since the day I up and hitched myself to her. I'm much obliged, Miss Margaret. I don't rightly know what I'd have done if you hadn't been a-willin' to tend my arm, seeing as how Doc's off birthin' another one of Kate's young'ns." He shook his head. "I swear that woman's fertiler than a cornfield full of fresh manure."

Replacing the stopper into the amber bottle of antiseptic and setting it carefully back in the wooden cupboard that housed Doc's medicines, Margaret bit back her smile, though she had difficulty repressing the pink blush dotting her cheeks. She should be used to Wooley's outrageous remarks after all these years; he

7

always had a comment to make about everything. The "Town Philosopher," that's what Doc called him.

In Kate Ferguson's case, Wooley was right. The woman had given birth to eight babies in the last nine years, and at the rate she was going, Kate would be worn out before she turned thirty. A twinge of envy tugged Margaret's heart. At least Kate would know the joys of motherhood before she died, she thought dejectedly.

Turning her attention back to the deputy, who was examining the bandage she had just applied, she finally replied, "You're quite welcome, Wooley. Just remember to keep that bandage dry until your arm heals. And be sure to change it frequently. No sense letting infection set in after all my hard work."

Rolling down his sleeve, Wooley eased himself off the table. "This town'd be lost for sure without you, Miss Margaret. I guess you've sewn all of us up at one time or another."

"I do what I can to help when Doc's not around." She rinsed out the bloody bandages she had left soaking in the basin and heaved a sigh. At least nursing was a suitable avocation for a spinster. And at twenty-six, with her prospects decidedly dim, there was little hope of changing her situation. Nursing seemed as good a chore as any. She'd been doing it long enough. Eight years. Ever since her mother had taken to her bed with a never-ending series of ailments and complaints.

"You goin' to the dance Saturday night? It's a retirement party of sorts for Tom Fraser."

Margaret smiled wistfully. A dance. She hadn't gone to a dance in years. Why, she had probably forgotten

8

how to dance. "I doubt it. With mother ill . . ." She shrugged, her words trailing off.

"Marshal Tom be mighty upset iff'n you wasn't there to bid him farewell, Miss Margaret. You know he's always taken a shine to you."

Avoiding Wooley's stare, Margaret busied herself rolling the pile of clean gauze strips that sat on the wooden counter. She felt her cheeks warm. Everyone in town knew of Tom Fraser's relentless pursuit of Margaret Parker. They'd been betrothed once—a lifetime ago—until her mother's illness had consumed Margaret's every waking moment, leaving little time for two young sweethearts to pursue a romance.

Tom had been patient for a while, but even his patience had run out in the face of Phoebe Parker's ill-tempered humor. It hadn't taken Tom long to find someone else—someone more available. He had married Betsy Gates three years ago. A union that, surprisingly enough, Margaret heartily approved of. Tom's happiness meant a lot to her, and he was very happy with Betsy.

Setting aside the neatly rolled bandages, she inhaled deeply of the familiar scents of antiseptic, sulfur, and the lingering odor of Doc's pipe tobacco. "I'll try to come, Wooley, but I can't make any promises. It's hard to find someone willing to stay with mother." She thought of Lupe, their high-spirited housekeeper, but immediately dismissed the idea. It was doubtful Lupe would be willing to give up a Saturday night.

Shifting the chaw of tobacco from one side of his mouth to the other, Wooley spit another stream of the brown liquid, his lips thinning in disgust. Phoebe

9

Parker. No one wanted to be around that witch. She was cursed. How she had managed to give life to a kind woman like Margaret was a mystery to him. He scratched his peppered beard, which most folks likened to lamb's wool, before turning toward the door.

"I'd best be mosey'n along. We're expectin' the new marshal to arrive anytime, and there's a pile of paperwork I've been meaning to get out."

"Well, let's hope Tom's replacement turns out to be as fine a man as Tom."

Wooley paused, his bushy brows furrowing in dismay. "I wouldn't count on it, Miss Margaret. I hear-tell Chase Gallagher's about as mean and ornery as they come. The Mexs call him, El Diablo de Ojos Plata—the Silver-Eyed Devil. He's got a reputation as long as the Grand Canyon and enough notches on his gunbelt to back it up. He ain't goin' to be an easy man to work with."

"You shouldn't repeat idle gossip, Wooley. It isn't fair to prejudge a man you haven't met."

"Maybe so, but Hank Waller was in Abilene back in '76 when Gallagher took down the Colter gang single-handedly. He says there weren't enough of them varmints left for the undertaker to scrape up."

Margaret's soft brown eyes rounded in horror at the image Wooley's words conjured up. She abhorred violence of any kind. Life was too precious to waste. Lord knows she'd wasted enough of her own.

"Sorry, ma'am," Wooley apologized, staring sheepishly down at the toes of his dusty boots. "Guess I got carried away. Well, leastways we ain't got no outlaws around here to worry about, unless you count old

Greybeard, that drunken Apache who wanders off the San Carlos reservation from time to time. Most likely, Marshal Gallagher's going to be plumb bored."

Bored. He'd been in town less than six hours and already he was bored to death, Chase thought, listening inattentively while Tom Fraser caught him up on the caseload.

Caseload. That in itself was a joke. Two pigs were missing from Elvira Thornburg's farm; a drunken Indian, who had busted the mirror at the End of the Trail Saloon, was sleeping it off in one of the empty cells in the back; and Lester Barnsworth had reported that his wife had run off with a traveling drummer. Hardly fodder for the folks at nearby Yuma Territorial Prison. He rocked back in the old wooden swivel chair which was positioned behind an equally old beat-up oak desk in Tom's office—his new office, he amended silently.

"Are you listening, Chase? I asked if you were free to have dinner with Betsy and me tonight?"

Chase rocked forward, his tooled black leather boots hitting the wooden planks of the floor with a thud. He noted the question in Tom's blue eyes, the concern, and felt a twinge of guilt. It wasn't Tom's fault that there was little need for a lawman in a land that was no longer lawless.

Forcing a smile, Chase smoothed the ends of his black mustache with his right thumb and forefinger. "Sounds good. I need to settle in at the hotel first. Wash some of this desert off." He swatted his pant leg,

11

throwing up a billow of dust to make his point. "What time you want me?"

"About seven. Chase . . ." Tom paused, perching himself on the edge of the desk. He hadn't missed the indifference in Chase's eyes. Had he been wrong in suggesting that Chase come to Purgatory? Chase was a loner—had been since they'd met. And though they were close, there was always a part of Chase that he kept to himself. But they were friends and Tom knew he had to try.

"I know Purgatory isn't quite what you expected. With the silver boom gone, it's just another sleepy town. I realize it lacks the excitement and challenge of Dodge City or even Tombstone, but give it a chance. You can make a good life here. You're not a kid anymore. It's time you settled down—time you hobbled that wandering itch you have."

Chase's right eyebrow arched; he pushed his Stetson back on his head, revealing ebony hair that was just beginning to gray at the temples. "I'm only thirty-five, for Christ's sake, Tom. I'm hardly ready for a rocker." Though the damned swivel chair he sat in could probably pass for one!

"I've known you a long time, Chase. I know there's something driving you—something that makes you restless, remote."

A cold mask descended over Chase's face. The clear gray eyes hardened into two silver dollars. "You don't know what you're talking about." He pushed himself out of the chair, pretending to study the outdated wanted posters on the back wall. The young face of Billy the Kid stared back at him. He shook his head.

The Kid had been killed by Pat Garrett six years ago.

"I won't press you, Chase. Just remember, I'm here if you want to talk." Tom crossed to the door, grabbing his hat off the wooden rack. "I'll leave you to get acquainted with your new job. Wooley Burnett, your deputy, will be along soon. He can answer any questions you may have. I'll see you at seven. And don't be late. Betsy frowns on tardiness."

Chase waited until the door slammed shut then swung about on his heel. Damn, but Tom was too sharp for his own good. Pulling a small leather pouch of Bull Durham tobacco and a prayer book of papers out of his vest pocket, he rolled himself a cigarette and lit it, drawing the aromatic smoke into his lungs.

Tom's assessment was more accurate than even Tom realized. He was driven—had been for more than eighteen years—and he had no intention of giving up. Not now. Not when the object of his quest was so close at hand.

Parker. Jack Parker. The name filled him with loathing and rage. The man had a lot to answer for: three lives to be exact. And he would leave no grain of sand, no clump of sagebrush, no boulder unturned that the slimy bastard could crawl under, until Gentleman Jack Parker was dead.

"Margaret! Margaret!"

Like the shrill, piercing cry of a crow, Phoebe Parker's voice split the stillness of the late afternoon.

Bent over the cookstove, Margaret paused, setting the wooden spoon down beside the copper pot of

13

rabbit stew she was stirring. Casting a quick glance at Lupe, who sat at the wooden work table peeling a pile of carrots and potatoes and looking blatantly relieved that it wasn't her name that had been called, Margaret dried her hands on the white apron around her waist and hurried out of the stifling kitchen to answer the summons.

Wiping her forehead with the sleeve of her calico dress, she ascended the steps to the second floor, barely noticing the torn and faded yellow wallpaper lining the stairwell or the well-worn runner beneath her feet.

The house had become an inferno, and she fervently wished for a soak in a tub of tepid water to cool off.

"Margaret, did you hear me? I said it's time for my medicine."

A resigned expression covered Margaret's face. The bath would have to wait. *Yes, Mama, I hear you,* she answered silently. Everyone within five miles probably had. Pushing open the door to Phoebe Parker's bedroom, Margaret entered to find her mother propped against the shiny brass headboard. Her pinched face was red with the exertion of her screams; her mouth was turned down in a habitual frown. The blue forget-me-nots on the wall behind her mother's head looked as wilted as Margaret felt at the moment.

"Where have you been, you worthless child? I could have died in the time it took you to get up here."

Margaret fought the urge to groan. Her mother was always on the verge of death—had been for the last eight years—her mysterious ailment coinciding with the disappearance of a husband who had taken off one day, never to return.

Margaret had reconciled herself to the loss of her father. And though it still hurt to think of the way he had run out on them, she couldn't blame him . . . not really. He'd been a quiet man with simple tastes, saddled with an extravagant, domineering wife who complained constantly. Knowing firsthand what his life had been like, she couldn't condemn him. If only her mother could face the fact that Jonathan Parker was not coming back, things would be so much easier.

Walking to the window, Margaret threw open the tattered lace curtains to allow some light to enter the room, then turned to face her mother. "I was fixing supper, Mama. Rabbit stew. Are you hungry?"

"Stew again? Why can't we have chicken? I like fried chicken."

Staring at the mounds of flesh that had accumulated on the petulant woman's body over the last eight years, Margaret didn't need to be reminded that her mother liked fried foods. If there was one thing Phoebe hadn't lost in the last eight years, it was her appetite.

"We had fried chicken last night. Don't you remember?"

"I don't care. I hate rabbit stew!" Phoebe crossed her arms over her corpulent chest. "I won't eat a bite. I'll just waste away and die, then you'll be sorry."

Reaching for the silver-handled brush that rested on the nearby walnut dresser, Margaret brushed her mother's gray-steaked, brown hair with long, soothing strokes, purposely ignoring the mutinous set of her chin. "You mustn't upset yourself so, Mama. You'll make yourself ill."

"Stupid girl! I am ill. Why do you think I stay in this

bedroom all day long? I swear, you're not only homely, you're stupid as well."

Margaret flinched at the unkind assessment of her looks. She knew she wasn't pretty and it didn't help to have her mother constantly remind her of that fact. Taking a deep breath, she continued her ministrations. "Doc Watson says your illness is all in your head, Mama. He says there's nothing wrong with you."

"There is!" Phoebe insisted loudly, clutching at the frilly, white ruffles edging the front of her nightgown. "That fool wouldn't know a sick person if he saw one. The man's not fit to treat a dog."

Bristling with indignation, Margaret bit the inside of her cheek to keep from replying. Doc Watson was one of the kindest, most caring men she had ever known. He was a fine doctor, but if Phoebe Parker was too stubborn to admit it, she wasn't going to waste her breath trying to convince her. Disagreeing with her mother never solved anything. She hadn't won an argument with her in the last eight years.

An hour later, Margaret found herself back in the kitchen, seated at the round oak table. The kerosene lanterns had been lit, lengthening the shadows now descending over the desert landscape.

Staring absently at the rabbit stew in front of her, she trailed the spoon back and forth through the thick chunks of meat and vegetables, her appetite gobbled up by her mother's venomous tongue.

"Why don't you eat, señorita? You will make yourself ill," Lupe admonished, standing over Margaret like a sentinel, her hands braced on her slender hips.

Looking up, Margaret forced a small smile to her lips as she returned the militant housekeeper's gaze. She and Lupe were nearly the same age, but Lupe's worldliness made her seem years older. Not that Lupe looked older. With her flowing black hair and flawless brown skin, Lupe was a beautiful woman. Many men vied for the favors of the flirtatious housekeeper, and Lupe disappointed very few. She was vain, volatile, and extremely loyal. Margaret couldn't have asked for a better friend.

"I'm not very hungry, Lupe. It's too hot to eat." At least there was some truth in that. The temperature had hovered around one hundred degrees most of the day, unseasonably warm for this time of year.

"*Sí*, it is hot, but that is not the reason you do not eat. It is your mama, no? She is lashing at you with that tongue of hers again. I hear her screaming. Why don't you stand up to her? Why do you let her torture you?"

Lupe's black eyes flashed fire as she spoke, her hands waving back and forth like a conductor leading an orchestra as she sought to make her point. Margaret almost smiled at the young woman's vehemence. Lupe's Mexican heritage was never more apparent than when she was angry or upset.

"She's my mother, Lupe. What do you expect me to do? I can't ignore her. She thinks she's ill."

"Bah! She is healthy as a horse and even looks like one, I think. You need to get out of this house. Make some friends. I could introduce you to some handsome *vaqueros.*"

17

"What would your handsome cowboys want with me? I am not pretty like you."

Lupe tossed her head back, the heavy curtain of hair falling about her shoulders like a black lace mantilla. "Who told you such a lie? You are *muy bonita*. You have lovely brown hair, smooth skin, and large, dark eyes. And you are very ... How do you say? *Abundante* ... ample on the top."

Margaret blushed as red as the checkered curtains flapping at the window. The warm breeze floating in only added to her discomfort. "Thank ... thank you. You are very kind."

With her flattened palm, Lupe slapped her forehead in disgust. "I am not kind; I am honest. It is your mother who puts these ideas in your head that you are not pretty. She is the one who is ugly, but her ugliness is on the inside where no one can see."

Margaret knew she should be offended by the things Lupe said about her mother, but she couldn't be. Everything Lupe contended, with the exception of her looks, was right. Phoebe Parker harbored an ugly side to her.

Pushing herself to her feet, Margaret walked to the cast-iron stove, scraping the dish of untouched stew back into the pot. Turning, she smiled softly at the young woman. "I know you mean well, Lupe, and I thank you for your kind words. But I am not able to leave my mother just now. Who would take care of her, if I were to go out as you suggest?" She thought of the dance, of the many dances she had missed, and sighed; it just wasn't to be.

"If you would agree to go out, I would find someone

18

to care for your mother. My own *madre* would be happy to help."

Margaret's eyebrows rose in disbelief. "Do you really think Isabel would be willing to stay with Mama? You know they've never gotten on all that well."

That was an understatement, Margaret thought. Isabel despised the ground Phoebe Parker walked on. And who could blame her? Ten years ago, when Isabel had been housekeeper, Phoebe had accused the faithful servant of stealing a piece of her jewelry. Isabel had repeatedly proclaimed her innocence, but Phoebe would not withdraw the accusation. After a brief investigation, the charges against Isabel had been dropped when the missing brooch in question had been found beneath Phoebe's mattress.

No one, including Margaret, had ever doubted Isabel's innocence, or the fact that Phoebe had purposely tried to frame the poor Mexican woman. The question was *why?* To this day, no one had been able to figure out Phoebe's motive.

"*Sí*, she will do it for me and for you, Margarita."

Her name on Lupe's lips brought Margaret out of her reverie. She turned her attention back to what the housekeeper was saying.

"She worries over you. And I think you already have somewhere in mind to go, am I right?" Lupe smiled at the blush on Margaret's face. Margaret's feelings were like glass—transparent and very fragile.

"Wooley said there's going to be a dance Saturday night to honor Tom Fraser. I would dearly love to go, if I could find someone to take care of Mother."

Throwing her arms around Margaret, Lupe's smile

19

widened. "Leave everything to me. I will arrange for *mi madre* to stay with yours." She fingered the gold cross at her neck, silently praying that her mother would agree. Phoebe Parker had many enemies; Isabel Diaz was one of them.

Margaret's smile suddenly faded. "But, Lupe, what will I wear? I haven't anything suitable for such an occasion." All of the dresses she owned were years out of date. There'd been little necessity to refurbish her wardrobe.

Surveying the faded green calico dress that Margaret wore, Lupe frowned, clucking her tongue in disapproval. *"Sí,* you are right. You will need to buy something new."

"Buy something . . . You know Mother would never allow that."

"Bah! She will never know. Besides, you are the one who earns all the money by helping Doc with his patients. You are the one who sells the eggs to buy the food. I think if you want to buy a new dress, Señora Parker will not object."

Margaret digested Lupe's reasoning, and the more she thought about it, the easier it went down. "You're right. Tomorrow I will go to Taylor's General Store and look for a dress . . . several dresses. It's time Margaret Parker got back to the business of living."

Frowning at his reflection in the mirror, Chase tied and retied the black string hanging around his neck. "Damn!" he swore, yanking on the string to untie the bow for the third time in a row. If there was one thing he hated, it was getting all dandied up to go out. He was much more comfortable in his denims and cottons than in the too-stiffly starched shirt and black broadcloth suit he had on.

The oil lamps hanging on either side of the cracked mirror flickered softly, illuminating his displeasure while reflecting the sparsely furnished room he had acquired at Hobson's Hotel.

The single spool bed was pushed against one wall, its faded blue gingham coverlet offering little to brighten the drab surroundings. No curtain graced the window; a torn, dirty shade hung in its place. There was a dresser, one ladder-back chair and little else. A chipped, blue floral pitcher and bowl rested atop the washstand, a chamber pot beneath the bed.

Engrossed in his efforts, Chase failed to notice the rather ominous-looking spider inching its way toward him, until it crawled up onto his sleeve and was making its way toward his neck. Sighting the bug in the mirror, his heart pounded with uncharacteristic fear. With a quick flick of his hand, he brushed the tarantula to the floor, stomping on it, crushing it beneath his boot heel. Shuddering, he took a deep breath.

"Damn ugly varmints!" He'd rather face a gang of outlaws with guns drawn than one of those hairy creatures. If there was one thing he hated, it was spiders.

"There!" he said, satisfied when the bow finally lay as he wanted. Surveying his appearance, he nodded in satisfaction, tugging at the bottom of his vest. The silver badge inscribed U. S. Marshal winked back at him in approval.

Checking his pocket watch, he noted the time. It was nearly seven. *Betsy frowns on tardiness.* Tom's words picked at his brain, causing him to grimace in disgust. Small wonder he had never married, though he'd come close once when he was young. Women had too many rules and regulations they wanted you to abide by. If he had wanted rules and regulations, he'd have joined the army.

Picking up his black Stetson off the nearby chair, he brushed the silver band with the edge of his sleeve until it shone, settling it atop his freshly washed hair. It had been a long time since he'd shared a proper meal with proper folks. Might as well get going and get it over with. He had faced worse in his lifetime—much worse.

Chapter Two

"I'm not going to any damn party and that's final!" Chase declared, stabbing his finger at the middle of Tom's chest. His voice rang hard, like the cool, salmon-colored bricks that comprised the walls of his office.

The morning sun shone in through the steel bars at the window, casting a striped pattern against the wooden planks of the floor but doing little to erase the chill permeating the room.

"You haven't changed a bit since the last time I saw you in Tombstone," Tom replied, running agitated fingers through his brown, wavy hair. "You're still a pigheaded, stubborn jackass."

"Maybe so," Chase conceded, folding his arms across his chest, "but I'm not going to any party."

Frowning, Tom shook his head. He knew Betsy's idea of inviting Chase to the party tonight was foolish. But once his darling wife took a notion in her head, there was no changing her mind.

Betsy had been so taken with Chase after meeting him at dinner last night, she was bound and determined to "rectify his lonely position as a bachelor," as she had put it. He had tried to explain that Chase wasn't interested in settling down, that Chase wasn't the marrying kind, but Betsy wouldn't hear another word. And so, now, here he was, arguing with a man who had no idea of the insurmountable odds he faced in the form of one Betsy Fraser.

Setting the blue speckled coffeepot on the potbellied stove, Wooley listened to the exchange going on between the two men, wondering if they were likely to come to blows. He hadn't seen Tom this mad in years, not since the night Tom had stormed into the End of the Trail drunker than a reformed preacher and had spilled his guts about Margaret's mother.

Wooley would never forget the hurt in Tom's eyes, nor the look of outrage plastered on his face, when he had explained how Phoebe Parker had summoned him to her house to inform him that she didn't want Tom calling on her daughter anymore. She had explained that Margaret's duty to family came before anything or anyone else.

Tom, being the gentleman that he was and not wishing to cause Margaret any more pain than she already suffered at Phoebe's selfish hands, had reluctantly stepped aside.

But from the determined look on Tom's face now, it didn't look like he had any intention of stepping aside this time.

The smell of freshly brewed coffee filled the air, stealing Wooley's attention. Grabbing the pot before it had a chance to boil over, he poured the steaming liquid into the tin cups, handing one to each of the men.

"I know this ain't none of my business," Wooley

ventured, taking a sip of his coffee, "but it don't seem like you two are making much headway with this argument." And by the stubborn set of both men's chins, it didn't seem likely they were going to any time soon.

"If a man can't count on his best friend to attend his one and only retirement party, who the hell can he count on?" Tom shouted, glaring at Chase.

"Don't blame me 'cause you decided to trade in your badge for a plow. What the hell are you going to grow in this dry, barren land? Cactus?" Chase retorted, seating himself behind the desk.

Tom gave Chase a sidelong look of disgust. "I'm wasting my breath here." He banged the cup down on the desk, causing the coffee to slosh over the rim. Turning to the deputy, he added, "Wooley, I'll see you tonight," before storming out of the office and slamming the door behind him.

"Whooeee! I ain't never seen the marshal so dang riled up before, 'ceptin' when he had that run-in with Phoebe Parker."

Chase's head snapped up from the papers he studied. "Parker. Did you say Parker?"

"That's right, Old Lady Parker." Pausing, Wooley pulled his handkerchief out of the back pocket of his pants, mopping at the spreading coffee stain. "Marshal Tom used to court her daughter, Margaret, before the old biddy put a stop to it."

The silver eyes sparked with interest. "How long ago was that?"

Rubbing his beard while he silently calculated, Wooley replied, "'Bout four ... five years ago, I reckon. Damn shame, too. Not that Mrs. Fraser ain't a fine woman, mind you. But Margaret, now there's a real lady."

"How old is this Margaret Parker?"

"Well, I don't rightly know. She was just a kid when I moved to Purgatory. Let's see, that was twenty years ago, so that should make Margaret . . . about twenty-six, I reckon."

"And is there a Mr. Parker?" Chase waited, tapping the pencil he held against the desktop.

Wooley shook his head. "Not anymore, there ain't. It seems Jonathan Parker took off one day. Nobody's seen hide nor hair of him since. Damn shame, too, the way he lit out leaving Margaret to contend with the old witch."

Chase jumped to his feet, toppling the swivel chair behind him. "How long has Parker been gone?"

Startled by the vehemence in the marshal's voice, Wooley took a step back. "About eight years. It's been a real hardship on Margaret; I can tell you that."

"Eight years," Chase repeated, mentally calculating the time frame. It fit. Parker had fallen off the face of the earth after the holdup in St. Louis eighteen years ago, then suddenly eight years ago he had resurfaced in Waco, Texas as the prime suspect in a bank holdup.

Could Jonathan Parker and Jack Parker be one and the same? Could that be the reason the trail had turned cold near Tucson? He knew he was getting close, but he never dreamt he was this close.

"How come you're so all-fired interested in Jonathan Parker?"

Noting the deputy's questioning gaze, Chase wondered if he should tell him the truth. Wooley was a shrewd old boy. Chase had sensed that right off.

Should he confide his suspicions to the deputy, taking the chance that he might run to Margaret Parker, or wait and see what he could find out tonight at the dance? Damn! He was going to have to go to that blasted party after all.

Pasting on an affable smile, he faced Wooley's curious stare. "I knew a man once down in Wichita. I thought it might be this Parker fella."

"And is it?"

Chase shook his head. "Don't think so. The man I knew wouldn't have been old enough to have a twenty-six-year-old daughter. He was only about thirty-five himself." Noting that Wooley wasn't entirely convinced, he suggested, "Why don't we go over to the saloon and have us a shot of red-eye? If I'm going to that dance tonight, I'd better have some fortification."

Wooley chuckled, his brown eyes glittering with amusement. "So, you've decided to go. Just as well. It wouldn't have been wise to buck Betsy Fraser. She's as single-minded a woman as ever I've met."

Chase groaned, remembering Betsy's concern that he was still a bachelor. "That's what I'm afraid of. There's nothing deadlier than an interfering woman."

"Well for heaven's sake! Margaret Parker. What are you doing here?"

Clutching the lavender-sprigged muslin gown tightly to her chest, Margaret spun on her heel to find Betsy Fraser standing right behind her. "Mercy me, Betsy!" She took a deep breath to stem the wild beating of her heart. "You took ten years off my life. I didn't see you come in."

27

The pretty blonde grinned impishly; the golden curls framing her heart-shaped face bounced beneath the blue-ribboned straw bonnet. "Well, I'm not surprised, the way you was admiring yourself in that mirror." There was a teasing quality to her voice that made Margaret smile and blush all at the same time.

"How you, Mr. Taylor?" Betsy called out to the bespectacled clerk behind the counter. The wiry old man waved back, then resumed stacking the bolts of colorful cloth on the shelf.

Turning her attention back to Margaret, her blue eyes twinkling mischievously, Betsy inquired, "You wouldn't be buying that dress for the dance tonight, would you?"

Knowing a loaded question when she heard one, Margaret hesitated before replying. Every unattached person in town had been the recipient of Betsy's matchmaking at one time or another. She had no intention of falling into that trap again.

The last time, it had been a traveling salesman who sold ladies' undergarments; the time before that, a drummer who had tried to lure her into the back of his wagon on the pretext of showing her his *merchandise*. *Thank you, Betsy, but no thank you,* Margaret said silently, but aloud she replied, "And if I was?" She handed Mr. Taylor a spool of lavender ribbon, instructing him to cut her a length.

Fingering an assortment of fans that rested in a nearby glass case, Betsy smiled innocently. "Why, I would be thrilled. Tom and I always say that you don't get out nearly enough, Margaret. You shouldn't stay cooped up in that house with your mother all the time. It just isn't healthy."

"I have little choice, Betsy. You should know that better than anyone."

Betsy blushed, taking Margaret's hands in her own. "I'm sorry. That was a thoughtless remark for me to make."

Observing the young woman's contrite expression, Margaret sought to reassure her. "Don't be silly. I'm just tired. I was up all night with Mother. She didn't take the news of my going to the dance all that well. It seems it brought on another one of her *attacks.*" It was difficult to stay angry at Betsy. Even if she was a bit thoughtless at times, her heart was always in the right place.

"Why don't you pay for your purchases, and we'll go have us a slice of pie over at the hotel," Betsy offered, seeking to make amends. "Mrs. Hobson makes the most delicious apple pies, and I'm just dying for a piece. It'll be my treat."

Margaret hesitated. "I don't know. I told Lupe I wouldn't be gone too long."

"I have a secret that I haven't told anyone. You'd be the first."

She smiled at Betsy's transparent tactics. They had shared many secrets—many things while growing up: childhood games and fantasies, pubescent crushes on older boys, and finally, Tom. She shook her head at the determined expression on Betsy's face. Arguing with Betsy was almost as difficult as arguing with her mother. "Oh, all right, just one piece, then I have to get back."

Walking down the wooden sidewalk, the heels of

their shoes clicking with each step they took, the two women chatted animatedly, discussing the plans for Tom's party. As they approached the saloon, they lifted their skirts, about to cross the street, when Betsy noticed the dark-haired man who had just stepped out of the saloon onto the sidewalk. He was accompanied by a cheap-looking redhead.

Grabbing Margaret by the arm, Betsy pulled her back against the side of the building.

A shadow of alarm touched Margaret's face. "Betsy! Whatever is the matter?"

"It's him," Betsy whispered, pointing toward the street. "The man with the redheaded woman."

"Him, who?" Margaret's eyes followed the direction of Betsy's finger, widening when they fell upon the tall, black-haired man with the menacing-looking Colt revolver slung low on his hip. Her mouth fell open. The woman, dressed garishly in a bright green satin gown that exposed a great deal of her anatomy, was rubbing his backside in a most provocative fashion, and he seemed to be enjoying it! Margaret's lips pursed in indignation at the vulgar public display. It wasn't difficult to guess what the woman's occupation was.

"Do you know that man?"

"Of course, silly. That's Tom's friend, Chase Gallagher, the new marshal."

"That's the new marshal?" *That womanizing, half-drunk cowboy with a day's growth of beard?*

"Yes. Isn't he gorgeous? I envy that red-haired woman. From the looks of it, he's taking her to bed."

Margaret gasped. "Betsy Fraser! Shame on you. What would your husband say?"

Betsy giggled. "Oh, Tom knows what I think of

Chase. I've already told him."

"Told him! Gracious me, Betsy, you're . . ." Margaret's words caught in her throat when Chase Gallagher picked up the half-naked woman and carted her across the street to Hobson's Hotel. Her heart seemed to jangle as loudly as the silver spurs attached to his boots as she watched the couple disappear into the wooden, two-story building.

"Mrs. Hobson's not going to like Chase bringing a whore into her place," Betsy said, straightening the white eyelet ruffle on the sleeve of her blue gingham dress. "Come on, let's follow. Maybe we'll see some fireworks."

"Are you crazy? I'm not going into that hotel now. Not after . . ."

"Oh, Margaret, don't be such a prude. You're a grown woman for heaven's sake. Men make love to women all the time."

"Well they don't do it in front of me."

Tugging on her friend's hand, Betsy pulled Margaret toward the hotel. "You promised to have one piece of pie and listen to my secret, remember? And besides, they're probably going to be upstairs for hours. From the looks of Chase Gallagher, he won't be easily satisfied."

Betsy's words drummed through Margaret's brain the entire time they were eating their pie, conjuring up images no decent woman would admit to having. She couldn't help the surreptitious glances she cast toward the stairs every time footsteps sounded in the hallway.

They'd been sitting in the dining room of the hotel

31

for over two hours and still the red-haired woman had not come down the stairs. And though she knew she needed to get home, Margaret didn't seem to be able to lift herself out of the chair. What could be taking them so long? she wondered. She'd seen animals mate and knew it didn't require this much time. Perhaps they were sleeping. Perhaps they were . . .

"Are you listening to me, Margaret? I said, who is going to stay with your mother tonight?"

Margaret's head shot up, her cheeks tinged with pink. She hadn't heard a word Betsy had said and from the expectant look on Betsy's face, she knew that her friend expected some type of answer. "I'm sorry. What did you say?"

Betsy stared at Margaret and then at the stairs; a calculating gleam entered her eyes. "Oh, nothing. It wasn't important. How's the pie?"

"Delicious," Margaret replied, taking another bite, though the tart apples lightly flavored with cinnamon and sugar couldn't satisfy her sudden hunger.

"You certainly must have been starved. I can't recall ever seeing you eat three pieces before. You'd think you were the one that was having the baby."

Margaret froze, her eyes widening, her fork paused in midair. "Baby!" The fork clattered to the plate, drawing the attention of the two cowboys seated at the next table. She smiled apologetically before blurting, "You're going to have a baby? Oh, Betsy, that's wonderful!"

Betsy smiled dreamily. "Yes, isn't it?"

"Does Tom know?" For a fleeting moment Margaret thought that if things had worked out differently this would have been her baby—hers and Tom's. She

32

pushed the disturbing thought to the back of her mind.

"Of course not, silly. You're the first one I've told."

Reaching across the blue-and-white checkered table-cloth, Margaret clasped Betsy's hand. "I'm so happy for you . . . for both of you."

"Are you, Margaret? I can't help but feel guilty about the way things turned out. I would never do anything to hurt you."

"Now who's being silly? Things happen for a reason. Tom and I weren't meant to be. You are his destiny, Betsy. You and the baby. Be happy. I'm thrilled for both of you . . . truly I am."

"Your day is coming, Margaret. I just know it is."

Margaret shook her head. "I'm a twenty-six-year-old spinster saddled with a sick mother. There's not many men anxious to take on that combination."

"What about Francis Brooks? I've seen the way he stares at you when he doesn't think anyone else is looking."

Thinking of Francis, the spindly-legged school-teacher, brought a sour smile to Margaret's lips. Francis had made a few overtures, but at the rate he was going, she would be aged and infirmed before he got around to making a declaration. And did she really want him to? Francis was kind, bright, hardworking, all those things a woman would want in a husband, but he was as dull as a well-used ax blade.

"I suppose Francis would be willing to put up with Mother. He's always spouting off about our Christian duty to our parents." How convenient that Francis's parents were dead, Margaret thought uncharitably, picking up her fork once again.

Absorbed in her pie, Margaret didn't notice Betsy's

sly smile as she looked over Margaret's head in the direction of the hotel lobby. Standing there, right next to the potted palm, looking none the worse for wear, was Chase Gallagher. It was indecent for a man to be so good-looking, Betsy thought. Tom was handsome, in a boyish sort of way. But Chase . . . Chase was all man.

"I wouldn't be at all surprised if you meet some handsome cowboy at the dance tonight," Betsy finally answered, her eyes traveling over the virile marshal. "Your destiny could be lurking right around the corner."

"Grab your partners and form a square," Wooley called out from the makeshift bandstand, bowing his fiddle while Hector Gomez, who stood next to him, plunked enthusiastically on his guitar.

Tapping her toe in time to the music, Margaret observed the dancing couples sashaying about the floor of the church hall. The plain white walls of the hall had been decorated with festive red, white, and blue streamers left over from last year's Fourth of July celebration. Long wooden tables, draped with white cloths and laden with every kind of food imaginable, were lined up against the back wall.

There had been a good turnout for Tom's retirement party. The large room overflowed with Tom's friends and neighbors who had come to pay homage to a man they respected. A man whose boots were going to be difficult to fill. Margaret thought of the new town marshal and cringed inwardly. Tom's retirement was going to have a profound effect on them all.

Pushing the unsettling image of the new marshal to

the back of her mind, Margaret returned her attention to what Alberta Bottoms and Marion Holmes were saying about the disgraceful way eighteen-year-old Cyndi Lang was fawning over the eldest son of Ben and Cora Mitchell.

Alberta and Marion, the two *biggest* gossips in town, their immense size doing equal justice to their mouths, took an intense pleasure in finding fault with just about everyone. No one, including Margaret herself, had been immune to their viperous tongues over the years. She clearly remembered them saying similar things about her and Tom when they were courting.

"I can't imagine how Myrtle Lang can let her daughter run loose like that," Alberta said, stuffing another doughnut into her mouth. "It's disgraceful the way some of these young people behave."

"I declare!" Marion chimed in, her double chin bobbing excitedly, "I have never seen such goings-on. Why, Cindi is practically lying all over Bobby Mitchell. It's simply disgusting!" Dabbing her forehead and cheeks with her hankie, she waved it in front of her face like a fan.

"I really think you ladies are overreacting," Margaret said, noting the affronted expressions her comment produced. "I think Cyndi and Bobby are just having themselves a good time. We were all young once." Though she doubted that was true in Alberta and Marion's case.

"Hmph! I can't believe I'm hearing such things from you, Margaret," Alberta argued. "After all, we older, more mature women, need to set an example for the young folks of this town."

Margaret swallowed her retort. How dare those two

old biddies compare her in age to themselves? The fat old cows. Why, she'd die before she'd turn into an opinionated, self-righteous busybody like those two.

Needing something to cool down her temper, she turned toward the refreshment table, ladling some lemonade into her cup. She was just about to take a sip when she heard Alberta's strangled gasp. Wondering what had offended the catty woman now, she twirled about, her eyes widening at the sight of the new marshal crossing the room in her direction. Remembering the last time she had seen Chase Gallagher, her cheeks flushed hotter than the desert during midday; she gulped down her lemonade.

"I can't imagine why that gunman is walking over here," Marion whispered, fanning herself with her hankie again. "Rumor has it, he's killed over fifty men. He shouldn't be allowed to mingle with decent folks."

"Mind your tongue, Marion," Alberta cautioned. "That man is no ordinary gunslinger. He's our new marshal. Isn't that right, Margaret?"

Nodding absently, Margaret observed the marshal's long-legged stride close up the distance between them. His motion was fluid—effortless, like a mountain lion stalking his prey. And though he was dressed like a gentleman, in a black, single-breasted frock coat, white shirt, and black string tie, there lurked a savage intensity beneath the polite exterior.

His arms and legs were muscular, and she remembered how effortlessly he had picked up the woman from the saloon and carried her to the hotel. Her chest tightened at the mental image of what they'd been doing there. Taking another sip of lemonade, she breathed deeply, pushing the disquieting thought to the back of her mind while studying the toes of her black leather shoes.

"Good evening, ladies."

The deep voice poured over Margaret like warm maple syrup. She looked up to find Chase Gallagher towering over her; the star on his vest hit her at eye level. Her eyes traveled up the muscular chest, landing on his deeply tanned face. It was then she noticed the faint scar on his cheek, running from the corner of his left eye to the bridge of his cheekbone; that, coupled with the neatly trimmed mustache, made him appear somewhat rakish. His hair was as black as Satan's heart, with just a sprinkling of silver at the temples. What was it Wooley had said they called him? "The Silver-Eyed Devil." Yes, it fit. At the sound of Alberta's voice, she turned her attention back to the conversation at hand.

"Why, hello, Marshal Gallagher. We were just talking about you. Weren't we, Marion?" The two women smiled smugly.

"Somehow, I thought you might be," Chase replied, not bothering to hide his sarcasm.

Margaret bit back a smile.

His answer brought a scarlet stain to Alberta's cheeks and an insulted gasp from Marion. Excusing themselves, the two overweight matrons swept across the room like an unwelcome prairie fire, leaving Margaret alone with the marshal.

"It seems your friends have deserted you."

Margaret stared at the backs of the retreating women and then up at the stranger who stared back at her with an expectant look on his face. Fidgeting nervously with the cameo at her throat, she finally

37

replied, "Yes . . . well . . . you'll have to excuse Alberta and Marion, Marshal Gallagher. They tend to be rather judgmental."

"You know who I am?"

"Why, yes," she answered without thinking. "Betsy Fraser pointed you out this afternoon when you crossed the street with that . . ." She clamped her mouth shut, mortified at what she'd been about to admit.

Locking his thumbs in his belt, Chase's right eyebrow cocked at a sharp angle. "So you saw me with Lillie Mae?"

She nodded; her apology lodged tightly in her throat.

"No need for embarrassment. Men have their needs, same as women." *Do you have needs Margaret Parker?*

His eyes traveled over her body, studying it, committing it to memory for future reference. She wasn't very tall, maybe five inches over five feet. She was slender, but rounded in all the right places. *Well* rounded, he amended, his eyes trailing over the two lush mounds. Her neck was long, smooth, and white; her face, delicate but determined. She wore her dark hair pulled back away from her face, the severe style making her warm brown eyes appear doelike. She had virgin written all over her, and she looked like trouble, but if she was Jack Parker's daughter, it was trouble worth getting into.

Margaret shifted nervously, chafing under Chase Gallagher's scrutiny. The way he stared at her with those quicksilver eyes, as if he knew what she looked like without her underclothes on, was unsettling. Taking a deep breath, she held out her hand. "Forgive my rudeness, Marshal. I'm Margaret Parker."

"I know."

Surprise touched her face. "You do?"

"Wooley Burnett's been singing your praises, Miss Parker. He's quite taken with you." Before Margaret could reply, he added, "Care to dance?"

She shook her head. "Oh, no, I haven't danced in years."

Taking the cup out of her hand, he placed it on the table. "Neither have I. But if you're willing to put up with a few crushed toes, so am I."

"But . . ."

Ignoring her objection, Chase grabbed onto her hand, leading her out onto the dance floor.

Mortified to find that people were staring, Margaret felt herself heat up like a teakettle about to boil over. "Really, Marshal Gallagher!" she protested through clenched teeth when she finally found her voice. "You should learn to take no for an answer."

Flashing her a smile that caused queer palpitations to form in her chest, Chase replied, "Darlin', that word's not in my vocabulary."

Chapter Three

Chase smiled inwardly at the rapturous expression on Margaret Parker's face. Her eyes were closed, as if she was having the most wonderful dream. They hadn't spoken much during the dance; he guessed she was still a little put out by the way he had practically dragged her across the room.

Damn stubborn woman! He knew she had wanted to dance. He'd been watching her from across the room for the past thirty minutes. The wistful expression she wore every time a dancing couple had passed by her had touched him in a strange way. She reminded him of a mongrel pup he once had. That dog loved to have his belly scratched, but he would snap and growl before he'd roll over on his back to let Chase pet him.

Getting close to Margaret Parker might not be as easy as he had originally thought. But get close to her he would. If she was Jack Parker's daughter, he'd be on her like a tick on a hound.

Placing his lips close to her ear, Chase whispered, "You seem to be enjoying the dance, even though I had a devil of a time convincing you of that fact." He smiled at the surprised expression she wore when she finally opened her eyes.

Margaret felt the beginnings of a blush creep up her neck. Truth be told, she was having the most delightful dream, and it had little to do with dancing. Being held in a man's arms again after all these years made her feel a little bit like Cinderella at the ball. Unfortunately, Chase Gallagher was no Prince Charming.

"I haven't danced in years, Marshal. I'm enjoying myself, despite the company I've been forced to keep." She still hadn't forgiven him for creating a scene in front of the entire room and was happy to see her remark had hit home.

"I doubt one dance is going to ruin your reputation, Miss Parker, even if it's with a man like me." There was a bitter edge to his voice.

The music ended before she could respond, but soon they were standing by the refreshment table and he was handing her another glass of lemonade.

"I thank you for the dance, little lady."

Chase started to walk away, but Margaret grabbed onto his arm, disturbed by the remark he had made but not knowing why. "Marshal, what did you mean by 'a man like you'? Are you so different from other men?"

He placed his work-roughened hand over her smooth one, and when he looked down at her his expression was unreadable.

"Darlin', I wouldn't want to shock your ladylike sensibilities."

She pulled her hand away; the heat from his innocent touch seared her skin like a branding iron. "What makes you think you could, Marshal? I don't shock easily."

"Would you be willing to put that to a test and let me walk you home after the dance?"

Margaret's throat suddenly felt parched and she didn't think it had a thing to do with the lemons in her drink. She hadn't been walked home by a man in years. What would people think? Did she care? "I . . . I . . ."

"That's what I thought. I saw the way you and those two old hags were talking when I walked up, like I might contaminate you or something."

She flushed guiltily. "That's not fair. Just because Alberta Bottoms and Marion Holmes are like that, doesn't mean I am."

"Then, you'll let me walk you home?"

Loneliness and confusion welded together to make her suspicious. "Why would *a man like you* want to walk *a woman like me* home? Surely, there are prettier, more accommodating females that would suit your purpose."

"I can't think of a one."

"Not even Lillie Mae?" she asked boldly.

He grinned, his teeth slashing white against his tanned skin. "Whores serve their purpose, darlin'. But with them, it's like a flash in the pan—a spark on a match. One burst and then it's gone. Like Tom says, it's time for me to think about settling in."

"And are you?"

He shrugged. "Depends."

She knew it was none of her business and she shouldn't even care, but for some strange reason she did and found herself asking, "On what?"

"On whether or not you're gonna let me walk you home."

She felt hot, foolish, and flustered all at the same time. Because her throat had swollen shut, she could only nod her acquiescence.

"See you later, Margaret Parker," he said before disappearing into the crowd of well-wishers that surrounded Tom.

Margaret didn't have a moment to sort out the meaning of Chase's words before Francis Brooks appeared in front of her asking for a dance.

"I never thought that brutish man would leave, Margaret. Are you all right?" Francis's greenish brown eyes, as indecisive as he was, peered into her face, as if expecting to find that some dread disease had befallen her.

Was she all right? She wasn't quite sure. All of a sudden she felt light-headed, giddy, and very warm. She smiled into Francis's concerned face. "I'm fine, Francis, but I would love a lemonade, if you wouldn't mind fetching me one."

While Francis's back was turned, she chanced a peek across the room and found Chase's gaze upon her. He winked, and she felt her cheeks turn scarlet.

"My dear," Francis said, handing her the glass, "whatever is the matter? You look quite flushed. Is there something I can do?"

"No." She shook her head. "No, there's nothing that can be done." And she knew it with a certainty.

With Francis standing guard over her like a faithful watchdog, the minutes turned into hours and the hours

43

seemed to drag. The music didn't seem quite as joyful; the food didn't taste quite as good.

Spying Betsy and Tom in the far corner of the hall, Margaret made her apologies to Francis and started across the room. Looking back over her shoulder, she was annoyed to find that Francis had not taken the hint and was following right behind. Betsy smiled in sympathy as Margaret approached, jabbing Tom in the side about something he whispered in her ear.

"Well, hello, you two," Betsy gushed, thinking that Francis really did resemble a character out of Washington Irving's "The Legend of Sleepy Hollow." Whether she would go so far as to say he looked like Ichabod Crane, the gangly schoolteacher from the story, as Tom had suggested, was another matter.

"You look lovely tonight, Margaret." Tom kissed her cheek. "That color becomes you."

Margaret glowed, smoothing the folds of her gown. She did feel pretty in the lavender dress. It was lovelier than anything she had worn in years. She fussed with the eyelet ruffle edging her neckline and smiled.

"I think our Margaret's turned many a head tonight. Isn't that right, Ica . . . Francis?" Betsy asked, catching herself just in time, ignoring Tom's chuckle.

The schoolteacher blushed. "Ye . . . yes, of course," he stammered, pulling his collar away from his protruding Adam's apple. "Margaret always looks splendid."

Margaret smiled sweetly at Francis before casting a thunderous glance in Betsy's direction.

"She certainly is a sight for these tired eyes," the deep voice sounded over Margaret's right shoulder.

Recognition came instantly. Gooseflesh sprouted

over Margaret's arms and neck. Turning her head, she found Chase standing beside her. He was staring strangely at Francis while holding out his hand in introduction. Francis's face paled as Chase's grip tightened around the schoolteacher's bony hand.

"Hope I'm not intruding, Brooks." Chase smiled inwardly as the greenhorn flexed and reflexed his right hand to get the blood circulating back into it. A pilgrim if ever he saw one, Chase thought, wondering what Margaret was doing in the company of such a man. She was certainly more woman than Francis Brooks could handle.

"Are you ready to go, darlin'? I'm afraid I'm about partied out." Ignoring both Margaret and Francis's gasps, he waited for her reply.

"I . . ." Before Margaret could complete her sentence, Francis butted in.

"I don't think it would be proper for Margaret to leave with you, Marshal Gallagher. It might start tongues to wagging. You being a . . . you being new here and all," he amended quickly, noting the dangerous glint in the marshal's eyes.

"I believe that's up to the little lady, schoolmarm." Chase turned a challenging stare in Margaret's direction.

"Well, I think it's awfully nice of Chase to offer to escort Margaret home. Don't you, Tom?" Betsy nudged her husband in the ribs again.

Tom stared at Chase, then at Margaret, wondering what in tarnation was going on. Margaret Parker was not Chase Gallagher's type of woman. And Chase was definitely not the man for Margaret. A strong feeling of protectiveness swept over him. His blue eyes impaled

Chase's gray ones.

"The important thing is that no harm comes to Margaret. I would never want to see her hurt." There was an implied warning in his words, but if Chase understood, he gave no indication.

"I would be happy to walk you home, Margaret," Francis offered, straightening to his full five-foot-four-inch height as he sidled up next to Chase.

Observing the two men standing side by side, Margaret couldn't help but notice the obvious difference in their stature. Chase stood almost a foot taller than the diminutive schoolteacher and was massively built. His muscles rippled beneath his shirt and pants, while Francis's were practically nonexistent.

Francis could only be described as slight. His body bespoke years of sitting behind a desk in the schoolhouse; his complexion hadn't seen the light of sun for years. He definitely paled in comparison.

Realizing how unkind she was being to compare two men who were as different as night and day, a guilty blush stole over her cheeks. "I thank you for your offer, Francis, but I've already accepted the marshal's escort home."

The statement brought a varying degree of responses. Francis stood wide-eyed, mouth agape and red-faced, as if he was about to have an apoplectic fit. Betsy, on the other hand, beamed from ear to ear.

Ignoring the scowl on Tom's face, Margaret focused instead on the grin that creased Chase's cheeks. Her heart fluttered and she took a deep breath, holding out her arm. "Shall we go, Marshal Gallagher?"

*   *   *

The night air was warm, surrounding them like a lover's embrace, as they stepped outside and headed west toward the main street of town. It was quiet, except for the steady rhythm of their heels crunching against the dirt-covered street and the beating of Margaret's heart, which pounded loud in her ears.

She was well aware of the man walking beside her, of the hand that rested possessively in the small of her back, of the scent of tobacco that lingered on his clothes. He filled her senses with longing, made her feel things she hadn't felt in years. And she didn't like it; she didn't like it one bit.

As they drew closer to the main part of town, the noise increased. The music of the saloons and the cantinas, coupled with the boisterous laughter of the cowboys enjoying a night on the town and the saloon girls making sure that they did, intruded into the quiet interlude that had developed between them.

"I knew it was too good to last."

Absorbed in her disquieting thoughts, it took a moment for Margaret to realize that Chase was speaking. "I'm sorry, did you say something?"

"The quiet. I knew it was too good to last." He frowned as a drunken cowboy fell through the swinging door of the saloon, landing unceremoniously at their feet.

"Oh, my!" Margaret exclaimed, jumping back a step. "I hope he's not injured."

Not particularly caring whether he was or not, Chase kicked the man in the ribs. "Get up you drunken cur, before I throw you in jail for littering up the street and making a nuisance of yourself in front of a lady."

When the man lifted his head, Margaret could see

47

that he wasn't a man at all but a boy, barely eighteen. The boy stared bleary-eyed at the tall man hovering over him; his wheat-colored hair fell over his forehead, reminding her of a sheep dog.

"I was just having myself some fun, Marshal. Is that a crime?" His voice held a note of defiance as he pushed himself to unsteady feet.

"The crime is that you can't hold your whiskey." Chase picked up the boy's hat, shoving it none too gently on top of his head. "Go home and sleep it off. And don't come back until you've grown a beard and can hold your liquor."

"I bet you wouldn't say that if I was Billy the Kid." The boy's words were thick and slow, as if his tongue were too large for his mouth.

"Billy's dead. Is that how you want to end up?"

In a flash, the brash young man was off the sidewalk, disappearing around the side of the building.

"You were a little hard on him, weren't you? After all, he's just a boy."

"So was Billy, remember?"

Margaret shuddered, remembering only too vividly the gruesome accounts of the murders that William Bonney, alias Billy the Kid, had perpetrated. Most of his victims had been unarmed or shot from ambush when they'd been gunned down. Billy had been seventeen when he killed his first man, twenty-one when he died at the hands of lawman Pat Garrett. Such a waste, Margaret thought, shaking her head.

"Just the same, I don't think you can lump that drunken cowboy and a ruthless killer into the same mold," she argued.

"You'd be surprised how deceiving looks can be

when it comes to killers, Margaret. I can call you Margaret, can't I?"

She inclined her head.

"Killers come in all shapes and sizes," he continued as they resumed their stroll toward her house. "Some are overt—psychotic like Billy. Others wear their cruelty beneath a facade of gentility." He thought of Jack Parker and clenched his fists.

Margaret didn't miss the pained expression on Chase's face and wondered at the cause of it. She placed a comforting hand on his arm. "You've witnessed a lot of evil in your lifetime, haven't you?"

The image of his mother and father lying in a pool of their own blood—Amy's sweet face, white and frozen in death—seared his memory, making his words harsher than he intended. "I've witnessed death. Lived with it most of my life. And I never forget, Miss *Parker.*" He emphasized her name, almost spitting it out. "Never!"

His venomous tone, coupled with the hatred burning in his eyes, chilled Margaret's soul.

They continued the rest of the way in silence. In the distance, the mournful howl of a coyote rang out against the diamond-studded darkness. The desert, so still and somber during the daylight hours, had come alive, its nocturnal creatures accomplishing the tasks they could not do in the heat of the day.

Upon reaching the two-story, clapboard house, Margaret felt relieved to be home at last. Chase made her feel uneasy—on edge. He was like a charged keg of dynamite, ready to explode at any moment, and she was eager to put distance between them as soon as possible. She paused before the rickety wooden gate.

"Here we are, Marshal. Thank you for walking me home."

The house was a shambles, sadly needing a fresh coat of paint and a lot of repair, Chase observed. The shutters hung lopsided at the windows; the front gate was falling off its hinges; and the pretty pink desert primroses that grew at the base of the fence looked hopelessly out of place. For some reason it bothered Chase to think that Margaret lived in such squalor. She was too refined—too genteel for such deplorable surroundings. The gate squeaked as he pushed it open.

"Looks like you could use a man's touch around here."

Seeing the house through a stranger's eyes, Margaret sighed. It was a sight, but it couldn't be helped. There was barely enough money for necessities, let alone the extra it would take to paint and fix up the place. "I'm afraid things have fallen into a bit of disrepair since my father left."

"He dead?" Chase tried to act nonchalant, hoping he'd learn something about Jonathan Parker. Pulling a cigarette out of his vest pocket, he lit it. He hated tailor-mades, but he didn't think he could roll a decent smoke right now if his life depended on it. "Mind if I smoke?"

She shook her head. "My father ran out on me and my mother. He's been gone a long time." She went on to explain about Phoebe Parker's illness.

"You must hate him for putting you through all that."

"Oh, no, I could never hate him. He's a wonderful man." Seeing the incredulous expression on Chase's face, she smiled softly. "I know that sounds crazy, but he really was a wonderful father when he was home,

50

which wasn't very often. He traveled a lot; he was a courier for a bank."

Chase took a long drag on the cigarette, trying to keep his emotions in check. The similarities between Margaret's father and Jack Parker were just too coincidental to ignore. He was positive that they were one and the same person. "Tell me about him."

Before Margaret could reply, a squealing, grunting creature came tearing around the side of the house, heading straight for Margaret. Dropping his smoke, Chase pushed Margaret aside and reached for his gun. "Get back! It's a wild boar."

Seeing what Chase was about, she screamed, clutching at his arm. "No, wait! Don't shoot."

He lowered the gun, his mouth dropping open at the sight of Margaret kneeling down to pet the animal. At closer range, he could see it wasn't a wild boar but a javelina hog. "What the hell is that?" He pointed an accusing finger at the animal.

Continuing to pet the pig, Margaret smiled up at the surprised expression on Chase's face. "This is Evelyn. She's a pet."

"A pet!" He stuffed his gun back into his holster. "You've got a musk hog for a pet?" He looked at the brown, coarse-haired creature, wrinkling his nose in disgust and was rewarded with a series of affronted grunts and snorts.

Straightening, Margaret cradled Evelyn in her arms, scratching the hog affectionately under the chin. "Evelyn is really a very smart animal. She's good company and hardly ever makes a mess in the house."

His eyes widened. "You let that pig in the house?" So much for the genteel, refined lady, he thought, shaking his head.

"Only during the day when it's too hot to leave her outside." She set the pig back down, smiling as it nudged inquisitively at Chase's boots. "At night she roams the yard, keeping watch on my chicken coops."

"Chickens? You raise chickens, too?"

She nodded. "I sell the eggs to Mrs. Perkins down at the grocery."

"Well, I'll be damned!" He ran his fingers through his mustache to hide his smile. *Who would have thought?*

They chatted for several more minutes until Phoebe's cry floated down from the upstairs window like a heavy blanket, smothering their enjoyment.

"Margaret, is that you? Who are you talking to? I hear voices."

Walking to the porch, which sagged pitifully under her slight weight, Margaret yelled up the stairs through the screen door. "I'll be right up, Mama. I'm saying good night to Marshal Gallagher."

"Well, hurry up. That crazy Mexican you left here to take care of me lit out over two hours ago. I could have died while you were off cavorting with your marshal."

Turning to look over her shoulder, Margaret smiled apologetically at Chase who had followed her up onto the porch. "I'm sorry about Mama; she's not herself."

The look of despair on Margaret's face touched him. It seemed she had her own burdens to bear. "You don't have to apologize. You're the one who's being hurt." He reached for her, holding her gently by the arm. He felt her tremble and saw the look of uncertainty—the fear mirrored in her eyes.

"I really must go in. Mama needs me."

He stared down at her, drawing her close to his chest, expecting her to bolt, surprised when she didn't. "I need you, too, Maggie."

Maggie. Margaret smiled at the nickname. No one had called her that since she was a little girl. Lifting her head, she looked up into Chase's eyes, surprised by the tenderness she saw reflected there. She knew she should leave—pull out of his embrace—but it felt so good to be held in his arms.

"Why did you call me that? No one's called me Maggie in years." His soft smile caused a fluttering low in her stomach.

"Margaret's too formal—too staid. You've got depths within you, Maggie. Depths that haven't been tapped as yet."

Suddenly, his smile faded, replaced by an ardent expression that excited and frightened at the same time. Margaret knew Chase was going to kiss her; she also knew that she wouldn't protest when he did.

When he lowered his head, capturing her lips with his own, her knees weakened. The touch of his lips, the musky scent of his skin, mingling with the taste of tobacco that lingered, the feel of his mustache, much softer than she could have imagined, sent her senses soaring.

Her heart pounded. When he kissed the pulsing hollow at the base of her throat, her cheeks, her forehead, the embers of desire banked dormant within her flared into a raging inferno.

Lost in a maelstrom of desire, it took a few moments for the sound of her mother's voice to penetrate her brain. When it finally did, she withdrew from the shelter of his arms—suddenly—guiltily. "I must go," she whispered, studying the toes of her shoes, not daring to look at him.

Chase tilted up her chin and saw the desire she tried so desperately to hide. "Must you?"

"Good-bye, Chase," she said, turning toward the door.

"Not good-bye, Maggie, only good night. For there will be other nights; I promise you that." With that vow, he stepped off the porch and walked away, without looking back.

Margaret stared after Chase, watching until he was swallowed up by the darkness. She touched her lips; the memory of his kiss lingered there. She touched her heart; the memory of his words warmed her: *". . . there will be other nights, I promise you that."*

Chapter Four

Removing the wire-rim spectacles from atop the bridge of his nose, Doctor Watson pinched the sides of his nose and blinked his eyes exactly three times. Margaret knew that it would be exactly three, never two, and certainly not four, for she had seen Doc do the very same thing hundreds of times since she'd been helping him out with his patient load.

The arrangement they shared was good. Since the day her father had left her and her mother high and dry, Margaret had been more than grateful for the employment. She spent as many hours a day as she could assisting Doc with his patients, and he, in return, gave her a priceless education and supplemented her meager income.

Margaret faced Doc across the small confines of his sitting room, noting how tired and worn-out he looked, wondering if perhaps there had been complications with Kate's delivery. "You were gone longer than I expected, Doc. Was there a problem at the Fergusons?" The lines across his forehead deepened at her question. The creases alongside his nose cut in like a canyon on a face well-mapped with each of his fifty-five years.

Leaning back in the well-worn brown leather chair that flanked the wood-burning stove, William Watson folded his hands across his chest, closing his eyes for a moment. When he opened them, there was a deep sadness within their blue depths.

"I told Kate that this had better be her last child. I told that husband of hers the same thing. Her body's just too spent to nurture and deliver another young'n. I fear she'll die if she gets pregnant again."

Margaret sat up straighter, her spine barely touching the back of the lumpy, horsehair sofa. "What did she say?"

"She said there wasn't anything she could do to prevent Willis from planting his seed in her. Said to deny him his rights would be cutting off her nose to spite her face."

"But she'll die!"

Tapping his pipe against his palm, Doc filled the bowl with tobacco and lit it before answering. The distinctive aroma of licorice permeated the room. "You're right, Margaret, but so is Kate. There's not much short of abstinence that Kate can do to prevent another baby, and I doubt Willis would agree to that."

"Did you explain that English doctor's rhythm method? The one you told me about?"

"I tried, but the concept of safe versus fertile days of the month seems too difficult for most of these women to understand. They're more apt to believe in old wive's tales and superstitions. Kate's no different. She thinks that as long as she's nursin', she won't get pregnant again."

Margaret shook her head, her face mirroring disgust. "One in the cradle, one at the breast, one on the way."

"Exactly."

"It's criminal that more women can't be educated about their own bodily functions. What could the government have been thinking when they passed the Comstock Law making it illegal for people to receive contraception information through the mail?" Margaret knew for a fact that books had been written on the subject of pregnancy prevention. She had even read one that Doc had given her: *The Private Companion of Young Married People,* by Charles Knowlton. But she also knew that these types of books were considered obscene, and that the authors had been prosecuted for writing on such a taboo subject.

"Things will eventually change, Margaret. And it will be young women, such as yourself, who'll bring about those changes."

"Like me? I'm not married, Doc. I've never even . . ." Realizing what she'd been about to admit, Margaret snapped her mouth shut, her cheeks glowing like two red coals.

Pushing himself out of his chair, Doc Watson took a seat next to Margaret on the sofa, cradling her hand in his. "Don't you go gettin' red-faced on me, Margaret Parker. I know you haven't been with a man, and there's no shame in that. Your time will come and when it does, you'll be a damned sight better informed than these other women around here. I'll see to that."

Chase Gallagher's virile form flashed through her

mind; she shifted nervously in her seat, pulling her hand out of Doc's grasp to wipe it on the skirt of her dress.

"I guess you know me better than anyone, Doc," Margaret replied, hoping he hadn't noticed her discomfort. "I've confided things to you that I've never even told my mother."

"And that pleases me, Margaret. You're the daughter I never had. I've always been too busy with doctorin' and such to allow myself time to court a woman and raise a family. You've more than made up for it. I'm just sorry that your own mother is too blind to see what a fine woman you are."

"Mama's too wrapped up in her own misery to pay me much mind. I've gotten used to it."

"Your mother pushed away the only husband she'll ever have. Too bad she can't see that she's doing the same thing to her daughter."

Margaret felt a stab of guilt. Were her feelings so transparent that one only had to look at her to see the hurt and animosity she harbored toward her mother? She loved Phoebe Parker, despite her lack of motherly devotion, but she would never forgive her for causing her father to leave.

"Did you know my father well, Doc?"

Rising to his feet, Doc walked to the window. His private quarters were situated on the second floor of the building that housed his pharmacy and surgery. The front window of his sitting room looked down upon the dusty main street of town. From it he observed a buckboard piled high with grain and bales of hay roll slowly by, but other than that, things were quiet on Main Street today.

"Not well," he finally answered, turning back to face her. "Jonathan and I spoke a few times, but he was quiet, kept to himself mostly. You seem to be a lot like him."

Doc's admission pleased her. She'd always strived to be like her father—kind, caring. She wanted none of the domineering, selfish traits her mother possessed and had done her best to master the irksome temper that sometimes surfaced when she was tired or annoyed.

She rose to her feet. "I'd best be getting home. Mama will fret if I'm late with her supper."

"Your mother could stand to lose a few pounds. It's not healthy the way she stays in bed all day and eats."

"I tried to tell her, Doc, but you know how Mama is. She won't listen."

He knew all right. Phoebe Parker was as big a hypochondriac as ever he'd seen. There would be no cure for what ailed her in this lifetime.

"Before you leave, Margaret, I have a favor to ask."

She paused, her eyebrow arching in question, while waiting for him to continue.

"I need to go to Tucson. There's a new abdominal surgical procedure being performed at St. Mary's Hospital. I'd like to sit in on a few operations and observe. I need you to keep an eye on things around here. I'll be gone about a week."

Uncertainty flashed across her face. "What if something comes up that I can't handle?"

Smiling, Doc put his arm around Margaret's shoulder, escorting her to the door. "There's not much, save for brain surgery, that you couldn't handle, Margaret. And seeing as how there's not many in this town with that particular ailment, I don't foresee that you'll have any problem. If you do, send me a telegram. I'll take the first stage back."

William Watson didn't doubt for a minute that his Margaret could handle any emergency that might arise in his absence. She had more common sense and ability than most of his learned colleagues. Her natural proficiency at healing never ceased to amaze him. The good citizens of Purgatory would be well-cared for left in Margaret's capable hands; he'd wager his last tin of pipe tobacco on that fact.

"You forgot to crown my king," Wooley accused, indicating with a nod of his head the black checker that had advanced to Chase's side of the board. "You wouldn't be tryin' to cheat me, now would ya?"

The regulator clock on the wall ticked off the fifteen seconds it took for Chase to pick up the checker and place it on top of Wooley's. He smiled. "Now why would I need to do that? I've already beat you three games in a row. I hardly think cheating's necessary."

Spitting a stream of tobacco juice into the spittoon that sat next to Chase's desk, Wooley maneuvered the wad of tobacco from one side of his mouth to the other while contemplating his next move.

"Did you get those signs painted like I told you to?" Chase asked. "We need to get those new ordinances posted as soon as possible."

Wooley looked up, a disgruntled expression on his face. "Yup. And I'm telling you right now, some of them rules is goin' to cause trouble. Most of the folks round here ain't goin' to like having a new set of rules to live with."

Chase leaned back in his chair, the checker game forgotten for the moment. "Once the people in this town realize that these new ordinances are for their own protection, they'll come around."

"You been here shy of a week, Chase. You should'a waited awhile afore changin' things."

"And let the streets turn into garbage dumps? It's time these folks took some reponsibility for this town. The place stinks; it needs cleaning. Do you know that other cities have built furnaces to burn their garbage? That garbage, eaten by pigs and other animals, can transmit diseases?"

Wooley scratched his beard and thought a minute. "And what about the gun law?" he continued, as if Chase had never spoken. "Tom never had a man surrender his weapon before. It ain't gonna be popular."

Chase sighed. If the rest of the town was as stubborn as Wooley, he certainly had his work cut out for him.

"Tom's not in charge anymore; I am. And it's my job to enforce the law. The surrendering of firearms is a territorial statute. Besides, it's a whole lot easier to keep things nice and orderly when a drunken cowboy or a disappointed suitor isn't packing iron. They can check their guns at the bar, or here at the marshal's office, and pick 'em up when they leave.

"There shouldn't be much of a problem. Most of the cowboys, except for a few working at the Bar H, will head for Tucson come a Saturday evening, where the drinks are cheap and whores plentiful. Most likely, those that come to Purgatory won't be interested in brawling."

Wooley looked skeptical. "I know for a fact that

61

we're never goin' to be able to enforce that law about pets being restrained and their owners bein' held accountable. Hell, even Margaret's pig cuts loose every once in a while."

Chase smiled at the memory of Margaret's "pet," then placed his booted feet on top of the desk, pointing to the bottom of his boot. "See that. I stepped in it today . . . on the sidewalk. You think the ladies of this town are going to want to put their dainty slippers in dog droppings?"

Wooley wrinkled his nose in disgust. "I ain't never thought when I hired on as deputy that I was going to be policing dog droppins and garbage. What's this world comin' to anyway?"

Chase smiled ruefully. "You and me are a couple of dinosaurs, Wooley."

"A couple of what?"

"Dinosaurs. Prehistoric creatures. We've lived too long—seen too much. We should have put out to pasture years ago, before we outlived our usefulness."

An affronted expression crossed the bearded face. "You sayin' we're useless?"

Chase nodded. "Pretty much. This here's the end of the line for me, Wooley. For all of us lawmen. The world's getting civilized. There are cities with electric lights, telephones, and cars that run on cables. The Arizona Territory just hasn't caught up with the rest of the country yet. But it will. Soon these vast open spaces will be gone, swallowed up by cities and people, all in the name of progress. I've seen it happen elsewhere."

"You're loco. Why, it's so open you can practically see from one end of this territory to the other."

"That's what the Indians thought and look where

they've ended up. On little patches of what was once their private domain. They've become obsolete; so will we."

The plight of the Indians had been a canker on Chase's soul that still festered. The so-called "savages" had been lied to, cheated, pushed, and pulled, from one part of the country to the next. Like the buffalo they had once hunted, they were a race of people on the edge of extinction. And it made him ashamed to be part of the race that had caused their demise.

Pushing himself out of his chair, Wooley stepped to the door, reaching for his hat. "You're damn depressing, you know that? And you've got a sneaky way of ending a checker game that I was fixin' to win."

Chase unfolded himself from the chair and stood, barely able to repress his grin. "Shall we go and perform our deputorial duties?" He pulled his gun from his holster, twirling the chamber to check the load.

"You ain't goin' to shoot no animals are ya?"

He shrugged. "Animals come in all shapes and sizes, Wooley. This Peacemaker's for the two-legged variety. I like to be prepared."

Gazing down the barrel of the Colt .45, then at Chase's eyes, which closely resembled the gunmetal color, Wooley shook his head. "I 'spect you do, Marshal."

"Dang gummit. I told you we was going to have nothin' but trouble with these new ordinances. We been hangin' signs for two days straight, and I ain't seen no improvement."

"Rome wasn't built in a day, Wooley," Chase

63

counseled as they headed up the main street toward the End of the Trail Saloon. "I've had several women— Alberta Bottoms for one—come up and praise me for trying to rid this town of its garbage."

Wooley scratched his head. "I don't know much about this here Rome. Is that back East somewheres?" Ignoring Chase's snicker, he continued, "Anyways, we still got that gun law to reckon with, and I saw Bear Donaldson and his two brothers ride into town this morning. They are a mean bunch of critters." He wiped his forehead with the back of his hand. "Damn if it ain't hot again today."

"This is Purgatory, after all. Is it not?"

"You got a funny way of talking, Marshal. I just hope them big words you use is going to be understood by that Donaldson bunch. They ain't as smart as me."

Chase bit the inside of his cheek to keep from smiling. Wooley Burnett certainly did have a way of growing on a body. But Chase couldn't quite decide if he grew like a patch of sweet strawberries that you couldn't get enough of, or an irritating fungus that needed relief. At the pleased expression on Wooley's face, Chase finally did give in to his smile.

The noise from the saloon drifted out and over the pair of swinging oak doors and into the street long before Chase and Wooley reached their destination.

The tinny sound of the honky-tonk piano blurted out the strains of "Oh, Suzanna" while an excited cowboy's whoop of pleasure seemed to indicate that he was having a winning streak at poker.

Armed with what Willy described as "more determination than sense," the two men hoisted their signs onto their shoulders and entered the saloon.

The room was crowded; the odor of Bull Durham, unwashed bodies, and cheap perfume filled the air. A roulette wheel, the saloon's most recent acquisition, spun in the corner like a well-oiled gun chamber. Green felt covered a couple of the tables, where men in groups of three and four gathered to try their luck at a game of poker or blackjack. There were only a couple of girls working the room. Most were upstairs sleeping off their last night's encounters and resting up for the ones ahead.

Chase smiled to himself. There were few things better than a good smoke, a stiff shot of whiskey, and a night between the thighs of a willing woman. Margaret's brown-haired, brown-eyed image rose up to taunt him, as it had so often since the night he had kissed her—a kiss that had surprised him as much as it had surprised her. Frowning, he pushed it away. He'd deal with the problem of Margaret Parker soon enough, but first things first. He turned toward the barkeeper.

"Howdy, Sam," Chase called out to the redheaded Irishman. "We're here to tack up the new gun ordinance."

Sam O'Rourke cast an anxious glance about the room then nodded. "Have at it, Marshal, though I'd appreciate you not be starting trouble inside me establishment." The words rolled off his tongue in a thick brogue.

Chase did his own survey of the room, sizing up the unfamiliar faces, nodding in greeting at those he knew. When his eyes finally landed on the large oil painting of a well-endowed nude woman hanging over the bar, he smiled. "I guess we'll put it right here next to this pretty

65

lady, Sam. The sight of a pair of full, ripe breasts always puts a man in a good frame of mind."

A chorus of chuckles and loud guffaws could be heard as Wooley tacked the wooden sign next to the painting. The ordinance read: NOTICE: All persons entering this house are requested to divest themselves of all weapons in accordance with Act 13, Section 7, of the revised statutes of Arizona.

"For those of you who can't read," Chase continued, "I'm going to tell you what this sign says. From now on, any man, or woman, coming into Purgatory will leave their guns either with the barkeep or at the marshal's office. When your business is done, you can pick up your weapons before riding out. Any questions?" He waited, relieved when there was only a smattering of grumbles before the men shook their heads and went back to their business. Though he was prepared for a fight, he didn't relish one.

From the rear of the room, a black-bearded, giant of a man stood, causing Wooley to groan out loud before whispering, "It's Bear, Marshal."

The man had an intimidating stance—hands splayed on his hips, his hands within reach of the two six-shooters he wore. "Why ain't you taking off your gun, Gallagher? Don't seem fair we got to give up ours while you keep yours."

At six feet four inches, Chase didn't have to look up to too many men, but in Bear Donaldson's case, it looked like he'd have to make an exception. "Didn't anyone ever tell you that life's not fair? It's Donaldson, isn't it?"

"That's right . . . Bear Donaldson. And these are my brothers, Moose and Skunk. We don't aim to give up

66

our weapons, Marshal."

Chase's eyebrow rose a fraction while he sized up the opposition. The biggest, Bear, had a thick barrel chest and arms the size of tree trunks. He was a blacksmith by profession, which accounted for his large biceps, though he'd been unable to hang on to a job for more than a few months. According to Wooley, Bear's fierce temper scared off the customers. Moose was stocky, mostly flab, and stood a good three inches shorter than his brother. He wore a mustache instead of a beard that drooped down almost to his chin. Skunk, the runt of the litter, didn't need size to repel his opponent. One sniff told Chase that he'd been well-named. The man looked and smelled as if he hadn't seen the inside of a bathhouse in years.

Hooking his thumbs inside his belt, Chase stared Bear straight in the eye. "I'm only going to say this once, so listen up. Those that want to stay in Purgatory put their weapons on the bar. If not, get out now and don't come back. That goes for you and your brothers, Donaldson."

"And if we don't?"

"Then I put a bullet in your brain with this gun." The Peacemaker cleared the leather holster with lightning-quick speed; a roar of approval drifted through the crowd. "That is, if you have one."

The room quieted, and one by one the weapons piled on top of the bar. The three Donaldson brothers stared at the menacing look on Chase Gallagher's face and then at his gun; they unbuckled their belts, placing the weapons on the bar with the others.

"You ain't won, Marshal, not by a long shot." Bear's tone was threatening. "It's easy to be a hero when you

67

got a gun to back up your words. I wonder just how brave you'd be without that Colt to give you courage."

"Is that a dare, Donaldson?"

The big man puffed out his chest and smiled, displaying a large gap where his three front teeth had been.

"Don't let him goad you into a fight, Chase," Wooley cautioned. "The man outweighs you by fifty pounds."

Chase knew the wisdom of Wooley's words. Bear was bigger. But he also knew that if he was going to exert his authority as marshal, he was going to have to make an example of Donaldson. "True, our friend Bear does have the brawn to win a fight, but does he have the brains?"

Bear's eyes narrowed. "Shall we step outside into the street, Gallagher? I'd be happy to show you just how *smart* I really am."

Moose and Skunk laughed, elbowing each other in the ribs before Skunk remarked, "That's telling him, Bear."

Chase held the door open for the three men and waved them on ahead. "After you, gents."

"Are you plumb loco?" Wooley asked after they were out of earshot, grabbing on to Chase's arm. "You're going to get whupped."

"Thanks for your vote of confidence, my friend."

"Them big words of yours ain't going to protect you against Bear. He talks with his fists not his mouth."

Chase's smile was feral. "Then we'll just have to teach him a new language, won't we?"

Chapter Five

Donaldson waited in the middle of the street, sleeves rolled up, his meaty fists poised to take action.

Unbuckling his gunbelt, Chase handed it to the deputy. "You're not to interfere. No matter what."

Wooley swallowed, then nodded, a hint of fear in his eyes.

As soon as Chase's boots hit the dirt, Bear was on him like a bee swarming over a hive of honey. A crowd gathered to line the street, egging the men on with taunts and jeers.

"Kill him, Bear," Moose shouted, raising his fist in the air. "Show him who's the better man."

Bear responded with a smile and a sharp blow to the marshal's face. A trickle of blood oozed out of the corner of Chase's mouth; he wiped it on the back of his hand.

A second later, Chase lunged for Bear's stomach, catching him square in the gut with a powerful blow. Bear grunted but didn't lose his footing.

"That's using your head," Wooley shouted, slapping

his thigh in delight.

A cheer went up from the crowd when Chase followed up his wallop with a well-aimed kick in the center of Bear's groin.

The big man paled, doubling over in pain. Before Chase had time to gloat, Bear rose up, pulling a menacing-looking blade out of the inside of his boot. He lunged for Chase.

"Chase, watch out!" Wooley yelled. "He's got a knife."

A woman screamed; someone let out a shrill whistle.

The steel blade glittered ominously in the afternoon sunlight, slashing through the air with accurate precision as it ripped across the front of Chase's chest. Soon, blotches of red blood soaked through the blue material of his shirt where the knife had found its mark.

Out of the corner of his eye, Chase saw Wooley draw his gun and step down off the sidewalk. "Stay back, Wooley," Chase ordered. "I intend to finish what I started."

"But you're cut!"

Chase grinned through his pain, though the effort cost him dearly. "Just a scratch."

Like a steel-coiled spring, Chase sprung at Bear, knocking the knife out of the startled man's hand. Bear brought up his other fist, attempting to club Chase alongside the head, but Chase was quicker and ducked, grabbing Bear about the throat.

Pressing his thumbs against Bear's windpipe, Chase watched in satisfaction as Bear's face turned red, then purpled. Droplets of perspiration poured off Chase's brow; his breathing grew ragged as the exertion of restraining the large man began to take its toll.

The two remaining Donaldson brothers made a move forward, but Wooley motioned them back with his gun.

"You fight dirty, Donaldson," Chase said, forcing Bear down to his knees. "Shall I break your neck? I could very easily, you know."

Reaching up, Bear attempted to pry Chase's hands away from his neck, but his action only caused Chase to squeeze harder. "Please," Bear begged, barely above a whisper. "I give in. You win."

"You'll play by my rules?"

Bear attempted to speak, but emitted only a raspy sound; he nodded instead.

Chase released him, pushing him into the dirt. "You and your brothers get your guns and get out of town. I don't want to see your faces around here again for a good long while."

Three pairs of hate-filled eyes stared at Chase; Bear struggled to his feet but said nothing as he made his way back to the saloon.

"All right, the show's over; let's break this up and get back to business," Chase ordered the onlookers.

"You heard the marshal," Wooley said. "Scat."

After the crowd had dispersed, Chase grabbed onto Wooley's arm; his breathing was labored, his complexion pasty white. "Get me to the doctor's," he demanded. "I'm bleeding to death for Christ's sake."

Pulling down the green canvas shade that covered the front window of Doctor Watson's pharmacy as she readied the office for closing, Margaret looked out to observe Wooley and Chase heading in her direction. As

71

they neared the building, she noticed the large amount of blood covering the front of Chase's shirt. She let out a horrified gasp, releasing the shade string she held; the shade flapped loudly as it rewound itself around the piece of wooden dowel.

Rushing to the door, she pulled it open, her eyes widening in alarm. "What's happened?"

"Marshal's been hurt, Miss Margaret," Wooley replied, helping Chase into the room.

"Afternoon, Maggie," Chase said, his tone nonchalant, as if he were paying a social call. "Is the doctor around?"

Margaret noted the thin layer of dust covering his face, which was now more white than tan. She also noted the beads of perspiration dotting his upper lip and forehead—a clear indication of the pain he was in. "Bring him to the back, Wooley." Locking the front door, she rushed ahead to relight the kerosene lanterns she had just extinguished. "Put him there, on the examination table."

Crossing to the sink, she scrubbed her hands with a bar of lye soap and ordered over her shoulder, "Take off his shirt, Wooley. I'll be there in a minute."

Chase brushed Wooley's hands away when the deputy tried to undo the buttons on his shirt. "I'm not crippled for Christ's sake, only cut."

"You're lucky you're not dead," Wooley retorted, eyeing the cuts and abrasions on Chase's face. The marshal was turning as colorful as the desert at twilight. The area around his right eye was turning blue, and he had an ugly purplish bruise on his left cheekbone.

Wiping her hands on a clean towel, Margaret turned

to face her patient. The sight of Chase's naked chest rendered her speechless for a moment. She stared wide-eyed at the tanned, rippling muscles lightly covered with hair; she took a deep breath, finally finding her voice. "Would someone mind telling me what's been going on?"

Chase smiled, noting her discomfort at his lack of wearing apparel. "A bunch of animals—a bear, a moose, and a skunk—didn't care for my new town ordinances. The bear, in particular, took exception. We had an altercation."

"I take it by the looks of your face that you lost." She dabbed at the blood on his lip with a piece of gauze, pulling her hand back when he winced. "Sorry."

"No, siree, Miss Margaret, Chase won. You shoulda seen it. Why . . ."

"Wooley," Chase interrupted, "why don't you go on over to the saloon and make sure our friends left town, then lock up the office. I won't be back today."

A disgruntled expression crossed Wooley's face at having been robbed of the opportunity to relate the gruesome details of Chase's fight. He paused by the door. "You sure you don't need me?"

"I'm sure Margaret is capable of assisting the doctor. Isn't that right, Maggie?" He stared meaningfully at her, noting the faint blush covering her cheeks when the door slammed shut.

Ignoring Chase's question, Margaret grabbed a clean white cloth, wringing it out in the basin. Approaching her patient with trepidation, she said, "I need to wash the blood off your chest."

Just as she was about to apply the cloth, he grabbed her hand. "Where's the doctor?"

"Doc Watson is out of town. I assure you, I'm quite capable of taking care of your needs."

His smile was blatantly sexual. "I don't doubt it for a moment, darlin'."

Margaret turned beet red and resumed her ministrations. It took her a few minutes to wash the blood that had crusted on Chase's chest, but after she did, she was relieved to find that his cut was only superficial. It ran across the width of his chest in a line about six inches long. It was red and angry-looking, but not deep.

"You won't need stitches. The wound's not that deep. I'll just put some antiseptic on it and bandage it up. It should be healed in a few days."

Chase stared at Margaret in admiration. She didn't so much as flinch at the sight of blood, but she wasn't nearly as stoic about the sight of a man's naked chest, if those pink blotches on her cheeks were any indication. He smiled inwardly.

Pouring some of the antiseptic onto the gauze pad, Margaret dabbed it gently against the laceration, pausing at the sound of Chase's indrawn breath. "Am I hurting you?" Without thinking, she blew on his skin to reduce the stinging sensation and was surprised when she heard him suck in his breath once again. Looking up, their eyes locked. They stared at each other for a moment, assessing, questioning, until Chase broke the spell.

"I'm in pain, Maggie, but it doesn't have a thing to do with this knife cut."

She lowered her eyes, noting for the first time the large, unmistakable bulge in Chase's pants. She stepped back quickly, turning toward the cupboard, making a great pretense of finding just the right size bandage.

The fullness of Margaret's breasts was clearly outlined through her thin cotton dress when she reached up to pull the roll of gauze down off the top shelf of the cupboard. To Chase it was a mesmerizing sight. The taut peaks of her nipples evidenced the arousal she sought so desperately to hide; he felt himself growing hotter and harder by the minute.

"I feel awfully warm, Maggie," he said, his voice husky. "Do you suppose I have a fever?"

Taking a deep breath, Margaret approached the table again, determined not to let the sight of Chase's virility interfere with her medical professionalism. Reaching up, she placed her palm against his forehead; it was cool. "You feel fine to me, Marshal. Now let's get this bandage on so we can both go about our business."

With quick efficiency, she wrapped the bandage around Chase's chest. The feel of his soft mat of hair against her fingers created a tingly sensation in the pit of her stomach. Touching him so intimately was doing strange things to her insides—things she had never experienced when treating other patients before. She swallowed, biting her lip, trying to concentrate on the task at hand.

"You're very good at what you do, Maggie. You have a gentle touch."

"Thank . . . thank you," she stammered, biting the gauze material to sever it, tying off the ends. "There, that should hold." She stepped back, eager to put distance between them.

"You seem awfully nervous, Maggie. Is something the matter?"

She shook her head, gathering up the supplies. "No . . . nothing." She sounded breathless, even to her own ears.

Chase slid off the table, coming to stand behind her. Placing his hands on her shoulders, he turned her toward him. "How will I ever thank you for tending me, Maggie?"

His hot breath on her face made her heart beat faster. The feel of his hands on her shoulders caused a quickening in her loins. Would he kiss her? The thought flashed through her mind as she stared up at the tempting curve of his lips—those same lips that had haunted her dreams since the night he'd first kissed her.

"Do you think Doc Watson might have a shirt I could borrow? Mine's ruined, and I hate to go parading around town half-naked."

She blushed, pulling out of his embrace, trying to hide her disappointment. "I'm sure he does. I'll just run upstairs and check." She bolted out of the room and up the stairs, failing to notice the self-satisfied grin on Chase's face.

Maggie was weakening. How long before he could get what he needed from her? And just what was it that he needed? he asked himself. As if drawn by a magnetic force, he found himself climbing the stairs after her. He found her in Doc Watson's bedroom, going through the doctor's closet.

"Find anything?"

Shrieking, Margaret spun about, startled to find Chase right behind her. "You scared me to death!" She held Doc's shirt up in front of her, as if it could shield her from the erotic glitter in Chase's eyes.

"Let me see." He held out his hand, placing it across

76

her chest, atop her heart. He felt the uncontrollable pounding. He moved his hand slowly, seductively in a circular motion over her breast. "You do feel scared, darlin'. Are you?"

Margaret swallowed the lump in her throat. The breast he so casually claimed had come alive under his fondling. Her nipple, rigid with desire, strained against the thin material of her blouse, pushing into his palm with an eagerness that alarmed her. She grabbed onto his hand. "Stop," she cried. "You mustn't. It isn't right."

Pulling her into him, he felt the evidence of her need pressing into his chest and heard her soft moan of desire. Nuzzling her neck, he breathed in deeply. "You smell good, Maggie, like lavender. Did you know lavender was my favorite scent?"

She shook her head, not daring to speak, not knowing if she could.

"Kiss me, Maggie. You know you want to." The silver eyes glowed with an unmistakable challenge as they stared into Margaret's brown ones, which were filled with uncertainty.

"Please, let me go. I have to get home." There was panic in her voice as she thrust the shirt at him and ran toward the door. His words halted her.

"You can run away this time, Maggie. I'm not going to push you. But be aware, I always get what I go after. And darlin', I'm coming after you."

The sound of her feet as she fled down the stairs brought a smile to Chase's lips. The kill was never as much fun as the hunt, except, perhaps, when the prize was Margaret Parker's virginity.

Margaret rushed home as if the devil himself were on

her heels. *El Diablo de Ojos Plata: The Silver-Eyed Devil.* Quickening her pace, she didn't pause to exchange pleasantries with Mrs. Perkins, who was standing just inside the doorway of the grocery, nor did she pay attention to the three Simmons boys who were piling up wooden crates alongside the horse trough in front of Hobson's Hotel and taking turns jumping in. Normally, the sight of that would have warranted a thirty-minute lecture on the evils of germs and bacteria, but not today. Today, Margaret Parker had other, more pressing, things on her mind.

"Kiss me, Maggie. You know you want to."

She covered her ears, trying to block out Chase's seductive taunt. His accusation had been all too accurate. She did want to kiss him—to be kissed by him—and he knew it. Damn it, he knew it!

When she reached her home, she kicked open the front gate with her foot to vent her frustration, but all she succeeded in doing was smashing her toes.

"Damnation!" she cursed, grabbing her foot, which now throbbed in pain.

At the sight of Evelyn rounding the dwelling at a feverish pace, she finally smiled, bending over to give the pig a gentle pat on the snout before entering the house. Lupe was in the kitchen, setting the table for dinner.

"Margarita, whatever is the matter? You look as pale as that apron you have on."

Margaret glanced down, dismayed to discover that she'd not had the presence of mind to remove her apron before leaving Doc's office. *That man! What had he done to her?*

"You are not sick, are you?" Lupe probed, stepping

around the table to feel Margaret's cheek.

"I'm fine, Lupe. Just tired. I had . . ." She paused, searching for a plausible explanation. ". . . an exhausting day at work."

Lupe eyed Margaret suspiciously before pushing her into a chair and shoving a glass of sangria at her. "Drink this. It will make you feel better."

The sweet, fruity wine punch did taste refreshing, but Margaret wasn't at all sure it could cure what ailed her.

"I hear there is a big fight in town today. The marshal, he fights that *bastardo* Bear. Did you see it?"

Margaret felt her cheeks warm. "No," she answered, a little too quickly. "I didn't."

"The marshal . . . they say he was cut." Lupe noticed how flushed Margaret's cheeks had become, and she didn't think it was caused by the sangria. "Did you perhaps treat his wound?"

Margaret nodded, taking another sip of wine.

"He is very handsome, no? Very big, very strong. I hear he beats that *bastardo* to a pulp."

"Yes, he's very big," she replied in a throaty whisper, remembering how massively muscled his chest was. How large the bulge between his . . .

"Margarita! Just exactly where was this man cut to make you blush so?"

Margaret's head snapped up; she grabbed her burning cheeks. "Lupe!"

Lupe laughed. "Aha. I knew it. You find this man to your liking, no?"

"He's just a patient. I treated his knife wound, which, I might add, was on his chest."

"This Marshal Gallagher, isn't he the one who walked you home after the dance?"

Margaret nodded mutely.

"I knew it." Lupe took a seat at the table across from Margaret.

"Knew what?"

"He is your man, no? You are his woman?" She clapped her hands in childish pleasure.

"I am his woman, NO!" Margaret replied emphatically. "And you had better keep your wild imagination under control."

"*Sí,* Margarita," Lupe said, a teasing smile curving her lips. "I will keep my imagination under control. But will you be able to keep yours?" She knew the look of a woman in love when she saw it.

A resigned expression crossed Margaret's face. Not a chance, she thought, feeling an unwelcome queasiness settle into the pit of her stomach. Clutching her middle to stop the fluttering, she stared down into her lap. *Not a chance.*

Chapter Six

Sandy Loomis watched the approach of the three riders as they traversed the narrow trail leading to the hideout. He could see clearly for almost a mile from his position atop the mountain where the cabin, which was little more than a one-room shack, was situated. There was only one way in and one way out, and it would be damned difficult for anyone to sneak up and catch him unawares.

Not that those three jackasses could sneak up on a blind and deaf beggar, he thought, his face twisting in disgust. He would never understand why the boss had insisted on hiring them in the first place.

They had gotten along just fine by themselves these past four years, pulling bank jobs in San Antonio, Santa Fe, Phoenix, and a host of other towns. Along with the money they had pulled from the bank robberies, they had supplemented their income quite nicely with an occasional episode of cattle rustling. They certainly didn't need the help of three dimwitted incompetents.

Tipping his chair back against the wooden planks of the cabin wall, Sandy locked his hands behind his head, smiling in satisfaction. It had been a good life so far, and the boss promised it was going to get even better.

As the three brothers approached the cabin, Sandy rose to his feet, lighting a smoke. Leaning his right arm against the porch railing, he pasted on an affable smile. "What took you boys so long? I expected you back yesterday."

"We had some trouble in town, Sandy," Skunk replied, fidgeting nervously with the leather reins in his hand. "There's a new marshal in Purgatory. Him and Bear got into it."

Sandy's smile soured. He looked up, shading his eyes to stare at the big man before him. He wanted to laugh. Bear's face was a sickly shade of purple; he had bruises at the base of his throat where his shirt lay open. It looked like the big bastard had finally met his match.

"Jesus! What the hell happened to you?"

Bear cast him a menacing look. "I gave as good as I got. I wouldn't worry about it, Loomis." Tying up his horse, he stepped onto the porch.

"Well, I am worryin' about it, you dumb son of a bitch." Sandy tossed his cheroot into the dirt, wishing it were Bear's head he was grinding beneath his boot heel. "The boss said we was to keep our noses clean. He doesn't want no trouble, not until he's ready to make his move."

"When we goin' to meet this fella?" Moose inquired. "You said when we hired on that we was goin' to be rich soon."

"The boss has it all worked out. When he gets back from Tombstone, he'll fill us in on the plan. Until then, we sit tight and stay out of trouble." He shook his head in disgust. "Shit! If I'd have known you boys were going to start a ruckus, I'd have never sent you in for supplies."

The three brothers cast quick, nervous glances at each other. Skunk stepped back, while Bear kicked at a knot in the board beneath his feet.

"We didn't get no supplies," Moose confessed. "The marshal kicked us out of town afore we could pick up our goods."

"Sheeet!" Sandy hollered. "You three are good for nothing. I told the boss you were a bunch of morons."

Bear's eyes glittered dangerously; he took a step forward, clenching his pawlike fists. "I don't like being called names."

In a split second the fair-haired cowboy drew his gun, leveling it at Bear's chest. "I say and do whatever I please, you dumb bastard. I'm in charge. If you don't like it, just say so."

Moose stepped between the two men, pulling on Bear's arm. "It weren't nothin' personal, Sandy. Bear's just had hisself a bad day."

The cowboy snickered, holstering his gun. "Seeing as how you three *morons,*" he emphasized the word, daring Bear to dispute it, "didn't get the provisions I sent you for, I'll have to go into town myself. What did you say this marshal's name was?"

"Gallagher . . . Chase Gallagher," Skunk replied.

Sandy's eyes widened imperceptibly before he shuttered them closed. "Gallagher, huh?" Shit! This was going to complicate matters. The boss said this might happen, but Sandy never really paid him no mind. Until now.

83

"You look kinda funny, Loomis. You heard of this Gallagher before?" Bear asked.

"Everyone with half a brain's heard of Chase Gallagher. He's killed more men than this desert's got cactus. You're lucky to be alive, Donaldson."

Bear blanched, as did the other two men.

"Try and keep out of trouble while I'm gone, boys. If you think Gallagher's mean, it's because you ain't met the boss yet." Sandy laughed at the anxious expressions on the faces of the three men and headed for the barn.

Seated in the far corner of La Cantina de Flores, Chase and Tom faced each other across the small wooden table, listening to the three Mexican guitar players strumming an enthusiastic rendition of "La Cucaracha." Outside, darkness had descended, blanketing the sky a velvet black, while inside, a fat, smoky candle in the center of the table flickered brightly, providing a glimmer of light in the noisy room.

Pouring himself a shot of tequila, Chase banged the bottle loudly on the table. "I tell you, Tom, I'm getting too old for this marshaling business. I never should have let you talk me into taking this damned job." He rubbed his right shoulder, which still felt stiff after his altercation with Bear Donaldson, despite three days of soaking in a hot tub. Truth was, his whole body felt as if he'd been trampled beneath the hooves of a stampeding herd.

Tom smiled, swallowing his *aguardiente*. The whiskey burned as it went down, causing him to squint. "You never did know when the deck was stacked against you."

"Is that so? Well, I distinctly remember a time down in El Paso when you weren't so smart yourself."

Tom grinned, thinking back to the fistfight he'd had with the biggest member of the Tyler gang, Nick Drummond. The three-hundred-pound Drummond had almost beat him to death, and would have, too, if Chase hadn't interfered and shot the gunman.

Being with Chase brought back old memories—memories of Santa Fe, El Paso, Sonora. They had shared many a drink in cantinas just like this one while performing their duties as U.S. marshals.

Those were good days, exciting times, but they didn't measure up to the feeling he'd had when Betsy had informed him about the baby. Nothing could measure up to that.

Thinking of Betsy brought Margaret to mind, as it often did. The three of them had shared a lot of remembrances over the years, some good, some not, but always they had remained friends.

Frowning, Tom cast a quizzical glance in Chase's direction. "Wooley tells me that Margaret fixed you up after the fight you had with Donaldson."

Chase sucked the lemon, licked the salt from his hand, then swallowed the shot of tequila. "Yeah. What about it?"

"I don't want to sound like an overprotective mama—Lord knows, Margaret's already got one of those—but I'd like to know what all this interest is that you've been showing toward Margaret. She's hardly your type of woman."

Chase's right eyebrow quirked. "And just what is my type?"

"Don't play with me, Chase. You know damned well that whores are more to your liking. You haven't had a relationship with a decent woman since I've known you. It's slam—bang—good-bye with you."

The candlelight reflected in Chase's eyes, making them appear hard and bright like diamonds. "Maybe, I haven't met the right one." *Or maybe the right one is dead.*

"You saying you've got honorable intentions toward Margaret?"

Chase shrugged. "Maybe. What difference does it make to you? I hear you and Maggie called it quits years ago."

"That doesn't mean that I don't still love her . . . care what happens to her."

His lips thinning in displeasure, Chase couldn't keep the sarcasm out of his voice. "Why don't you go home to your wife, Tom, before I lead you astray?" He took another shot of tequila, welcoming the stinging sensation all the way down to his gut.

"Don't be such an ass, Gallagher. We're friends, remember? Besides, I can't go home. Betsy's hosting the Women's Guild meeting at the house."

"The what?"

"A bunch of the town women meet once a month to discuss social issues, beautification projects, that sort of thing."

Chase snickered. "When a bunch of women get together there's only three things they discuss: men, babies, and sex. And not necessarily in that order."

"You think so?" Tom pondered a moment, then shook his head. "Nah. Alberta and Marion would rather have their tongues pulled out. Those two old hags are too prudish to engage in anything so sordid."

"I got five dollars says I'm right." Chase pulled out the money, laying it flat on the table.

Staring at the money, then at Chase, Tom grinned, pushing himself to his feet. "You're on, amigo. Let's go."

The monthly meeting of the Purgatory Women's Guild was about to begin. Every chair in Betsy Fraser's front parlor was filled, including the green-and-pink floral chintz-covered sofa that Betsy had acquired from her mother only last month.

Tapping her spoon against her china teacup, Esther Perkins brought the meeting to order in a voice that was quiet, yet firm. The same gravelly voice that had chased dozens of candy-stealing children out of her grocery. "Now, ladies, if you will kindly quiet down, we need to discuss the particulars of this year's fund-raising event. Do we have any suggestions?"

"How about a bake sale?" Marion Holmes suggested. "I believe my applesauce cake would bring a high price, as it does every year." She smiled smugly, folding her hands primly in her lap, as if the matter were settled.

"We've done bake sales two years in a row, Marion. We need to come up with something different."

"Bertie's right," Betsy concurred. "And I think I've got just the answer, though it's a bit risqué."

Excited giggles and twitters floated through the room. Marion looked down her bulbous nose at the younger members of the group, crushing them to silence. As past president and founder of the Women's

Guild, she wielded a great deal of influence among the women present. Those who weren't intimidated by her biting tongue, soon found her immense proportions too formidable to contend with.

Betsy continued, "Since we're going to need a substantial sum of money this year to repair the roof on the schoolhouse and purchase the garbage incinerator that Marshal Gallagher has suggested, I propose we hold an auction."

"An auction? What's so risqué about that? We held one a few years back," Esther reminded them.

"What I'm proposing is a different type of auction." Betsy paused, unsure of how to explain the outrageous plan she had just concocted. Patting her softly rounded tummy three times for luck, she said, "I'm suggesting that we auction off some of our unmarried women."

The ladies of the room exchanged startled glances before Marion blurted out in a shrill voice, "What?" Her cheeks turned as pink as the velvet cushions she was seated upon; she fanned herself anxiously with her napkin. "You mean like those soiled doves who work in the saloons?"

"Marion Holmes, of course Betsy wasn't suggesting any such thing. Were you, Betsy?"

Smiling weakly at Bertie, and then at the surprised but anxious faces of the others in the room, Betsy was saved from answering when the door flew open and Margaret entered. Margaret looked flustered and out of breath, like she had run all the way from her house.

"Sorry, I'm late, but Mama wasn't feeling well tonight." She removed her coat, hanging it on the oak and brass hall tree.

A chorus of sympathetic murmurs ensued, followed

by a discreet exchange of pitying looks.

"That's quite all right, dear," Esther assured her. "Betsy was just about to suggest a plan for our fund-raiser this year . . . a risqué one, I believe she said."

Margaret searched Betsy's face, noting the telltale mischief in her eyes. Good Lord, what had the impulsive woman come up with now? Seating herself on the sofa next to Audra Simmons, the wife of the only lawyer in Purgatory, she waited for Betsy to continue.

"As I was saying, I propose that we auction off several of our most eligible women."

A collective gasp went up. Marion paled as white as the lace curtains hanging behind her head.

Betsy, fearing that the overweight woman was going to faint and demolish the mahogany tea table resting in front of her—the only really new piece of furniture that she possessed—added quickly, "Now, it's not as improper as it sounds. True, many men do purchase whores for their amusement . . ."

"I'll say," Audra butted in, leaning forward in a conspiratorial fashion. "I heard just the other day from Myra Cummings that her son, Tommy, had engaged the services of a slut by the name of Lillie Mae. Myra said, Tommy claimed she had the biggest . . ."

"Audra Simmons! For shame. This is hardly proper conversation for maiden ladies," Alberta exclaimed, patting her flushed cheeks.

All eyes turned on Margaret who blushed profusely. Not because she was the only *maiden lady* in the room, but because Audra's words conjured up visions of Lillie Mae in Chase Gallagher's arms—visions of Lillie Mae's ample endowments pressed provocatively against Chase's chest.

"Margaret, are you all right? You look a little funny." Betsy bit back the smile that threatened to cross her lips. She'd bet her last dollar that the "funny" look on Margaret's face was jealousy.

Margaret flashed her an indignant look. "I'm fine. Why don't you finish telling us about your preposterous plan."

"My plan is simple: The single women of this town will be auctioned off to the highest bidder. They will then be required to spend the remainder of the day with the gentlemen who purchased them, as his companion. All the proprieties will be strictly observed, of course."

"Didn't I tell you, Tom?" Chase whispered, elbowing his companion in the ribs. "They're in there talking about selling off women like they were a herd of cattle."

The two men stood below the open window of the parlor, listening intently to the discussion going on within.

"They haven't discussed anything indecent, yet."

"How do you know? We just got here."

Before Tom could respond, Marion's agitated voice floated out the window and over their heads.

"What if the bidder ravishes the woman? What if he tears off her clothes and has his way with her?"

Chase smiled smugly, holding out his hand.

Grudgingly, Tom dug into his pocket, withdrawing a five-dollar bill.

"Really ladies, you are letting your imaginations run

90

wild. Nothing like that is going to happen." Betsy thought she saw a flicker of disappointment cross Marion's face, but she couldn't be certain. "Well, what do you think?"

"I think it's a horrible idea. And since I happen to be the only unmarried woman in this room, save for the Widow Holmes, I vote no," Margaret said, folding her arms firmly across her chest, a pinched expression marring her features.

"I know Cyndi Lang would agree and Hannah Morgan, too," Bertie said, ignoring Margaret's protestations.

"Yes, and I bet the two Adamson twins would participate."

"Those two horse-faced creatures would jump at the chance to accompany anything in pants, Betsy, and you know it," Margaret retorted. That ridiculous drowning ploy they had pulled last Founder's Day while swimming half naked in the San Carlos River hadn't fooled many people, especially Margaret. Why, they'd parade stark naked down Main Street if they thought it would help them snare a husband, she thought uncharitably.

All eyes looked up as the front door slammed shut and Chase and Tom entered the room.

"Ladies," Chase said, bowing his head in greeting. "Tom and I couldn't help but overhear your discussion when we came through the door. We'd like to help."

Margaret flushed at the sight of the man whose face and body had tormented her every waking moment for the past three days.

"Why, Marshal, how nice to see you," Alberta gushed. "And of course, you, too, Tom. Do come in

91

and join us."

"I hardly think that would be appropriate."

"Oh, don't be so rude, Margaret. Where are your manners? Marshal Gallagher is new here. He's not familiar with our monthly meetings, and he's graciously offered his assistance."

Chase smiled triumphantly, ignoring Margaret's double-edged glare, which was divided between himself and Alberta Bottoms. "I have a suggestion as to how we can settle this little difference of opinion." He pulled a gold coin out of his pants pocket.

Tom's eyes widened at the sight of the familiar coin, but he refrained from speaking, swallowing his smile.

"We'll flip. Heads—you ladies in favor of the auction win. Tails—Miss Parker does. Does that sound fair?"

All eyes turned on Margaret again. Feeling outnumbered, and not wishing to appear annoyed, though she certainly was, she nodded her acquiescence.

Chase flipped the coin in the air, catching it in his palm. "Betsy, would you care to do the honors?" He splayed his fingers to reveal the coin.

"It's heads," Betsy said, smiling excitedly, then noting Margaret's furious glare, she sobered immediately.

Wonderful, Margaret thought, staring at the coin and then at the aggravating man who held it. Now she would be paraded before the town like some whore exhibiting her wares. She bit her lip to keep from voicing those very thoughts.

When everyone but Margaret had adjourned into the kitchen to partake of cake and coffee, Chase crossed the room, seating himself next to her on the sofa.

"You don't look very happy. Come on, be a good sport. After all, it's for a worthy cause."

Margaret was so furious she could hardly speak. Trying hard to keep her anger in check, she retorted in a voice as reasonable as she could muster, "Really, Marshal Gallagher! I don't need your advice on how to react or behave. Just because I don't relish the prospect of being paraded in front of a group of men like a prize bull . . ."

"Heifer," Chase corrected.

She shot him a withering glance. "Like a prize animal up for auction, doesn't mean that I'm not a good sport. I'll have you know that I've been pelted in the face with cream pies, made a complete and utter fool out of myself during the sack races last Fourth of July, and was nearly killed during a cherry pie-eating contest when I swallowed a pit. So don't tell me about good causes. I've done my share."

Awe then admiration crossed his face. Margaret was certainly full of surprises. She had more layers to her than an old maid in a full set of underwear, and he would love to peel each one back to discover the real woman beneath.

"I stand corrected. But you needn't worry about being embarrassed," he said, rising to his feet. "You won't be auctioned off to just anyone."

A kernel of suspicion took root and began to grow; Margaret shifted uncomfortably in her seat, her eyes narrowing suspiciously. "How do you know?"

Chase grinned, crossing to the door. "Because I intend to buy you."

"You!"

"That's right, darlin'. You'll be all mine, to do with as

93

I please." He winked, blew her a kiss, and walked out of the room.

Margaret's jaw almost hit her chest as she stared in stupefaction at Chase's retreating back. When the full import of his words finally registered, she vaulted to her feet and rushed to the door, eager to tell him just what she thought of his monstrous conceit.

But it was too late; he was gone.

Turning on her heel, a murderous gleam lighting her eyes, she marched to the kitchen. Betsy Fraser would pay for this; she would pay dearly.

"Marshal Gallagher?"

Chase looked up from the wanted posters he studied to find a white-haired gentleman standing in the doorway of his office. The man was neatly dressed, but his clothes were badly wrinkled, as if he had slept in them. In his hands, which were gnarled but well-manicured, he clutched a pearl-gray felt bowler.

"I'm Chase Gallagher. Can I help you?"

Shutting the door behind him, the man stepped forward, thrusting out his hand. "William Watson, Marshal. It's a pleasure to finally meet you."

Chase shook his hand, returning his smile. "We've already been introduced, in an odd sort of way." Reaching into the bottom drawer of his desk, he retrieved a paper-wrapped parcel marked Wong's Laundry, handing it to the doctor.

Doc's brows wrinkled in confusion as he stared at the parcel. "I'm afraid I don't understand."

"I had to borrow one of your shirts a few days ago. Mine was cut up a bit."

The corners of Doc's mouth turned up into a smile as comprehension dawned. "Ah, yes, I seem to remember Margaret telling me something about that, but I was so tired when I arrived home this morning, all I could think about was taking a nap. I'm afraid I didn't pay her much mind."

"Thanks for the loan."

Doc reached into his coat pocket, extracting his pipe. "Margaret treated you in my absence?" Tapping some tobacco into the bowl, he lit it.

Chase nodded. "Just a slight knife cut. She patched me up—did a real fine job, too." There was hardly a scar, not that it would have mattered. He already had a number of others, one more would have made no difference.

"Margaret's a good girl. I couldn't get along without her."

"Why don't you sit, have a cup of coffee." Chase pointed to the chair by the potbellied stove.

Doc complied, setting the parcel down on his lap. "I've only got a minute, but I wouldn't mind a cup. Thanks."

"Maggie . . . Margaret worked for you long?" Chase asked, filling the two cups with coffee, handing the doctor one.

Doc didn't miss the casual use of Margaret's name; his eyebrows rose a fraction at the slip. "About eight years. Her father left Margaret and her mother in a rather precarious financial situation. I stepped in to help." He smiled to himself. "Best move I ever made. Margaret's a fine woman. Loyal to those she loves"—he frowned—"to a fault, I'm afraid."

"You're speaking of her mother?"

Surprise touched the wrinkled face. "She told you?"

"A little. I heard the woman's screeching firsthand. She's quite demanding."

"Demanding and demented. Phoebe's as crazy as a loon. I don't blame Jonathan Parker for leaving. Had I been in his shoes, I might have done the same thing."

"You know her father?" Chase asked, staring into the depths of his coffee cup, trying to keep the excitement out of his voice.

"Met him a time or two. He looked to be a nice sort. Fancy dresser. Cultured speech. Never seemed like he belonged here in the territory. Too polished."

Chase's head rose up sharply. "What do you mean?"

"Parker looked as if he belonged in some drawing room back East. His hands were soft, like he never did a day's work—I notice things like that about people—and he had a fondness for jewelry. He always wore a diamond stickpin on his tie. I never could figure out where he got the money for it. He carried a pocket watch, was never without it; it was the prettiest watch you'd ever want to see. Very expensive-looking. Gold—engraved with a . . . ."

"Shamrock," Chase whispered absently.

"That's right! How'd you know?"

He shrugged. "Just a guess. My father had one like it." He balled his fists, trying to keep his emotions in check.

"What a coincidence." Doc shook his head, pushing himself to his feet. "Before I forget, Marshal, the sheriff down in Tucson asked me to deliver a message. Apparently, there was some trouble in Tombstone—a bank robbery. He thought you'd be interested in knowing."

Chase's mouth tightened a fraction. "Did Sheriff Brown give you any details?" If Mike Brown had gone to the trouble of sending a message, something was up.

Rubbing his chin, Doc thought for a moment. "Come to think of it, he did. Sheriff said you might want to follow up on this one. Said that the description of the robber matched the man you've been looking for."

Chase jumped to his feet, fingering the handle of his gun. Noting Doc's puzzled stare, he forced a smile to his lips and his hands back down to his sides. "Thanks for the message, Doc. It looks like I'll be taking a trip to Tombstone."

"Trouble?"

His face became a mask of stone. "Only for the man who robbed the bank."

Chapter Seven

Perched high on a plateau between the Dragoon and Whetstone Mountains, Tombstone had passed its heyday as the prosperous silver-rich community it once had been. Once larger, more cultured and sophisticated than San Francisco, it was now just another has-been—a quiet city on the verge of extinction.

Exiting the stage, Chase slapped his Stetson against his pant leg, throwing up a billow of dust. He felt tired and dirty. The ride from Tucson had taken seventeen hours and had hardly been worth the ten-dollar fare he'd paid. More than once, he had cursed himself for not riding Lucifer. His horse's company would have been far preferable to the odoriferous drummer and the taciturn lawyer he'd shared the stagecoach with.

Glancing down Allen Street, the main thoroughfare of the town, a dozen memories assailed him. It'd been years since he'd stepped foot in the "Town Too Tough To Die," as the early inhabitants had labeled Tombstone.

Tombstone was a wild, uninhibited place back then.

98

The silver strikes had brought, not only miners, but claim jumpers, con artists, whores, gamblers, and gunmen—the cream of a degenerate society.

Heading north, away from what was once known as the "decent" part of the street, Chase passed the notorious Bird Cage Theatre, where a man could indulge in all types of entertainments from vaudeville acts to prostitutes, who plied their trade behind the twelve curtained cages lining the perimeter of the room. For twenty-four hours a day, seven days a week, the amusements never stopped.

Continuing, he passed the infamous O.K. Corral where the Earps, along with Doc Holliday, had allegedly fought it out with the Clantons and the McLaurys six years before. The gun battle had actually taken place on Fremont Street, a block away, in front of Fly's Photographic Gallery, but Chase supposed that a picture-taking establishment didn't possess quite the allure a livery stable did for the dime novelists who portrayed the incident.

Entering the Alhambra Saloon, which was virtually deserted this early in the day, he sidled up to the long mahogany bar, placing a dollar down in front of him. His throat felt as parched as the miserable arid country he had just rode through, and a stiff shot of whiskey was just the cure for what ailed him.

"Help you, mister?" the fresh-faced boy behind the bar inquired.

Things had surely changed, Chase thought sadly, staring at the brown-haired, pimply-faced lad. Not a familiar face in sight, and a boy still wet behind the ears tending bar.

"Whiskey . . . and it's Marshal, not mister." He

threw open his duster, displaying the silver badge on the front of his frock coat. "Clark around? I need to talk to him."

The boy's eyes rounded at the sight of the badge. He swallowed, trying to keep his hand steady while he poured the drink. "Sure thing, Marshal. I'll fetch him straightaway."

Chase grabbed the bottle along with the glass of whiskey and took a seat at a table in the corner of the room, his back against the wall. Old habits died hard, he thought, but he wasn't fixin' to end up like Bill Hickcock with a bullet in his back. He sipped slowly on his drink, waiting for Richard Clark to join him.

From the red velvet curtains on the windows to the black-and-red diamond-patterned Brussels carpet on the floor, it looked like Dick was doing well at his chosen profession. There were few who could beat Dick Clark at a game of poker; he was a player extraordinaire—a master of the game.

"Chase Gallagher, you dog. What the hell brings you back to Tombstone?"

Chase looked up, swallowing his surprise at how Dick's appearance had changed in the last few years. His brown hair had grayed considerably, and there was an unhealthy pallor to his complexion. "You look like shit, Clark. What the hell happened?"

Pulling out a chair, Dick seated himself at the table, calling for another glass. "I've got the TB, Chase. It's killing me . . . slowly but surely."

"It ain't killed that bastard John Holliday yet. Don't be too sure you won't make it."

Dick's hand shook as he poured the whiskey into his glass. "I got other problems, as well."

Noting the redness of Dick's eyes, the gauntness of his face, Chase frowned. "You don't have to worry about dying from tuberculosis, Clark. The morphine you're addicted to will kill you long before that. Why don't you sell this place and settle down on that cattle ranch you bought in the San Pedro Valley? It'd be a whole lot healthier."

Dick's smile was downright naughty as he confessed, "I only bought the ranch so's I could attend the cattlemen's conferences. Fleecing them fools has put a tidy sum in my pocket."

"You'll never change."

"Nor you. You're still wearing that marshal's badge, though you swore last time we met that you were retiring."

"I thought so, too, until Tom Fraser talked me into moving to Purgatory."

"Purgatory!" The gambler's laugh was followed by a spasm of coughing. He shook his head, spitting discreetly into his handkerchief before wiping his mouth with the square of white cotton. "Holy Jesus, you are a glutton for punishment. How the hell's Fraser? I haven't seen hide nor hair of him in years."

"Respectable. He's gone and married a pretty little blonde. They're expecting their first baby."

"Fraser married! That do beat all. Shit, I can still remember all the trouble you two used to get into. Sheriff Behan threatened to have both your badges more times than I care to remember."

Chase hid his smile behind his hand as he smoothed down his mustache. "We've matured."

"Haven't we all? My hair's as gray as old Barney's over at the tonsorial parlor, and I can't see nearly as well as I used to."

Chase sobered instantly. "I was counting on your powers of observation, Dick. I heard the bank was robbed a few days back."

Dick's smile faded. "It was Parker. He played faro in my place the night before the robbery."

Chase's eyes turned glacial; he grabbed the whiskey glass so forcibly it shattered in his hand. "The bastard's always a step ahead of me."

"Vengeance can kill a man as surely as a bullet, Chase. Why don't you give it up? Parker ain't worth all the years you've wasted on him."

"He killed my family . . . my fiancée. I won't give up until he's dead."

"Well, he's eluded you again. My sources tell me that Parker rode out right after the heist. Headed for the mountains north of here. You'll never track him down."

Chase knew Dick was right. He'd tracked Parker many times before, had even used an Indian guide to help him, but he'd never been able to find the bastard. Parker was as slippery as snot on a doorknob.

"Why don't you spend a couple of days and relax. Maybe, play a little poker before you ride out."

Chase's eyebrows rose; the light from the crystal chandelier overhead illuminated his incredulity. "With you? You think I'm nuts? Hell, you've beaten just about everyone in the territory and beyond. I'm not in your league."

Dick leaned back in his chair, drawing a well-used deck of cards out of his coat pocket. "Remember when I took Horace Tabor for all he had? I even won that carload of silver ore that stood outside on the track." He shuffled the cards, spreading them facedown in front of him. "It was the closest I ever came to owning a mine." With a skill honed by years of practice, he extracted the four aces from the deck, holding them up for Chase's inspection.

"Yeah, I remember, which is exactly why I'm turning down your offer. Besides, I've got some pressing business to conduct in Purgatory."

"What kind of business? I never figured you for no businessman."

"I'm about to make the biggest, most important, purchase of my life."

Clark was visibly impressed and asked, "A mine?"

Chase chuckled, shaking his head. "A woman."

"I don't know why I let you talk me into things, Betsy Fraser. This is by far the most scatterbrained of all your schemes. And believe me, you've had some winners." Margaret reached for another piece of yellow ribbon, fashioning the satin material into a bow while she spoke.

She and Betsy were seated at the table in Margaret's kitchen, preparing the decorations for Saturday's festivities. The kerosene lantern on the table flickered softly, illuminating Margaret's displeasure.

"I'm sure to suffer the biggest humiliation of my life," she added.

"Oh, posh!" Betsy cast off her comment with a wave of her hand. "Quit being so dramatic. You're starting to sound like your mother." She ignored the scathing look Margaret threw at her, adding, "Hand me those scissors, will you?"

"My mother is going to go into a permanent decline when she hears that her only daughter is to be auctioned off like a common strumpet."

"She won't know. Besides, it's for a good cause."

"Won't know! Why you've got handbills plastered on every street corner and building in this town. What if Lupe or one of Mother's churchgoing friends happens to mention it?"

Betsy sighed. "I don't mean to be unkind, Margaret, but you're a grown woman for heaven's sake. It's time you quit worrying about what your mother thinks. Nothing you've done has ever pleased her; she's always going to find fault, no matter what you do. Haven't you figured that out yet?"

Margaret opened her mouth to reply, but was saved from answering by a knock on the front door. "I wonder who that could be?"

Betsy smiled wickedly. "Maybe Chase is back from Tombstone. He probably missed you and has come to call."

Margaret sighed, pushing herself to her feet. If only it were true, but she didn't have any illusions about Chase Gallagher. He was the kind of man who craved excitement—thrived on it, and she wasn't what a man would call an exciting woman.

"It's probably Doc, or one of Mother's do-gooders come to pay their obligatory call," she said, secretly praying with every step she took toward the door that she was wrong and Betsy was right. Opening it, her face fell, for it wasn't Chase, but Francis Brooks who stood in the doorway.

"Evening, Margaret. Hope I'm not interrupting your dinner."

Swallowing her disappointment, Margaret faced the banality of her existence. "Come in, Francis. You haven't interrupted anything but an annoying conversation I was having with Betsy."

He paused by the door, looking ill at ease. "I can come back another time."

Guilt, fed by years of bowing to others' wishes, forced her to be kind. "Don't be silly. We were just making bows to decorate the platform for the Founder's Day auction."

Twirling his hat nervously in his fingers, Francis cleared his throat. "Actually, the auction is the reason I'm here."

Margaret kept her features deceptively composed, hiding the annoyance that threatened to consume her. Here it comes, she thought. The lecture on the impropriety of the auction—the chastisement for her unseemly participation in such a pagan event. "Really?" she asked.

He swallowed, causing his Adam's apple to protrude more than usual. "I'm planning to bid on you, Margaret. I just wanted you to know that my intentions are strictly honorable."

Margaret's mouth fell open; she snapped it shut, fearful that she would laugh in his face. Francis's intentions were never anything but strictly honorable. The fact that he was going to the auction to bid on a woman was ludicrous enough, but for him to think that he had to explain his motives . . . it was really too much. She bit the inside of her cheek at the sight of the red, telltale blotches now covering Francis's face—blotches that always appeared whenever he was the least bit nervous.

"I hope I haven't offended you." Francis reached for her hand. "That was never my intention."

She shook her head.

"It is for a worthy cause, after all. And after I prayed and deliberated on the propriety of such an . . . an unusual event, I've decided to participate." The words came out in a rush, as if the telling of them took every ounce of his strength.

What a sanctimonious toad! Margaret thought, pulling her hand out of Francis's limp and clammy hold. At least Chase was honest in his motives, however misguided they were.

"Well, I really must be going. I promised Mrs. Simmons I would tutor Chad this evening."

Mumbling her farewells, Margaret shut the door and leaned against it, trying to hold back the spasms of laughter threatening to explode; it was no use. Grabbing herself about the middle, she doubled over, giving in to her hysteria, which was how Betsy found her a few moments later.

"Good heavens! Are you ill?" Betsy asked, rushing forward.

Betsy's concerned expression set Margaret off again. "No . . . I . . ." She shook her head, unable to answer.

"Who was at the door?"

"Fra . . . Fra . . . Francis."

Betsy smiled, needing no further explanation.

"He's . . . he's going to bid on me."

Betsy laughed aloud at that. "I'm surprised . . . as tightfisted as he is. I always expect moths to fly out of his change purse whenever he opens it."

Margaret composed herself, wiping her tears on the edge of her sleeve. "Me, too."

"You'll probably raise the most money, Margaret. I heard Pete Forrester is going to bid on you, as well as Henry Persall."

And Chase Gallagher, Margaret added silently, smiling to herself. She wasn't about to confide that fact to Betsy, however; the woman had a predilection for meddling.

"I wouldn't be at all surprised if the marshal enters the bidding. He's sweet on you, Margaret."

A guilty, hot blush swept over Margaret's cheeks. Without answering, she hurried back to the kitchen, heading straight for the pitcher of iced tea that rested on the counter.

"You know something that you're not telling me, Margaret Parker," Betsy continued, close on Margaret's heels. "I want to know what it is."

Turning, Margaret smiled innocently. "Care for some tea?" She pressed the glass into Betsy's hands, then resumed her seat at the table.

Studying Margaret's face intently, Betsy's eyes narrowed. "Is something going on between you and Chase that I don't know about?"

Margaret looked aghast. "Heavens no!"

Setting down her glass, Betsy gathered up her supplies, stuffing them into her satchel. "Well, you sure act as if there is. And don't think I haven't missed the way you two stare at each other. Those looks have been hotter than the inside of a cookstove."

Covering her cheeks, which were as hot as Betsy had just described, Margaret jumped up, shaking her head. "You are positively awful. Chase Gallagher is not interested in me. Why a man like that could have any woman he wanted. What would he want with the likes of me?"

Betsy's eyebrow arched. *What indeed!* Patting Margaret tenderly on the cheek, she replied, "You're a lovely woman, Margaret. Any man would be lucky to have you for a wife."

"A wife?!"

Betsy nodded. "Tom says Chase is thinking about settling down. It seems perfectly logical to me that he's decided to court you."

Margaret refused to acknowledge the fluttering in the pit of her stomach. "And what if I don't wish to be courted?"

"Then you're crazy. Who wouldn't want to lie beneath that big hunk of man every night? Lord, it gives me goose bumps just thinking about it."

Margaret's heart started racing so fast she thought she was going to faint. She grabbed for the back of the chair.

"Are you all right?" Betsy asked, alarmed by the pallor on her friend's face. She wagged her head, clucking her tongue in disbelief while helping Margaret back into the chair. "Good Lord! If just talking about bedding Chase makes you faint, what are you going to do when it actually happens?"

Reaching for the glass of iced tea, Margaret gulped it down, holding the cold glass next to her forehead. "It's not going to happen," she choked.

"Girl, you've got a lot of growing up to do. If you think a man like Chase is going to be dissuaded from getting what he wants, think again. He's a lawman; he always gets his man." With those prophetic words, Betsy slammed out the door, leaving Margaret to stare openmouthed after her.

Was everyone crazy? Margaret wondered. First, Betsy comes up with that ridiculous idea for an auction, which everyone thought was just wonderful. Then, ever-practical, dull-as-dishwater, Francis Brooks comes by to inform her that he's going to bid on her. And now, she's expected to be ecstatic because Betsy suspects that Chase Gallagher, a ruthless, gun-toting killer, who uses up women like bullets, intends to court her.

She slapped her forehead, a gesture she had seen Lupe do countless times. If this was sanity, God save her from the rest of the lunatics.

Chapter Eight

Seated demurely in one of the wooden folding chairs, her hands folded primly in her lap, Margaret stared nervously out at the crowd from her position atop the platform. The participants were seated in front of Hobson's Hotel; the auction scheduled to begin at any moment.

The sun at its zenith made Margaret hot, adding to her own nervous perspiration. She had purposely worn one of her older gowns—a thin, red lawn, embroidered with tiny white roses. Being years out of date, it was not terribly stylish, but cooler than many she owned.

Observing the sea of anxious faces staring back at her, Margaret swallowed. It seemed as if the entire town of Purgatory had turned out for the auction, which the handbills had touted as the most daring and innovative fund-raiser this side of the Colorado River.

As Betsy had predicted, Pete Forrester, the blacksmith, and Henry Pursall, from the land office, were in attendance. She fought the urge to groan aloud as she stared at the two men. Both winked and waved simultaneously, causing Margaret to blush and shift uncomfortably in her seat. She'd curl up and die if either one of them made a successful bid for her, she thought.

Pete was short and stocky with blond curly hair and a long, drooping mustache. He had hands as big as bear paws that loved to pinch and pet, as she had found out firsthand after accompanying him to the church social last May. Her posterior had been black and blue for a week, as had Pete's right eye, where she had pelted him with her reticule.

Henry Pursall was as thin and tall as a pencil, with a bald pate that resembled an eraser tip. She had been the recipient of his ardent affections one winter's day last December, when he had marched into Doc Watson's office, stripped down to his long johns, and demanded to be examined, all the while making lewd suggestions. She had been spared further embarrassment when Doc walked in, looking angrier than she had ever seen him. He'd sent her out of the room and administered a strong emetic. The sound of Henry's repeated retching had been music to her ears.

"Isn't this exciting, Margaret?"

Her reverie broken, Margaret turned to find Penny Adamson addressing her. Penny's hawklike nose was so close to Margaret's face it was practically stuffed into her left ear.

"I'm just praying that Henry Pursall bids on me. He's a darling man, don't you think?" Penny continued, ruffling the golden curls around her face, which Margaret was certain came directly from the use of bleaching powder. No one had hair that yellow!

"I think you and Henry are perfectly suited. I'll keep

111

my fingers crossed for you." That seemed to placate the foolish woman for she turned to speak to her sister, Flora, seated on her other side. Perhaps Penny and Henry could run off to the river together and strip down to their altogethers, Margaret thought, smiling to herself. They seemed to have a penchant for such goings-on.

Taking another gander at the crowd, Margaret was disappointed to discover that Chase was not in attendance. Perhaps he'd been detained in Tombstone, or perhaps he had changed his mind about bidding on her. The latter, being the more likely reason he'd failed to show.

She'd been foolish to get her hopes up. Chase wasn't interested in her, despite his teasing remarks and Betsy's hopeful predictions. Still, she had harbored a tiny hope in the corner of her heart that he would be here today to bid on her. She could see that he'd been toying with her, and she hadn't been smart enough to realize it. Well, she realized it now, for the auction was about to begin and there was no Chase Gallagher in sight.

Chester Simmons, dressed in a brown-and-gold checkered suit, climbed onto the platform. He looked more like a hawker peddling his wares than the respectable lawyer he was. Chester called for the crowd's attention, and Margaret's stomach knotted into a tight ball.

Why hadn't she listened to her mother? Mama had warned her last night that no man would bid on her—that she was too plain, too old, to be taken seriously by any man looking for something other than a maid or a companion. Her mother's cruel remarks had hurt, as had her condemnation of Margaret's participation in such a scandalous event. Phoebe Parker had been aghast to discover that her daughter was going to be humiliated in front of the entire town.

"You'll be the last one left. All the others will be bought, and you'll be the last one left."

Phoebe's words rang in her ears. And as Margaret's attention returned to the auction, she feared her mother would be proven right. There were only three of them left, and Cyndi Lang was walking toward the front of the stage. It didn't take Bobby Mitchell long to make his bid, and off Cyndi went, leaving only her and horse-faced Flora Adamson to finish out the auction. Even Henry had deserted her by bidding on Penny.

Despair filled her, until she remembered Francis's promise to bid on her. She sat up a little straighter. At least she wouldn't be totally humiliated . . . not totally. She took a deep breath, rising to her feet when Chester called out her name.

She was last!

Oh, Lord, even Flora, who'd been purchased by Pete Forrester, had been auctioned off before her.

Chester smiled, shouting encouragement as Margaret walked to the front of the stage amid a round of applause. Looking down at the throng of people, she caught sight of Francis who looked hopeful as he smiled up at her. She breathed a sigh of relief.

"As you all know, this is Miss Margaret Parker," Chester began. "Margaret's a fine nurse, a wonderful companion to her bedridden mother—"

Oh, why didn't he stop? He was making her sound like some charity case.

113

"What am I bid for this paragon of womanhood?"

"Fifty cents!" came Francis Brooks's offer.

Fifty cents! My God! Why she'd die before she'd be sold for such a paltry sum. Perhaps she should bid on herself. No, she couldn't do that.

"One dollar."

Margaret scanned the crowd, her gaze falling on a sandy-haired cowboy she had never seen before. He winked at her. *Bless you, whoever you are.*

"One dollar and fifty cents," Francis shouted, smiling proudly up at Margaret, who had the sudden urge to spit in his face.

"Two dollars," came the stranger's counterbid.

"One hundred dollars," came the deep voice from the rear of the crowd.

A hush fell over the assembly, then murmurs of excitement and speculation ensued, followed by whistles and lewd comments.

Margaret reddened. Rising up on her toes, she strained to see who the mysterious bidder was. The crowd parted, allowing the man to approach the platform.

"There's been a bid of one hundred dollars," Chester said, winking slyly at Margaret.

Following Chester's gaze, Margaret's mouth fell open. Standing on the street below, looking up at her with a rakish grin on his face, was Chase. Her heart flip-flopped in her chest. And at that moment, she had never felt more grateful to anyone in her life. She smiled sweetly.

"Are there any other bids?"

The sandy-haired stranger shook his head.

All eyes turned on Francis.

"Well, schoolmarm," Chase asked, "you aim to bid again?"

The schoolteacher flushed bright red and shook his head, smiling apologetically at Margaret.

"Looks like you're all mine, darlin'."

Her cheeks flooding with color, Margaret gasped when Chase reached up and grabbed her about the waist, swinging her down off the platform.

A cheer went up from the crowd.

The gratitude felt moments before was short-lived.

Pulling out his money, Chase handed it to Chester, then turning toward Margaret, said, "That should do it, darlin'. Are you ready to go?"

Margaret was struck momentarily speechless. Was there no end to her humiliation? Chase was still holding on to her, as if she weighed no more than a sack of potatoes. She remembered the last woman he held so provocatively and pushed herself out of his grasp. "I can walk by my own power, Marshal. I don't need to be carried."

Ignoring her protestations, Chase grabbed her firmly about the waist and dragged her toward a waiting buggy. "Get in."

She looked at the buggy, then at him, folding her arms firmly over her chest. "I'll do no such thing. I demand to know where you're taking me."

He smiled. "Well, according to what I was led to believe, anywhere I want. I paid my money, now I expect you to do your part."

A strangled sound emerged from her throat. "Whatever do you mean?"

"I mean, darlin', that if I want to take you back to my hotel room and make mad, passionate love to you, I

115

will. I paid for that privilege."

Her cheeks flushed as scarlet as the cotton dress she wore. "Now wait just a minute! All the proprieties are to be strictly observed."

"First I'm hearing about it."

"You . . . you weren't at the auction when it began. If you were, you would have heard the rules. Obviously, you have been grossly misled. I'd ask for my money back if I were you."

His stance was as firm as his voice when he spoke. "Get in."

Her expression remained mutinous. "I will not. I'm not some woman of the streets you can purchase for your pleasure. I may be considered an old maid, Marshal, but I assure you, I'm not *that* desperate for a man."

"Nobody's accusing you of being an old maid, though with your sour disposition and stubborn hide, I can see why you still are." Ignoring her sputtering indignation, he continued, "Now get in, or I will pick you up forcibly and deposit you upon that seat. Do I make myself clear?" He stepped forward, daring her to refuse.

"You won't get away with this. I'll have the law on you," she said, climbing reluctantly aboard the buggy.

Chase laughed. "I am the law, darlin'. Do you want to file a complaint?"

Folding her arms across her chest, Margaret stared straight ahead, not daring to speak all the epithets that came quickly to her lips. To think that she had actually been grateful. *Grateful!*

The feel of Chase's knee pressing tight against her thigh when he took the seat next to her caused her to squirm restlessly.

"Why don't you relax, Maggie? I'm not going to ravish you. I promise."

Tilting up her chin, she refused to look at him. "I might have to be in your company, Marshal Gallagher, but I don't have to enjoy myself."

"You like my company and you know it."

"I do not. I . . ."

Before Margaret could voice another protestation, Chase pulled her tight against him, planting his mouth firmly over hers. He kissed her soundly, thoroughly, until he heard a mewling sound come from deep within her throat. He relaxed the pressure, savoring the sweetness he drank from her lips. A moment later, he raised his head, smiling into her flushed face. No old maid he knew ever kissed like that!

"I guess that's one way to silence you."

Feeling faint, flushed, and flustered, Margaret pressed her lips tightly together, refusing to acknowledge his presence.

They traveled east for thirty minutes, past stands of cactus, mesquite, and tumbleweeds that looked like yellow cannonballs as they drifted by. Overhead the sun shone brightly, hotly, against the clear blue sky, making the short ride very uncomfortable. Droplets of perspiration trickled down between her breasts, and Margaret was certain that the underarms of her dress were going to be permanently stained. She was, therefore, grateful when the San Carlos River finally came into view.

The blue water stood out in vivid relief against the muted colors of beige and yellow sand. The stream meandered restlessly, weaving its way through the dry desert floor.

Their destination came as no surprise to Margaret. Chase had finally told her, in his usual authoritative and irksome manner, that they were going to picnic on the banks of the river. And though it secretly thrilled her, for she hadn't been on a picnic in years, she wasn't about to admit that to him.

In fact, she wasn't about to admit a great many things to him: like how his kisses made her heart ache and her blood boil; how his commanding presence thrilled and irritated at the same time; how his musky scent filled her senses with longing; how the sight of his muscular body created a stirring deep within her breast, and other, more intimate, parts of her body.

"Are you getting overheated? Your face is as red as an apple."

Reaching up, Margaret grabbed her burning cheeks. "I'm probably having a heatstroke," she lied. "You rushed me away before I could get my bonnet."

Chase pulled the horse to a halt beneath the shade of a tall cottonwood tree. "Perhaps we should go for a swim." He stared at her knowingly and smiled. "To cool ourselves off."

"I . . . I didn't bring my bathing suit."

His eyebrow arched. "You have one?"

She nodded. "I ordered it from the Montgomery Ward catalogue, though I've never had the courage to wear it." Her mother considered it scandalous, likening it to something only a cheap woman would wear.

Extending his hand, he caught hold of a curl that had escaped from her bun, wondering what she'd look like with her hair down. "You seem to lack courage about a great many things."

118

She stiffened, yanking her hair out of his grasp. "I beg your pardon."

"Men scare you. Your mother scares the hell out of you. And your own feelings scare you."

"You are insufferably rude, Marshal. I demand to be taken home at once." She crossed her arms over her chest, refusing to look at him.

Jumping down off the seat, Chase tied the horse to the tree, then came around to her side of the buggy. "Demand all you want, darlin'. I bought you fair and square. Paid a goodly sum, I might add." He reached up to drag her off the seat, despite her squirming protests. "Hope you're going to be worth it." He chuckled at her outrage, then released her, doubting if Miss Margaret Parker had ever been teased before.

Grabbing the quilt and wicker basket out of the buggy, he strode toward the river, spreading the patchwork material along its bank.

Still fuming over Chase's less than flattering assessment of her character, Margaret made no move to follow, until the stare he directed at her proved too challenging to ignore. She wasn't a coward—cautious perhaps—but never cowardly. She advanced toward the river, damning Chase Gallagher and her own perverse desire to prove him wrong.

"Hungry? I fixed us some lunch." He smiled sheepishly. "Well, actually, I had Mrs. Hobson fix it." He patted the space next to him on the blanket.

Doing her best to ignore him, she dropped down on the quilt, careful to occupy the space at the very corner, away from where he sat. "How nice," she replied, unable to keep the sarcasm out of her voice.

At least it was cool by the river, she thought. A small

119

consolation for having to share the enjoyment with him. The water drifted past her, looking cool, wet, and immensely inviting. She stared at it longingly, wishing she were brave enough to chuck propriety and jump in. Of course, then she'd be no better than the Adamson twins.

"Why don't we go for a swim? It's hotter than a prairie fire out here and that water looks mighty inviting."

She turned to stare at him, wondering if he was a mind reader. "I couldn't. I told you, I don't have my bathing costume."

"So? Neither do I." He grinned. "We'll just swim in our underwear. There's hardly a bit of difference between a bathing suit and underwear." Removing his jacket and vest, he began to unbutton his shirt.

Margaret's eyes widened; her heart beat as wildly as the flapping cottonwood leaves overhead as he pulled the shirt tail from his pants. He was doing it! He was undressing in front of her. "Marshal, you can't mean to take your clothes off in front of me." Her voice held a note of panic.

His smile was wicked as he took off his shirt and hung it on a low branch of the tree. The sight of his naked chest, so achingly familiar, made her stomach clench. She distinctly remembered what it felt like to run her hands over the warm flesh, to feel the soft mat of hairs whisper beneath her fingers, to . . .

"If you want to suffocate, darlin', that's your choice. Me, I'm goin' swimming."

He reached for the buttons on his pants and her mouth dropped open, as she suddenly realized that Chase might have on beneath his pants what he had on under his shirt, which was absolutely nothing. "Stop! You mustn't."

Stepping out of his pants to reveal a pair of cotton drawers, he chuckled. "Scared you, did I?"

"No. I . . ."

"Don't you have any underclothes on beneath that dress, Maggie?" The thought brought an instant hardening to his loins, which he could do little to hide. Margaret must have noticed it, too, for she flushed red from the roots of her hair to the tips of her toes, turning quickly away.

"Of course, I do." What kind of woman did he take her for? What kind of woman was he used to dealing with? But she knew the answer to that; her lips thinned in displeasure.

"Well, then, take off your duds and let's get wet."

She stared longingly at the water, then heaved a sigh, shaking her head. "I can't."

"Margaret, when are you going to stop worrying about what everyone else thinks? There's no one here but you and me."

She swallowed. That was the problem.

"Tell you what. I'll turn my back until you strip and get into the water. Once you're in, call out and I'll join you. That way, you can still preserve your modesty."

Perspiration trickling down between your breasts was a strong incentive to cast away years of convention, Margaret thought, biting her lower lip in indecision. "Promise you'll keep your back turned?"

"Cross my heart and hope to die of heatstroke."

With fumbling fingers, she worked at the buttons of her dress, glancing quickly over her shoulder to make certain Chase was holding to his word. He was, which

121

made her all the more surprised when he said, "I told you I wouldn't look. Don't you trust me?"

Not in a million years, Margaret answered silently, but aloud she replied, "I'm almost done." Easing out of the dress, she folded it neatly and laid it on the quilt. Removing her shoes and stockings, she stood beneath the tree clad only in her white cotton, lace-edged camisole and drawers. She never wore petticoats . . . well, hardly ever. It was just too darned hot, and they were too impractical, not to mention downright itchy.

Walking to the water's edge, she stuck her big toe in. "Yipes!" The water was colder than she thought it would be.

"Are you in yet?' Chase asked impatiently, slapping at a mosquito that was feasting on the back of his neck. "I'm frying over here, and I'm being eaten alive by bugs."

"Not quite," she called out.

"I'm counting to five, then I'm turning around. If you're not in by then, too bad."

"But . . ."

"One . . ."

Margaret looked at the water and grimaced.

"Two . . ."

She put her right foot in and stifled her scream.

"Three . . ."

Without another word, she plunged into the chilly water, immediately breaking out in gooseflesh. "Okay, you ca . . . can . . . come in now," she chattered. As soon as the words were out of her mouth, she realized her mistake. The water was only thigh deep, and even if she sat down completely, which she hastened to do, it didn't cover her breasts, which were bobbing on top of the water like two buoyant corks. Staring at the floating mounds in dismay, then at the man who was running toward her, Margaret opened her mouth to explain, but it was too late.

With a warrior's yell that would have done Geronimo proud, Chase jumped into the water, landing inches from where Margaret sat. When his head came up out of the water, it was obvious from the sensual glow in his eyes that he realized Margaret's predicament.

He grinned lasciviously, his eyes raking over the lush, wet mounds that were totally transparent to his view. Her breasts were full—ripe like two mouthwatering melons. The rose peaks, taut from the cold, puckered impudently as they strained against the wet material. He licked his lips, not realizing where his hand strayed until he heard Margaret's sharp intake of breath. Pulling his hand back down, he moved closer to her, his words causing Margaret's body temperature to rise considerably.

"Darlin', you were definitely worth every one of those one hundred dollar bills." He reached for her.

Chapter Nine

"Ouch!" Chase yelled as his knee scraped over a jagged rock on the riverbed. "Damn!" He released his hold on Margaret's waist and grabbed onto his leg.

Not taking the time to question her good fortune, Margaret scampered out of the water and up onto the river bank. She was breathing deeply but dared not rest, for when she gazed over her shoulder, she could see Chase was close on her heels.

"Don't you dare touch me, Chase Gallagher!" She backed away, a defiant expression on her face.

Her hair had loosened in the scuffle, cascading down her back like a magnificent waterfall. The sunlight filtered down through the cottonwood leaves, dancing brightly on her cheeks, making them appear translucent. Chase stared, mesmerized, totally ignoring the blood that trickled down his leg as he gazed at Margaret's body so temptingly displayed before him. Some old maid! The woman was a goddess. Her pink, firm flesh, clearly visible through the thin, wet garments, was molded to perfection.

"You're beautiful!" he said, a touch of reverence in his voice.

Margaret felt warmed by the compliment no man had ever paid her before, until she noticed his eyes straying to the area below her abdomen; quickly, she covered herself with her hands. "Have you no shame?"

An infuriating grin split his cheeks. "None whatsoever, darlin'." He limped forward, and it was then that she noticed his knee.

"You're bleeding!"

"Just a scrape."

Years of medical training soon replaced modesty, and she ordered, "Sit here on the blanket. Let me look at that knee."

He obliged, leaning back on his hands while she ripped open the material encasing his left leg. The loose, wet strands of her hair tickled his exposed flesh when she bent over to examine it more carefully.

"I'll need to wash this out. There's gravel and dirt embedded; you'll get an infection if it's not cleaned proper." She hurried down to the river, wetting one of the napkins she had grabbed from the picnic basket, affording Chase a delightful view of her fetching posterior when she leaned over to complete her task.

A peach—a succulent peach. He licked his lips to savor the thought.

"Now hold still," she ordered when she returned, grabbing on to his leg. "This may hurt a bit."

He observed the way she pulled her lower lip between her teeth as she concentrated on cleaning his wound. Her camisole gaped open as she bent over, exposing her unfettered breasts to his view. He was in pain, all right! And if her hand moved up his leg any higher, she was going to get a feel of just how pained he was. He sucked in his breath, saying, "You always seem to be nursing me."

"Nursing's what I do, Marshal."

With those breasts to suckle, a man could nurse and never get his fill, Chase thought wickedly. He looked up and their eyes locked. His eyes must have reflected his thoughts, for when Margaret gazed into them, she blushed. Without a word, he reached for her and was surprised when she didn't protest. He laid her down on the blanket, leaning over her.

"You're quite a woman, Margaret Parker."

She swallowed, wondering at the insanity that had suddenly overtaken her. "I am?"

Slowly, so as not to frighten her, he covered her body with his own. Gently, he kissed her, tasting the sweet honey from her lips, sucking the nectar as he plunged his tongue deep within her mouth.

Margaret moaned; she felt hot, despite the wet garments pressing into her flesh. She had never been kissed like this before. Chase's tongue, probing in and out of her mouth, licking and tasting, teasing and tormenting, created a strange tightening in her loins. She could feel his male hardness pressing into her mound, and she had the strongest urge to press herself against it.

His hands covered her breasts, gently massaging the aching globes through the wet material. Soon the ribbons of her camisole were unfastened, and his fingers covered her burning flesh, pulling on her nipples until they jutted forth like two stiff peaks. His tongue replaced his fingers, suckling and laving the swollen mounds, while his hands traveled down to

126

untie the ribbon of her drawers.

Please, you must stop! her mind cried out, but her voice was unable to voice the denial.

Slowly, his hands moved downward to draw the material with them and the lower half of her body was left totally exposed to his view. She squeezed her eyes shut, as if that could somehow shield her from the embarrassment she felt.

Chase's gaze feasted upon Margaret's nakedness, marveling at the total perfection before him. He was rock hard, ready to burst, and fearful that he would disgrace himself. He couldn't tell what Margaret was thinking for her eyes were closed.

Like a feather trailing over her flesh, Chase's fingers caressed her legs, her abdomen, tickling her already sensitive nerve endings until she wanted to scream for release. Finally, she opened her eyes to find him staring down at her, a questioning look in his eyes.

"I want you, Maggie. I want you in the worst way. But not if you're not ready to have me."

God, why did he have to leave the decision to her? She wanted him; there was no denying it. But she couldn't tell him that. She was respectable . . . or at least she used to be. She couldn't give him permission to have his way with her. They weren't married. It was wrong. Hadn't her mother always counseled her on the evils of the flesh?

"I . . . I . . ." How could she answer when his hand was pressing over her most intimate part, cupping it, massaging the pebble-hard flesh?

He kissed her again, trailing his tongue down her face, her neck, over her breasts, down her stomach, until it was almost to her woman's mound.

"Stop! You mustn't. It's wrong." She made a half-hearted attempt to push him away, but he ignored her, separating the folds with his fingers, placing his mouth at the apex of her thighs.

Oh, God! She clutched the edge of the blanket, her legs opening to the delicious torment his tongue inflicted, her head lolling back and forth as she tried to keep a grip on reality. As his tongue laved at the tiny bud of her passion, causing it to harden, she moaned aloud, lifting herself off the blanket to press her body against his mouth. His mustache abraded the sensitive skin, creating more pleasure than she ever realized existed. Suddenly, a wetness flooded her thighs and she felt herself tighten and expand. Soon she was climbing—climbing so high she was sure to reach the heavens. And then she exploded, shattering into a million, glittering stars.

Chase stared at the rapt expression on her face, awed by the power of her fulfillment. Margaret positively glowed, shining like the brightest star in the heavens. He smiled, easing himself down to draw her into his embrace.

"You're an exciting woman, Maggie," he whispered, brushing the damp strands of hair away from her face.

Slowly, she opened her eyes to find Chase's face only inches from her own. She could smell her musky woman's scent upon him and she blushed.

"I . . . I never considered myself exciting before," she confessed. How could she sit here talking with him as if nothing had transpired between them? What strange, wonderful affliction had she succumbed to? She wanted to caress his face—to tell him what their lovemaking had meant to her—but her hands felt weighted to her sides and her words, like flies to paper, stuck in her throat.

"You're that and much more, darlin', and don't ever forget it." He kissed the tip of her nose. "You're my woman now, Maggie. I've laid my brand on you, staked out my territory. No man but me will ever plant his seed within you." He palmed her mound with his hand. "No man will touch you here but me. Do you understand?"

She felt her cheeks grow warm again and nodded mutely, her heart beating so fast she thought she would explode. But did she really understand? Did she really know what Chase wanted? For she would be no man's plaything—no man's whore.

Chase was used to dealing with women of loose virtue. Did he think her one of them? How could he not, after the wanton way she had behaved? The glow of their lovemaking faded, reality crashing in on her like a ton of boulders. She attempted to cover herself, but he grabbed onto her hands.

"Why do you hide yourself from me? There's no shame in what we did."

"I'm not a woman of easy virtue. What happened between us was wrong."

"It wasn't wrong, and it's going to happen again, and again, and again."

She shook her head. "No." Pushing herself up, she forced the edges of her camisole together. "I'll be no man's whore." No matter how wonderful Chase made her feel, what had occurred between them today could never—*would* never happen again.

"I don't consider you a whore." He brushed the curls away from her face and cupped her cheek. "I told you once, I'm looking for something more lasting—more permanent."

Permanent. What was he telling her?

"I'm not much good with words. Better with actions." He grinned, wiggling his eyebrows suggestively.

She drew her arms over her chest to hide the involuntary affirmation to his comment.

"I want to court you, Maggie Parker. I want to take you for my wife."

Her mouth dropped open. Pulling away from him, she grabbed the quilt from beneath them, wrapping it about herself. There was no way she would discuss something as important as marriage while sitting stark naked out in the middle of nowhere.

"You know, once we're married, you'll have to get over your modesty. I'll probably insist that you wear nothing beneath your clothes, so I can flip up your skirts and have my way with you whenever I want."

Though she could see he was teasing, she couldn't control the throbbing between her thighs or the beet red flush covering her face. She reached up to quiet the burning, forgetting she had hold of the quilt.

Chase's grin was erotic. "That's the idea," he said, chuckling. "I always enjoy feasting my eyes on a bare breasted woman."

She shrieked, grabbing for the quilt once again. "Really, Marshal . . . Chase, you mustn't say such things."

He rubbed his chest in an abstracted circular motion with his right hand while contemplating her words. Her eyes followed the movement; she swallowed. "I'll need time to consider your proposal."

Bending over, he picked up her drawers, running the pink satin ribbon over his lips. "Don't take too long, darlin'," he replied, handing them to her. "I'm not a patient man."

She felt as hot as the burning sun overhead. Grabbing the garment, she stuffed it beneath the quilt. "No . . . no I won't. Now, if you will turn around; I'll get dressed."

"I like you better naked, but if you have to . . ." He shrugged, gathering up his own garments before turning around.

Scampering into her clothes as quickly as she could, Margaret felt an overwhelming shyness wash over her when Chase turned back to face her a few minutes later.

"Feel better? Not quite so vulnerable?"

Vulnerable. He had hit the nail on the head. She did feel vulnerable. Not because of her nakedness, but because she was laying herself open to hurt—to a great deal of pain. If things didn't work out between her and Chase . . . She shivered. For she knew with a certainty that she loved him—had loved him since the moment he had taken her in his arms and dragged her out onto the dance floor. And she was scared. Lord, she was scared.

He said he wanted to marry her. But he didn't say anything about loving her. Was she merely an object of his lust? She smiled inwardly at that. Her, Margaret Parker, an object of lust! It was too absurd.

Or did he have some feeling for her?

She searched his face and saw only amusement and kindness there. He *was* kind, she realized, in his own gruff sort of way. And fun. She hadn't enjoyed herself

131

this much in years. And he desired her. Of that, she was certain.

She smiled and saw the question in his eyes as she walked forward to stand before him. "I've decided to accept your suit."

Chase's face split into a grin. He pulled her into his chest, planting a kiss firmly on her mouth. "You won't be sorry, Maggie," he said, when he finally lifted his head.

Margaret prayed with all her heart and soul that Chase was right. But at the moment, held tightly in his arms, she just didn't care.

Later that night, as he lay on his bed, hands clasped behind his head, staring into the flickering flames of the kerosene lamp on the dresser, Chase pondered the path he had taken today.

There would be no turning back. He had set his course for revenge, and there would be no deviation from it.

There couldn't be. Maggie had accepted his suit. He smiled thoughtfully as he thought of her naked and writhing beneath him, experiencing her woman's passion for the first time. He was glad he had been the one to give it to her. She had been wonderful—wonderful, warm, willing, wet.

Christ but it had been hard—damned hard—not taking her. He massaged his aching groin, wondering just who had done the seducing today.

His smile turned confident. Soon he would have her. Soon Maggie would become Mrs. Chase Gallagher and he would plant his staff deep within her velvety softness.

Closing his eyes, her sweet smile hovered over him, her lips brushing his in a warm caress. Guilt assailed him. His eyes flew open and he frowned.

What kind of a man would take advantage of such an inexperienced woman?

Reaching for the bottle of whiskey on the nightstand, he poured himself a drink. Gulping down the fiery brew, his guilt momentarily assuaged, he felt better. He *was* doing the right thing. Shit! He was marrying her for Christ's sake, wasn't he?

What more could she ask? What more could he give?

He poured himself another drink and shook his head before tossing it down. The whiskey burned—burned the guilt—burned the pain—burned the image of a pair of doelike eyes in a trusting face. He threw the glass across the room, watching it shatter against the wall.

Nothing. He could give her nothing.

Chapter Ten

The morning sun shone brightly through the upstairs bedroom window, teasing Margaret into wakefulness. She cocked one eye open, staring at the beehive clock on the mantel: seven o'clock! She gasped, bolting upright. She had overslept. Bounding out of bed, she crossed to the window, lifting up on the sash. A warm breeze floated in, doing nothing to alleviate the closeness of the room.

It was going to be another sweltering day—a sweltering but wonderful day, Margaret thought, an ebullient smile lighting her face. Chase wanted to court her—to marry her. Holding out the sides of her nightgown like a graceful ballerina, she pirouetted on tiptoe.

Yesterday had been magical. She had experienced a woman's pleasure for the first time in her life. Her nipples hardened at the memory of where Chase's hands and mouth had been. Palming her cheeks, which burned at the erotic images, she ran to the cheval mirror that stood in the corner of her room and stared at herself. Did she look different? Would anyone be able to tell she was in love? Was that really her—Margaret Parker, spinster and nursemaid—who stared back with the bloom of roses in her cheeks and a twinkle of excitement in her eyes?

"Margaret? Are you up yet? I'm simply famished."

Margaret's smile faded. Mama. How could she have forgotten her breakfast? Grabbing her wrapper off the foot of the bed, she hurried to her mother's room.

Phoebe was up, seated in the rocking chair by the window when Margaret entered. The glower on her face told Margaret she was not pleased to have been kept waiting. Ignoring the scowl, Margaret smiled cheerfully. "Morning, Mama. Did you sleep well?" Her only answer was a snort.

Phoebe eyed her daughter suspiciously. Something was amiss. Margaret never wore her hair down, and she never neglected to bring up her breakfast on time. "What's got into you? Why, you look like a harlot with your hair loose and falling about your shoulders like that. Where are your slippers? Where is my breakfast?" The questions poured forth, with hardly a pause between each one.

Feeling herself warm, Margaret turned away from her mother's probing stare to fluff the pillows on the bed and smooth out the sheets. "You must be feeling better, Mama. I see you're up and in your chair earlier than usual today."

"Don't change the subject, Margaret. Why aren't you dressed? You know I rely on you to feed and bathe me. Am I to starve while you indulge yourself in petty pleasures?"

Spinning on her heel, Margaret turned back to face

135

her, her eyes darkening. "I hardly think oversleeping is indulgent, Mama. After all, it is Sunday. Am I to have no day of rest?"

"Hmph! I expected you to look a lot more dour after that ridiculous auction you participated in yesterday. You were the last one sold, were you not?"

Margaret hated the smugness that tightened her mother's lips. "I was . . . but I also brought the most money."

"What kind of women consent to be auctioned off? Whores and pitiful spinsters, such as yourself?"

A familiar burning sensation smoldered in the pit of Margaret's stomach. She took a deep breath to calm herself. "It was for a worthy cause, Mama. We raised almost three hundred dollars for the new garbage incinerator."

"And who, pray tell, bought you? That scrawny schoolteacher, I suppose."

"Actually, it was Marshal Gallagher."

"Marshal . . ." Phoebe paled, clutching her chest. "Bring me my vial of smelling salts. I fear an attack coming on."

Seizing the green vial off the dresser, Margaret waved it under her mother's nose; the strong odor of ammonia poured forth, seeming to revive her. "What's the matter? Do you want me to call Doc Watson?"

Phoebe's recovery came quicker than expected. "I have an ungrateful daughter, that's what the matter is. You left me here all alone so that you could cavort with that gunslinger who calls himself a marshal. Don't think I haven't heard about him. Just because I'm confined to this room, doesn't mean I don't hear things. I'm privy to most of what goes on in this town."

Margaret knew of Phoebe's infamous "spy" network. The so-called Christian women who came to call filled her mother's head with gossip and exaggeration. She fought to keep her face impassive and her voice even. "Marshal Gallagher is a very nice man, Mama. I don't think you should prejudge someone you haven't met."

"I heard the way you went off with him yesterday. Did he fill your head with pretty words and compliments? A man like that uses women like you. I should know; your father treated me the same way."

Margaret's voice rose sharply. "You don't know anything of the kind." She took a deep breath and forced her anger down. "Now, why don't you tell me what you want for breakfast."

"You've upset me. I couldn't possibly eat a thing. How can I eat when my daughter behaves like a harlot with a known killer? Did he kiss you? Did he put his hands on your flesh? We do have a reputation to maintain, Margaret, though you seem to have forgotten that fact."

Margaret's cheeks reddened. "Why must you always berate me? Don't you want me to be happy?"

"No daughter of mine is going to consort with a gunslinger. I forbid you to see this man again."

Lifting her chin, Margaret stared defiantly at her mother. "I'm afraid that's not possible."

Phoebe fanned herself with her hankie, her agitation becoming more apparent. "You mean to disobey me?"

"Chase Gallagher wishes to court me, Mama. He wants to marry me."

Phoebe's mouth fell open, then she threw back her head and laughed—a vicious, vile sound that made the hairs on Margaret's arms stand straight up on end.

"Stupid girl. Men like that don't marry homely women like you. He only wants one thing from you, Margaret. Mark my words, once he has his way with you, he'll toss you aside like yesterday's garbage."

"Are you speaking of me, Mama, or of yourself?" Margaret could see her barb had hit, for Phoebe's eyes filled with tears. She felt a small stab of guilt—very small.

"Your father said he loved me, then he left, without so much as a good-bye—left me to raise a daughter all by myself."

"I'm sorry for you, Mama, truly I am. But I don't think you can compare all men to Papa. What he did was wrong. But that doesn't mean the same thing will happen to me."

Phoebe's face twisted into a demonic mask. "Men are deceitful—evil. They make you perform unspeakable acts of perversion. Your marshal will be no different. Once he's had his fill of your flesh, he'll go. It doesn't matter that you're not pretty or desirable."

Margaret flinched, rocking back on her heels as if she'd been slapped; she said nothing, allowing her mother to continue her diatribe.

"Men are like animals. They rut with anyone to fill their insatiable needs. It's the curse of Satan that comes over them." Phoebe began to rock back and forth, wringing her hands as she stared straight ahead, seeing nothing.

Shaking her head, Margaret heaved a sigh and headed for the door. Mama was ill, but no amount of medicine could cure her. She had a sickness of the soul, and Margaret refused to let her poisonous attitude contaminate her happiness. Not this time. She had given up Tom to please Mama; she wouldn't give up Chase.

Pausing by the door, she looked back. "I'll bring your breakfast, Mama." But Margaret knew that her mother didn't hear her; Phoebe was in another world—another time: a place where Jonathan Parker still loved his wife.

Quietly, she closed the door behind her.

Jonathan Parker folded his neatly manicured hands on the scarred pine table in front of him and stared intently at the four members of his gang. He was dressed stylishly, as befitting his nickname Gentleman Jack, in a suit of black superfine with a gold brocade vest. In his tie, he sported a large diamond stickpin, taken off a dead man whose identity had long ago faded from his memory. In his vest pocket hung a gold engraved watch, whose owner he wasn't likely to ever forget. Not with Chase Gallagher dogging his heels for the past eighteen years.

A single candle burned brightly in the center of the table, highlighting the anger on Jack Parker's face when he spoke. "I gave orders that you boys were to stay out of trouble while I was gone. Now Sandy tells me that you've gone and caused trouble with Gallagher. If you've messed up my plans, I'll see each and every one of you three bastards dead." The words were cold—precise, like the pointed blade of a double-edged sword.

"We didn't mean no harm, boss," Moose explained. "That new marshal is a mean son of a bitch. He wouldn't let us keep our guns."

Loomis shook his head, giving Parker an I-told-you-so look before saying, "Shut up, Donaldson. The boss ain't interested in your pitiful excuses for screwing up. If you and your brothers can't follow instructions, maybe we should look for someone who can."

Parker held up his hand in a conciliatory fashion, causing Sandy's eyebrows to raise. "Now, Sandy, let's not be hasty. I'm sure these boys have learned their lesson. Isn't that right, boys?"

"Sure thing, Mr. Parker," Bear conceded quickly, loosening the blue bandanna around his throat, which suddenly felt as tight as a hangman's noose. "We don't aim to cause you no more trouble."

Parker smiled sinisterly. He reached for the knife on the table, causing three pairs of eyes to widen slightly. Picking up the apple in front of him, he began to peel it with quick, methodical strokes. The Donaldson brothers breathed a collective sigh of relief.

"If everything goes according to plan, you boys are going to get rich." He popped the slice of apple into his mouth, noting the foolish grins on their faces. They were dumb bastards, but expendable. They'd serve their purpose well enough. Even with their limited intelligence, he'd be able to use them for his scheme to recover the gold.

"When you aiming to put your plan into action, boss?" Sandy asked, leaning back in his chair.

"There are plans to make; we've got to lay the groundwork. Gallagher's presence puts a crimp into the situation. I've got to work around that. That son of a bitch has been on my tail for years. I won't let him screw this up for me."

"You plan to kill him?" Bear asked, a bit too eagerly.

Parker cut another slice of apple, chewing and contemplating at the same time. "I've been in this business a long time. I take it slow and careful. Gallagher's no fool. We're going to proceed cautiously. Gallagher will meet his Maker when I say so and not before. Is that clear?"

The group nodded.

"Donaldson . . ." Jack directed his attention to Bear. "You and your brothers step outside. I've got to talk business with Sandy in private." His tone brooked no refusal.

After the three men had left, Parker leaned across the table, lowering his voice. "Those three fools won't be privy to all the plans. They'll be told only as much as necessary to allow them to perform their duties. Understood?"

"Sure. I never could figure out why you wanted me to hire them in the first place. They're as dumb as homemade soap."

Jack smiled smoothly. "Even soap has its uses, remember that." His smile faded quickly when he added, "I understand you attended the auction last Saturday that my daughter participated in."

A self-satisfied smirk covered Sandy's face. "Yeah. I felt sorry for her. Her being the last one left up on the platform."

"And did it ever occur to you what you would have done if you hadn't been outbid?" Though the words were calmly spoken, the anger on Jack's face was anything but.

Sandy swallowed. "No. I was just doing it for fun."

"Your job is to do what I say, when I say. You could

141

have messed up my plans by your stupid actions."

"I'm sorry. I didn't think."

Parker banged his fist on the table, causing Sandy to cower. "I don't want you to think, Loomis. I want you to follow instructions. What progress did you make with the housekeeper?"

"The greaser gal likes me fine, boss. I got me a few kisses and feels. It won't take long to get into her drawers; she's one hot little chili pepper."

A trait common to all the Diaz women, Jack thought, smiling to himself. Isabel had been a tasty morsel, especially when compared to that frigid bitch Phoebe.

"Good," Jack finally replied. "I want you to get as close to the woman as possible. She'll know everything that goes on in the house. We need that information."

Sandy smiled confidently, his blue eyes lighting with lust. "Leave the little Mexican gal to me, boss. I'll have her writhing beneath me, spewing forth information, in no time."

Parker stared at Loomis in disgust. He hated a man who thought with his dick and not his brain. That's what made Gallagher such a worthy adversary. The man was smart . . . and relentless. But as smart as Gallagher was, he wouldn't catch Jack Parker. Jack had waited a lifetime to reclaim the gold from the St. Louis bank robbery. And no one, not Gallagher, not Sandy, not even his own daughter, was going to come between him and that gold.

"I am ready to go, Margarita, if you are done baking the cookies." Lupe removed the last batch from the oven, setting the tin sheet on the counter. She shook her head, wiping her forehead with her apron as she stared at the pile of oatmeal cookies. "Why you would want to bake in such hot weather makes no sense to me."

Margaret sighed, grateful that the task was completed, grateful, too, that Lupe had arrived unexpectedly to help. What had started out hours ago as a way to take her mind off her mother's hateful comments, had ended up as a major cooking chore.

"All finished." Lupe wiped her hands on the apron. "Twelve dozen cookies and no one to eat them but you and your *madre.* Do you not think it would be easier to take out your anger on your mama rather than on the stove? It would take a lot less time." She dared Margaret to refute the statement.

"I appreciate your help, Lupe, but you needn't have stayed so long. It's nearly suppertime. Isabel will be wondering what's happened to you."

Lupe shrugged. "Mama is angry with me. I don't think she cares if I come home or not."

Margaret was surprised by the comment. She had always envied the close relationship Lupe shared with her mother. "I'm sure you are mistaken. Isabel dotes on you."

"Not anymore. She is so *furioso,* I am afraid to step foot in the house."

"So that's it? I wondered what brought you over here on a Sunday afternoon. You're usually out with one of your many admirers."

"*Sí.* That is the trouble. I have met a new man. He is so handsome, but an Anglo. My mama, she no like him. She say I should stick with my own kind—that

143

gringos bring nothing but trouble and bad luck."

Margaret's smile was sympathetic. "It seems our mothers are of a like mind. Mama doesn't want me to see Chase anymore."

Forgetting her own problems for the moment, Lupe asked, "You and the marshal?"

Margaret nodded.

Lupe's grin split wide. Throwing her arms about Margaret's middle, she hugged her. "I told you he was your man. I was right, no?"

"*Sí,* you were right," Margaret replied, kissing Lupe on the cheek. "Chase has asked me to marry him."

"Aiyeee!" Lupe jumped up and down excitedly. "I am so happy for you, Margarita. You deserve much love and happiness."

"Thank you, Lupe; you are a good friend." Though she wasn't sure how much love and happiness she would receive by marrying Chase.

"When is the wedding?"

"I have no idea. We only decided to court yesterday."

"He is a powerful lover this Marshal Gallagher, no?"

A wistful expression crossed Margaret's face. "He makes me feel things I've only dreamed of."

"You have been alone too long, Margarita. It is time you took a man to your bed."

The brown eyes widened. "We've never . . ."

"But you will. And once you experience the joy, you will hunger for it. It will get into your blood like a sickness."

It already had, Margaret thought, for her every waking moment since she had lain in Chase's arms had been filled with thoughts of little else.

"I must go. I promised to meet *mi amante* down by

the livery stable."

Concern filled Margaret's voice when she asked, "Should you openly defy your mother, Lupe?"

Wrapping her *rebozo* about her shoulders, Lupe smiled before retorting, "Should you, Margarita?"

Before Margaret could reply, a knock sounded at the kitchen door.

"Are you expecting someone? A man perhaps?" Lupe's smile teased.

Margaret blushed. "No. I . . ." Her heart raced as she hurried to open the door. Chase stood on the back step, a bouquet of prickly poppies, primroses, and tidytips clutched in his right hand. She stared at the flowers, awed by the gesture. No man had ever brought her flowers before. Warmth flowed through her.

"Why, Chase, I wasn't expecting you."

His right eyebrow cocked. "No? Why I thought since we were affianced, we should be seeing each other on a daily basis. Can I come in, or should I give these pretty wildflowers to some other gal?"

Margaret's cheeks glowed; she stepped back quickly, allowing Chase to enter.

"*Buenas tardes,* Señor Gallagher," Lupe said when Chase entered the room.

Margaret apologized for her rudeness and hastily completed the introductions. After a few minutes of polite chitchat, Lupe gave Margaret a conspiratorial wink and departed, leaving Chase and Margaret alone.

"Your housekeeper's a pretty little thing," Chase remarked, removing his hat. He tossed it on the chair.

An unfamiliar stab of jealousy pierced Margaret's breast but soon dissipated when he added, "But not as pretty as you, Maggie." Stepping further into the

145

room, Chase dropped the bouquet on the table then swept her up in his arms.

"I've missed you, darlin'. I can't seem to get the taste of your lips and the feel of your warm body out of my mind." He kissed her then—an all-consuming kiss that seemed to go on forever. When it finally ended, he looked into her eyes and smiled. "You smell good—like cinnamon and nutmeg." He licked her ear, her neck, and she felt her knees buckle.

"I've been baking," she choked out.

He glanced at the cookies on the counter. "I can see that. Having a bake sale at the church?"

She shook her head, embarrassed to explain, "No. I just like to bake."

"And I like to eat." He nibbled her lower lip, rubbing his hands in a circular motion over her bottom. "You taste mighty sweet, darlin'."

Every pulsing point in Margaret's body began to throb. It was as though her blood had boiled and was seeking a means of escape. Of their own volition, her arms crept up to wrap themselves around his neck. She pressed herself into him and felt his arousal against her stomach.

Margaret felt pleased—empowered by the knowledge that she had the ability to arouse Chase, as he did her. Tentatively, she placed her tongue against his lips and probed gently, seeking entry. When he opened to take her tongue inside, she was lost in a whirlwind of desire.

She wasn't quite sure how she ended up sprawled atop the kitchen table, wasn't sure that she cared, until she felt Chase's hands climb up underneath the skirt of

146

her dress and press on the center of her being. She moaned.

"I want you, Maggie. Lift up and let me slide your drawers off."

Sanity returned at the sound of his voice; her eyes flew open. "No, wait!" She pushed at the granite-hard wall of his chest, her mother's vile words ringing loud in her ears: *"He only wants one thing from you, Margaret. Mark my words, once he has his way with you, he'll toss you aside like yesterday's garbage."*

"What's wrong? I thought you wanted to make love."

Ignoring the pained expression on Chase's face, Margaret righted herself, smoothing down the folds of her dress, then her hair. "I'm sorry. This never should have happened. It's all my fault. I don't know what came over me."

"I'm what's come over you, Maggie. You want me. It's a natural, biological fact of life."

"But it's wrong!"

Chase heaved a sigh, plowing his fingers through his hair while he stared at her. Maggie's cheeks were flushed; her eyes glazed like chocolate frosting. Her nipples protruded, telling him better than words that Margaret Parker's body wanted him—needed him— even if Margaret Parker's mind wasn't ready to accept it.

Crossing to the counter, he grabbed a handful of cookies and took a bite of one. It was good—warm, spicy, tasty—just like Maggie herself. "I don't know what's wrong in two people desiring each other. We're going to be married, aren't we?"

147

"Yes . . . but we must observe the proper rules of courtship." She was certain making love on top of the kitchen table wasn't one of them.

His forehead wrinkled. "Rules? I thought the man wooed then wed. I didn't know there were rules."

She took a deep breath, wondering how she was going to explain etiquette to a man who lived life by his own rules. "It is usually customary for the man to seek the intended's parents' permission. In my case, due to Mama's illness, that won't be necessary. But you should be aware, Mama isn't happy with your suit."

"Well, that's good, 'cause I'm not marrying your mother." He shoved another cookie into his mouth, waiting for her to continue.

"I read that . . . that a lady shouldn't be too demonstrative in her affections during the days of her engagement."

"Where in hell did you read a thing like that?"

Excusing herself, Margaret hurried into the parlor, returning a moment later with a gilt-embossed book entitled, *A Treatise on Decorum—Etiquette and Dress.* "It's all spelled out in this book." She handed it to Chase. "I'm afraid my conduct has been grossly inappropriate."

Flipping through the pages, Chase's frown deepened as he read: "An honorable man will never tempt his future bride to any such demonstrations of affection . . . No lover will assume a domineering attitude over his future wife." He slammed the book shut, setting it on the table.

"Ten to one some fancy-dressed easterner who has never had himself a woman penned this hogwash. No real man would believe this . . . no real woman either,

148

for that matter."

Margaret looked clearly disturbed. "But . . ."

"Margaret . . ." His voice grew firm. "Quit letting your emotions be ruled by books, and, I suspect, your mother's dire warnings about the male species. I'm not getting any younger and neither are you." He winked when she blushed. "I want a short engagement—no more than a month."

Her mouth fell open, and she exclaimed, "A month!"

"That's right; I can't live like a monk longer than a month, and I don't expect you'll be able to either. Not if your actions today are any indication of your affectionate nature."

Margaret turned away to avoid Chase's knowing smile, but he grabbed her around the waist, pulling her onto his lap. "One month, Maggie, darlin', and not a moment longer. We'll play by your rules, with only an occasional kiss now and then." Cupping her chin, he turned her head to face him. "Agreed?"

Swallowing hard at the ardent expression she saw in his eyes, and wondering how she was going to survive a month with only a chaste kiss now and then, she nodded mutely.

He kissed the tip of her nose. "Now, I'd best be going. I need to soak in a tub of cold water."

She blushed when she felt his hardened member beneath her buttocks and rose abruptly, causing him to chuckle. Picking up his hat off the chair, she handed it to him. "Shall I set a date with Reverend Dorsey?"

"I'll leave the wedding arrangements to you. It's the honeymoon that I intend to take charge of." He brushed her lips gently with his own. "Sweet dreams, darlin'."

Feeling hot and irritable as she watched Chase walk away, Margaret fixed the latch on the screen door, then searched the porch for the old copper washtub. She wouldn't arouse her mother's suspicions by running the water into the upstairs bathtub, but she was definitely going to cool off. Chase's comment about soaking in a tub of cold water had become downright appealing. In fact, it had become a necessity.

Chapter Eleven

In a town the size of Purgatory, one wasn't usually afforded the privilege of keeping a secret, and so, the courtship of Margaret Parker and Chase Gallagher had become common knowledge by the time Margaret entered the Methodist Church the first thing Monday morning.

She had been embarrassed to discover that Reverend Dorsey already knew of her plans to wed. The wrinkled, white-haired clergyman with the myopic eyes had wasted no time offering his heartfelt congratulations while making the most of the opportunity to expound on her duties and obligations as a wife, warning her about the evils of the flesh, sounding very much like her own mother.

When their interview had finally ended and she'd secured the date for the wedding ceremony, which was to be the last Sunday in June, Margaret's sigh of relief had almost been audible. She was a private person used to keeping her own counsel. She neither sought nor wanted advice about her upcoming marriage, and she especially didn't need any more advice on the intimacies of marriage. Between her mother, Lupe, Chase, and the Reverend Dorsey, she'd learned enough to write a book on the subject. She smiled to herself. Maybe she should call it, *A Spinster's Guide to Matters of the Flesh*. She laughed aloud at that.

Pausing outside on the steps of the church, Margaret retied the green satin ribbons of her straw bonnet while staring at the white clapboard schoolhouse directly across the street.

Chewing her lower lip indecisively, she wondered if Francis had already heard of her plans to wed Chase. She had to tell him—decorum dictated that she must. But what would she say? She knew it was a foregone conclusion in Francis's mind that they would wed one day. She had pretty much resigned herself to that fate, too. But that was before Chase had entered her life—before Chase had made her feel like a woman should feel in a man's arms.

The ringing of the school bell interrupted Margaret's thoughts. Glancing up, she saw that the children were out in the yard taking a recess from their lessons. Now was as good a time as any to face Francis, she supposed. Picking up the skirt of her green muslin dress, she hurried across the street.

Exchanging smiles and waves with the Simmons brothers who tarried on the steps of the schoolhouse shooting a game of craps, which she was sure their teacher wasn't aware of, Margaret entered to find Francis writing the day's lesson on the blackboard. He was dressed very soberly in a black broadcloth suit, looking every inch the stern taskmaster she knew him to be. Taking a deep breath to fortify herself, she stiffened her spine and strode forward past rows of small desks, upon which sat the childrens' main text, McGuffey's *Eclectic Readers*.

"Good morning, Francis."

The schoolteacher turned, surprise then pleasure lighting his eyes. "Why, Margaret, what brings you here?"

Her shoulders slumped. *He didn't know.* "I have something of importance to discuss with you. I thought, perhaps, if you had a few minutes, we might talk."

He set down his chalk and eraser. "You know I always have time for you, Margaret. Besides—" he checked the time on the regulator clock that hung on the wall—"the children still have fifteen minutes left of their recess."

Fidgeting nervously with the strings of her reticule, Margaret searched for the right words; when none came, she blurted, "I'm getting married."

Francis's smile faded, his face whitening to the color of the chalk on the blackboard. "Married?" He groped blindly for the desk behind him, perching himself on the edge when he finally found it. "To whom?"

"Chase Gallagher has asked me to marry him. I have accepted."

"Cha . . ." His mouth fell open; he vaulted to his feet. "You're going to marry that gun-toting marshal? But why? Surely, you can't love him."

Margaret stiffened. "Actually, Francis, my feelings for Chase are no one's business but my own. But to answer your first question, I'm going to marry him because he asked me. I'm twenty-six years old; I'm not likely to get another offer."

153

"But surely you knew that I was going to propose."

Her tone softened, as did her expression. She didn't want to hurt him, and hoped she wouldn't have to. "Francis, please try to understand. Although you have often hinted at the fact that we would one day marry, you never made an honest-to-goodness proposal. There was no formal understanding between us."

He came forward, grabbing onto her hand. "But I love you, Margaret. I just assumed we had all the time in the world."

Withdrawing her gloved hands from his grasp, she noted his forlorn expression and smiled sadly. "I'm afraid you assumed too much, Francis—took too much for granted."

"I never realized . . ."

"I hope we will remain friends," she interrupted, needing to end their awkward conversation before it got out of hand. "I value our friendship very much."

Before he could answer, the door flew open and the children started filing in. They were boisterous and noisy, giving her just the excuse she needed to leave.

"I'd better go and leave you to your students. Take care, Francis." Turning toward the door, she halted when she heard him say, "I wish you well, Margaret, though I fear you are making a grave mistake. The marshal isn't the right man for you."

Without looking back, she exited the building, hoping the spitball that whizzed by her ear a moment before had landed on Francis Brooks's forehead.

Entering Doc Watson's office a few minutes later,

Margaret hung her bonnet on the hall tree. Removing a freshly washed white starched apron from the stack of linens on the shelf, she covered her gown with it.

"What's the matter, Margaret? You look like you're ready to spit nails."

Margaret turned at the sound of Doc's voice and smiled wanly at his assessment; it was exactly how she felt at the moment. She was getting tired of everyone telling her not to marry Chase. Why didn't they just mind their own business?

"I just had an unpleasant exchange with Francis Brooks," she explained.

"So you told him about the wedding?"

Her eyes widened. "You, too? Is there anyone in this town that doesn't know my business?"

Coming forward, he draped his arm about her shoulders. "It's a small town, Margaret. People talk. Most are excited about the news. Why Betsy Fraser almost exploded at the telling of it this morning when she came in for her monthly visit."

Margaret smiled at that. Betsy would be happy for her. She was probably taking credit for the entire set of circumstances. And she was probably fit to be tied that Margaret hadn't confided in her yet. "I'm not surprised, as nosy as Betsy is. How's she doing?"

"I suspect the baby will be born some time in December. Speaking of babies . . ." Doc paused, leading her to the pair of Windsor chairs by the window. "You will be careful not to end up like Kate Ferguson, won't you?"

Margaret felt her cheeks warm. "I hadn't really given it much thought, Doc. You know how much I want a baby. The thought of preventing one's never crossed

155

my mind."

"You're twenty-six and in good health. But good health soon fades under the burden of childbearing."

"You needn't worry that I'm going to produce a child every year, Doc. Why, Chase and I haven't even discussed children; I have no idea if he wants any." Her face clouded with unease. Lord, what if he didn't? She desperately wanted a child—could never marry a man who didn't.

"Your marshal looks mighty virile to me, Margaret. I don't expect he'll shoot many blanks." He smiled at her shocked expression, then added, patting her hand, "Just be careful."

"I will," she answered absently, wondering how she was going to approach Chase about the subject of having a child.

Chase laughed at Wooley's astonishment when Tom blurted out the news of Chase's impending marriage to Margaret. The three men were seated around the potbellied stove in Chase's office, sharing a cup of coffee, as had become their daily ritual each morning.

"Well I'll be hog-tied and roasted on a spit," Wooley cried, slapping Chase on the back. "Whoever would have guessed you was sweet on Miss Margaret."

"Looks like Chase is full of surprises," Tom said, smiling with pleasure. "I never would have believed he'd settle down."

"I just had to find me the right woman, that's all," Chase interjected, sipping thoughtfully on his coffee.

"Miss Margaret is surely that," Wooley concurred. "I've never known a sweeter dispositioned woman in my life. Why, next to Margaret, Concita's a venomous snake."

Tom laughed. "Why'd you marry that gal, if she's such a handful? I told you marrying someone fifteen years younger than yourself was going to get you in a heap of trouble."

Scratching his beard, Wooley's smile was full of mischief. "There's some benefits to living with a she-cat." He winked broadly.

"You old dog," Tom said, his blue eyes twinkling. "I should have known *that* was the reason your disposition changed so dramatically after you married. Why you went from vinegar to honey within a day of the wedding night."

"I suppose we all have our reasons for getting hitched. Ain't that right, Marshal?"

Feeling uncomfortable at the turn the conversation was taking, Chase ignored Wooley's question and rose to his feet. He had no intention of getting into a discussion on why he was marrying Margaret Parker. Crossing to the door, he grabbed his hat off the rack. "I don't have time to sit here jawing with you boys all day. I've got work to do." Without a backward glance, he strode from the office.

Staring at the door after Chase had departed, Wooley shook his head. "I wonder what's gotten into the marshal. He's seems a mite on edge. Must be gettin' cold feet."

"I expect it's a bit more than that, Wooley. Chase told me this morning that he'd found a note from Margaret under the door when he came to work this morning. He's to meet Phoebe Parker this evening."

Wooley whistled, his eyes rolling in disbelief. "That

explains it, then. I guess a man who's about to meet the spawn of the devil has a right to be on edge."

The smell of fried chicken wafted out through the screen door as Chase approached the front porch of the Parker residence. The sounds of clanking dishes, banging pots, and Margaret's soft voice as she hummed a refrain of "Green Grow the Lilacs" greeted his arrival.

He'd dreaded this moment since he'd found Maggie's note under his door this morning, inviting him to dinner "to meet Mother," it had stated.

He should have refused—made an excuse. He must be nuts putting himself through this torture. And for what? This whole scheme of his could backfire in his face. He could be stuck with a wife, a mother-in-law who despised him, and a ramshackle house that was most likely going to fall over during the next big thunderstorm.

What made him believe that one day Jack Parker would try to get in touch with his daughter? Gut instinct, pure and simple, he thought. It had saved his life many times; it just might get him the revenge he sought.

The sound of Margaret's voice as she broke into song at the top of her lungs interrupted his musing. He smiled. At least marrying Maggie was palatable. She was full of fire. She would be an exciting bed partner. He sniffed. And she knew her way around a kitchen. Thoughts of Maggie in bed had given him a powerful appetite. Banging on the door, he waited but a moment for his knock to be answered.

Margaret's eyes lit with pleasure as they fell on Chase

standing at her door. He looked very handsome in his dark suit and string tie. She could tell he had taken great pains with his appearance, and it brought a funny ache to her breast. His hair, shining like wet obsidian, was neatly combed; he smelled of shaving soap and bay rum, and it was all she could do not to throw herself at him. "Hello," she said softly. "I've been expecting you."

He stepped into the hallway, taking a quick look around. "Is your mother here?" For a man who'd faced countless outlaws it seemed stupid to be apprehensive about facing one old battle-ax, Chase thought. But he was.

Margaret's smile faltered a bit. "Mama's in her room. She won't be joining us for dinner. I thought perhaps we could go up and get the introductions over with, then eat."

"Maybe we should eat first," Chase suggested. Who knew if they'd have an appetite when Phoebe Parker got through with them.

"Margaret! Margaret! Is that marshal here yet? I hear voices." Phoebe's distinctive whine echoed down the stairwell, bringing an apologetic smile to Margaret's lips.

"Mama doesn't like to be kept waiting."

Neither did a black widow before she swallowed her prey, Chase thought, but he wasn't going to mention that. He nodded. "Lead on."

Placing her hand on his arm, Margaret stared pleadingly into Chase's eyes. "Please don't be upset if Mama should say something that offends you. She's quite outspoken and often rude."

He covered her hand with his own, feeling the tension that flowed through her body, noting the concern that clouded her eyes. "Darlin', I've faced cattle rustlers, Indians, and murderers. How bad could your mother be?"

But he found out a few minutes later when he was ushered into Phoebe Parker's inner sanctum. The gray-haired woman was seated in a spindle-backed rocker that looked ready to collapse under her massive weight. Her lap was covered with a rose-patterned quilt, and Chase thought she looked like everybody's image of a sweet old grandma—until she opened her mouth.

"So, you're the man who's proposed marriage to my daughter." She eyed him from head to toe, her lips pinching into a thin line.

Chase stepped forward, extending his hand. "Pleased to meet you, Mrs. Parker." She totally ignored the gesture. Her eyes were cold and flat like a snake's, offering not a hint of welcome or acceptance.

"You don't fool me for one minute, Marshal. I know the only thing you want from my daughter is what she's got between her legs."

Margaret gasped, her hands flying up to cover her mortification. "Mama!"

Chase hid his anger behind a polite smile. "On the contrary, Mrs. Parker, I find your daughter to be beautiful and kind. What you're suggesting I can find in any whorehouse. Margaret's appeal is much wider than that."

"We both know Margaret's plain, Marshal. No need to sugarcoat with me. I wasn't born yesterday."

"If you think your daughter plain, perhaps you need eyeglasses."

Margaret swallowed her surprise and her smile. Chase was holding his own.

Phoebe's lips pursed so tight, she looked as if she'd swallowed a lemon, whole. When she finally spoke, her words were as acerbic as her expression. "Hmph! You're a rude man. I don't want you marrying my daughter. She's too good for the likes of you."

Grabbing Margaret around the waist in a proprietary fashion, Chase pulled her into him, delighting in Phoebe's gasp of surprise. "You're probably right, Mrs. Parker. I'm sure Margaret is too good for me, but we're still getting married. Margaret's old enough to make her own decisions, though we'd like to have your blessing, if you're inclined to give it."

Phoebe paled, clutching her chest. "Margaret, my smelling salts."

Chase shook his head as he watched Margaret rush forward to do her mother's bidding. Why didn't she just let the old bitch die? He would.

"Don't get upset, Mama," Margaret said as she waved the vial under her mother's nose. "You wouldn't want to miss out on dinner tonight. We're having fried chicken."

The cure was instantaneous. Apparently, Margaret wasn't as taken in by her mother as Chase had originally thought.

"I'm much better," Phoebe said, "but I think you had better take your marshal out of here. It upsets me too much to have him around."

Margaret stared beseechingly at Chase who nodded. "It was a pleasure meeting you, Mrs. Parker . . . or would you rather I call you Mama?"

She screamed at that and Chase smiled inwardly before departing the room. He knew it was wrong to torment the old woman, but he just couldn't help it.

Who the hell did she think she was talking about Maggie like that?

A few minutes later, Maggie joined him in the kitchen, looking tired and defeated, muttering her apologies as she busied herself with getting dinner on the table.

The anger that had festered like a boil at Phoebe's rudeness toward her daughter finally burst. "How do you stand it?" Chase blurted, noting the hurt in Margaret's eyes as she placed the bowl of mashed potatoes on the table. It made him wish he had kept his big mouth shut. "I'm sorry. I shouldn't have said that."

Margaret took the seat next to him. "I don't expect you to understand, Chase. It's a burden I have to bear. If Mama is going to be a problem, I'll understand if you wish to break our engagement." She felt the tears rush to her eyes—tears she wasn't accustomed to shedding. It was a luxury she didn't allow herself.

"Damn it, Maggie, I'm sorry. I'm such an ass." He pulled her out of her chair and onto his lap. "Don't even think that your mother is going to come between us. She isn't. I can handle her. Admittedly, not with kid gloves as you do, but I can still handle her."

Blinking back her tears, she nestled her face into his neck. "I'm sorry about Mama. You were wonderful. I only wish I could stand up to her like you do."

He rubbed her back gently, sensing the moistness on his neck and feeling like a damned heel. "You're kind and gentle. It's what makes you who you are. I wouldn't want you any other way." She looked up; the tears spiking her lashes reminded him of diamonds as they sparkled in the candlelight.

"Really?"

He kissed the tip of her nose. "Really."

"I've never known anyone like you before," she confessed.

He grinned. "Darlin', they broke the mold after I was born."

She smiled at his quip, placing her hand tenderly on his cheek. "I guess they did."

Feeling a queer tightening in the region of his heart, Chase turned his face to place a tender kiss in the middle of her palm. The ardent expression in Margaret's eyes worried him—excited him, made him dream of things that could be—that must never be. He knew he had already lost his mind. Had he lost his heart, as well?

Chapter Twelve

"You know I should never speak to you again, don't you?" Betsy said, handing Margaret one of the dinner plates to dry. They had just finished a scrumptious meal of roast pork, mashed potatoes, and baby carrots, and Margaret was too stuffed to argue the point.

"I wasn't purposely trying to keep anything from you," she tried to explain. "It's just that the whole town knew of our courtship before I had a chance to tell anyone about it." She placed the china plate atop the growing stack on the counter.

"Well, I do feel responsible for this whole turn of events. Why, without my auction, you and Chase might never have gotten together."

Margaret smiled, knowing full well that Betsy thought exactly that. "I appreciate all your efforts, and I'm especially grateful for the delicious dinner you prepared for Chase and me tonight. It was very thoughtful of you to have gone to so much trouble." Chase must have thought so, too, for he had eaten three servings of the pork and potatoes. He had quite an appetite for a great many things, she thought, smiling wickedly.

"It was the least I could do. After all, I am going to be the matron of honor and Tom, Chase's best man." Betsy's smile bubbled effusively. "I'm so excited, Margaret. I can't wait to purchase a new dress for the occasion."

Staring at the increasing girth of Betsy's waistline, Margaret wondered if it would be wise for her friend to spend the money needlessly to purchase a new dress. There wouldn't be another opportunity for her to wear it after the baby was born. "Do you think it's wise to buy something new? With you being pregnant and all, I wouldn't want you to waste your money."

Betsy's mouth dropped open, staring at Margaret as if she had lost her mind. "Waste my money . . . are you kidding? I look for any excuse to buy a new dress. Besides, you can borrow it when you get pregnant. We're of a like size."

Betsy's comment bothered Margaret, and she made a great pretense of putting the dishes away in the cupboard so she wouldn't have to answer her. She hadn't had an opportunity to speak to Chase about having a baby, and was still unsure how he felt. In fact, she was planning to broach the subject when he escorted her home this evening; the thought made her exceedingly nervous.

"Speaking of dresses," Betsy continued, "have you decided what you're going to wear?"

Folding the dish towel neatly, Margaret hung it on the rack to dry. "Mama is insisting that I wear her old wedding gown."

"You're kidding! Has she reconciled herself to this marriage?"

Unable to keep the disappointment out of her voice, Margaret replied, "No. She's still very much opposed. I think she ranks Chase only one step above the devil."

Betsy smiled at that. Knowing something about Chase and Tom's former escapades, Betsy thought Phoebe very astute, but for all the wrong reasons. She asked, "Then why?"

Margaret had asked herself that very question. She'd been bowled over when her mother had suggested that she go up into the attic and bring down the wedding gown. "If you're going to go through with this horrible wedding, then you might as well look respectable. We can't afford to spend any of our hard-earned money on the likes of him. You can wear my dress," she had insisted.

The dress had proven exquisite. It was champagne satin with row upon row of delicate seed pearls. Margaret had never seen anything quite so lovely, and when her mother had suggested she try it on, she couldn't resist. The tight-fitting sleeves and bodice hugged her body like a glove. It was difficult to imagine that her mother had actually fit into such a small gown. Obviously, Phoebe had been a great deal thinner when she had married Jonathan Parker.

"I'm not sure about Mama's motives," Margaret finally confessed. "I suspect it's her way of keeping a hand in things, even though she's not planning to attend the ceremony."

Betsy withheld her comment about Phoebe's selfish

motives. The woman had never gone out of her way to be a real mother to Margaret; why should she start now? Hoping to spare Margaret's feelings, she thought it better to let the subject drop.

"Whew! Finally finished," Betsy said, wiping her forehead and hands on her apron. "I guess we can join the men in the parlor for coffee and dessert. I'm certain Tom has bent Chase's ear about his new idea to open a mercantile."

"He's giving up the idea of farming?"

Betsy nodded. "Tom's not cut out to be a farmer. And with the lack of abundant water and the poor condition of the soil, we just decided it was too big a risk to take."

"That's probably wise. But what does Tom know of operating a mercantile? He's been a lawman all his life."

Handing Margaret four dessert plates and forks, Betsy smiled confidently. "Do you know anyone more capable than me to run a store? Shopping is my forte. I was born to it."

Giggling, Margaret shook her head. "Come to think of it, I guess there're fewer people better qualified."

Betsy smiled smugly. "My thoughts, exactly."

A few minutes later they joined the men, who were in the middle of a heated discussion regarding Tom's plan to operate a mercantile.

"You're nuts! This town can't support another store. It's already got two," Chase argued. "Are you sure you've given this idea enough thought?"

"Probably as much as you've given to getting married. It was quite a sudden decision, wasn't it?"

Chase pinned Tom with a heated glare, but before he could respond, Margaret, who had overheard the entire conversation, stepped in. "I guess our decision was rather sudden, Tom. But neither of us is getting any younger. Why should we wait?"

Tom flushed, embarrassed that Margaret had overheard his comment; he smiled apologetically. "You shouldn't. I was just being perverse because Chase has more opinions than Alberta Bottoms and Marion Holmes put together. He's worse than an old woman."

"I'm sure Chase just has your best interests at heart," Margaret supplied, turning to stare at her fiancé, who was muttering nasty invectives under his breath. "Isn't that so, Chase?"

He shrugged. "Don't matter to me if this fool wants to risk all he's got."

"Coffee anyone?" Betsy interjected, thrusting the cup of hot liquid into her husband's hands before he had a chance to comment. She gave him a warning glance. Chase might be opinionated, but he was still a guest in their home, and she wasn't going to ruin the evening because of two stubborn, mule-headed men.

After another thirty minutes of brooding stares and awkward conversation, Margaret and Chase finally expressed their regrets and took their leave. The walk home to Margaret's house was almost as strained as the last few minutes of their visit to the Frasers' had been. The quiet was deafening. And although the night sprung forth with the sounds of its inhabitants, it wasn't enough to fill the embarrassing silence that existed between the two people who walked side by side.

Margaret chanced a sidelong glance at Chase, whose reticence in speaking seemed to indicate that he had a great deal on his mind. She was loath to bring up the subject uppermost on *her* mind: that of having a child. When Chase finally did speak, Margaret was so startled she almost tripped over her own feet.

"I'm sorry about tonight. I'm not usually so eager to butt into other people's affairs." He reached out to steady her.

"I expect you're not used to living in a town the size of this one, where your personal business becomes everyone else's, and you're obliged to listen to well-meaning advice. It grates on a body after a while."

"You're pretty perceptive, you know that? And I guess I had no right to interfere in Tom and Betsy's plans."

"I'm sure they'll just pass it off as prenuptial jitters. It isn't every day a confirmed bachelor decides to get married."

Her remark surprised him. "Who says I'm a confirmed bachelor?"

"I . . . No one really. I just assumed, because of your age and the fact you've never married, that you didn't wish to." Her obvious mistake only pointed out how little they really knew about each other.

"I was engaged once . . . many years ago. I was just a kid."

Margaret felt stunned and a little jealous. "I didn't know. What happened? How come you didn't marry?"

Chase's eyes clouded in pain. Pausing at the gate

fronting Margaret's house, he replied softly, "She died."

"I'm sorry."

He shrugged, pushing the wood-slated gate open. "It was a long time ago. I got over it."

Noting the hurt in his eyes, Margaret wondered at the truth of his words. He must have loved the woman very much to still grieve for her. The thought brought a heaviness to her chest. "Time lessens the pain, but it never really makes it disappear, does it?"

"If you're wondering if I'm still in love with Amy, the answer is yes." He saw her flinch and added, "I'll always love her; we grew up together. But I won't let her memory stand between us, Maggie. She's dead, and you're very much alive." He drew her into his arms, his mouth covering hers hungrily. Suddenly, his hands were everywhere—on her breasts, cupping her bottom, insinuating themselves between their bodies to press against her swollen desire. She couldn't control the moan that escaped, nor the insistent thrusting of her hips as she sought an end to her torment.

Feeling Margaret's response, hearing her moan of pleasure, Chase forced himself to stop, feeling guilty that he hadn't been able to restrain himself. He heaved a deep sigh. "I'm sorry. Damn it, Maggie! I can't seem to control myself where you're concerned. I promised you I'd wait, but it's hard . . . damn . . . I'm hard as a rock."

It took a moment for Chase's words to finally penetrate her passion-fogged brain, but when they did, Margaret colored fiercely, feeling the evidence of his arousal pressing against her stomach. "What if I don't want to wait?" she replied, unable to believe that she'd actually voiced her thoughts aloud. Lord, what was wrong with her?

If her question surprised Chase, he didn't show it. "We've only got two more weeks. I made a vow; I intend to keep it."

She nodded, stepping back, hugging herself to squelch the torment his caresses had inflicted. "I guess that would be best."

"I doubt it would be best, darlin', but I guess it would be the most proper." He smiled grimly, wondering if he was doomed to be frustrated forever. It seemed as if it had become his natural state of late.

Summoning up her courage, Margaret finally remarked, "Chase . . . there's something I've been meaning to ask you."

"What's that, darlin'?" He escorted her the rest of the way up the walk. "Another detail about the wedding that you've neglected to tell me?" Seating Margaret on the porch swing, he sat down beside her, waiting for her to answer.

"Actually . . ." She bit her lip, unsure of how she should proceed. "This detail has something to do with after the wedding."

He grinned. "Aha. The honeymoon—my area of expertise."

She blushed. "Indirectly."

"Don't tell me you're scared? Why, after what we just went through, I won't believe that for a minute."

The swing started moving at a rapid pace as Margaret kept time with her own nervous thoughts. This was harder than she'd expected, and Chase wasn't

171

making it any easier. "I want to have a baby," she blurted.

The porch swing stopped abruptly, and Chase's mouth dropped open. "A baby?" That was one possibility he hadn't considered.

"You do want to have children, don't you?"

He observed the apprehension in her eyes, the way her hands fluttered nervously in her lap, and he knew that his answer was very important to her. "I hadn't really thought about it," he answered truthfully.

"I realize it's a bit premature to be discussing this, considering the fact that we haven't . . . that we haven't . . ."

"Consummated?"

She nodded. "But I need to know your feelings on the subject. It's very important to me."

His feelings. What were his feelings? He'd never thought much about having a child—never believed he would ever get married. His kind of life never lent itself to settling down. There'd always been too many loose ends; there still were. What kind of a father would he make? Probably a damned sight better one than Jack Parker.

Reaching for her hand, he brought it to his mouth for a kiss; then, placing it on her abdomen, he covered it with his own. "Maggie, if my seed takes root within you and grows, then that's God's will. And I can tell you in all honesty, the thought of planting that seed gives me nothing but pleasure. I promise to do my share to get you with child. If I have to devote my every waking moment to the task, then I will."

Her eyes widened. "Tha . . . thank you."

172

He caressed her cheek, thinking that if he searched the rest of his life, he'd never find a more perfect treasure. "It'll be my pleasure."

Time passed by quickly for Margaret. There were so many last minute details to attend to before the wedding and she only had two more days to get everything done.

Two more days! Would she really be Mrs. Chase Gallagher in only two more days? She couldn't believe it was actually happening. Everything was falling into place. The church hall had been rented for the reception; Betsy and Mrs. Perkins were taking care of the food; Alberta and Marion had generously offered to supply the flowers and decorations; and even Chase had cooperated by keeping a respectable distance. It wouldn't do to get too distracted now, she thought, not with only two days left. Everything was going to be perfect.

"Margaret!"

Well almost everything, she thought, setting the pen down and pushing herself out of the kitchen chair. She would have to complete the list for the last minute items tomorrow morning. It was getting late, anyhow—nearly midnight. Stretching to ease the tension in her neck and back, she turned down the kerosene lantern and trudged up the stairs.

"I'm out of my medicine," Phoebe stated when Margaret entered. Her mother reclined against the pillows of her bed; a Beadle dime novel entitled, *Hurricane Nell,* rested on her lap. "Run to the doctor's and fetch my pills."

"But it's late, Mama. Doc is out at the Fergusons'. He won't be back until tomorrow." She thought of the distressing news Doc had told her this morning and sighed deeply: Kate was pregnant again.

"I can't wait that long; I'll die without my pills." Phoebe wept softly into her hands, adding, "You're just so caught up with your wedding plans, you don't care if I live or die."

Realizing that she was being manipulated, but not possessing the energy to argue over a box of stupid pills—pills that were in reality only candy—a placebo, Doc had called them—Margaret said, "Very well, I'll go, but I hope no one sees me dressed like this." She had already bathed and donned her nightclothes before setting to the task of making out her list. Who knew she'd be required to gallivant about in the middle of the night?

"You're not intending to go out dressed in your night clothes, are you? Why, it's highly improper!"

"I have no intention of getting dressed to walk such a short distance. I'll put on my shawl. There shouldn't be anyone out and about this time of evening." Most likely all the sane people had retired to their beds already. Too bad she hadn't been as wise; it would have spared her from doing her mother's bidding.

Phoebe was about to voice another opinion on the subject, but Margaret's heated stare made her think twice about it.

Margaret cursed beneath her breath the entire way over to Doc Watson's office. She cursed at the fact that there was no moon to guide her, causing her to stub her toe on the sidewalk; she cursed her mother's selfishness at asking her to go out at such an ungodly hour; but most of all, she cursed herself and her own lack of self-assertiveness that had allowed her to be dominated—exploited. Would she never stand up to her mother?

Entering through the rear of the building, Margaret felt her way to the examination room, lighting the kerosene lamp on the counter. Tossing her shawl on the table, she proceeded to hunt through the cupboard that housed Doc's medicines. Although most of Doc's prescriptive medicines were kept out front in the pharmacy, she knew the container of sugar pills was kept separate, so there would never be any mix-ups.

Spying the container she suspected held the pills on the top shelf of the cupboard, she was just about to reach for them when a noise behind her made her turn. She gasped, her eyes widening in fright, at the sight of the nefarious-looking man standing behind her. He was dressed in a long black duster with a felt slouch hat pulled low on his forehead, and he was holding a gun.

"Well, ain't you a purty little thing." He smiled, displaying teeth that were rotted, several of which were missing, and waved his gun. "Come on over, little gal. Let old Brandy take a gander at you."

Fear, stark and vivid, raced through her body. Trying desperately not to show it, she demanded with far more bravado than she felt, "What do you want? Why are you here?"

"I expect I'm after the same thing as you."

Margaret's brow creased in confusion, until she noticed that his eyes searched frantically over the shelves of the cupboard—eyes that were red and dilated. Drugs. He wanted drugs. She had never actually seen an addict until now, but Doc had told her stories—horrible stories about men and women in the throes of their addiction. She shuddered.

"Where's the opium, little gal. I don't have a lot of time to waste."

"I don't know," she lied, taking a step back as he advanced toward her.

"You're quite a looker, you know that? I bet under that concealing nightgown, you are one prime piece of meat." He chuckled. "I ain't had me nothing prime for weeks. The whores I've been taking my ease with are a dried-up bunch of cronies." He licked his lips, wiping his mouth on his sleeve. "You look mighty fresh, gal, like maybe you ain't been rode too hard."

Scream, she told herself. *Scream at the top of your lungs.* But the little voice inside her head that controlled her reason told her that to do so would be committing herself to death. He had a gun and it was pointed at her heart.

"You'll leave, if you know what's good for you. I'm to be married to the marshal of this town. He'll kill you if you try anything."

"So, you're the marshal's piece, huh? Well, he's got good taste, I'll say that for him. Lift up your gown. I want to see what's beneath all that pristine material."

Margaret began to shake. Digging her nails into the palms of her hands, she stared down at the floor. *Please God! Spare me. Anything but this.*

He motioned with his gun. "Lift 'em, sweetheart. I got me a hankerin' to see what your marshal finds so

176

interesting between your legs."

No one saw the tall figure who seemed to come out of nowhere, nor the menacing Colt revolver pointed at the stranger's back. "Why don't you ask the marshal, you mangy lowlife?"

Margaret's head shot up. "Chase!" Tears of relief filled her eyes. "Thank God you've come."

"Drop the gun and reach for the ceiling," Chase ordered the would-be robber.

After the intruder did as instructed, Chase motioned for Margaret to come to his side, never taking his eyes off the man. "Are you hurt? Did this bastard touch you?" The words dripped cold and lethal, chilling everyone in the room, including Margaret who rubbed her arms to warm herself.

"No . . . I'm fine."

Chase ran his free hand over her to satisfy himself that she was telling the truth, then shouted to the stranger, "You . . . turn around."

The man did so, shaking like a willow in a heavy wind, whether from fear or his addiction, Margaret couldn't be certain.

"What's your name?" Chase demanded.

"Brandy . . . Brandy Jennings."

"Well, Mr. Jennings, you're under arrest. Now head for the door . . . slowly. And don't try anything. It would give me nothing but pleasure to put a bullet between your eyes."

Margaret gasped, watching in relief as the man followed Chase's order.

"Lock this door and wait here," Chase said, casting a sidelong glance at Margaret. "I'm going to lock up this

177

scum, then I'll be back to escort you home."

"There's no need . . ."

Like storm clouds, the silver eyes darkened ominously. "Do as I say. I'll deal with you when I return." Pushing the robber out the door in front of him, Chase departed.

After locking the door, Margaret plopped down on the chair, unable to control the violent spasms that racked her body. She had almost been raped tonight—Chase was furious with her—and she wasn't sure who was going to receive the worst punishment—her or Brandy Jennings.

Chapter Thirteen

The waiting was interminable. Margaret had almost given up on the idea that Chase was coming back when she heard the loud rap. Crossing to the door, she rested her hand on the knob, calling out, "Who's there?"

"It's me, Chase."

Breathing a sigh of relief, she unlocked the door, admitting Chase into the room. The angry look on his face told her that he was still madder than a wet hen. She had never seen him really livid before and it gave her pause.

"You all right?" he asked, giving her a quick once-over.

She nodded, afraid that if she spoke and he heard the tremble in her voice, he wouldn't believe her.

Removing his hat, he combed agitated fingers through his mass of ebony hair. "What you did tonight was pretty damned stupid!"

She opened her mouth, about to agree, but clamped it shut when she heard him add, "I can't believe that a grown woman would wander the streets half-naked in the middle of the night. I thought you had more sense than that. Were you looking for trouble? 'Cause you certainly found it."

Her brown eyes darkening to midnight, Margaret almost choked with fury. How dare Chase insinuate that she'd been looking for trouble? Perhaps she'd been foolish to venture out in her nightclothes, unescorted, but she was hardly naked! "I don't like your tone, nor what you're implying. I have a perfectly logical explanation for being here so late. If you'd bothered to ask, before going off half-cocked, I'd have told you that I came for Mama's pills."

His face reddened, and the pulse at the base of his neck throbbed ominously. "Did I go off 'half-cocked' before or after I saved your pretty little ass?"

Anger, mixed with the strain of her ordeal, surged through her body like a fire out of control. For the first time in her life, she lifted her hand in anger, fully intending to slap Chase Gallagher across his arrogant mouth. But he was quicker, grabbing on to her hand.

Expecting Chase to respond in kind, Margaret was taken totally off guard when he pulled her up against him, crushing her lips with his own in a kiss meant to punish.

And Chase, whose desire had hardened instantly when he came in contact with Margaret's soft lips and pliant body, couldn't decide who was punishing whom. After a few more moments of delectable torture, he lifted his head, his voice shaking slightly when he spoke. "Christ, Maggie, you scared the hell out of me! If I hadn't seen the light when I made my rounds, you might be dead." He hugged her fiercely.

Tears welled up instantly, forming a large knot in her

throat. "I'm sorry. You were right; it was stupid of me to go out alone."

He ran his hands gently, comfortingly, over her body, annoyed by the amount of material the voluminous folds of her nightgown contained. Had he really said half-naked? There was enough material covering Maggie's lush form to conceal the entire Grand Canyon! "Ssh," he crooned softly into her ear. "I shouldn't have said what I did; I was just afraid for you."

When she looked up at him with tears spiking her lashes and a tremulous smile on her lips, it was his undoing. He kissed her again, parting her lips to plunge his tongue deep inside her mouth. In and out, he thrust, matching the movements with his pelvis, pressing his hardened member into her soft belly. When he felt her go limp in his arms, he carried her to the examining table, setting her on top of it. Taking several deep breaths to calm himself, Chase tried to get himself under control, noting that Margaret was attempting to do the same.

Margaret's pulse skittered alarmingly at the ardent, determined expression she saw in Chase's eyes. The silver orbs sparkled like multifaceted diamonds as his hands came up to undo the buttons at the top of her gown. When he reached for the stethoscope hanging on the side of the table, and she saw the hint of mischief in his eyes, she swallowed. Was he intending to examine her? The thought caused a tingling sensation in the very core of her being.

"I felt you go faint in my arms," Chase whispered, opening the front of Margaret's gown, ignoring the blush that spread over her cheeks like red satin. "I think

I should listen to your heart . . . just to make sure you're all right."

Inserting the stethoscope into his ears, he placed the disc against her heart. The feel of his hands against her flesh, rough, yet tender, wreaked havoc within her. Her breasts surged at the intimacy of his touch, the nipples stiffening even harder than before.

"You seem to be having some problems," he teased, noting the rigidity of her breasts. "Perhaps, like any good doctor, I should attempt to cure what ails you."

Liquid heat pulsed through her veins. "Do you think you can?" she asked in a breathy whisper.

His smile was incredibly sensual. "I'm sure of it." Hanging the stethoscope back in its place, he pushed the top of her nightgown down to her waist, baring her breasts to his view. Cupping the soft, perfectly formed mounds, he bent his head, exploring first one taut dusky nipple, then the other.

Margaret sighed in ecstasy, gripping the sides of the table with her hands when his tongue left her breasts to venture lower, skimming across her stomach.

"You drive me crazy with desire, darlin'. I want you . . . here . . . now."

Running her fingers through his hair, across the firm, rigid muscles of his back, she whispered, "I want you, too. Make love to me, Chase."

"With pleasure." Pushing her back against the leather of the examination table, he proceeded to climb on top of her.

At that moment there was a loud banging at the door. Exchanging a look of mutual frustration with Margaret, Chase groaned aloud as Doc's voice floated in through the door.

"Margaret, are you in there? Margaret, open up, it's Doc."

"Christ!" Chase yelled, righting himself, refastening his trousers. "We have company."

Her face turning alternate shades of red and white, Margaret bolted upright, working furiously to button her nightgown. Good heavens! How was she going to explain what they'd been doing . . . and on Doc's own examining table, no less?

"I'll let him in," Chase said, grabbing her shawl off the table and tossing it to her. She smiled weakly and nodded.

"Margaret." The banging on the door became more insistent.

Glancing back over his shoulder to make sure Margaret was decent, Chase readjusted his own discomfort and opened the door. The startled expression on Doc's face would have been funny under any other circumstances. Unfortunately, tonight Chase's humor had fled.

Looking from Chase to Margaret as he entered, then back to Chase again, Doc asked, "What's going on? No trouble, I hope." His probing eyes seemed to take in everything, narrowing suspiciously at the sight of Margaret's haphazardly buttoned gown, causing her to blush profusely.

"We did have some trouble a little while ago, but it's all taken care of now." Chase went on to explain the situation involving Margaret and Brandy Jennings, bringing a deep scowl to Doc's face.

"I'm surprised at you, Margaret. You should know better than to risk your life over your mother's foolish whims."

Margaret colored fiercely, then suddenly realizing why she had ventured out in the first place, blurted, "Mama! I completely forgot about her." She flashed Chase a guilty look; but instead of finding guilt on his face, she found only amusement. "I have to get home."

"I'm sure Marshal Gallagher will be happy to see you home, Margaret," Doc said, his eyes twinkling at her embarrassment.

Chase nodded, grabbing Margaret firmly about the waist. "I'll see that no harm comes to her, Doc."

Doc threw back his head and laughed, bringing a bright pink stain to Margaret's cheeks and a hearty chuckle from Chase when he said, "Two more days till the wedding, huh, Chase? I know that you've vowed to keep Margaret safe, but who's going to protect her from you?"

Two days later, the wedding went off without a hitch.

Standing in the middle of the church hall, which had been decorated with white satin streamers and bouquets of wildflowers, Margaret surrounded by her friends, with her husband by her side, felt happier than she had ever thought possible. The strains of Wooley's fiddle sang through her veins, making her as giddy as the champagne she had drank in great quantities. She was in love; she was married. And there was nothing that could destroy her newfound happiness.

"If your smile gets any wider, darlin', people are going to think that we've already had our honeymoon," Chase whispered.

"I don't care what anyone thinks." She stood on

tiptoe, brushing a kiss across his lips; the silky feel of his mustache tickled. "I'm too happy to care."

A twinge of guilt tugged at his conscience; he pushed it away, saying, "If you keep torturing me, Mrs. Gallagher, we're going to have to leave this shindig rather abruptly; I fear something's coming between us."

Lowering her gaze, she gasped at the large unmistakable bulge between Chase's legs.

"Your thoughts betray you, Maggie, darlin'. Are you ready to leave?"

She blushed, her eyes widening. "What of the cake? We haven't eaten any of it, or opened any of the presents." She stared at the lovely tiered wedding cake that Betsy had baked. It was covered with creamy white icing and surrounded by gaily-wrapped packages.

He pulled her to a secluded corner of the room, ignoring the snickers, laughter, and ribald comments that followed them. "Darlin', I've got a gift that's going to give you so much pleasure, you won't need any of these things. And as for the cake . . ." He bent low to whisper in her ear. "Well, I can think of something else far sweeter to nibble on."

Margaret swallowed, casting a nervous glance about the room. Everyone seemed to be having a wonderful time. Betsy and Tom were dancing; Alberta and Marion were at the refreshment table stuffing food into their mouths like it was their last meal; and Wooley was fiddling his heart out.

Gripping Chase's hand, she smiled up at him—a smile so blatantly seductive it made the breath catch in his throat. "How far did you say it was to Tucson?"

Bending over, he kissed her tenderly on the lips. "The

ride of your life awaits you, little darlin'. And I'm not talking about the buggy ride to Tucson." With that, he picked her up, tossed her over his shoulder and strode from the room amid a chorus of whistles and cheers.

A soaring, white-winged dove dipped its wing against the cloudless blue sky as the buggy approached the flat desert town of Tucson.

Considering the dove to be a good omen, Margaret smiled happily to herself as she observed the stark countryside surrounding them. Tall, gnarled saguaro cactus, their arms raised in greeting, stood like primitive sentries amidst green paloverde trees, mesquite bushes, and prickly pear. Glistening rocks lined the dusty road like priceless jewels, as the soft wind whispered through the tawny tumbled hills.

In the distance, surrounding the town on all sides, were six ranges of jagged, purple-colored mountains, providing a sharp contrast to the squat, white-washed adobe buildings that comprised the town.

"The desert has a beauty all its own, doesn't it?" she commented, marveling at the breathtaking sight.

"It does; but it doesn't hold a candle to my beautiful wife."

Margaret smiled. "Perhaps you have been drinking the waters of the Hassayampa River." At his look of puzzlement, she explained, "Indian legend says that once a man drinks Hassayampa water, he will never tell the truth again. You are kind, but I am not blind, and your effusive compliments embarrass me."

"Then you will just have to go around being embarrassed, because I'm not going to lie just to please you. I speak the truth when I say you're beautiful."

"Thank you," she answered shyly, quickly changing the subject by asking, "How much longer?"

"Fifteen more minutes and you'll be lying between the sheets of a comfortable bed in the Palace Hotel. Hope you're not too tired." He grinned. "You won't be getting much sleep."

Chase's words drummed through Margaret's brain as they made their way up the winding staircase of the lavishly decorated Palace Hotel and down the wide hallway to their suite. Much to her mortification, Chase had made no bones about announcing to the clerk behind the front desk that they were newly wedded, wanted the best room in the house, and didn't want to be disturbed for any reason. Chase had stared so menacingly at the bald-headed, mustached man when he enunciated the last edict, the poor clerk had almost fallen off his stool in his haste to accommodate him.

"We're here, darlin'," Chase announced, unlocking the door with his brass room key and throwing it open. Before Margaret could take one step, he swooped her up in his arms and carried her across the threshold. "Wouldn't do to break with tradition, now would it?"

When they entered the large, beautifully decorated suite, Margaret didn't notice the room's rich red damask drapery or its gilt-edged furnishings. All she could see was the enormous brass bed that fully took up one half of the room. Her eyes widened, and she swallowed nervously. "It's . . . it's lovely."

Noting her reaction, Chase lowered her carefully to the floor, sliding her down the length of his body. "You're not scared, are you?" He tilted up her chin

187

when she attempted to avert her eyes.

"A little," she confessed. "I've never . . . I've never been with a man before." He seemed pleased by her answer.

"I thought as much, but with your ardent response to my lovemaking it was difficult to tell at times."

She turned the color of the drapery. "You make me feel things I've never felt before—make me act in ways totally alien to everything I've been taught."

Kissing her lightly on the lips, he retrieved the bags from the hallway and locked the door. "You can use the bathroom first, if you'd like."

Presenting her back to him, she said, "Would you mind unfastening my gown? I don't think I'll be able to reach the buttons." At Betsy's insistence, she had purchased a lovely blue dimity traveling dress to wear on her honeymoon. Unfortunately, she hadn't forseen the problem that the tiny bone buttons down the back would present.

The feel of Chase's lips on her bare flesh alerted her to the fact that he was done, and the tingling in her toes made her realize that she was ready to get this honeymoon underway. "I'll be back in a moment."

Discarding his coat and tie, Chase walked to the window and rolled a cigarette. Staring out, he observed the purple shadows that streaked across the sky as the sun began its descent into the horizon. A faint roar of thunder could be heard in the distance, signaling an approaching storm, a common occurrence during the summer months.

Listening to the sounds of splashing water coming from the bathroom, he smiled, his heart beating fast in anticipation. Maggie was on the other side of the door, naked and in her bath. The thought made him as hard as a brick. Stripping out of his shirt, he tossed the cigarette out the open window and strode toward the bathroom door. She was his wife now, and it was time to consummate that fact.

Reclining in a tub full of lavender-scented bubbles, Margaret's eyes widened as the bathroom door creaked open and Chase entered. She slid beneath the bubbles, hoping to conceal her nakedness.

"I thought you might need some help, darlin'," he said, kneeling beside the tub. Ignoring her gasp of surprise, he held out his hand. "Hand me the soap and I'll scrub your back for you." Without waiting for her to comply, he reached over her, his arm lightly brushing against her breasts, and picked up the bar of soap off the dish.

Shutting her eyes to alleviate her embarrassment, Margaret was soon entranced by the sensual feel of Chase's hand as it glided the soap over her back in wide circular motions. Lulled by the movements, the heat of the water, and the incredibly erotic feelings she was experiencing, Margaret drifted off into her own world. She was brought back abruptly when Chase's hand moved from her back to slide across her breasts.

"We wouldn't want to neglect the front, now would we?"

Her eyes flew open as did her mouth, but no sounds of protestations came forth, only moans of pleasure as his hand moved lower across her abdomen to administer to the now pulsing area between her legs. The feel of his fingers as they abraded the sensitive flesh of her thighs, her woman's mound, her nub of pleasure, caused her to cry out in ecstasy. Just when the tension

189

began to build, his hand stopped and withdrew.

Casting aside all modesty, she grabbed onto it. "Don't stop. Please don't stop," she begged. He smiled, pulling her up and out of the tub to wrap her in a warm, fluffy towel.

"Patience, little darlin'," he crooned. Cradling her in his arms, he carried her to the massive bed, laying her beneath the sheets. "I'll be back in a moment."

What seemed like hours was in reality only minutes until Chase exited the bathroom. Margaret's eyes riveted on the powerful, muscled body walking toward her. Chase was still wet, and his flesh glistened like dew on the petal of a flower. His hair gleamed like black velvet in the glow of the lantern, his rigid member jutting forth proudly, telling her better than words that the time for waiting was over.

The mattress sagged beneath his weight as he crawled in beside her. She felt suddenly shy, vulnerable to be so close—so intimately exposed to his nakedness. But when he reached for her and covered her lips with his own, all thoughts of shyness fled, replaced by an urgent need to explore and be explored.

"You smell so good, darlin' . . . so damn good," he whispered, nibbling on the lobe of her right ear. Inserting his tongue, he licked at the orifice until her breathing grew rapid and she thought every nerve ending in her body must be on fire.

"It's the lavender," she choked. "You said it was your favorite scent." She had bought the bar of soap as a last minute thought and was happy now that she had.

"It's not the lavender; it's you . . . your muskiness . . . your woman's scent that tells me that you're wet and ready for me."

190

"I am ready for you." With a boldness brought about by her own need, she caressed his chest, exploring the hard muscled mounds of flesh, delighting in the feel of his soft hairs beneath her fingertips. Lowering her head, she traced her lips where her fingers had been moments before, laving his nipples, listening to his soft moan of pleasure. Pleased by his response, she moved lower, trailing her tongue over his stomach, down his abdomen, until she reached the tumescent tip of his desire. Hearing his indrawn breath, she grew bolder, lightly flicking her tongue across the tip, tasting the saltiness of it.

"God, Maggie, you're killing me," Chase cried.

Quickly, she raised her head, alarmed at the agony she saw registered on his face. "I'm sorry; did I hurt you?"

"God, no! But if you continue in that fashion, the honeymoon is going to be over rather quickly."

"Oh," she said, unsure of what he meant.

Rolling Maggie onto her back, Chase enveloped her body with his own, staring down into the brown eyes that were so full of passion and innocence. "You really are inexperienced, aren't you?"

Margaret didn't have time to respond because Chase began to suckle her breasts with a singlemindedness that brought a gasp to her throat. His lips and tongue were suddenly everywhere—her breasts, her stomach, her legs—everywhere but where her need was the greatest. Frantically, she arched, thrusting her pelvis, hoping he would end the pulsing torment that surged through her woman's mound. She remembered how good it felt the last time to have his tongue on the very bud of her being, and she opened her legs as his mouth caressed the inside of her thighs.

"Not this time, darlin'," came the muffled response against her leg. "This time we're both going to fly." With that, he inserted his finger into her, readying her for what was to come.

A moment later with his comforting weight upon her, he eased himself into her, filling her, possessing her. There was only a brief moment of pain to be replaced by an agony of a different nature as he thrust in and out, in and out, taking her higher and higher with every powerful stroke. Their sweat-glistened bodies harmonized in the age-old rhythm of love-making—their motions becoming one as the hot tide of passion consumed them, heating their blood as they climbed toward the pinnacle of their fulfillment.

Suddenly, her body began to vibrate and she exploded, crying out as she attained her climax. "I love you," she confessed, her words smothered by Chase's lips as they covered hers.

Closing her eyes, her body melted against his and she fell into a lethargic slumber. She didn't see the unguarded look of tenderness in Chase's eyes, didn't hear the gentleness of his voice when he replied, "I love you, too, darlin'."

Gazing down into Margaret's sated features as she lay in repose, a lump of tenderness rose in Chase's throat. And in that moment, he realized it was true. What had started out as a means of revenge had ended up giving him the greatest gift of all—Maggie's love.

He loved her.

But would she continue to love him when she discovered he was after her father—the man she thought so highly of? What would she do if she had to

ENJOY ALL THE PASSION AND ROMANCE OF...

Heartfire

Heartfire Romance

ROMANCES from ZEBRA

After you have read HEART-FIRE ROMANCES, we're sure you'll agree that HEARTFIRE sets new standards of excellence for historical romantic fiction. Each Zebra HEARTFIRE novel is the ultimate blend of intimate romance and grand adventure and each takes place in the kinds of historical settings you want most...the American Revolution, the Old West, Civil War and more.

SUBSCRIBERS $AVE, $AVE, $AVE!!!

As a HEARTFIRE Home Subscriber, you'll save with your HEARTFIRE Subscription. You'll receive 4 brand new Heartfire Romances to preview Free for 10 days each month. If you decide to keep them you'll pay only $3.50 each; a total of $14.00 and you'll save $3.00 each month off the cover price.

Plus, we'll send you these novels as soon as they are published each month. There is never any shipping, handling or other hidden charges; home delivery is always FREE! And there is no obligation to buy even a single book. You may return any of the books within 10 days for full credit and you can cancel your subscription at any time. No questions asked.

Zebra's HEARTFIRE ROMANCES Are The Ultimate In Historical Romantic Fiction.
Start Enjoying Romance As You Have Never Enjoyed It Before...
With 4 FREE Books From HEARTFIRE

TO GET YOUR
4 FREE BOOKS
MAIL THE COUPON BELOW.

Heartfire Romance

FREE BOOK CERTIFICATE

GET 4 FREE BOOKS

Yes! I want to subscribe to Zebra's HEARTFIRE HOME SUBSCRIPTION SERVICE. Please send me my 4 FREE books. Then each month I'll receive the four newest Heartfire Romances as soon as they are published to preview Free for ten days. If I decide to keep them I'll pay the special discounted price of just $3.50 each; a total of $14.00. This is a savings of $3.00 off the regular publishers price. There are no shipping, handling or other hidden charges. There is no minimum number of books to buy and I may cancel this subscription at any time. In any case the 4 FREE Books are mine to keep regardless.

NAME

ADDRESS

CITY   STATE   ZIP

TELEPHONE

SIGNATURE   HF 102

(If under 18 parent or guardian must sign)
Terms and prices subject to change.
Orders subject to acceptance.

GET 4 FREE BOOKS

HEARTFIRE HOME SUBSCRIPTION
SERVICE
P.O. BOX 5214
120 BRIGHTON ROAD
CLIFTON, NEW JERSEY 07015

choose between them? Whom would she choose?

Running his hands possessively over her heated flesh, he kissed her into wakefulness, delighting in her soft whimpers of pleasure. The night was still young, and he hadn't had his fill of her. He would never have enough of her. Not ever!

Chapter Fourteen

At the same time the newlyweds were affirming their marital vows, another couple lay naked in the hayloft above the livery stable entwined in each other's arms. The sandy-haired cowboy swore silently his own sinister vow while stroking the silky, coffee-colored flesh of his companion.

Outside, against the stillness of the night, could be heard the bark of a lonely dog and the hoot of a pair of night owls. But inside the barn, only breathless whispers and moans of ecstasy were discerned as the sweat-slicked bodies of its inhabitants reached for satisfaction. Their musty scent mingled with the stale odor of the hay, perfuming the air with the essence of their passion.

"You excite the hell out of me, baby. These past few days have been filled with pleasure." There was much truth in what he said, Sandy Loomis thought, staring down at Lupe Diaz's heavy-lidded gaze. The bitch was insatiable. Like a mare in heat, he had ridden her hard and she'd enjoyed every minute of it. She gave as good as she got, he'd say that for her. He hadn't felt this good in years. He'd miss the little *puta* when he was done with her.

Lupe smiled, snuggling against the lanky cowboy. The hay beneath the blanket crinkled as she adjusted her position. "You are all man, *mi amante*. You know how to pleasure a woman."

Flicking his tongue out over her nipple, he smiled in satisfaction at her moan of pleasure. When he had her hot and bothered, he withdrew, pleased by her pained expression. "Someday, I'm going to give you things—take you away from this two-bit town."

Her smile was trusting and full of happiness. "You love Lupe?"

Caressing her firm buttocks, he smiled smoothly, "I'm crazy about you, baby. I've got plans—plans to make us rich."

"There is no more silver in the mines near here, *querida*. How will you get so rich?"

Forcing her legs open with his knee, he positioned himself between them. "I'm talking about gold not silver. But right now, baby, I'm thinking about mining another kind of treasure." He shoved himself deep within her, causing her to cry out as she encased his hardened manhood.

"The treasure is yours, *querida*. Take it—take it all."

A calculating gleam entered his eyes as he thrust one final time convulsing in ecstasy on top of her. His passion spent, he recovered himself, whispering into her ear, "Don't worry, baby. I intend to."

Staring in rapt concentration at Chase's naked

physique as he stood before the dressing table mirror shaving, Margaret sighed, drawing the sheet up under her chin to hide her body's predictable response. She watched the straight razor as it scraped the soap from his cheeks and chin, every so often shifting her gaze down to admire the taut muscles of his back and buttocks. Shifting uncomfortably as her thoughts brought a familiar wetness to her thighs, she decided it would be prudent to take her mind off the persistent throb hounding her and said, "You're very good at that." She was startled by the angry curse he threw at her.

"Goddamn!" Chase examined the fresh nick on his chin, wiping at the blood with a towel. Turning toward Margaret, who was pressing herself against the pillows, trying to make herself invisible, he said, "Don't you know better than to bother a man while he's shaving? You broke my concentration."

"I'm sorry."

Noting her contrite expression, he sighed, wiping the remainder of the soap off his face. "I'm a bear in the morning. I'm not fit to be around until I've had my coffee."

"I didn't know. Shall I get you some?" She started to rise but he motioned her back down.

"Already ordered it. The maid should be bringing up a pot directly. Sorry I snapped. I'm not used to sharing a room, I guess."

Margaret's eyes widened at that remark. Drawing her knees up under her chin, she was silent while Chase dressed, mulling over his comment. There was a lot about her new husband that she didn't know, but she was determined to rectify that situation.

The knock at the door proved to be the maid with the pot of coffee. Watching in amusement as Chase grabbed the pot out of the maid's hands, scaring the daylights out of her before shooing the poor woman away, Margaret swallowed the laughter bubbling up in her throat. Once Chase had poured himself a cup of the steaming liquid and resumed dressing, she deemed it safe to resume their previous conversation.

"Didn't you ever spend the night with the whores you bedded?"

The coffee Chase had just swallowed spewed forth across the room like a shower of brown rain. "What?" He stared at her as if she'd lost her mind.

"You said you weren't used to sharing a room. Didn't you share one with Lillie Mae?"

"No, I didn't. And why are you so all-fired interested in Lillie Mae and whores in general? They're hardly a fit topic of conversation for a lady."

She giggled. "Now you sound just like Mama."

He rolled his eyes, shrugging into his shirt. "God forbid!"

"What's it like being with a whore?"

Brushing the hair back out of his eyes, he sighed. "You're not going to let go of this, are you?"

She shook her head, smiling impishly.

"You want details or generalizations?"

She blushed. Although she was curious to know how she compared to Lillie Mae, she wasn't brave enough to ask for details. "Generalizations will be fine."

"Whores are just regular women who are down on their luck. Most of them sell themselves out of necessity—to buy clothes, pay rent, put food on the table. There are a few . . ." He paused; a faraway look entered his eyes that made Margaret wish she had never asked. ". . . that do it just because they like it."

She contemplated his words then said, very matter-of-factly, "I think if I were a whore, I'd do it just because I liked it."

Chase's mouth dropped open; he stared in disbelief at the little bundle on the bed before a grin split his face. Striding toward Margaret, a lascivious glint in his eyes, he asked, "So, you like making love?"

"Oh, yes! It was wonderful. Can we do it again sometime?"

He threw back his head and roared, then fearing he had insulted his new wife, attempted to bring himself under control. But Margaret, who wasn't the least bit insulted, just smiled coyly and threw off the sheet that covered her. The sunlight shimmered across her body, revealing every delectable curve and mound.

The laughter died in Chase's throat. He took a step forward. But Margaret, noting the determination in his eyes, scampered out of bed, running toward the bathroom. "I'd better get dressed. You did promise to take me to see the mission," she tossed out over her shoulder.

She had only seen Mission San Xavier del Bac once when she was a small child. The pristine white building with the carved shell and arabesque decorations had captivated her child's imagination. It was like some grand Spanish castle out of a fairy tale, and she had vowed if she ever came to Tucson again, she would revisit it.

The low growl emanating from Chase's throat made her eyes widen. She turned to find him closing up the distance between them.

"I've seen enough sights," he said.

Noting his intention, and realizing that there would be no sightseeing if Chase had his way, Margaret ran into the bathroom, slamming the door behind her. "I'll just be a moment."

The sound of the bolt being thrown as Chase reached for the knob brought a scowl to his lips. "You're a tease," he shouted.

Maggie's laughter floated out through the closed door, followed by a mocking retort. "Can we do it again sometime?" The laughter became louder, more high-pitched.

"All right, that's it. I've heard enough. Open this door or I'm going to break it down."

Before Chase could make good on his threat, a knock sounded at their door. Staring down at the bulge in his pants, he grimaced. "Who is it?" he yelled, impatience and frustration evident in his tone.

"Telegram, sir. It just arrived," came the hesitant reply.

Grabbing his hat off the chair, Chase held it in front of him as he moved to answer the door. The messenger, a boy just shy of manhood, took one look at Chase's face and thrust the paper at him, scurrying down the hall.

"Wait! Don't you want your tip?" Chase called out after him. But the boy disappeared. Shrugging, he shut the door, ripping open the missive. The words that greeted him brought a rush of anger through his entire body.

At that moment, Margaret entered, fully dressed, a teasing smile on her lips. One look at Chase's face told her that something was dreadfully wrong. She sobered instantly, fear knotting her chest. "What is it? What's happened?"

"A telegram just arrived from Wooley. I'm needed back in Purgatory." He stared at her, his eyes as cold as an arctic glacier. "The goddamn bank's been robbed."

The following day, pacing the confines of his office, Chase frowned, staring down at the diamond stickpin in his palm that Wooley had found the day of the bank robbery. It had been stuck between the planks of the bank's flooring, directly in front of the safe.

"It was almost as if it was left there on purpose," Wooley said, scratching his bearded chin. "Like a calling card or something. You know what I mean?"

Chase stopped, perching himself on the edge of his desk. "I know exactly what you mean."

"They didn't take much—only about five hundred dollars. But it's got the town folk pretty riled up. The money for the garbage incinerator was included in what was stolen, and that's got Alberta Bottoms and Betsy Fraser fit to be tied."

"Did anyone see anything . . . anything at all?"

Wooley shook his head. "Nope. The varmints sawed their way in from the rear of the building. Let's face it, the bank wouldn't have presented much of a problem for someone with experience. It was built as a temporary structure. We fully intended to brick it one of these years."

"Well, perhaps now the good people of Purgatory won't be tempted to wait another twenty-five years before they do so," Chase replied, sarcasm thick in his voice. He had never seen a town so lackadaisical about their welfare. They were just lucky that someone hadn't come along long before this to rob them.

Of course, just any old someone hadn't robbed the bank. He knew it was Parker. And obviously, Parker knew he was the marshal. It was a dare—a perverse challenge of sorts. That's how Parker operated. He thought himself too smart to be caught, but he would be, Chase vowed silently. Eventually, he would catch the slimy bastard.

"You sure seem lost in thought, Marshal, like you have something real important on your mind."

"Well, I did have my honeymoon interrupted, in case you've forgotten."

Wooley smiled sheepishly. " 'Tweren't my fault. You said I was to wire you if we had any problems."

"You did right, Wooley," Chase admitted, staring thoughtfully at the diamond. It sparkled prettily, reminding Chase of Maggie's eyes the last time he made love to her. "I'd best be getting home. I'm not quite settled in yet and Maggie's been after me to clear out of the hotel and move into her house this afternoon."

"As fine a woman as Margaret is, I don't envy you having to live in the same house with her mother. Phoebe Parker's nuttier than a Christmas fruitcake."

"How come you dislike the old hag so much? What she ever do to you?"

Spitting into the cuspidor, Wooley wiped the remaining spittle on his sleeve. "Ain't what she's done to me, but to Miss Margaret. I've watched that gal grow up under that conniving woman's thumb. And I can tell you, it weren't a pretty sight. Phoebe did her best to wring out every ounce of spirit and independence Margaret had within her. She ruined

Margaret's chances of ever making a match, until you came along. There's nothing motherly about the bitch. Why, a female dog has more love for her pups than Phoebe ever showed toward Margaret."

Chase smiled knowingly, pushing himself off the desk to wrap his arm about Wooley's shoulder. "You love her, don't you?"

A red flush covered the older man's cheeks. "Reckon I do. But it ain't what you think. I don't love her like I do my Concita—more like a father or an uncle."

"You feel protective towards her?"

"If anyone tried to harm a hair on Miss Margaret's head, they'd have me to contend with."

Chase debated silently about whether or not he should trust Wooley with the information he had on Jonathan Parker. Deciding that Margaret's life might one day depend on that trust, he said, "Sit yourself down, Wooley. I've got something to tell you. It's very confidential, and if you breathe a word to anyone, including Maggie, I'll have your hide."

Wooley's eyes widened slightly as he straddled the chair. Folding his arms across the back, he listened intently to everything Chase had to say, stopping him now and then to ask a question. When Chase was through with his narrative, Wooley shook his head in disbelief.

"I knew there was something fishy about why you asked so many questions about Margaret's father. Now, I guess I know."

"You can see why it was so important for me to keep everything a secret. Parker's back for a reason. He'll show his hand when he's ready and not before. We've got to be ready for him."

202

Pushing himself to his feet, Wooley stood toe to toe with Chase. "Tell me something, Chase, and tell me true. Did you marry Margaret to get close to her father?"

The silence that followed Wooley's question was uncomfortable. Chase wasn't sure exactly how he should answer, but deciding that honesty was probably the best way to handle things, he replied, "That was the reason I first started to court her, but that's not the reason I married her. I love Maggie."

Wooley grinned and slapped his knee. "Whooey! That's a relief off my mind. I didn't want to have to get into it with you, Marshal."

Chase chuckled and walked to the door, pulling his hat off the rack. "Keep your eyes and ears open. I'm going home for a while. All this talk about Maggie's given me a powerful hankerin'."

As he watched Chase depart, Wooley wiped his nose on his sleeve, then dabbed at the moisture forming in the corner of his eyes. Yessir, but the boy was going to work out all right, he thought. He'd had his doubts when he'd first heard about the marriage. But now that he knew the marshal loved Maggie, everything else would work out all right. Damned if it wouldn't, or his name wasn't Woolford Ambrose Aloysius Burnett.

Chapter Fifteen

Chase paused on the porch of his new residence, listening to Phoebe's shrill diatribe as she issued orders from her upstairs bedroom. A moment later, he observed through the screen door Margaret scurrying up the stairs to attend to her mother's latest whim.

Damn selfish bitch! he fumed silently, loathing Phoebe Parker for the callous treatment of her daughter. He couldn't allow Maggie to continue being treated like some damn lackey. There would have to be some changes made. He wasn't going to stand by and watch his wife work herself into a frazzle over that fat, conniving, bitch of a mother of hers.

Entering the house, he slammed the screen door behind him, dropping the leather saddlebags he had just retrieved from the hotel by the front door. About to march up the stairs to make his feelings known, his boot paused on the first tread at the sound of Lupe's voice.

"Señor Gallagher, it is you. You gave me such a fright. I forget that you live here now." She smiled, then noting his thunderous expression, sobered instantly. "What is wrong? You look *muy furioso.*"

Latching on to the surprised woman's arm, he hauled her into the kitchen. "How long has this nonsense between Maggie and her mother been going on?"

Comprehension dawned clearly in Lupe's eyes, and she smiled sadly. "A very long time, señor. It is very bad for Margarita, no?"

"I'm going to put a stop to it. I can't stand the way Phoebe orders Maggie around. Maggie'll be the one sick, if this continues."

Closing the door that led into the hall, Lupe shook her head, her eyes filled with concern. "You must not interfere, Señor Gallagher. It would only cause trouble between you and Margarita. I have tried many times to speak to Margarita about the way her mother treats her. It is no use; she continues to defend Señora Parker. It is her mama."

Chase listened, his frown deepening. What Lupe said made sense. But how was he going to live in a home where some bedridden, crazy woman ruled with an iron hand? No self-respecting man could put up with that indefinitely. "I appreciate your advice, Lupe. I realize you are more familiar with the situation in this house than I am, but I can only hold my tongue for so long. The bitch grates like a burr beneath my saddle. And you can believe it when I say I'm not the one who's going to be thrown when the horse bucks. No sir! Maggie's my wife, and Phoebe Parker had damned well better get used to the idea."

"I am sorry for your trouble, señor, but you must learn to do what I do and keep your distance from the señora. It is the only way to keep peace in the family."

Unfortunately, as the days went on Chase discovered that keeping his distance from Margaret's mother was not going to be as easy as Lupe had suggested. Phoebe had suddenly improved enough to leave her room for short periods of time each day—a circumstance that Maggie stated as being "nothing short of miraculous."

His mother-in-law had even granted them the pleasure of her company at dinner on two different occasions—occasions when Chase had completely lost his appetite.

Slapping the paintbrush against the weathered boards of the house as he endeavored to make the place presentable—no wife of his was going to live in a hovel—Chase wished he could paint Phoebe's mouth shut as easily as he had painted the upstairs windows closed—an occurrence that had taken him a full day to rectify—so he would never have to hear her say, "Tell me, Marshal, is being married to Margaret everything you thought it would be?" She would then smile slyly, as if she knew some deep, dark secret. God, he despised the woman!

"Chase, are you almost done? It's nearly time for dinner."

Maggie's voice floated up, jarring him out of his unpleasant ruminations. Staring down at her sweet face, Chase sighed, wiping the sweat from his face and neck with the red bandanna he pulled from his back pocket. "Is your mother joining us this evening? 'Cause if she is, I'd sooner stay out here and work."

Margaret's smile was full of understanding. Chase'd had the patience of a saint the past week. She couldn't blame him for disliking her mother; Phoebe had done her best to alienate him with her acerbic comments. They hadn't had much time alone, either; it seemed Mama's recovery had been aided immensely by Chase's presence in the house.

At night, alone in their bed, Mama's soft snores had been a constant reminder of her presence, acting as effectively as a shower of cold water upon their ardor. They had slept, side by side, like some old married couple, not touching, but fully aware that the other lay only a hair's breadth away.

"Mama isn't feeling well," she finally explained. "She's taking dinner in her room this evening."

The smile of relief that crossed Chase's face was touching. Returning it with one of her own, she said, "Don't be too long. I have something extra special for dessert tonight." She winked and reentered the house.

Hallelujah! Chase thought, scrambling down off the ladder. The wicked witch was going to remain in her den, and he would have Maggie all to himself this evening.

The darkness of the bedroom was relieved by the single candle that flickered softly on the nightstand and the brightness of the moon that shone in through the open window. The soft chirping of the crickets serenaded Maggie and Chase as they lay naked, entwined in each others' arms, whispering quietly, trying desperately not to disturb Phoebe who slept only a few feet away in her own bed across the hall.

Trailing her finger lightly over the furred mat of hair on Chase's chest, Margaret sighed deeply. "I've missed you—missed being with you."

"But we've been together every day."

"I meant, being with you like this."

He smiled into the darkness, kissing her forehead. "Perhaps you can purloin some laudanum from Doc. We could give it to your mother the nights we're planning to make love."

Running her lips tenderly over his chest and shoulder, Margaret smiled wickedly, asking, "Do you think it would harm Mama if we gave it to her every day?"

A low growl emanated from his chest. Before Margaret knew what was happening, Chase had her pinned beneath him, her arms held firmly over her head.

"I have you at my mercy, woman. Do you wish to beg for your release?"

Her smile was teasing, seductive. "That depends on whether or not you intend to spear me with that fierce weapon of yours."

He grinned, enjoying their banter. "Most definitely, my beautiful captive. I intend to do to just that." Nudging her legs open with his knee, he positioned himself between her thighs, rubbing his organ provocatively against her opening.

Margaret's breathing grew rapid; her heart beat wildly in anticipation. She could see the effort to bridle his passion was costing Chase dearly, for he was biting his lower lip as if to concentrate all his energies on holding back. Margaret opened her mouth to encourage him to continue. But the sound that came forth didn't come from her lips but from her mother's across the hall.

"Margaret, come quick. I need to use the chamber pot."

A look of horror crossed Margaret's face. "Mother of God!" she cried out in a hoarse whisper, tears of frustration filling her eyes.

"God has nothing to do with this," Chase retorted angrily, his passion deflating as rapidly as a hot air balloon. He rolled off Maggie onto his back, covering his eyes with his forearm.

"I'm sorry, Chase. I've got to help Mama."

The silence that permeated the room was deafening as Margaret eased herself off the bed and searched the covers for her wrapper. Shrugging into it, she walked, shoulders slumped, towards the door. She was about to turn the brass knob when Chase's voice froze her in her tracks.

"If you know what's good for your mother, Maggie, you'll buy that laudanum. For as God is my witness, I intend to shut Phoebe up . . . permanently, if I have to."

"They're married?!" Jack Parker stared incredulously at his partner, unable to believe what Sandy had just revealed to him. His face reddened in anger as he paced the confines of the small cabin.

"That's right, boss. I got it straight from Lupe. They was married a couple of weeks back. Gallagher's living in the house."

"Son of a bitch!" Jack paused, leaning his palms against the table, banging his fist, nearly upsetting the kerosene lantern centered there. "Gallagher's been a thorn in my side for as long as I can remember. It's time I put a stop to his interfering ways." Pulling up a chair, Jack eased himself into it, a calculating gleam entering his eyes as he ran his fingers absently over the dents and nicks across the tabletop while mapping out his plan.

Sandy had seen that look twice before: once when they'd plugged the old miner in Tombstone, and the other while holding up the bank in Laredo. Rubbing his palms together, he smiled in anticipation. Parker was fixin' to kill Gallagher, and Sandy had every intention of being there when it happened. "You got a plan to take Gallagher down?" he asked.

Jack smiled confidently. "Sandy, my boy, you're most astute." At the cowboy's puzzled frown, Jack clarified, "That's exactly right. And I think I know just the way to do it."

A murderous lust entered Sandy's eyes; there was a childish eagerness to his voice when he asked, "We're going to ambush him, right? Riddle his body with bullets?"

Jack laughed and poured himself a whiskey from the half-empty bottle on the table. "Nothing as sordid and simpleminded as that, my good man. Gallagher will be killed in due time; but first, we have to gain access to the gold. That is our main objective. When we've accomplished that, then we take care of the marshal."

Disappointment rang as loud as a bell when Sandy spoke. "I don't get it. If Gallagher's in our way, how come we're not eliminating him first?"

"There's more than one way to skin a cat. And I think that way lies with my daughter, Margaret."

Sandy's brows wrinkled in confusion. "Your daughter? You haven't laid eyes on her in years. What makes you think she'll help you?"

"Margaret and I were as close as any father and daughter could be. She's a very trusting soul—very loyal to those she loves. I think I can play upon her sympathies very nicely." His smile never reached his eyes. "After all, I'm still her daddy; that fact alone should be useful for something."

Sandy's look was skeptical; he scratched his head. "I don't know . . . you said yourself that you took off without saying good-bye. She might hate you." At Jack's confident smile, he added, "And don't forget, that wife of yours has surely poisoned her mind against you by now."

Jack's smile faded, his lips snarling like a mad dog's. "Phoebe has no doubt tried to poison Margaret's mind; she tried often enough when I lived there. But Margaret was always more my daughter than Phoebe's. She'll do what I say when the time's right."

"I hope you're right."

Jack pushed the bottle of whiskey across the table. "Have a drink and calm down. You sound like a jittery old woman. Haven't I always been right? Have I ever let you down?"

Sandy shook his head.

Pushing himself to his feet, Jack resumed his pacing. "Well, then, what do you have to worry about? The plan's in the works. I'll need to make contact with Margaret before too long. Do you think your little *puta* will carry the message to her?"

"When my dick's inside Lupe, she'll do anything I tell her. The bitch is hot for me; she thinks I love her."

Jack laughed, slapping Sandy on the back. "You're

211

all right, boy. You remind me of myself at your age. I had quite a way with the ladies back then."

Sandy didn't doubt it for a moment. Jack was still a handsome man, despite his graying hair and the slight limp to his left leg that an old bullet wound from a heist they'd pulled a few years back had caused.

"Did you send the Donaldsons for the supplies I told you to get?"

"Yea. They're in Tucson . . . left this morning. I warned them not to get into any trouble. Said I would cut off their balls and serve them up for supper one evening if they did." Sandy laughed. "Made quite an impression on old Skunk."

Jack cast Sandy a sidelong look of disgust. The man's crudity was, at times, distasteful. He'd given up on ever turning the crass cowboy into something other than what he was: a liar, a thief, and a murderer. He'd never been able to convince Sandy that using one's brain could be as effective as using one's brawn.

"We're going to have to create a diversion to force Gallagher out of town when I meet with Margaret. See what you and the boys can come up with." At Sandy's nod, Jack added, "And don't wait too long. It's already July. I planned to be back in New York long before this."

"You're still planning to head back East?"

Jack nodded. "Once I get what I came for, there won't be anything to hold me here in this godforsaken country. Arizona Territory will see the last of Gentleman Jack Parker."

"And your daughter? What of her?"

Jack shrugged. "Maybe I'll take her with me. After all, she'll be a widow when all this is said and done."

The insane laughter that followed Jack's comment rose the hackles on Sandy's neck. He almost felt sorry for Margaret Parker. She seemed a nice sort, and she was a looker. He'd seen her big breasts the day of the auction. Like melons they were, full and ripe. Compared to Lupe's plum-size appendages, they were a feast a man could sink his teeth into. He licked his lips, smiling inwardly.

Maybe, just maybe, he'd pull a few surprises of his own where Margaret Parker was concerned. He'd be rich and she'd be a lonely widow. And everyone knew that a widow couldn't do without a man's hard dick within her for too long. He pushed down on the hardened member straining within his breeches and grinned. A nice big bonus awaited Margaret and she didn't even know it.

Chapter Sixteen

"I think our little rodeo might just rival Buffalo Bill's Wild West Show, Miss Margaret," Wooley commented, tacking the red, white, and blue bunting across the front of Mrs. Perkins's Grocery. "Main Street sure looks mighty festive and there's been lots who've already signed up for the competition, including me and Chase."

Margaret smiled, handing the deputy another nail. Wooley was on loan from Chase; the gesture made after she had complained that there was little time to complete the decorations for this year's Fourth of July celebration and not a soul had come forth to volunteer. She knew that if Chase thought she was seeking his assistance, he'd be only too glad to volunteer Wooley's services.

The hot afternoon sun beat down unmercifully, making this July one of the hottest on record. It had been so hot the week before, the Purgatory Women's Guild had decided to postpone the annual celebration for a week in the hope that it would cool off a bit. It had, if you could consider one hundred degrees cool!

"How many more of these drapes you fixin' to hang, Miss Margaret? I'm gettin' plumb parched in this here heat."

Shading her eyes from the sun's glare, Margaret glanced down the wide, dusty street. All the storefronts, save for the jail and Fitzgerald's Hardware, were finished. "Looks like just two more, Wooley, including the jail."

Climbing down off the ladder, Wooley pulled a twist of tobacco out of his back pocket and sawed off a piece with his teeth. Working the plug around his mouth, he softened it up a bit, then spit, taking care to avoid hitting Margaret's shoes. "Beggin' your pardon, Miss Margaret, but I get a mite fidgety without my tobacco to chew on."

"Wooley, you can chew and spit as much as you like," she said, thinking she was grateful that Chase had never succumbed to the nasty habit, "if only you'll get those last two buntings hung."

Why she had let Betsy talk her into yet another project was beyond her ken. A week ago they'd been sitting in Betsy's parlor sharing a pot of lemon tea when Betsy had blurted out her intention to oversee the rodeo arrangements. "It would be such fun, Margaret," she had said. "But of course I wouldn't be able to do everything alone, not in my present condition. It would be wonderful if you could help."

Margaret groaned aloud at the recollection, prompting Wooley to ask, "Something the matter?"

"No more than usual, Wooley," she replied offhandedly, wondering how Betsy had the time to devote herself to so many tasks with the opening of the

215

mercantile just a few weeks away, and wondering, too, when she and Chase were going to have some time alone together.

Since that awful night when her mother had interrupted their lovemaking, she had walked on eggshells around Chase. It seemed his temper had worsened with each day and *night* that passed, and she realized that she was going to have to take some drastic action to salvage their strained relationship. She wasn't about to let her mother win this time.

"A husband deprived of his marital rights is like a bear with a thorn in its paw. The more the paw festers and the pain builds, the meaner the bear gets," Betsy had counseled wisely when Margaret had broached the awkward problem of Phoebe's unending interference. "Chase is right," Betsy had added. "Drug the woman and lock her in her room, or you'll never share a moment's peace with your husband."

Betsy's words repeated over and over in Margaret's mind as she walked with Wooley toward the jail. Spying the hotel on the other side of the street, a delicious thought entered her mind. Excusing herself, she hurried across the street, returning a few minutes later with a secretive smile on her lips. "Are you ready to decorate the jail, Wooley?" she asked, noting the deputy's questioning gaze but hoping desperately he wouldn't ask what she'd been up to.

"'Spect so. Might as well get this over and done with."

Her thoughts exactly as she stared at the imposing brick building, wondering how wise it would be to beard the lion in his den.

"You want I should hang this here, Miss Margaret?"

Wooley asked, holding the bunting over the door.

She nodded. "Yes, please. I'm going to go inside for a moment to speak with Chase. I'll be right back."

"I wouldn't if I were you, Miss Margaret," Wooley cautioned. "Marshal's been as mean as a rabid dog lately. I don't know what's got into him." Though from the telltale blush on Margaret's cheeks, and the knowledge that Phoebe was doing her best to bust up the marriage, he had a pretty good idea.

"It's been difficult with my mother," Margaret tried to explain. "You know how she can be at times."

"Yup, and I also got me a notion what's been ailing the marshal. He's been walking a mite stiff-legged lately."

Margaret felt the heat creep up her neck. Did everyone in town know that she and Chase hadn't been intimate lately? The thought gave her the added courage she needed to proceed with her plan. "I'll be back in a minute."

"Take your time." He was going to suggest that Margaret and Chase use one of the cells in the back room, but after seeing how mortified Margaret had been at his last comment, he thought it best to keep his mouth shut and nodded instead.

The scent of lavender teased Chase's senses. He looked up from his paperwork to find Margaret standing quietly in front of his desk. His heart gave a queer little lurch. She was dressed prettily in a yellow-and-green calico print dress. Her hair was pulled back, fastened at the nape by a matching yellow ribbon, but left dangling down her back, just the way he liked it. She had taken to wearing her hair down since their wedding night, when he had run his fingers through the

217

thick tresses and had commented on how beautiful it was. He smiled at the memory, then remembering their present state of affairs forced the recollection away.

"What brings you here today, Maggie? I thought you and Wooley were readying things for tomorrow's celebration."

Margaret's smile, as well as her words, were tentative. "We are; I just stopped in to say hello. And, I thought if you were free, I'd take you to lunch."

His right eyebrow lifted. "You want to take me to lunch?"

She nodded. She had a little more than lunch in mind, but he didn't need to know that yet. "I've put away some of my egg money for special occasions. Is there a problem?"

Shaking his head, he pushed himself up from the desk. There was no accounting for the peculiarities of a woman's mind. They'd hardly spoken in days and here she was wanting to take him to lunch. "Where'd you have in mind?"

"The hotel," she answered without hesitation, taking a deep breath. "I've reserved a room." Observing the way his mouth dropped open at her comment, she blushed hotly, adding, "Sort of an indoor picnic." She looked down quickly at the toes of her black, high-button shoes.

Standing so close that their chests touched, Chase tilted up Margaret's chin. "And may I inquire as to the menu for today's luncheon?"

Her heart pounded loud in her ears; Chase's nearness was unsettling. It had been too long since they'd been together as man and wife, but she aimed to rectify that,

218

answering boldly, "Me."

He smiled, his eyes lighting with a sensuous flame. Reaching first for his hat, then her waist, he replied, "I'm a starving man, darlin'. I hope you've got enough to satisfy me."

Gazing up, she smiled seductively. "More than you could possibly handle, Marshal."

He brushed her lips, causing her toes to tingle. "Don't count on it, darlin'. I've spent most of my life in the saddle; I'm used to riding hard and long. Where do you think I got these bowed legs?"

She glanced down, but all she could see was the large bulge in his crotch, not the bow in his legs. Smiling, she took his hat from his hands and set it on his head, saying, "Ride'em, cowboy."

The series of competitive events for the Fourth of July celebration was to take place north of town, just past Miller's Livery. A large corral had been constructed for the bronc riding and calf roping contests, and a series of hay bales had been stacked to accommodate the marksmanship competition.

Margaret and Betsy strolled, arm-in-arm, chatting companionably as they made their way toward the arena. Both Chase and Tom were to compete in this morning's events and the two women were eager to cheer their respective husbands on to victory.

Passing Alberta and Marion, who had volunteered to oversee the refreshment area which was set up in front of the blacksmith shop, they waved. Betsy smiled dubiously as she remarked under her breath, "I don't know how smart it was to put those two in charge of the food. There might not be anything left when it's time to eat."

Sighting the whole steer that was roasting on a spit over a bed of coals, Margaret shook her head. "I'm sure that with your prodigious appetite you'll be able to find something to eat."

Glancing down at her protruding abdomen, Betsy's voice was full of dismay when she confessed, "I have been eating like a cow, lately. Doc says if I don't quit, the baby's going to grow too big to push out."

"Well, I envy your fatness. I just wish it was me that was carrying a babe."

A teasing smile tipped the corners of the pregnant woman's mouth. "I take it things have improved between you and Chase?"

"They couldn't be better." Margaret blushed, thinking of the wanton way she had behaved yesterday afternoon at the hotel. The rickety, old brass bed in the room she had rented had nearly collapsed due to their impassioned hours of lovemaking. It was a day she would remember for a long time.

"I can see by that satisfied grin on your face that you took my advice."

"The bear's paw is all healed now," Margaret quipped, causing Betsy to giggle.

"Glad to hear it. Come on, there's Chase and Tom." Betsy pointed at the large crowd of men that had gathered. "Let's go watch. Tom hasn't ridden a bronc in years. I have a feeling he's going to get something more than his ego bruised today."

Approaching the two men who were leaning against the corral fence, Margaret and Betsy yelled out in unison, waving as they made their way through the throng of competitors. Cowboys from as far away as Phoenix had come to compete for the prize money.

"I never expected this large a turnout, did you?" Margaret asked, trying to elbow her way between two brawny men. She recognized some of the cowboys from the Bar H and the sandy-haired man who had bid on her the day of the auction, but other than those few, the rest were strangers.

"When it comes to games, men are like little boys, always having to prove who's best."

"I guess we're going to find out; the first cowboy's mounting up."

"Where've you two been?" Tom asked when the two women finally reached the fence. "I was afraid you were going to miss our grand exhibition." He kissed Betsy on the nose, caressing her stomach tenderly.

"I'm not anxious for my wife to watch me fall on my butt," Chase admitted, draping his arm about Margaret's shoulder.

Both Chase and Tom wore numbers pinned on their shirtfronts, indicating in what order they would ride. Chase had donned a pair of leather-fringed chaps over his trousers, decorated on the front with silver conchas, while Tom was attired in a pair of sturdy Levi's.

"It's not your posterior I'm worried about," Margaret replied brazenly. "I'd still like to have a baby, you know."

Three pairs of eyes turned on her and she blushed furiously, covering her cheeks with the palms of her hands.

"My wife seems to have a one-track mind lately," Chase said, chuckling. "You'll have to excuse her."

There was no more time for conversation for Tom's

number had been called. Everyone wished him luck, and Betsy sent him on his way with a passionate kiss and a command to be careful.

Having just bucked off the previous two riders, the horse that waited for Tom had an air of confidence about him. The bay stallion's only accoutrements were a cow saddle, bridle, and bucking strap, which wound around his flank—one of the most touchy parts of his anatomy—causing him to buck harder.

Staring at the snorting, wild-eyed beast, Margaret had her doubts about the wisdom of such a contest. The rider was supposed to stay on the horse's back for a full three minutes; his success indicated by the firing of the judge's gun. The cowboy who rode the horse for the duration would win the prize money of fifty dollars. A hefty amount for most cowboys, who usually didn't earn more than thirty dollars for a month's pay, but not enough to entice anyone of sound mind to participate, which didn't say much about Tom or Chase's faculties.

The horse waited impatiently in the far corner of the corral, snorting and pawing the ground while being restrained by two men who had hold of his lead ropes. It was going to be necessary, Chase had explained, for Tom to climb the fence and ease himself down on top of the ferocious beast, which Tom was attempting to do at this very moment.

"Give'em hell, Fraser," Chase shouted as Tom positioned himself atop the animal. When Tom nodded his head, signaling that he was ready, the men released the rope and Tom was immediately propelled forward, up, down, and around. The horse emitted grunts and snorts and loud bawls of rage, indicating his displeasure with having a rider on his back.

222

Betsy stared wide-eyed, her mouth covered to prevent the screams that rose quickly to her throat from escaping when approximately sixty seconds later, Tom was effectively bucked off the triumphant creature. "Good heavens!" she blurted, "I hope he's not injured." A moment later, she breathed a sigh of relief when Tom stood and ran to the fence, climbing safely out of the way.

"Chase," Margaret asked, grabbing on to his forearm, "are you certain that you want to go through with this? It looks terribly dangerous."

"Hell, no! I'm not certain. But I damned well better unless I want to be called a coward."

A tight twist of fear entered her stomach when Chase's number was called and he moved to the other side of the corral.

"He'll be all right, Margaret," Betsy said, patting her friend's hand in a comforting gesture. "Chase has ridden broncs before."

Margaret's eyes widened. "He has?"

"Sure. Tom said Chase broke his own horse the same way. Lucifer was a wild mustang that Chase broke to rein."

That knowledge made Margaret breathe a little easier, but not much. Observing Chase's descent upon the horse's back, she cringed, biting her lower lip.

Chase held tight on the rein with his left hand, his right held high above his head. With a nod of consent, he was sent pitching and spinning, like a pinwheel, in all different directions.

His primary objective was to outfox his horse and hold his seat. He had studied the movements of the animal while the other riders were upon him and was confident he would be able to contemplate the changes in rhythm and beat. Riding a bronco was a little bit like dancing, and he sure as hell didn't want to miss a beat and end up landing on his butt or worse, his head.

He kept careful watch on the horse's back muscles. A great deal could be told by the way the horse's muscles flexed and tensed. The muscular ridge at the base of the horse's neck, termed the fin, momentarily swelled before each buck jump, and by studying it, he could also ascertain which direction the horse intended to leap.

Damn but he hoped this ride was going to be over soon, Chase thought, unsure how much longer he was going to be able to hold out.

"Look!" Margaret yelled, pointing at her husband. "His nose is bleeding."

"That's pretty common, Miss Margaret," Wooley said, sidling up next to Margaret. "It's all that bucking and twisting. Makes a body's head bounce a bit too much."

When the ride went over the two-minute mark, the cowboys began to whoop and holler their encouragement, waving their hats and whistling loudly, all except the sandy-haired cowboy who watched with a malevolent gleam in his eyes.

Sandy Loomis could barely contain the look of jealousy on his face as he observed Gallagher riding into victory. When the gun went off, signaling the successful completion of the ride, and the crowd roared its approval, he swore silently under his breath.

Gallagher had beat him in this contest, but he wasn't going to beat him again, Sandy vowed. He wasn't going to look like a damned fool in front of his little Mexican señorita. Glancing down at Lupe, whose eyes were shining bright with happiness as she clapped in approval for her employer, he frowned, yanking on her arm.

"Come on; let's go get us a drink. I'm tired of watching Gallagher show off."

Lupe stared at him strangely, then shrugged. Sandy was full of impossible moods. She never knew what to expect from him one minute to the next. He was like a stick of dynamite, and she was never sure when he would explode. But it was also what made him so attractive, so macho. And except for the one time when he had slapped her for teasing him about his plans to get rich, he had been good to her. He loved her; he had told her as much. And as soon as he was ready, she would leave Purgatory with him. It would be soon, he had said. But he had given her no further explanations.

She hadn't told Margarita yet, but she would. When the time was right, she would explain everything to her. She knew Margarita would understand and be happy for her, for Margarita was very much in love with Señor Gallagher.

Upon their return, Chase and Tom were greeted with a steady stream of congratulatory comments and an effusive show of affection from their wives. Chase's blue checkered shirt was lightly speckled with blood from his nosebleed, but other than that, he was uninjured from his ride.

Wooley, who had watched Margaret and Betsy's affectionate display with something akin to a blush, had shaken his head in disgust and sauntered off to find some "men-type amusements," as he called them, throwing the two women into a fit of hysterical laughter.

When Betsy had recovered enough to talk, she suggested, "Let's go get some supper before Alberta and Marion eat it all. I'm so hungry I could eat that entire steer by myself."

"From the looks of your stomach, I thought you already had," Tom responded. His comment was met with a swift punch from his wife who glared angrily at him. "Ow! What'd you go and do that for," he asked, grabbing hold of his arm.

"This is your baby, in case you've forgotten," Betsy said, her eyes filling with tears. "Don't blame me for looking so grotesque."

"Now, honey," Tom cajoled, "don't go gettin' all weepy-eyed on me. I was just joshing you."

Chase caught the look of envy on Margaret's face as she watched Betsy and Tom banter back and forth. The unadulterated longing for a child was so plainly written there, it made his heart ache. He decided, then and there, he would step up his efforts to get Margaret with child. And damn Phoebe Parker if she stood in his way. They would make love on the front porch, in the backyard, or in their bed if they damn well pleased. And after yesterday's encounter at the hotel, he damn well pleased.

His little spinster was one hell of an exciting woman. She had more tricks up her sleeve than all the whores put together at Lillie Mae's brothel. He grinned, thinking of the arousing bath they had shared together.

Damn! Wouldn't this celebration ever get over with? he wondered. He had a hankerin' to get beneath those skirts she wore. And he knew for a fact, she didn't have a stitch of underwear on beneath them.

"Chase Gallagher, what on earth are you thinking about? Your smile is positively indecent," Betsy chided.

Chase blushed like a schoolboy who'd been caught with his hand in the cookie jar.

"Son of a bitch," Tom said, throwing his head back and laughing aloud. "First time I've ever seen a blush across your face, Gallagher."

"Are we going to eat or stand here all day gawking at each another?" Chase retorted, not bothering to hide the annoyance in his voice. Taking hold of Margaret's hand, he led her toward the food, trying to ignore the loud burst of laughter that followed in his wake.

"For heaven's sake, Chase, slow down. You're yanking my arm off," Margaret scolded, pulling her embarrassed husband to a halt before the refreshment table.

He smiled sheepishly. "Sorry. I just needed to get away from Tom. He can be so childish at times."

Margaret thought the pot was calling the kettle black, but she didn't say so. Instead, after noting how much food her husband had loaded onto his plate, she asked, "You're not planning to run in the foot race, are you?" She stared at the piles of beef, tortillas, refried beans, and tamales and wondered where he was planning to put it all. "You're likely to explode after eating all that food."

"I haven't eaten a thing all day," he said, stuffing a meat-filled tortilla into his mouth. "I was afraid I'd puke if I got up on that horse with a full stomach. I'm fair to starving now."

After they'd eaten their fill, which wasn't until Chase

227

had filled his plate two more times, Margaret and Chase headed toward Main Street, where the foot race was about to begin. Wisely, Chase decided to forego the competition and cheer Wooley and Tom on instead.

There were only six contestants, all of them men. Wooley and Tom were lined up on the far right and standing next to Wooley was none other than Francis Brooks.

"Looks like the schoolmarm is fixin' to run in the race, Maggie," Chase commented, eyeing the skinny schoolteacher with distaste. "Never figured him for much of an athlete."

Neither had Margaret, who stared wide-eyed when the starting gun went off to see Francis take off like a fox after a jackrabbit. "Apparently, we misjudged him," she replied, noting that Francis was far ahead of the other runners as he made the turn toward the finish line.

"Too bad he wasn't fast enough to catch you, darlin'. But then, I guess the best man always wins." Chase grinned, kissing the tip of her nose, then her mouth, which produced an instantaneous blush when Margaret observed Alberta and Marion, who were standing only a few feet away, staring at them with mouths agape. She knew they were whispering about her; she could see their jaws flapping faster than Francis's feet slapping the dirt as he crossed the finish line. And she was suddenly determined to give them something really titillating to talk about.

Wrapping her left arm around Chase's waist, she let her hand drop, slowly and purposely, to caress his bottom in a provocative fashion before grabbing hold and giving him a pinch.

Her action had the desired effect, for without so much as a look or a word, Chase swung her up in his arms, in front of Alberta, Marion, God, and everybody, and proceeded to walk straight toward the two busybodies. Noting their appalled expressions, it was all Margaret could do not to laugh in their faces.

When Chase reached the two women, whose jaws were well on their way to reaching their ample bosoms, he paused, a devilish grin lighting his face. "Are you having fun, ladies? I hope so, because we certainly intend to." He winked, and without another word, carted Margaret the rest of the way home, fully intending to make good on his statement.

Chapter Seventeen

Standing in the doorway of the Parker home, Lupe stared nervously at the departing buggy, wringing her hands in agitation as she observed Margaret leaving with Doc.

Having told her only this morning that she would be accompanying Doc to the Fergusons' place, Margaret had explained that there had been a complication with Mrs. Ferguson's baby and that she, Margaret was unsure how long she would be detained.

Lupe had almost cried with relief at the news that Margaret would be gone for a few days, for she had no desire to deliver the message that Sandy had insisted upon.

Yesterday, when Sandy had been so upset about losing the bronc riding competition to Señor Gallagher, Lupe had sought to comfort him by agreeing to deliver a message to Margarita. Sandy had explained that it was from an old acquaintance of Margaret's who he had met during his travels, never revealing, until after Lupe had agreed, that the message was actually from Margaret's father.

Knowing that a message from Señor Parker would upset Margaret, Lupe had tried to refuse, but Sandy had been adamant, threatening to leave her if she didn't do what he demanded.

Shaking her head sadly as she watched the buggy disappear into a trail of dust, Lupe pondered her predicament. How could she tell Margarita that her father had returned and wanted to see her? It would upset her too much. Margaret had been devastated when her father had left without saying good-bye. It would open up all those old wounds to have him show up again after all these years.

Turning back to enter the house, Lupe closed the door behind her. Heaving a sigh, she dropped onto the wooden stool, leaning her arm against the kitchen counter. Her mama was right: Anglos caused too many problems. But what could she do? She loved Sandy. And though she loved Margarita, too, that love wasn't enough to keep her from delivering the message.

She would do nothing to anger Sandy. She was determined to leave this town with him. He was her man—her love, and she must keep him happy. There was nothing else she could do; she had promised.

Rocking back and forth in the old wooden rocker that rested by the side of the bed, Margaret stared at the lifeless form before her and felt the anguish and anger that surfaced whenever she gazed upon Kate's emaciated body. It was all so senseless—so sad. Kate was dying, and, according to Doc, it wouldn't be much longer before she slipped away.

Doc was surprised she had lasted this long. He had said as much this morning when he'd come back to check on Kate. The child growing within her had died, and Kate was going to die with it. She had lost too much blood and had developed puerperal fever. There would be no recovery—no miracle. Only a slow and painful death as Kate's body raged with fever and her lifeblood seeped away.

It had been almost three weeks since she had first come to nurse the dying woman and help care for the children. Three weeks of cooking, scrubbing, changing diapers, offering hope to Willis, Kate's husband, and Beth and Will, Jr., the two eldest children, and she was exhausted.

Chase had been angry last night when he had come to find her looking haggard and ill herself, her energy spent. He had threatened to carry her home bodily if she didn't come willingly. She had never seen him so angry before, and it had gladdened her heart to know that he truly cared for her. He had visited her every evening. And every day that she saw him made her realize how much she missed him and wanted to go home.

But she couldn't leave. Who would stay and take care of this poor family that was falling apart? Who would offer comfort to a dying woman?

Wringing out the rag in the basin of cool water, she gently sponged Kate's brow. The woman made a pitiful mewling sound, deep within her throat, but didn't awaken.

No. She would stay—stay and pray that God would find it in his heart to take this wretched woman with him to a better place—stay and pray that it would be soon.

Margaret watched dry-eyed as the pine box was carefully lowered into the plot of ground that had been prepared for it. Her prayers had been answered. Kate Ferguson had died two days before, looking like a whispery shadow of her former self as she was laid to rest in her wooden coffin. God had been merciful, and Margaret could shed no tears for a woman who was better off dead.

Staring at the solemn faces of the Ferguson family, a heaviness settled in her chest. She gripped Chase's hand tighter, grateful that he stood beside her in this time of tragedy, and felt comforted as he gently squeezed her hand.

Chase was pensive, his expression giving no indication as to his feelings. She guessed he wasn't as affected by the funeral as she. Chase was used to death, having lived with it most of his life. But when she looked up to stare at his somber profile, she could see the teardrop at the corner of his eye—see the tautness that pulled his lips into a straight line across his mouth, and she was relieved. Relieved that he hadn't become immune to a part of life that would surround them the rest of their days.

The heavy black bombazine dress she had donned for the funeral was making her very uncomfortable, absorbing the August sun instead of repelling it like so many of her light cotton dresses would have. Removing her hankie from her reticule, she dabbed at the droplets of moisture forming on her brow. Suddenly, the ground beneath her feet began to shake, and she heard a strange buzzing noise in her ears. "Chase," she whispered, just before everything around her went black.

Doc's expression was grave as he moved his hand over Margaret's forehead. "I won't kid you, Chase; Margaret's burning up with fever. We need to get this gown off her and start sponging down her body to lower her temperature."

Chase stared at Doc, then at Margaret who lay fitfully upon their bed. Having heard her feeble cry for help, he had caught her just before she fainted and had carried her into the house just a short time ago.

"What's wrong with her?" Chase asked, a tight knot of fear forming in his chest as he began to remove Margaret's clothing. "Why is she so still?"

"She fainted; I know that much. As to the reason . . ." Doc shrugged, asking, "Has she been vomiting lately? Complained of tenderness in her breasts?"

Chase's eyes widened as they fell on Margaret's abdomen. "You think she's pregnant?" His heart beat faster at the thought.

"I'll have to examine her to determine that. Why don't you go downstairs and help Lupe with those basins of cold water . . . and fetch some witch hazel. I should know something by the time you return."

Ten minutes later, Chase reentered the room just as Doc was pulling the sheet up over Margaret's fevered body. Setting the basins down on the table by the hearth, he crossed the room to stand beside the bed, handing Doc the bottle of witch hazel.

"Well, did you find out what's wrong with her?"

Doc nodded, pulling the sheet down partway to reveal Margaret's chest. "See those tiny red dots that look like blisters?" He pointed to the three that were centered between her breasts.

"Yeah. So what?"

"It appears that Margaret has contracted a case of the chicken pox, probably from the Ferguson children."

"Chicken pox!" Chase's face registered disbelief. "That's a child's disease for Christ's sake. I had them when I was a kid."

"Apparently Margaret didn't. I've already checked with her mother, and Phoebe has assured me that Margaret never had them."

Chase plopped down on the edge of the bed, unsure of whether or not he should feel relief that Margaret only had the chicken pox. Margaret would be disappointed to learn she wasn't pregnant. Hell! He felt disappointed himself.

"I guess it's not too serious, then?" Chase finally asked.

Sponging Margaret's brow with a cloth that had been soaked in witch hazel, Doc shook his head. "On the contrary, the chicken pox can be very serious when contracted by a woman of Margaret's age. It's a lot harder on an adult than a child."

"But what can we do for her? I remember when I had them; they itched like crazy. Is Maggie going to have the same type of reaction?"

"Most likely, because of her age, she'll have a worse case than you did—heavier, more acute. We'll need to keep her comfortable, try to bring the fever down. Sponging her body with witch hazel will help. And I'll

235

have Lupe prepare a pot of boneset tea. That will bring on the sweats and help break the fever. Other than that, there's not a heck of a lot we can do." For all the advancements that had been made in medicine, there were still some diseases that just had to run their course.

A feeling of dread overtook Chase when Doc's comments finally sunk in. He didn't know anything about nursing a sick woman. "But who's going to care for her? I don't have any experience with that sort of thing."

"Margaret's going to need you, Chase. Once her fever breaks, she's going to be cantankerous and demanding, even more so than her mother." Noting Chase's horror, Doc smiled reassuringly. "You'll do just fine. I'll check in on you every few days, and Lupe will be here to help with the meals and such. I'm sure you'll have everything under control in no time."

Chase did have everything under control—everything but his temper, that is. Margaret's foul moods seemed to be in direct proportion to the number of pox she had on her body, which were numerous. It had been six days since she'd first come down with the disease. And in those six days, she had cried, screamed, cursed, and thrown things at him. And he had been patient. In fact, he had exhibited the patience of Job . . . up until now.

Staring at the mutinous expression on Margaret's speckled face as she reclined against the bed pillows, Chase's voice was firm when he ordered, "You'll eat every bit of that mush, or I'll pour it down your throat myself." He folded his arms over his chest. "And don't go narrowing those brown eyes at me; it'll do you little good. Doc says you need to eat more, and I aim to see that you do." He impaled her with an icy stare, until finally, realizing she was defeated, Margaret picked up the spoon and began to eat.

"You're being hateful! If you knew how much it hurt to eat, you wouldn't make me. I've got those things inside my throat, inside my mouth, and they hurt," she said between mouthfuls of mush.

As sympathetic as Chase felt toward Margaret's predicament, he wasn't about to show it. He'd already found that she had no compunction about playing upon his sympathies, as long as she got what she wanted.

"They certainly haven't affected your speech," he countered. "You've been fussin' and carrying on worse than your mother. And your language! Really, Margaret, I've been shocked these past few days." He swallowed his smile at her outrage, ducking just in time to watch the oatmeal splatter haphazardly over the wall behind his head.

"Get out," she demanded. "You're making me feel worse than I already do."

Staring at the mess on the wall and floor, he gritted his teeth, trying to keep his temper in check. "I should leave that mess there until you're well enough to clean it up yourself, but God knows how long that will be."

His comment brought tears to her eyes, and she wept softly into her hands. "I'm sorry. I know I've been hateful. You probably wish I had died."

Taking a seat on the edge of the bed, Chase took hold of Margaret's hand. "Darlin', you know that's not true.

Haven't I tried to take good care of you? Haven't I attended to your every whim?" Which were numerous, he might add. How many times had he risen during the middle of the night to fetch her water or bring the chamber pot? He'd lost count, as well as a lot of sleep.

"Yes," she replied in a small voice. "You've been a saint."

Having never been put up for sainthood before, Chase had to smile at Margaret's assessment. "I'm not sure how much of a saint I am, but I'm sure as hell tired of playing the monk. When you're well, Mrs. Gallagher, you're going to have a lot to make up for."

The idea of making love with Chase didn't sound particularly appealing at the moment, Margaret thought dejectedly. The most private parts of her anatomy were infested with the blasted pox. "I'm afraid it's going to be a while longer."

He kissed her hand. "Good things come to those who wait. Didn't my mama always tell me that?"

"What was she like? You never talk much about your family, except to say that they're dead."

A faraway look entered the silver eyes, making them look softer, almost pewter in color; his voice was full of tenderness when he spoke. "She was a lovely woman—kind, generous. She loved to bake . . . like you. And she had a fondness for children, also like you. I guess you're a lot like her in many ways."

The comparison made Margaret smile. "And your father?"

"He was a lawyer, owned the most successful law firm in St. Louis."

"That's where you're from? St. Louis?"

He nodded.

"And you became a lawman because of your father?"

His eyes hardened. "Indirectly."

"You said your parents and your fiancée were dead, but you never said how they died. Were they killed in a terrible accident?"

"It was terrible, but it was no accident."

Margaret looked at Chase questioningly, but Chase rose before she could probe further. Now was not the time to get into the reasons behind his parents' deaths. But he would have to tell her soon. He wanted no lies between them. He loved her too much for that.

"It's time I checked on things at the jail. I'll be back at noon to look in on you. We'll do your baking soda bath then." He winked. "Seeing you naked is the only damn benefit about this nursing business, far as I can tell."

"But I look so ugly," she protested. The horrible spots were everywhere. And they itched like the dickens. She had used every ounce of restraint she possessed to keep from scratching them, including wearing gloves at night. She'd seen the effects of pox on those who had scratched themselves, and she had no desire to be marked for life with hideous scars.

"Darlin', that pig of yours, who, by the way, has developed the annoying habit of following me around, is ugly. You, my darling wife, are beautiful. A couple of hundred red spots aren't going to change that fact."

Margaret started crying again, in earnest this time, which alarmed Chase who rushed forward to comfort her. "What's wrong? Aren't you feeling well?"

She shook her head in denial, smiling tremulously. "I . . . I feel fine. In fact, I'm deliriously happy."

Staring at his wife, who was smiling and crying at the same time, and whose face had become one large red dot instead of a mass of tiny ones, he shook his head.

If he lived to be a hundred, he would never understand the workings of a woman's mind. There was no rhyme or reason to it. Women were a contradictory species set on the face of this earth to plague men. Ever since Eve had bitten that damn apple, men were doomed. And Margaret, who had infested his mind and body like a disease, was surely to be the death of him yet!

Chapter Eighteen

"I want Gallagher dead!"

Sandy stared in dismay at Parker's rage-mottled face and shook his head. "But, boss, you said we was going to take things slow. It ain't my fault that your daughter's been sick and Lupe hasn't been able to deliver the message."

"I said we were going to go slow, but I didn't say we were going to stand still for God's sake. It's August. I wanted to be out of this hellhole by now. And here I sit, like some goddamn reptile, crawling inch by inch, and never making a lick of progress."

The door opened and Bear stuck his head in. "You want I should put the dynamite into the barn, boss?"

Parker's eyes narrowed at the sight of the hired hand. "I don't give a damn if you shove it up your ass, Donaldson. Now get the hell out of here. Loomis and I are having a private discussion." The door shut as quickly as it had opened. "We're going to have to do something about the Donaldson brothers," Parker said after Bear had left. "I'm not sure they fit in with my plans now."

Parker wasn't sure if Sandy fit in with his plans now either, but he wouldn't voice that opinion just yet. He needed Loomis to deliver the message to Margaret. But once that was done, he would eliminate both the Donaldsons and Loomis altogether. Why should he share what was already his in the first place?

"What you plan on doing with that dynamite, boss? Is that how we're going to get the gold?"

A humorless smile twisted Parker's lips. Fool, he thought. Loomis actually believed that the gold was hidden in the well behind the Parker house; it's what he had told him. But it was much more accessible than that. Getting his gold back was going to be like stealing candy from a baby . . . from his baby, he amended silently. Margaret was sitting on a fortune, and she didn't even know it.

"That's right, Sandy, but first things first." Parker's voice hardened ruthlessly. "I want that message delivered without delay. If you can't handle that Mexican *puta,* perhaps I should take a turn at her. Maybe you're not man enough to convince her."

Grabbing his hat off the table, Sandy pushed himself to his feet, his nostrils flaring with fury. "No one messes with Lupe but me." He fingered the handle of his gun.

"I'll get your message delivered, then you and me are going to get some things straight, Parker. I don't take kindly to threats, and you've been doing a lot of threatening lately. I hope you remember why you hooked up with me in the first place. I know how to use this gun, and I'm fast."

"Not as fast as Gallagher, or so I'm told," Parker taunted.

Sandy's gun cleared the holster with lightning quick speed, causing Parker's eyebrows to raise. "I'm fast enough. And if you think otherwise, you'll be making a deadly mistake."

"Calm yourself, Sandy, my boy. I'm well aware of your unique capabilities, but I'm also aware of your failings. I can't take the chance that you've been sidetracked by what's between your little whore's thighs. You've got to quit thinking with your dick, Loomis. We're going to be rich, man! Are you with me?"

His anger subsiding, Sandy nodded, easing his gun back into the holster. "Sure, boss, sure."

Unfolding himself from the chair, Parker crossed to the door, putting his face against Sandy's as he spoke. "Then get the message delivered. And don't come back until it's done. I want that gold; I want Gallagher dead. Do you understand?"

The cowboy stepped back, his bravado suddenly fading. "Sure, boss, sure."

"Then do it. And don't fail me, boy. I've waited a lifetime to get that gold. But time's running out. We've got to make our move."

When the door slammed shut, Parker turned, reaching for the bottle of whiskey on the table. Pouring himself a stiff drink, he held the glass out in front of him in mock salute. "To your death, Gallagher," he toasted. "May it be swift and soon!"

The sign over the store read Fraser's Mercantile. Margaret smiled happily as she paused on the wooden sidewalk to read it, commenting to her husband who

243

had accompanied her to the grand opening, "Looks like they've done it. Betsy and Tom have finally opened their store."

Like several of the Fraser's closest friends, they had been invited to the grand opening party this Sunday evening. The official opening of the store wasn't scheduled to take place until nine o'clock tomorrow morning.

Chase grunted, disapproval etched clearly on his face. "They're damn fools, the both of them. I tried to tell Tom he was out of his mind to invest all his money in such a risky venture. Serve them both right if they lose their shirts."

Margaret folded her arms, her foot tapping against the wooden planks as she stared up at her husband. "This is my first outing since recovering from the chicken pox, and I'll thank you to keep your comments to yourself, Chase Gallagher. Tom and Betsy are our friends. And no matter how this venture of theirs turns out, we'll support them one hundred percent."

Chase bowed, bringing her hand to his lips for a kiss. "Yes, dear," he replied, a bit too sarcastically.

"And I'll thank you to leave your henpecked husband imitation out here where no one can see it. It hardly suits you anyway," she retorted, pulling her hand out of his grasp.

"Now don't go getting yourself in a snit. I was just teasing."

Her anger quickly abated, and she smiled contritely. "I'm sorry. I don't know what's come over me."

"I expect it's not what's come over you but more what hasn't gone into you." At her puzzled expression, he went on to explain, "We haven't made love in over three weeks, darlin', and you know what a passionate woman you are. And what a wonderful lover I am." Locking his thumbs in his belt, he stood there grinning at her.

Margaret's cheeks bloomed with color. "Your conceit astounds me, Marshal."

His right eyebrow cocked. "Do you deny it?"

The sexual tension had been building between them for weeks, drawing them tighter than a string on a fiddle. That string was about to snap. She could see it in the way Chase's eyes sparkled like silver fire; she could feel it in the way her nipples grew taut at the very thought of being held naked in his arms. "No," she finally replied. "But I won't feed your ego by affirming it, either."

"Then I guess we'll just have to put it to a test."

Chase's seductive grin was making her feel very uncomfortable. Before he had a chance to change his mind about attending the celebration, she pulled him forward to enter the building.

Betsy and Tom were standing behind a long, wooden counter, serving punch to the guests who'd already arrived. Wooley and Concita were there, as were Alberta, Marion, and Audra Simmons.

Glancing about the attractively furnished establishment, Margaret was impressed by the pleasing displays and homey atmosphere of the store. Betsy, with her usual good taste, had done a marvelous job of decorating the interior.

At the two large windows that fronted the building hung white eyelet curtains, pulled back on each side to give a draped effect. The shelves along the back wall were neatly lined with bolts of colorful cloth, in patterns ranging from gingham to calico, as well as shoes, boots, and other dry goods. There were barrels in all different sizes containing everything from nails to pickles. Glass cases along the left wall enclosed pieces of jewelry, combs, and gloves; while to the left, hanging on two long racks, were ready-made dresses for women and ready-made suits and shirts for men. From the ceiling hung bacon, hams, luggage, and Stetsons, as well as several farm implements and coils of rope.

"I can see by that delighted look on your face that you're quite impressed with Fraser's Mercantile. I can also see that this business of theirs is going to cost me a pretty penny."

"Oh, Chase, don't be silly. Why, see for yourself." She pulled him toward the rack of dresses. "These dresses are all very reasonably priced. And the selection is far superior to Mr. Taylor's."

"That's right, Gallagher, don't be so cheap. Buy the little lady something," Tom Fraser goaded, a twinkle lighting his blue eyes as he stepped from behind the counter to greet his friends.

Margaret smiled at Tom's conspiratorial wink, moving away to inspect the row of leather-bound books on the shelf.

Chase shook his head. "I never thought I'd see the day when you'd be wearing an apron, Fraser. If those desperadoes you put behind bars could see you now, they'd laugh themselves silly."

"And I never thought I'd see the day when you'd be wearing a ring through your nose," Tom retorted.

"Come along, Chase," Margaret said, tugging on her husband's shirtsleeve when she'd finished browsing over the reading material. She hadn't heard Tom's comment and had no idea why Chase's cheeks were reddening. "Betsy is signaling to us from across the room. I think she wants to show us something."

Tom smiled. "I rest my case."

Chase glowered at his friend. "At least I haven't let my wife talk me into opening up a dress shop."

"Give it time, Marshal. After all, you haven't been married that long. Women can be very persuasive when they set their minds to it. Isn't that so, Margaret?"

Margaret shot them a reproachful look. "You two *men,* and I use that term loosely, remind me of a couple of schoolboys. I've never seen such carrying on between two adults before."

"Speaking of schoolboys, look who just entered the store."

Margaret and Tom followed Chase's gaze, observing Francis Brooks accompanied by a woman neither Margaret nor Tom recognized. She had ink black hair, curled up in ringlets, and a bow-shaped mouth that, at the moment, was turned up into a smile as she responded to something Francis was saying. She was diminutive, about the same height as Francis, and had a pleasing figure that was shown off to perfection by the green lawn gown she was wearing, making Margaret wish she had worn something other than the serviceable brown twill skirt and white cotton blouse she had on.

Being in the same room with the woman made her feel a little bit like a cactus standing next to a magnolia in full bloom, and she hoped desperately that Chase wasn't making the same comparison.

"It seems Francis has made a new acquaintance," Margaret remarked, unable to take her eyes off the couple. Had Francis grown taller, or was that just her imagination?

"You two have been so busy with your respective situations, or else you would have known that Purgatory has acquired a new milliner. That's Laurette Appleton. She only arrived in town a week ago," Chase explained.

"Well, Francis hasn't wasted any time," Tom remarked, observing the way the schoolteacher hung on the milliner's every word. "Looks like he replaced our Margaret without a second thought."

Both men laughed, which made the color in Margaret's cheeks heighten. "I think we should go over and introduce ourselves instead of standing here ogling them."

But that wasn't necessary, for Francis had spotted Margaret and was crossing the room with Laurette Appleton on his arm at this very moment.

The awkwardness that Margaret had come to expect from Francis was missing as he made the introductions. Instead, he spoke smoothly, without a blush, stammer, or any other sign of embarrassment.

The way Chase and Tom were admiring the newcomer made Margaret want to kick them both soundly in the shins. The woman was attractive, but she certainly wasn't beautiful. Of course, she probably didn't have pockmark impressions over her entire body, either.

"Welcome, Miss Appleton, I'm Margaret Gallagher. My *husband,* Marshal Gallagher, tells me that you've opened a millinery shop."

The woman smiled prettily, exhibiting two perfectly formed dimples on either side of her cheeks. "Why, yes, and I hope you'll stop by to see my creations. If I do say so, they're far superior to anything this store has to offer."

The words poured slowly out of Laurette Appleton's mouth as sweet and thick as maple syrup. Her Southern drawl, which Margaret assumed to be Georgian, grated on Margaret's nerves, as did the woman's insulting comments. She wasn't about to let this interloper demean her best friend's merchandise. But rather than chastise Laurette Appleton herself, she would leave that chore to Betsy who would do a far superior job.

"This is Tom Fraser, Miss Appleton; he owns this store. Perhaps you can counsel him on what type of apparel he should be carrying. Or better, yet, see that blond woman over there." Margaret pointed at Betsy who was serving up a glass of punch to Esther Perkins. "She's Mrs. Fraser—the one that does the buying. I'm sure she'd be grateful for any advice you would care to give her."

Chase and Tom exchanged worried glances before Tom took hold of the woman's elbow, saying, "Allow me to introduce you to my wife, Miss Appleton. I'm sure Betsy would be delighted with any suggestions you would care to make." He cast Margaret a reproachful look before departing.

Francis followed behind them like a faithful puppy dog, making Margaret, who observed the look of adoration on his face, reevaluate her opinion of his increased stature.

When they were alone once again, Chase escorted Margaret to the corner behind the front door where the mailboxes were located. "I'm assuming you already know that you've just fed poor Laurette Appleton to the wolves; that was your intention, wasn't it?" The corners of his mouth tipped at the look of innocence on Margaret's face.

"I have no idea what you mean. I'm sure Betsy would be happy to discuss improvements in the millinery section."

"Like hell! That woman's got about as much flexibility as a concrete corset, and you know it."

"Really, Chase, the way you're defending Miss Appleton would make one think you have some interest in her."

"So that's it? You're jealous of Laurette Appleton."

"I am not! How dare you suggest such a thing! Why, I only met the woman a few minutes ago. How could I be jealous of her?"

"Darlin', I gave up long ago trying to figure out the workings of a woman's mind. Life's too short to solve that puzzle." He ignored her snort and continued, "You've got no call to be jealous of anyone, Maggie. I've got eyes for no one else but you."

"It's not your *eyes* I'm worried about," she tossed out.

Chase threw back his head and laughed, giving Margaret a swift slap on her behind. "Get you out that door, woman. We've got some pressing matters to take care of at home."

Dropping into a curtsy, she lowered her thick lashes, before replying meekly, "Yes, dear."

Holding hands like two young lovers as they crept stealthily up the stairs, Chase and Margaret whispered quietly, trying to keep the noise to a minimum until they could reach the safety of their room. But as Margaret's foot hit the top step, a loud squeak sounded, followed by a familiar but unwelcome voice.

"Is that you, Margaret? I've been waiting up to talk to you." Phoebe's words hurtled through the closed door like a cannon ball, hitting her targets full on.

Margaret blanched, gazing over at Chase, whose lips were thinning in displeasure; she patted his cheek reassuringly. "I won't be a minute; I promise."

"I'll hold you to that." He kissed her lightly on the lips, disappearing into their bedroom.

Drawing a deep, frustrated breath, Margaret entered her mother's room to find Phoebe wide awake and sitting in her rocker. "Mama, why are you still up? I thought you'd be asleep hours ago." She seated herself on the edge of the bed.

"I waited up for you, Margaret. You know how I worry when you go out alone."

"I wasn't alone, Mama. Chase was with me."

Phoebe fussed with the crocheted afghan atop her lap. "Oh, him. I'd completely forgotten all about him."

"I know for a fact that you've spoken to Chase several times in the last few weeks, Mama. He told me that you'd been inquiring after my health."

"Of course, I inquired. You are my only daughter. I had to make certain he was taking proper care of you."

It was as close to an admission of caring that Margaret was ever going to get from her mother. She'd learned a long time ago that Phoebe was neither generous with her affections nor her praise. She dealt out both like a miser did his money.

251

"Chase took good care of me, Mama. He truly cares for me."

"Hmph! Deception is the calling card of the devil, Margaret. Always remember that."

Margaret sighed in exasperation. She had no intention of engaging her mother in another discussion on the evils of men. "Did you wish to speak to me about something, Mama? It's late; I'm tired and anxious to get to bed."

Phoebe's lips twisted into a sneer. "You don't fool me. I know why you're so anxious to leave. It's him. You want to fornicate like some Jezebel. Well go on. But don't come crying to me when he leaves you high and dry. I've tried to warn you."

Pushing herself off the bed, Margaret took her mother's hands in her own, squeezing them gently. "I'm sorry that Papa hurt you so badly, Mama. I love you, but I love Chase, too. Please don't ever make me choose between you." Leaning over, she placed a kiss on the wrinkled cheek and walked to the door, never seeing the string of tears that fell from her mother's eyes.

"Everything all right?" Chase asked when Margaret entered. He was reclining against the headboard, hands locked behind his head, as naked as the day he was born.

The sight of Chase's firm, muscled body in the glow of the candlelight made Margaret pause; her heart quickened. Though she had seen him naked countless times, it never failed to excite or impress her. He was like some perfectly chiseled marble statue that graced the halls of a museum. But unlike a statue that was cold and inanimate, Chase was warm and very alive. And the rising proof of that now jutted forth proudly to greet her.

"I can see that you're happy to see me," she said, closing the door behind her.

"If you'll take off those duds, I'll show you just how happy I am."

The weeks of forced abstinence heightened the anticipation. With slow, precise movements, Margaret unbuttoned her blouse, never taking her eyes off Chase for a moment. Removing it, she stepped out of her skirt, folding it carefully and laying it on the chair by the window. Next came her shoes, then stockings, which she unrolled, one by one, tossing them onto the pile.

She heard Chase's sharp intake of breath when her hand went up to touch the ribbons of her chemise. Smiling seductively, she pulled on the string, allowing the material to fall open and her lush mounds to spring forth.

Observing the way his eyes followed her every movement, she casually strolled to the dressing table and picked up her hairbrush. With long, smooth strokes, she pulled the brush through her thick tresses; the motion caused her breasts to bounce in a most provocative fashion. She caught his eyes in the mirror and smiled, licking her lips as she turned to grasp the tapes of her drawers. With one pull, she loosed them and they fell in a puddle of cotton at her feet.

Completely naked, she crossed the room, standing proudly before the bed. The glow of admiration in Chase's eyes made her feel truly beautiful.

"You're temptation and desire all rolled into one," he whispered, holding out his hand. He thought of Eve and that apple, and knew that Adam never had a chance.

Margaret placed her hand in his, climbing onto the bed. With a quickness that surprised him, she straddled his lap, pushing him back into the pillows. "You're at my mercy, now. And since I was so very impressed with your bronc-riding abilities, I've decided to see for myself what it's like to have all that unleashed masculine power between my thighs." She heard his gasp of surprise, caught his pleased expression, before easing herself over the length of him, taking him full within her.

With a rocking pelvic motion, she began to ride him, reveling in the intense pleasure she saw registered on his face. The feel of his hardened shaft as it impaled her soft woman's core was exquisite torture. She threw back her head, writhing in ecstasy as the feeling within her intensified. Taking hold of his hands, she placed them on her breasts, encouraging him to massage the aching globes, all the while never breaking stride as she moved up and down on the pulsating member.

"Ride me, baby, ride me hard," Chase ordered, pulling on her taut nipples, delighting in the moan of pleasure that escaped from Maggie's throat. She was magnificent, like some creature out of Greek mythology, some pagan goddess, all wild and uninhibited. Her sweat-slicked body undulated uncontrollably and it was all he could do not to give in to the potent pleasure that was building inside of him. He grabbed onto her hips, rotating them, urging her to move faster and harder.

"Oh, God, darlin', I can't hold out much longer."

Faster and faster Margaret rocked, to and fro, as she

reached for fulfillment. Her breathing grew shallow, her motions frenzied. When Chase moved his fingers from her hips to the hardened nub between her legs, the tension built unbearably within her. Tighter and stronger it grew, making her feel like a clock that had been wound too tight and was ready to spring. Able to stand it no longer, she cried out, convulsing in spasms on top of him.

With one final stroke, Chase rode the crest of his own fulfillment, exploding deep within her. He had never felt so sated—so totally at peace with himself. Reaching for Margaret, he brought her head down to smother her moans of pleasure with his lips. Rolling her onto her back, he continued to shower her face with kisses, licking the sweat off her upper lip, smoothing the damp strands of hair away from her face.

"I love you, Maggie," he whispered. "I love you so much, it scares the hell out of me."

Margaret's lashes flew up and she smiled radiantly. No matter how many times he told her, she never tired of hearing it. "I love you, too. And I'm not scared a whit."

"There's things we need to talk about—things I need to tell you."

She placed her fingers over his lips. "Ssh! I'll not waste my evening with talk, Chase Gallagher. Not when I've got you right where I want you."

He felt her pelvis thrust against him, and his eyes widened. "You don't mean to . . ."

Her smile was erotic, full of promise. "That's exactly what I mean. I want you again. I feel insatiable tonight."

"But, darlin', I'm an old man. I'm not sure I can

accommodate your desires." But the readily stiffening manhood between Margaret's thighs belied Chase's protestations.

"That old horse you rode during the competition had more than one rider on his back. If he was good for a number of rides, then I'm sure you are, too."

A mock look of horror crossed his face. "Why, Margaret Gallagher! I'm shocked. Wherever did you learn such things?"

Running her hand up his thigh, she trailed her finger over the tip of his manhood, feeling the moist evidence of his desire, smiling at the way his eyes darkened to pewter. "Why, I had an excellent teacher, Marshal. And I've always heard that practice makes perfect."

He groaned. "Darlin', if you get any more perfect, you're going to kill me."

"But, Chase," she argued, wrapping her hand around his swollen member. "It'll be such a pleasurable death."

"Oh, God!" he cried out, "I'm going to meet my Maker."

Chapter Nineteen

"Margarita, I've been waiting hours for you. I didn't expect you to sleep so late this morning."

Margaret could barely meet Lupe's eyes as she stepped into the kitchen. She hadn't meant to oversleep, but after the night of arduous lovemaking she had just experienced, she could barely drag herself out of bed this morning. Chase, too, was suffering the effects of their romantic encounter. He had been as surly as a flea-bitten dog when he'd forced himself out the door an hour ago.

Heading straight for the pot of coffee on the stove, she poured herself a cup; the strong, black liquid seemed to revive her. "I'm sorry, Lupe. I was up rather late last night; I guess I just overslept."

"Your mama, she is ill again?"

Margaret colored and shook her head. "No, not this time."

"You blush like a new bride, Margarita. I think perhaps you and Señor Gallagher have been making up for lost time." Lupe giggled at Margaret's mortification, setting a plate of bacon, eggs, and toast in front of the embarrassed woman. "Eat. You need to keep up your strength. The marshal, he is *muy* macho. If you do not eat, you cannot keep up with him."

"Lupe Diaz, you are incorrigible! Am I to have no secrets from you?" A strange look passed over the housekeeper's face, prompting Margaret to add, "Is something wrong? You look whiter than bleached muslin."

Taking a seat at the table, Lupe pleated the folds of her red-and-blue madras skirt, searching for just the right words. "Margarita, there is something I must tell you."

Margaret's fork paused in midair. "You know you can tell me anything. We are friends—amigos."

"You know that I have been seeing the gringo?" At Margaret's nod, Lupe continued, "His name is Sandy Loomis, and I am very much in love with him."

Smiling with pleasure, Margaret reached out, patting Lupe's hand. "I'm very happy for you. Will you and Mr. Loomis be getting married?"

Lupe's face glowed for the first time that morning. "*Sí*. Sandy says he loves me. I think we will get married eventually."

"That's wonderful! I'm so happy for you."

"But, Margarita, you do not understand. That is not what I have to tell you, only a small part of it."

Noting Lupe's anxiousness, a flicker of apprehension trickled through Margaret's body. Was Lupe in trouble? Was she going to have this Sandy Loomis's baby? Not able to keep her suspicions to herself a moment longer, she blurted out, "You're pregnant!"

Lupe smiled softly. "No, Margarita, this is not about

me, but about you."

Margaret's forehead crinkled in confusion. "Me? What does Mr. Loomis have to do with me? I've never even met the man."

Lupe took a deep breath. "He is acquainted with your *padre*. He has asked me to deliver a message from Señor Parker."

A moment of shocked silence ensued before Margaret's mouth dropped open and she exclaimed, "My father?!"

"*Sí*. Your father has returned; he is in the area and wishes to meet with you."

Her meal forgotten, Margaret rose to her feet and began pacing back and forth. Her father had returned? Now, after all these years? She paused before Lupe's chair. "I don't understand. How is Mr. Loomis acquainted with my father?"

Lupe related what Sandy had told her, adding, "Your father is ill. He wishes to see you again before he dies."

"Dies." The word came out in a whisper. Tears filled her eyes, bringing Lupe to her feet.

"I'm so sorry, Margarita. I didn't want to tell you; I knew it would hurt too much. Sandy says there are reasons your papa hasn't come before now. But Señor Parker wouldn't tell Sandy what they are. He will tell only you."

Margaret dropped back down in the chair. Her father was ill—dying. He had come back to say good-bye. "Where is he? When can I meet with him?"

"Because of your illness, I told Sandy that the meeting would have to be delayed. Señor Parker is living somewhere close by. I do not know exactly

259

where. If you are willing to meet him, I am to make the arrangements with Sandy."

Margaret nodded absently. "I will have to tell Chase and my mother."

Lupe shook her head emphatically. "No! You cannot! For some reason your papa does not want anyone to know of his arrival. He told Sandy that you were to come alone—that you were to tell no one of his visit."

"But I don't understand."

Lupe reached into the pocket of her apron, drawing out a sealed envelope. "I was asked to give you this. It is from your *padre.*"

Margaret stared at the envelope, recognizing the handwriting immediately. A tremor of excitement shot through her veins.

"I will leave you to your letter, Margarita. I must go to Mrs. Perkins's Grocery to fetch the rabbit for tonight's dinner. You will be all right?"

Looking up, Margaret nodded. "Yes, I'll be fine. Go on. When you return, we'll finish pickling the cucumbers."

Lupe pulled a face, but Margaret didn't see her. She was too preoccupied by the missive she held tightly in her hand. She stared at the white envelope for several seconds before opening it. As if the last eight years had never been, Jonathan Parker's words came forth, bringing a rush of tears to her eyes:

My dearest Margaret, Though it has grieved me to be away from you these many years, I have kept track of your welfare through various sources. It is my fondest wish that we become reacquainted, and I hope you will find it in your heart to forgive me for leaving as I did.

I would like to meet with you as soon as possible. I can disclose nothing further, except to say that I love you and will explain all when we finally meet. If you are agreeable to such a meeting, please leave word with your housekeeper. My friend, Loomis, will be in touch. Your loving father, Jonathan Parker.

Margaret wiped the tears from her eyes, then carefully refolded the letter, stuffing it into the pocket of her skirt. Her heart ached with both happiness and sadness at the prospect of seeing her father again. He was alive, but not for long. He still loved her, but she could tell no one. Why was he being so mysterious? Why wasn't she supposed to tell anyone of his visit?

And what possible excuse for her absence was she going to give Chase when she finally went to meet her father? She didn't want to lie to him—hated having to keep things from him. A new closeness had formed between them—a closeness built on trust and love. How, then, could she deceive him?

Biting her lower lip, she withdrew the envelope from her pocket once again, pressing it against her breast. Chase would understand. He knew how much she missed her father. He wouldn't want her to miss what might be her only opportunity to see him.

Convinced she was right, Margaret decided then and there that she would keep her father's presence a secret. She would meet with him—find out why he had stayed away so long. And Chase would understand. He would have to.

*   *   *

Chase stared at the telegram that had just arrived
from Warden Clements at Yuma Prison. His eyebrows
knitted in puzzlement. Why would the warden of
Yuma send him a telegram? Ripping open the missive,
his brows furrowed even more deeply as he read the
contents. One of the inmates claimed to have knowledge of the Purgatory bank robbery. He was willing to
talk, but only to Chase.

"Bad news?" Wooley inquired, checking the barrel of
his revolver. As was his practice every Monday
morning, Wooley had just spent the last twenty-five
minutes cleaning his gun. His theory: one never knew
when there might be cause to use it, and he was going
to be ready just in case.

Chase shrugged. "It's puzzling that an inmate in
Yuma Prison would have knowledge about the
robbery here. I'd bet my last dollar that Parker pulled
that bank job. It has all the earmarkings of one of his
heists."

"You goin' to ignore the telegram?"

Heaving a sigh, Chase shook his head. He would
have to leave, and just when things were getting good
between him and Maggie. Damn! Why'd he take this
stupid job in the first place? He was getting too old to
go traipsing off on what was probably just a wild-goose
chase. "I've got to follow up on it. It's doubtful
anything will come of the visit. But as long as there's a
chance, I've got to go."

"You want me to come along? I'd welcome the
change of scenery."

Chase's lips twitched. "It's hotter than hell in Yuma.

262

Hardly an ideal location for a change of scenery." He wagged his head. "No, you'd better stay put. There's no telling when our friend will show his hand. I want someone here in case he does."

"How long you figurin' on being gone? It seems every time you leave something happens."

Chase had had similar thoughts, but he doubted if Parker would be so brazen as to show his face in town; Wooley knew what he looked like.

"You fixin' to change your mind, Marshal?" There was a note of hopeful expectancy in Wooley's voice as he asked the question.

"Nope. I've got to go. I'll head on home and pack my gear." Crossing to the door, he reached for his hat. "I shouldn't be gone more than five, maybe six, days. If there's a problem, you know where to reach me."

Wooley nodded. "Sure, Marshal. Everything will be fine. You go on along. Just be careful. Don't let one of them sidewinders get you." Wooley's assurances waned as Chase made his exit. Something didn't feel right about this whole setup. Chase might be walking into a trap. That Parker fella might be waitin' for him outside of town somewheres. Maybe he should follow Chase for a spell, make sure he got out of town safely.

Realizing the absurdity of his fears, Wooley shook his head and snorted. There was only one person that could get the drop on Chase Gallagher, and she wasn't about to do him any harm. He chuckled. No siree! Margaret might love Chase to death, but she wasn't about to kill him.

Up to her elbows in pickle brine, Margaret thought

263

about Chase's sudden departure and sighed. He'd only been gone a few hours and already she missed him terribly.

When he'd come home unexpectedly announcing his trip to Yuma, she'd been relieved at first. His absence would mean she wouldn't have to make up any lies about where she was going and who she was going to meet. But then, when she'd thought about him being gone days on end, riding over harsh terrain, all alone, a terrible surge of guilt assailed her. She didn't want him to leave—had actually begged him not to. But of course, he had paid her no mind. Explaining the importance of his mission, Chase had kissed her soundly on the lips, patted her behind "for luck," he had said, and rode off on his big black stallion.

Placing the lid on the brown earthenware crock that housed the newly made pickles, Margaret wiped her hands on her apron. Lupe had still not returned from her errand to Mrs. Perkins's Grocery and Margaret had the sneaking suspicion that the housekeeper was doing more than buying rabbit.

As if conjured up by her thoughts, Lupe strolled into the kitchen, holding an assortment of white paper-wrapped parcels. "I am back, Margarita."

The woman's face was flushed, her lips slightly swollen. It was obvious to Margaret that Lupe had just been kissed, and it didn't take a detective to find out who had done the kissing. Sandy Loomis was back in town.

"I am sorry to be so late." She stared at the crock of pickles and was unable to hide the relief that crossed her face. "I see you are all finished with the pickles."

"Yes, I'm finished. Isn't that what you were counting

on?" Margaret smiled inwardly at Lupe's guilty expression. "It's no secret that putting up pickles and preserves isn't one of your favorite pastimes," she added.

"Please forgive me. I . . . I was with Sandy."

Lupe's blush surprised Margaret. The worldly housekeeper wasn't given to episodes of embarrassed behavior. "I thought as much. Well, no matter, they're all done now. Besides, it gave me something to do. Took my mind off Chase's trip."

Lupe's eyes widened. "Señor Gallagher is gone?"

Margaret nodded. "He had to go to Yuma on business. He'll be back in a few days."

Lupe lowered her gaze in confusion. How could Sandy have known that the marshal would be gone when he asked her to deliver the message? she wondered, shaking her head. Deciding it was just a coincidence, she pushed the question to the back of her mind. "It is probably for the best, Margarita. Your papa has sent word. He wants to meet with you."

Margaret's heart thudded loud in her ears. "When?"

"This evening after supper. You are to accompany Sandy. He will bring the buggy and pick you up."

Excitement mingled with apprehension. "But I don't know Mr. Loomis. It wouldn't be seemly for me to be seen riding out with him, especially when Chase has just left."

Lupe smiled. "Believe me, Margarita, Sandy knows how to be very discreet. We have been meeting for weeks in the livery and no one has been the wiser. No one will see you."

Margaret bit her lower lip indecisively. It was one thing to deceive Chase about meeting her father, but

265

quite another to ride out alone in the dark with a total stranger. Her reputation would be ruined if anyone saw her. "I don't know."

"I will let you wear my *rebozo*. It will cover your head and face. We are of a like size. If anyone sees you, they will just think it is me."

"But what about Mama? She'll get suspicious if I leave."

"I will stay and tell her that Doc has had an emergency and that you were needed at his office."

"Do you think this meeting is a good idea, Lupe?"

Noting the confusion in the young woman's eyes, hearing the uncertainty in her voice, Lupe hesitated a moment before answering. "Only you can decide that, Margarita. It is your papa who wishes to see you. Do you want to see him again?"

"Oh, yes, more than anything," Margaret answered without hesitation. "I've missed him so much."

"Then you must go. It will be all right. You will see. Your fears are all for *nada.*"

But as Margaret sat stiffly on the leather seat of the buggy next to Sandy Loomis, who turned out to be the same man who had bid on her the day of the auction, she wasn't sure Lupe was right. For some strange reason, Mr. Loomis made her feel uncomfortable. They hadn't spoken a word since Lupe had first made the introductions, a circumstance Margaret was heartily thankful for. She had nothing to say to the cowboy, and the nervous lump lodged in her throat made speaking next to impossible anyway.

Her thoughts turned to her father. What would she

say to him when she finally saw him? What possible explanation could he have for leaving like he did?

"Guess it's been a while since you've seen your old man."

Mr. Loomis's voice sounded loud against the stillness of the night, jarring Margaret out of her reverie. "Yes," she croaked, "almost nine years."

Sandy breathed in the scent of lavender that clung to Margaret Gallagher's hair, smelled her sweet cinnamon breath as she spoke. His crotch swelled, straining against the denim of his pants. He wanted her—wanted to be in her—to feel her soft, lush mounds pressed up against his naked chest. And he would have her, every delectable inch of her. But not yet.

"It's not much farther," he said, trying to keep the excitement out of his voice.

Margaret looked about but could see nothing in the darkness. The lights from town had long since faded, leaving only the shimmer of a thousand stars and the last quarter of the moon to light their way.

Another fifteen minutes of silence passed before an isolated building came into view. As they drew nearer, Margaret could make out the form more clearly. It was a small house, sadly in need of repair. The fence surrounding the structure had fallen, lying on the ground dejectedly, as if there had been little purpose for it to remain standing. There were no signs of life— no animals—no crops, or any other indication that anyone resided there. Pulling up to the front of the dwelling, Sandy drew the horses to a halt.

"Your father's inside the house waiting for you."

Margaret cast another apprehensive look at the building. There was a single light coming from the

267

window in the front room, but she could distinguish no shapes or forms that might be within.

Sandy jumped down, coming around to her side of the buggy to help her alight. Observing the ardent look in his eyes, she felt uncomfortable and pulled back when his hands reached up to grasp her waist. But his grip was strong and he swung her down, letting her body slide down the length of him.

She gasped as her body came into contact with his, pulling back immediately. She had felt the unmistakable bulge pressing against her thigh and it repulsed her. Her voice rose sharply as her feet hit the ground, and she extricated herself from his embrace. "I can make my own way from here, Mr. Loomis. Thank you for your assistance."

Hearing the censure in her voice, Sandy realized his mistake at once and smiled contritely. "Beg pardon, ma'am. I lost my footing."

Margaret's eyes narrowed suspiciously, but then noting the boyish smile and the sincere apology in the man's voice, she decided she might have been mistaken. After all, Mr. Loomis was a friend of her father's. "No need to apologize, Mr. Loomis. It's pitch black out here and easy for a body to stumble."

"Yes, ma'am. If you'll just follow me, I'll lead you to your father."

Pausing outside the house, Margaret breathed in deeply, wiping her sweating palms on the skirt of her calico dress. She had worn blue, remembering it was her father's favorite color.

"Don't be nervous, ma'am," Sandy said, trying to reassure her when they'd reached the front door. "He's just an old man who's been missing his daughter."

268

Margaret smiled at the cowboy's kindness. "Thank you, Mr. Loomis. It's kind of you to say so."

He reached across the front of her and opened the door, allowing her to enter first. It took a moment for her eyes to adjust to the brightness of the room, but then she saw him, standing with his back to her, next to the fireplace.

Her father looked much older. His hair had grayed, and there seemed to be a permanent stoop to his shoulders as he stood staring into the flames of the fireplace. He leaned against a black, gold-tipped cane.

"Papa," she called out, barely above a whisper.

He turned then, tears filling his eyes as he looked upon his daughter for the first time in eight years.

"Margaret? Is it you? Is it really you?"

The smile that lit Margaret's face could have illuminated the entire house. Brushing at the tears streaming down her face, she replied, "Yes, Papa, it's me."

He held out his arms and she rushed into them, hugging him to her breast.

Sandy stared in disgust at the whole exchange, though he did his best to hide it. Parker was quite an actor; he'd have to give the old man credit for that. Margaret had fallen into his arms with no thought of hesitation. Lucky son of a bitch, he thought, noting how her big breasts were pressed up against her father's chest.

With a shake of his head, he exited the room, needing a breath of fresh air to dispel the sudden anger he felt. Parker was a bastard. To deceive his own flesh and blood as if she were nothing more than a faithful dog. He spat, kicking the dirt with the toe of his boot. It wouldn't give him a moment's pain when he double-crossed Parker and took his little girl away from him. No sir! Margaret would be a whole lot better off with him than with that lying, smooth-talking, bastard of a father of hers.

Striking a match against the heel of his boot, he lit a cigarette, inhaling deeply. Once he had the gold and the woman, he'd buy a spread, settle down, maybe even raise himself a passel of kids.

He smiled to himself. Soon he would have it all—everything he had ever wanted. He had bowed and scraped to Parker, and others like him, for the last time. Parker thought him a fool. But he was no man's fool—no woman's either. He would take the gold, take the woman. And Parker be damned!

Chapter Twenty

"I can't believe it's really you, Papa," Margaret said, running her hand gently over his face. Now that she'd had a chance to see him up close, she discovered that he wasn't as old or decrepit as she'd originally feared. True, his hair had grayed considerably, and he walked with a pronounced limp, but his face was tanned, almost healthy-looking, and the years since she had seen him had been kind. "You've aged gracefully," she added, noting how the tiny lines around his eyes crinkled when he smiled. He led her to the only pieces of furniture in the room—a table and two chairs.

"Thank you, my dear. But I'm afraid that, though I look perfectly fine, I have an ailment that, in time, will kill me."

Tears filled her eyes as she reached across the table to grasp on to his hands. "Have you seen a doctor? Perhaps Doc Watson can help; he's very good at curing people."

He shook his head sadly. "There's no cure for what ails me, Margaret, though seeing your beautiful face again has made me feel immeasurably better." He could see that his words pleased her. "I've got a cancer that's eating away at my innards. The process is slow but deadly." He squeezed her hands, which had suddenly turned clammy. "It's why I had to see you again. Why I've come back."

Margaret swallowed the lump in her throat. "But I don't understand why you left to begin with—with no word—no good-bye. Mama was devastated; we both were. We've missed you."

"Your mother was part of the reason I left. Living with her was intolerable." His voice reflected the aversion that he felt, as his thoughts traveled back to his former life with Phoebe. "She was greedy, always wanting what I couldn't oblige her, demanding more of me than I wanted to give. I realize I took the coward's way out. I'll understand if you can't forgive me. But I had to leave."

Margaret digested all that he told her. His confession merely affirmed what she had concluded long ago: Her mother had driven him away. "You said Mama was part of the reason you left. Was there another?"

"There was, but we won't talk of it this night. I want to hear all about you. Your life. What you've been doing since I've been gone."

Margaret spent the next thirty minutes relating what her life had been like the past eight years. She told him how her mother had fallen ill after he'd left—which produced another sneer—how she'd been working for Doc Watson, and about the loneliness and despair she had oftentimes felt at his absence.

He made no comments, asked no questions, until she had concluded her narrative. "Sandy tells me that you've married. Do you have children?" He tried to keep the disgust out of his voice at the thought of his daughter producing Gallagher's brat. Although he had to admit, the irony of the situation was amusing; a small smile crossed his lips.

Margaret's face glowed with happiness as she told of her courtship and subsequent marriage to Chase. "I feel so lucky, Papa. I have a husband who loves me, and now, you have returned to make my life complete."

Patting her hand, Parker smiled smoothly, pushing himself to his feet. "I'm afraid we'll have to cut our first meeting a little short, my dear. The pain in my gut has worsened. I need to rest."

Noting the sudden pallor of his complexion, the way he clutched his middle, Margaret grew instantly concerned. "Do you have medicine to relieve your suffering?"

"Yes, though it does little good." Eager to bring the conversation around to their next rendezvous, he changed the subject. "I'll send word when I'm able to meet with you again."

"But how long will I have to wait? I want to spend as much time with you as possible."

"It will only be a day or two. I'll send word with Sandy."

Rising to her feet, Margaret took a good look around at the empty room she was standing in. Surely her father couldn't be living in this barren, miserable hovel. "Do you live here?"

He smiled, escorting her to the door. "No, I'm staying with Loomis. But his place is hardly suitable for a young lady of refinement."

And this was? she wondered silently, but aloud she

replied, "I understand. I will wait to hear from you."
She kissed his cheek, inhaling the familiar spicy scent
of his cologne—a scent she associated with walks in the
garden, stories read while seated upon his lap, happy
memories she'd had while growing up.

"Remember, Margaret, no one is to know that I'm
here. I'll explain more the next time we meet. Until
then, you must trust me."

"I do, implicitly," she assured him, before exiting the
building.

Parker smiled and waved as the buggy departed,
feeling quite pleased with the way his first meeting with
his daughter had turned out. Margaret trusted him. He
laughed aloud at that, shutting the door behind him.
Poor, gullible Margaret. Still a daddy's girl.

He shook his head. She reminded him too much of
her mother. Margaret was like Phoebe had been when
he'd first met her: pretty, naive, soft spoken. Would
Margaret change into a shrewish harpy? he wondered.
Would she grow intolerant of her husband's infi-
delities? Was she as frigid as a block of ice when she
made love to Gallagher?

His laughter was mocking as he pulled a flask out of
the inside front pocket of his coat and took a swallow.
Margaret wouldn't have to worry about Gallagher
cheating on her, and she wouldn't have to worry about
making love with him much longer, because Gallagher
was going to be dead.

Standing sideways in front of the dressing table
mirror, dressed in her chemise and drawers, Margaret
placed her hands on her abdomen and smiled. She had

missed her last two monthly periods and was almost positive that she was pregnant.

Hugging herself, she giggled in childish anticipation, wondering what Chase was going to say when she told him. He would be back in a few days, and she couldn't wait to tell him the news that he was going to be a father. He would happy, of that she was certain. And proud! Men set a great store by such things. And he would make a wonderful father.

Catching a glimpse of the time on the mantel clock, she gasped. It was nearly eight o'clock, and Doc was expecting her to assist him with some minor surgery this morning.

Rushing over to her closet, she grabbed a serviceable cotton navy skirt and white blouse. She'd best hurry. It wouldn't do to keep Elvira Thornburg's bunions waiting. Giggling at the absurdity of such a thought, she dressed and hurried out the door.

Doc was just pulling up the shades of the pharmacy windows when she entered. "Morning, Doc. Isn't it a beautiful day?" She hung her shawl on the hook by the door and put on a clean, white apron.

"You're certainly in a euphoric state this morning. That husband of yours didn't happen to come home last evening, did he?" His smile was teasing.

She felt her cheeks warm and shook her head. "No, Chase is still in Yuma. I don't expect he'll be back before Saturday or Sunday." She followed Doc into the examination room, setting the leather instrument case he would need for Elvira's procedure out on the counter.

Doc eyed her suspiciously. "You've got a glow about you, Margaret. Is there something you want to tell me?"

275

She smiled. "Can't I ever keep a secret from you, Doc?"

Drawing his pipe from the back pocket of his trousers, he lit it, puffing slowly, waiting for her to confirm his suspicions.

The clouds of aromatic smoke drifting over Margaret's head turned her skin a sickly shade of green. Bile rose up in her throat. Rushing over to the far corner of the room, she grabbed the emesis basin and vomited the contents of her breakfast into it.

"I thought so," Doc said, chuckling. "No woman glows unless they're in love or unless they're with child." He handed her a cool cloth. "I already know you're in love, so that leaves . . ."

"You're too smart for your own good," she said, once she had recovered herself. "Please don't breathe a word of this to anyone. I want Chase to be surprised."

"My lips are sealed. But you'd best take some oat or chamomile tea for your nausea, else your mother and Lupe will know something's wrong."

"This is the first morning I've been truly sick. I've felt a bit queasy at times, but I've never vomited before."

"I'd like to reassure you that it will be the last, but I'm afraid you're in for several more weeks of this."

She grimaced, and he laughed aloud. "It's all part of the joys of motherhood. Once you're holding your new babe in your arms, you'll forget all the minor discomforts you've had to endure."

Her smile was ebullient. "I can't wait, Doc. It seems that everything in my life has suddenly turned perfect."

Removing his surgical instruments from their case, Doc placed them to soak in a solution of carbolic acid; a procedure which would disinfect them. "I sense that we're not just talking about Chase or the baby. Am I right?"

Margaret's face clouded with unease. Doc was a very perceptive individual; she should have realized that before shooting off her mouth. Lord! She was getting as bad as Alberta and Marion. "I . . . I can't say what's made me so happy, Doc, so please don't ask. I'd have to break a confidence, and I'm not willing to do that just yet."

"I won't press you, Margaret, but know that I'm here for you if you need me."

Tears filled her eyes as she crossed the room. Wrapping her arms about Doc's middle, she hugged him, feeling comforted by his presence. He'd always been there for her; he always would be. "I love you, Doc."

"Here, now," Doc said, his cheeks reddening in an uncharacteristic blush. "What's Elvira to think if she comes in here and sees a beautiful, young girl making over an old man like me? It would create the biggest scandal this town's ever seen."

Margaret brushed away her tears and laughed, releasing her hold on the older man. "The Widow Thornburg's had her sights set on you for years. I think she'd be jealous as all get out."

At that moment the door opened and the two hundred and fifty pound Widow Thornburg waddled into the examining room.

"Morning, William." Her voice lost its warmth as her gaze fell on Margaret. "Margaret."

Doc and Margaret exchanged knowing glances then burst out laughing, leaving a startled Elvira to wonder if perhaps they'd been secretly sipping the medicinal brandy.

Later that same afternoon, while Margaret was bent over the cookstove preparing a pot of chicken soup that she hoped would help alleviate her nausea, Lupe entered the kitchen, slamming the screen door behind her.

Startled by the noise, Margaret shrieked, spinning on her heel. Observing Lupe standing in the doorway, she breathed a deep sigh of relief.

"Lupe Diaz! You took ten years off my life. What on earth are you doing, sneaking in here like that?"

Lupe smiled apologetically. "Margarita, you must have been lost in thought. I enter this house many, many times each day. It has never frightened you before."

True, Margaret thought, but then, she'd never had so many secrets to contend with before. It was making her jumpier than hot grease on a griddle. "I'm sorry I snapped. I just have a lot on my mind."

"I have a message for you from your *padre.*"

"Ssh! Not so loud." She cast a nervous glance over her shoulder. "I heard Mama pacing upstairs a while ago. She's been getting out of her bed more frequently lately."

"That is good, no?"

Margaret shrugged. "It would be if I didn't have to keep Papa's presence a secret. I'm so afraid that she'll come downstairs unannounced and overhear us talking."

"I think the señora will lose what is left of her mind if she learns that your papa has returned."

"Shut the door, then we can talk."

278

Lupe closed the door leading into the front hall, then took a seat next to Margaret at the table.

"Mama would be devastated if she learned Papa had come back and did not want to see her. I believe, deep in her heart, she thinks he'll come for her one day. It's very sad."

"He will not come. My *madre* she say that it is very bad between the Señora and Señor Parker when he live here. They fight all the time. Mama say, he had many women. Your mama, she no like to . . . to make love with him."

Surprise siphoned the blood from Margaret's face. "Lupe! That can't be true. Papa would never have been unfaithful to Mama."

Lupe shrugged. "I'm just telling you what my mama told me. I don't think she would lie."

Margaret patted Lupe's hand. "I'm sorry. I didn't mean to imply that Isabel would lie. I'm just shocked to think that Papa would ever do such a thing."

"Men have their needs, Margarita. If they don't find what they're looking for at home, they go elsewhere."

"I suppose you're right," Margaret replied absently, not quite ready to believe that Isabel Diaz had her facts correct. Surely, the former housekeeper was mistaken. After all, Isabel and Mama had never liked each other. And how on earth would Isabel have been privy to such information?

"It is all in the past anyway, Margarita. There is no sense in worrying about what happened many years ago. What you need to worry about is now. I have another message from your *padre*. He wishes to see you again."

"When?"

"This evening. Sandy is to take you down by the river. He will meet you there."

"The river? But that's out in the open. What if someone should see us?"

Lupe slapped her forehead. "Margarita, you are making both of us crazy. It will be dark. Who will be out by the river after dark?"

Margaret thought of the few times she and Chase had gone there to relive their first encounter, but she wasn't going to mention that to Lupe. "I guess you're right," she conceded reluctantly.

It was pitch black out when the buggy carrying Margaret and Sandy finally reached its destination. Sandy had been quiet and introspective, hardly saying a word the entire journey there. There had been no repeat of their first encounter—no ardent looks or familiar clutches. He had been reserved and respectful and Margaret had been both relieved and grateful.

Spying her father standing beneath a tall cotton-wood tree at the edge of the riverbank, Margaret strode forward, holding out her hands in greeting. "Hello, Papa, it's nice to see you again."

Jonathan Parker smiled warmly, kissed his daughter on the cheek, then led her to a fallen log that he'd been using for a seat. "Sit down, Margaret. I'm glad you were able to come tonight."

She smiled. "Of course, I came. Did you think I wouldn't?"

"I was hoping you would. There are things that I need to discuss with you. Things that will explain my reasons for leaving like I did."

280

Margaret's heart drummed loud in her ears. "What kind of things?"

"First, I just want to say that you were never the reason for my sudden departure. I've always held a special place in my heart for you, Margaret. And though your mother and I did not get along well, I never lost my love and deep abiding affection for you."

Margaret wiped at her eyes with the hem of her skirt. "Nor I you, Papa. I always knew that you'd come back some day."

Parker's eyes widened at her conviction, but he didn't comment on it, saying instead, "What I have to tell you may cause you more pain. I didn't come back to hurt you, my dear. If you'd rather not know the entire truth, I can leave now and never return."

Her head jerked up. "Leave? You would leave me again?"

"My dear, I know that you are a happily married woman. But what I didn't know was the name of the man whom you married. Once I found out, I have agonized over whether or not to confide in you."

Margaret's forehead wrinkled in confusion. "Chase? What you're going to tell me has something to do with my husband, Chase Gallagher?"

He leaned heavily on the cane before him and sighed. "Margaret, your husband is the main reason I have not been able to come home."

"But I've only known Chase a short time. We've only been married three months. How could he have prevented you from coming home? I know once he meets you he will welcome your return as I do."

Taking her hand, he held it firmly in his grasp. "I must start at the beginning, so that you can understand

281

the entire sequence of events."

The croaking of the bullfrogs seemed to keep pace with the pounding of Margaret's heart. She nodded mutely, allowing him to continue.

"As I already told you, Phoebe was always wanting more than I could give her. She had highfalutin ideas. Only the best was good enough for her. The salary I earned while working as a courier for the bank was small, hardly enough to keep your mother in the style she preferred."

"I don't understand."

"I embezzled a small amount of money from a bank in St. Louis. In my position as a courier, it was easy to remove the money from the courier's pouch and pocket it. I thought if I had the extra funds, it would make your mother happy and my life a little easier."

"You stole?" There was accusation, disbelief in the question.

"I'm not proud of it, Margaret. Looking back, I see that what I did was wrong. It's a crime that's haunted me for the past eighteen years."

Margaret pushed herself to her feet and walked to the river's edge, her father following. The water slapped against the bank, then receded in a soothing motion. But Margaret's nerves were too frayed at the moment to be soothed. "I don't know what to say."

"Say that you'll forgive an old man for his foolish indiscretion."

She turned back to face him. "But what of Chase? You said he was involved."

"Your husband is a United States marshal, appointed by the president of these United States. He's empowered by law to travel all over the country, hunting down wanted criminals. He's been hunting me for the past eighteen years."

She gasped. "No! I don't believe you."

He grasped her shoulders, shaking her gently, as if he could jar the truth into her. "Chase Gallagher wants me very badly, Margaret. I'm the one criminal that has eluded him all these years. It's a black mark on his record. He would do anything to get his hands on me." He let the full import of his words sink in, noting the grief on her face when they did.

"Including, marrying your daughter?"

"I never dreamed he would go this far. Never thought he would use an innocent woman."

She shook her head in denial; her words were thick with tears when she spoke. "No! Chase loves me. I know he does." Why then did her father's words penetrate her soul so deeply? Why did niggling doubts eat slowly at her newly found joy?

"Perhaps he does. Perhaps he's changed. Perhaps this is all a mistake and I'm grievously wrong."

Her mind traveled quickly over all their past conversations when Chase had inquired innocently about her father. Her hand flew up to push back the bitter bile that rose to her throat. Turning on her heel, she fled from the look of pity on her father's face—fled from the truth that stared at her, so ugly and condemning: Chase had married her for revenge.

Chapter Twenty-One

Kneeling between the neat rows of carrots and cucumbers, Margaret scraped at the dirt with her fingers to loosen the weeds that had grown amidst the vegetables. The straw bonnet she wore did little to shade her from the morning sun, which was already near its zenith. Beads of perspiration dripped from her brow, mixing with the tears that fell from her eyes.

She had come out to her garden at first light to work out the demons that plagued her soul. But no matter how hard she hoed, how many weeds she pulled, she couldn't exorcise the bitterness that pervaded her body at the knowledge that Chase had betrayed her.

She loved him. She thought he loved her.

How could he have done such a despicable thing? To use her—marry her—just to get close to her father. It was unconscionable; it was vile.

She pounded the ground with her fist, shaking her head in utter desolation. Their love—their marriage—had been a lie, a cruel hoax, and she'd been the butt of it.

Reaching into her pocket to retrieve the telegram that was waiting for her upon her return last night, she reread it:

Darlin', I'll be home sometime Sunday evening. I've missed you like crazy. Be ready and waiting for me. I've got a powerful hunger. Chase.

Holding it up in front of her face, she smothered her wail of misery, then wiping her eyes on the edge of her apron, she forced herself under control. Chase was coming home . . . tonight. She must steel herself for what was to come. He must never suspect that she'd been to see her father; he would arrest him, maybe even harm him.

Chase had kept her father from her for eight years, but he wouldn't keep him away any longer. She would continue to visit Papa, spend his last remaining days with him, and Chase would never be the wiser. She would do what she had to to protect Jonathan Parker. She would deceive her husband, as he had deceived her, and she would get her revenge.

For like the separation she and her father had been forced to endure, Chase would never know the joy of having his child—never experience the thrill of holding his son or daughter to his breast.

Chase had married her for revenge. Well, two could play that game. She would exact her own retribution for his deception. She would use him, as he had used her, then she would cast him from her heart—from her mind—from the very depths of her soul . . . forever.

* * *

The sun had disappeared into the horizon by the time Chase rode Lucifer into the livery stable and deposited the travel-weary horse with Mr. Martin, the proprietor.

Hoisting the well-worn leather saddlebags over his left shoulder, he bid his farewells to the lanky man, then began the short walk home.

The streets were pretty much deserted, most folks having retired to their homes for supper. An idea that sounded extremely appealing to Chase at the moment whose stomach was growling its concurrence. He just hoped Maggie had fixed his favorite: chicken and dumplings. That woman knew her way around the kitchen—he smiled to himself—and the bedroom. He picked up his pace as the two-story house came into view.

God, he was glad to be home. He had missed Maggie while he was gone to the degree that he thought he might even be able to tolerate her mother for a few days.

Patting the pouch of his saddlebags, he felt for the present he had purchased for his bride, relieved to find that the lovely pair of pearl earrings still rested inside.

They weren't fake either, but genuine pearls he had bought off a traveling drummer. A man by the name of Mr. Peacock whom he had just spent the last two days traveling with. They'd parted on the trail, the drummer deciding he could do a more profitable business in the bustling community of Tucson.

As Chase pushed open the gate, which now hung straight on its hinges—he was proud to note—a snorting, grunting sound assailed him. Evelyn sped straight for him on her short, stubby legs.

"Hello, girl," he said, bending over to scratch the hog behind her left ear. "Did you miss me?" He glanced up quickly at the door and windows, making sure no one had observed his affection toward the animal. He didn't want Maggie to think the annoying creature had won him over completely. Evelyn nuzzled his boot and snorted again, indicating she had.

Entering the house, he dropped his bags by the door and entered the kitchen, pleased to find Maggie in the midst of dinner preparations. He snuck up behind her, planting a kiss on the back of her neck. "Hello, darlin'."

Startled, Maggie yelped as the knife she was using cut straight into her thumb. She immediately plunged her hand into the basin of cool water in the sink.

Chase stepped back, horrified at what he'd caused her to do. "Darlin', I'm sorry. I didn't mean to scare you." Grabbing a clean dish towel, he handed it to her, feeling like a damn fool.

Margaret stalled as long as possible, then finally turned to face him. The sight of Chase's smile, so achingly familiar, brought a sharp pang to her breast. He smelled of horse, leather, and bay rum, and the scents stimulated rather than repulsed her. Grabbing a wad of gauze from the top shelf of the kitchen cupboard, she wrapped it around her thumb, forcing a small smile to her lips. "How was your trip?"

"Damn the trip! Don't I get a kiss?"

Panic assailed her momentarily until she remembered the stakes she was playing for. "Of course."

He drew her into his arms then, plying her lips with a kiss that contained all his pent-up frustrations and desires. The feel of those lips, so warm, so persuasive, rendered Margaret weak-kneed. Finally, unable to stand the torment he was inflicting a moment longer, she broke the contact, saying, "I'd best get your supper on the table. You must be hungry." She retreated to the safety of her stove, while Chase, casting her an uncertain smile, removed himself upstairs to wash.

He returned a few minutes later, carrying a small package wrapped in white paper and tied with string. Handing it to her, he smiled. "This is for you."

She stared at his hand, at the box, and didn't want to feel the excitement that blossomed in her breast. He'd brought her a present. Tears rushed to her eyes, but she blinked them away. This wasn't going to be easy. Chase wasn't going to make what she had to do easy.

"Thank you," she said softly, unwrapping the box and opening it. Her eyes widened at the beautiful gold and pearl earrings. "They're lovely." Having never seen such an exquisite piece of jewelry, she held them up to the light of the lamp, admiring their perfection before replacing them in their bed of red satin.

"Do you really like them?"

"Oh, yes! I've never had such a wonderful present before." About to lean over and kiss him, she caught herself just in time. Setting the package down on the table, she thanked him again. "Why don't you sit down; supper's ready."

Casting her a quizzical glance, Chase said nothing, doing as she requested.

Margaret thought the meal would never end. The tender chicken and moist dumplings stuck in her throat like balls of cotton as she listened to Chase making small talk about his trip, all the while wondering how he could have deceived her like he did, wondering, too, why he would bring her presents and pretend to love her.

"I've got to go over to the jail; make sure everything is okay," he said, wiping his mouth on the linen napkin when he'd finished his meal. "Why don't you go on upstairs and wait for me." His grin was suggestive. "I'll only be a minute."

Margaret nodded, grateful for the small reprieve she was receiving as she watched Chase depart. How on earth was she going to lie in Chase's arms and pretend nothing had happened? How was she going to resist the pleasure she knew awaited her?

With a grim purpose in mind, she cleaned up the dishes as quickly as she could and climbed the stairs to her bedroom. Stripping out of her clothes, she donned her most concealing nightdress, turned off the lamp and slid beneath the covers to wait.

Thirty minutes passed before Chase's cheerful whistle played along her nerve endings like an instrument out of tune. The insistent sound of his boots hitting the treads as he mounted the stairs made her heart beat loud in her ears. Squeezing her eyes shut, she forced herself to take deep, even breaths. When she heard the door open, she stiffened.

"Maggie?" Chase frowned into the lightless room, closing the door quietly behind him. "Maggie, are you awake?" The room was pitch black as he stumbled in the darkness, feeling his way across the room to the bed. Staring down at the inert form beneath the covers, his frowned deepened: Maggie was asleep.

He let out a string of curses under his breath. Why the hell hadn't he waited until tomorrow to check on the jail? Nothing important had happened anyway.

Now he was doomed to spend the entire night with a warm woman by his side in a state of unfilled desire.

He didn't have the heart to wake her. She was sleeping so soundly, she must have been exhausted. Pulling off his boots, he shed his clothes, climbing into the soft feather mattress. Pulling Maggie's backside up against his chest, he drew the covers up and over them. Tonight was going to be pure torture, but he couldn't bear to be without her one more second.

Margaret was having similar thoughts as she lay stiff as a corpse nestled up against her husband's warm, muscled chest. Her eyes eased open and she stared straight ahead into the black velvet night that enveloped them. When Chase's hand came around to cup the fullness of her breast, she bit her lip to keep from moaning in pleasure.

It was going to be a long night . . . a very long night.

"You goin' to tell me about your trip to Yuma, or are you just going sit there staring at that plate of steak and eggs?"

Chase glanced up, smiling apologetically at Wooley who was seated across from him in the dining room of Hobson's Hotel. They were sharing an early morning breakfast, Chase having decided to let Margaret sleep so that she would be fully rested for the evening ahead.

Last night had been a disappointment. His homecoming was not quite what he had expected. True, Margaret did seem to like the present he had brought her, but the usual excitement and animation in her response was missing. Something was wrong, but he couldn't put his finger on it.

"Sorry," he finally replied. "Guess I'm just tired. It was a long ride."

Wooley sipped thoughtfully on his coffee. The marshal's thoughts were definitely not on his work. "And the informant? Did he have anything new to add about the bank robbery?"

Chase's features hardened in anger. "There was no informant. Sean Clements thought I was out of my mind when I showed up demanding to see the prisoner. He claims he never sent any telegram."

Wooley whistled and shook his head. "So you was sent on a wild-goose chase."

"Yeah. Now all I've got to do is figure out why."

"There ain't been no trouble here to speak of. A bunch of cowboys from the Bar H wandered in, drunker than a bachelor on the night before his weddin'. They caused a bit of a ruckus when Sam wouldn't serve them any more liquor, but they left peaceably. Other than that, it's been quieter than a cemetery at midnight."

"Have you noticed anyone new in town? Someone that might not be from around here?" If Parker's gang was close by, he'd be sending in one or two of his men to scout out the place.

Wooley scratched his whiskered chin. "Nope." He shook his head. "Not unless you count that sandy-haired cowboy. You know, the one you beat in the shooting match. He's been hanging around quite a bit. I've seen him with Miss Margaret's housekeeper, Lupe, a time or two. They seemed pretty close, if you know what I mean."

Chase frowned. Loomis was the cowboy's name. And Chase had little use for him, especially after the man had accused him of cheating during the shooting match. Good thing Maggie and Tom had been there to calm him down, or he would have filled Loomis's thick skull with lead. "He claims to work for the Bar H, doesn't he?"

"Yup. But it seems like he does more drinking and gambling than cowpunching."

Gulping down the last of his coffee, Chase wiped his mouth with his napkin, pushing back his chair. "Check it out, Wooley. Ride out to the Bar H and speak with Harley Hawkins. If Loomis is employed there, Harley'll know."

"Where you going? You ain't even finished your breakfast?"

Pushing the plate of half-eaten steak across the table, a distracted look on his face, Chase said, "You finish it for me. I'm going home for a few minutes. I have some questions that need answering."

Entering his house a few minutes later, Chase was pleased to discover both Margaret and Lupe seated at the kitchen table, having a cup of coffee.

"Morning, ladies. Any of that coffee left?"

Lupe rose, returning a moment later with a steaming mug of the dark brown liquid. She was about to excuse herself, but Chase halted her departure.

"Don't go just yet, Lupe. I've got a couple of questions to ask you."

"Is there a problem, Señor Gallagher?" Lupe asked, staring at him quizzically, resuming her seat.

"What do you know about a man named Loomis?"

Lupe swallowed, casting a nervous glance in Margaret's direction. "Loomis? Do you mean Sandy Loomis?"

Chase leaned back in his chair, sipping thoughtfully on his coffee. He hadn't missed the way Lupe's hands fidgeted nervously with the spoon on the table. "That's right. Wooley tells me that you two are acquainted."

"*Sí*. Sandy and I have been seeing each other. We are to be married."

Chase's eyes widened at that remark. Loomis didn't seem the type of man who'd relish giving up his freedom to settle down. He turned his attention on his wife. "You met this Loomis fella, Maggie?" he asked, noting how she lowered her eyes rather than meet his gaze.

"Only once. He . . . he came to pick Lupe up. He seemed a nice sort."

"Why do you ask so many questions about Sandy, Marshal? Has he done something wrong?"

Placing his palms flat on the table, Chase pushed himself to his feet. "I always make it my business to investigate the new people in town, Lupe. I don't like any surprises."

"You didn't do much investigating when it came to Laurette Appleton," Margaret snapped. "You certainly welcomed her with open arms."

Chase grinned, leaning over to place a kiss on her cheek. "Have I been neglecting you, darlin'? You're getting a mite high-strung again."

Margaret bolted to her feet, casting Chase a furious look. "I'll thank you to keep your vulgar remarks to yourself, Chase Gallagher. I'm no longer interested in hearing them." With that, she spun on her heel and stormed from the room.

"Maggie, wait!" he shouted. But it was too late. She was gone. Scratching his head in confusion, he turned his attention back to the housekeeper, whose expression was just as stunned as his own. "Is there some problem I'm not aware of, Lupe? Has Phoebe been picking on Maggie again?"

"No, señor, not that I know of."

He shook his head. "Women!" he said. Who could figure them out?

Grabbing his hat, he shoved it on his head and slammed out the door, never seeing the tear-stained face of the woman who stared after him from the upstairs bedroom window.

Chapter Twenty-Two

"That's the third report of trouble in about as many days," Wooley advised Chase. "First, Harley reported ten head of cattle missing, then Sam discovered his strongbox busted and his cash gone this morning. Now, Mrs. Perkins claims her store's been broke into." The deputy scratched his head. "It don't seem logical that we've had so much trouble lately."

Seated on the sidewalk in front of the jail, Chase leaned his chair back against the brick wall, puffing repeatedly on his cigarette as he listened to Wooley recount all the problems that had plagued the quiet little town recently.

Observing the inhabitants of Purgatory going about their normal afternoon routines, he waved at Lyle Wallace who was sweeping and the sidewalk in front of his barbershop across the street, and smiled at the look of outrage on Esther Perkins's face as she shooed the Simmons boys out of her store for the second time that day. Glancing down the street toward the saloon, he caught sight of Myra Cummings who was yanking her son Tommy out of the clutches of a petite blonde.

Everything looked normal; but it wasn't. Things were happening in Purgatory. There'd been a rash of robberies, shootings, and the like since he'd returned from Yuma, and it didn't take a Pinkerton detective to figure out who was behind the trouble.

"I suspect Parker's the cause for all of our problems," Chase finally replied. "But there's no way to prove it. I'm goin' purely on gut instinct."

Wooley spit a stream of tobacco juice, narrowly missing Chase's boot and smiled apologetically before replying, "Parker. Now that seems logical."

Unfortunately, the problems that plagued Purgatory at the moment seemed trivial compared to the difficulties he was facing at home, Chase thought, frowning. Nothing seemed logical about the way Maggie had been behaving since his return. She'd practically ignored him—had gone out of her way to avoid him whenever possible. They'd hardly exchanged more than polite pleasantries. Maggie had been touchier than a bitch with a new litter of pups.

Something clicked in Chase's brain and he rocked forward, feeling stunned, as if he'd just been struck by a thunderbolt of lightning. *A new litter of pups.* Maggie might be pregnant. That would account for her moodiness. Shit! It had to be something like that. He hadn't made love to her in over a week and that just wasn't normal.

Rising to his feet, he stared down at Wooley, who was engrossed in the latest edition of the *Arizona Star*. Wooley had always shown a special interest in Maggie. Perhaps he'd sensed something—heard something that might account for her strange demeanor.

Chase asked, "Wooley, have you noticed anything odd about Maggie's behavior?"

Lowering the paper, Wooley stared at the anxious expression on Chase's face and wondered at the cause of it. He shook his head. "Can't say that I have . . . except maybe that she's been a mite nervous lately. Sort of on edge. I thought maybe . . ." He paused, a red blush covering his whiskered cheeks. "When Concita acts out of sorts, it's usually because of female trouble."

Chase's eyes widened in understanding. He chuckled and chided himself for being an insensitive fool. Why hadn't he figured that out? Maggie was probably having her monthly. That would account for her moods and the fact that she didn't want to be touched.

Mentally calculating the days since he'd been home, he grinned. If his figuring was correct, Maggie should be back to normal by tomorrow.

"I take it you figured out what her problem is?" Wooley remarked, a teasing twinkle in his eyes.

Chase felt the heat creep up his neck. Kicking the legs of Wooley's chair so that the chair and Wooley toppled forward, he ordered, "Get up and over to Mrs. Perkins's place." He smiled at the annoyed expression on the older man's face when Wooley attempted to right himself. "I'm going to ride out to the Bar H. Hawkins may be back from Tombstone. I want to question him about Loomis."

"I told you, Chase, Charlie Dominguez, Hawkins's foreman, says that Loomis never worked there. And Charlie ought to know, since he's the one that does the hirin' and firin'."

"Just the same, Harley may have heard something. He's been at the Cattlemen's Association meeting. If more than one rancher's been rustled, Hawkins will know of it." And besides, he added to himself, it was time he scouted the area. One of Parker's men might not be as careful or clever as Parker himself would be. There may be a sign, a clue, as to the whereabouts of their hideout.

Bidding Wooley good-bye, Chase stepped off the sidewalk, heading in the direction of the livery.

Margaret caught sight of Chase just as he stepped off the sidewalk. He was directly across the street from where she stood in front of Laurette Appleton's millinery shop, and it was providence that he hadn't spotted her yet. Turning quickly, she pretended to study the vast array of hats so attractively displayed in the window. Through the reflection in the glass, she observed Chase rounding the side of the building and breathed a sigh of relief.

Avoiding him the past few days hadn't been easy, especially at night in the small confines of their bed when it had taken every ounce of her strength not to succumb to her body's desires. She had used every excuse imaginable to avoid intimacy with him: headaches, tiredness, and last night, she had purposely picked a fight.

How much longer could they go on like this? What would happen when he no longer accepted her excuses and forced the issue of their lovemaking?

Sighing deeply, she willed the burning behind her eyelids to cease, willed the ache surrounding her heart to stop, and proceeded the rest of the way to Fraser's Mercantile.

The bell over the front door tinkled merrily, in direct contrast to Margaret's mood, as she entered the store, drawing Betsy's attention away from the colorful bolts of material that she was stacking on the shelf.

"Why, Margaret, how nice to see you. It's been ages. Have you come to shop or just visit?"

Margaret fidgeted nervously with the strings of her reticule. To be perfectly honest, she wasn't sure why she had come; she just knew she needed to see a friendly face. "I thought if you weren't too busy, we might have a cup of tea."

"What a splendid idea!" Betsy smiled widely, stepping carefully down off the stool. "I'm not busy at all. In fact, it's been quieter than a deserted mine shaft in here. Tom's gone to Tucson to pick up the new plow that Willis Ferguson ordered, and there hasn't been a customer since Bertie came in this morning to purchase twenty yards of green satin material. Bertie aims to get a head start on her Christmas dress this year, or so she claims. Says she's planning to throw a gala party this Christmas season."

"Twenty yards?" Even with Margaret's limited knowledge of sewing, she knew that it didn't take twenty yards of material to sew a dress.

"I expect she'll need every bit of it to make a gown big enough to fit her. I swear, Bertie's gained even more weight since the Fourth of July rodeo . . . and she's not even pregnant." Betsy patted her increased girth and giggled. "At least some of us have an excuse, right?"

Margaret's face paled as white as the crisp, cotton blouse she wore. "What?"

The blue eyes narrowed suspiciously. "I thought I was speaking about myself, but maybe I wasn't." Giving Margaret's form a cursory once-over, Betsy added, "Is there something you want to tell me?"

At Betsy's prodding, Margaret burst into tears, covering her face with her hands, sobbing piteously into them. Growing instantly alarmed, Betsy rushed forward to drape her arm around her best friend's shoulder.

"Mercy me! Whatever is the matter?" Guiding Margaret to the table and two chairs that stood in the far corner of the room, Betsy ordered her to sit. "I'll be back in a moment."

Before Margaret had time to dry her eyes, Betsy had pulled down the shades at the front window, hung the Closed sign on the door and locked it.

"There, now we won't be disturbed," Betsy said, seating herself next to Margaret. "Now, tell me what's upset you so. Is it Chase? Have you two had a fight?"

Betsy's innocent questions only caused Margaret to start crying again, which prompted Betsy to rise once more and retrieve a bottle of sherry and two glasses from the back room. Setting them on the table, she poured a generous amount of liquor into each glass. "Drink this," she ordered, placing the glass in Margaret's hands. "It's the best cure I know for the weeps. And Lord knows, since I've been carryin' this baby, I've had my share of them."

"Tha . . . thank you," Margaret sobbed, taking a small sip of the amber liquid. The sweet liquor warmed her, making her feel a little better.

Betsy waited a moment for Margaret to compose herself, then said, "We've been friends a long time, Margaret. I'd like to think that you could confide in me, if you needed to."

"Oh, Betsy, everything is such a mess. Nothing has turned out like I expected."

"Has Chase mistreated you? I can have Tom speak to him if that's the case."

Margaret's eyes rounded in horror. "You mustn't breathe a word of this to Tom. He would go straight to Chase."

Betsy's brow furrowed in confusion. "I don't understand any of this, Margaret. Chase doesn't know that you two have had a disagreement?"

Shaking her head, Margaret reached out, clasping her friend's hands, which she noted were slightly swollen. She'd been so distracted with her own problems, of late, she hadn't had the presence of mind to check on Betsy's pregnancy. "Is everything okay with the baby? Your fingers and hands look a little puffy."

"Don't change the subject on me, Margaret. You're good at evasive tactics, but they won't work this time. Tell me what's wrong."

Margaret heaved a deep sigh. "Chase has deceived me."

Betsy gasped, her hand flying to her throat. "With another woman?"

"No. Nothing like that. I thought he cared for me, loved me, but I've discovered that he married me to seek revenge."

"Margaret," Betsy chided softly, "I know Chase loves you. One only has to look at the man to know that."

"No!" Margaret shook her head emphatically. "He pretended to love me, to care for me, because . . ." She paused, uncertain if she should confide in Betsy. As good a friend as Betsy was, she wasn't known for her discretion.

"Because?"

"If I confide in you, you must swear on the life of your unborn child that you will never reveal what I'm about to tell you to anyone."

"Of course, I swear. I may have a big mouth, but I know when to keep it shut."

Despite herself, the corners of Margaret's lips twitched.

"See . . . I've made you smile. Now, tell me what all this is about."

Taking a deep breath and another swallow of the sherry, Margaret proceeded to tell Betsy of her father's visit and the truth regarding her marriage to Chase. Betsy listened intently to everything Margaret said, then when the narrative was finished, she leaned back in her chair and wagged her head, a disgusted look upon her face.

"I can't believe you would actually think that Chase is so shallow he would marry you for revenge. He loves you, Margaret. Which is a lot more than I can say for that father of yours." Margaret stiffened, which prompted Betsy to add, "I know you love your father. You should; he's your flesh and blood. But don't be blinded to his faults. He left you and your mother without a thought to your welfare.

"Look what he's done to your mother—look what he's doing to you. How can you be so sure that he's telling the truth? Maybe he's lied to cover his own hide—to make himself look better in your eyes."

Margaret lifted her chin, meeting Betsy's gaze head-on. "I just know. Besides, why should he lie? What good would it do him, now? He's dying."

Betsy thought long and hard, but had no reasonable

explanation for Jonathan Parker's motives; she only knew that she didn't trust him—had never trusted him, even as a child. But she also knew that Margaret did, and therein lay the problem. "I don't know what Jonathan Parker is up to . . . why he's come back. I only know that Chase loves you. And if you throw that love away, you'll be making the biggest mistake of your life."

Despair clouded Margaret's eyes. "I've already made the biggest mistake," she said, barely above a whisper. "I'm pregnant."

Betsy's eyes lit with pleasure and she smiled. "That's wonderful!"

"Is it? I can't stay with Chase now that I know why he married me. I'll have to raise the child alone."

"I take it that Chase doesn't know about the baby."

"He must never know, Betsy. You must never tell a soul."

"But he's bound to find out sooner or later. You can't hide a thing like that. Why, when he holds you in his arms . . ." Betsy halted, noting the crimson blush covering Margaret's cheeks. "You don't mean to tell me that you've locked him out of your bedroom?"

"Not in so many words. But I have been avoiding him."

"Girl, have you lost whatever sense you once had? That in itself is reason enough for Chase to divorce you. Think of your baby. Do you want it branded a bastard?"

Margaret bit her lower lip, shaking her head. "I don't know what I want. I'm so confused."

Pushing her bulk out of the chair, Betsy came to stand behind Margaret, placing her hands on her shoulders, kneading them gently. "I'll do what I can to help because I'm your friend. But know this, Margaret, Chase is not the one at fault here. If you ruin your marriage, your chance at happiness, the blame must rest squarely on your shoulders. A man like Chase comes along only once in a lifetime. Remember that before you make any decisions that you'll regret."

Margaret nodded mutely, the tears in her throat too thick to allow the words to come out. Betsy spoke what she believed to be the truth. But what was the truth? Was her father lying to protect himself? Had she accused Chase unjustly, even if it was only in her own mind? She needed to confront Chase, make him tell her that their marriage wasn't based on lies. But how could she? To do so would endanger her father's life.

She was trapped. Trapped by the attachment she had for her father—trapped by the all-consuming passion she had, would always have, for one man. She was a prisoner of her own feelings, and there was no escape.

Seated in the large, comfortable red leather wing chair in Harley Hawkins's office, Chase waited impatiently for the owner of the Bar H to make an appearance. He had been ushered into the study over thirty minutes ago by Charlie Dominguez, foreman of the ranch. The big burly Mexican *vaquero* had confirmed Wooley's contention that Sandy Loomis had never worked for the Bar H.

It seemed as though the investigation on Parker was running into a dead end. Except for the fact that Loomis had lied about his employment, there was nothing to connect him with Parker—nothing except Chase's instincts.

"Sorry to keep you waiting, Marshal, but my prize heifer's in labor and I was needed out at the barn," Harley Hawkins said upon entering. He took a seat behind the massive oak desk and lit a cigar, offering Chase one.

"No thanks," Chase replied, noting the expensive cut of the man's jacket and wondering if he had worn such fancy duds to check on a cow. Pulling his pouch of tobacco and papers out of his inside coat pocket, Chase rolled himself a cigarette and lit it.

"Charlie said you wished to speak to me about one of my hands."

"Actually, your foreman has already cleared up that piece of the puzzle. What I'm really interested in finding out is whether or not you've had any more cows rustled, and if you've heard similar complaints from some of the other ranchers who were at the Cattlemen's Association meeting. If there's a gang of rustlers operating in this area, I want to put a stop to it."

Leaning back in his chair, Harley puffed contentedly on his cigar before folding his hands over his corpulent stomach. The afternoon sun shone in through the double-hung windows of the office, dancing brightly off the gray of his hair and mustache. The owner of the Bar H looked to be a man whose years were catching up with him; Chase figured him to be pushing sixty, maybe even sixty-five.

"Several of the ranches have been hit, but the losses have been small, usually five or six head," Harley responded. "It doesn't appear to be a major operation, and the men doing the rustling seem inexperienced, not

305

at all professional. Several cows and calves have been deliberately shot." He shook his head, his distaste for the deed clearly etched on his face. "A man earning his living by selling stolen cattle would never cut into his profits like that."

Chase pondered the older man's words for a moment, then asked, "So you think we're dealing with a bunch of amateurs?"

Hawkins nodded. "One of my men spotted three men the day before yesterday on the northern-most end of my property. They were camped out in the open, like they didn't have a care in the world. Dusty was by himself, so he thought it best to ride for help. When he and several of my men arrived, the three trespassers were gone."

"Any descriptions?"

"As a matter of fact, Dusty reported that one of the men was unusually large." Harley chuckled. "'Like a giant grizzly,' was how Dusty described him."

Chase's eyes narrowed. "Bear Donaldson," he muttered under his breath.

"You have an idea who this man is?"

Chase unfolded himself from the chair, pushing himself to his feet. "I've got my suspicions, and I'd appreciate it if you'd keep me informed about anything else that may come up." Holding out his hand, he shook the older man's hand.

"Sure thing, Marshal. Nothing sickens me more than a man who would steal another man's cows."

Chase's eyes hardened into chips of ice, the look on his face so feral it caused Harley to shudder inwardly. "Only a man who would kill another human being."

Puffing thoughtfully on his cigar, Harley watched

the marshal depart, shaking his head. Chase Gallagher was a man with a mission, if ever he saw one. And he didn't think his mission just involved catching a bunch of two-bit cattle rustlers. No sir! Harley had lived too long—seen too much—to believe that. The marshal of Purgatory had one thing on his mind. He'd seen that murderous gleam in his eyes when he'd talked of one human being killing another.

A shiver of apprehension ran up his spine as he gazed out the window to observe the lone rider atop the big black stallion. "Vengeance is mine, sayeth the Lord," he whispered. But vengeance wasn't the Lord's this time; it was Chase Gallagher's.

Chapter Twenty-Three

The following morning found Chase rummaging through the bottom drawer of his dresser. Margaret was nowhere to be found, and he needed to find a clean shirt before his meeting with Sandy Loomis this morning. He intended to interrogate the cowboy, who he knew to be staying at Hobson's Hotel, before ruling him out as an accomplice of Parker's.

"Son of a bitch!" he cursed, pulling out a garment that he thought to be a shirt, only to discover that it was actually one of Maggie's blouses. Staring at it, he held the white cotton fabric to his nose, breathing in the scent of lavender. His gut twitched. Christ, Maggie, what was wrong? What had he done? he asked himself silently, refolding the blouse.

As he went to return it to its rightful resting place in the drawer, he spotted an envelope. His brow wrinkled in confusion. Why would Maggie have stuck an envelope in the bottom drawer of the dresser beneath her clothing? he wondered. He couldn't remember her mentioning that she'd been corresponding with anyone. Curiosity, long a part of his nature, rose to the forefront, and he couldn't resist taking a gander. Removing the piece of paper from the envelope, he began to read: "My darling daughter, . . ."

Disbelief then anger rushed through him like a freight train out of control. He shook with suppressed rage. Parker. He knew it. That goddamn bastard had been in touch with Maggie. Reading further, he grew more incensed to discover that Maggie had actually met with her father, probably more than once.

Crumbling the note in his hand, he took deep breaths, trying to get his anger under control. This explained a lot of things. Why Maggie had been avoiding him for one. There was no telling what filthy lies that bastard had told her. Had she believed him? he wondered. She'd certainly gone out of her way to keep Parker's presence from him. A feeling of betrayal swept over him. Why hadn't she confided in him? Trusted him? He was her husband for Christ's sake.

Shoving the note into the pocket of his trousers, Chase yanked a shirt from the drawer. He would confront her—get to the bottom of things. Maggie might be Jack Parker's daughter, but she was *his* wife. And if there was one thing he wouldn't tolerate, it was disloyalty. A man should be able to expect devotion—fidelity from the woman he loved. And besides, Jack Parker was a dead man.

"Are all the supplies in order, Margaret?"

Margaret turned at the sound of Doc's voice to find

309

him standing right behind her. She'd been inventorying the medical supplies while Doc sutured up the laceration on Chad Simmons's leg.

She nodded. "I've just finished. We need to order more laudanum, and we're getting low on tincture of iodine."

"I'll see to it," he replied, filling the basin with water to scrub his hands. "The Simmons boy is fine. I sent him home to rest. I'm sure he won't mind missing a day or two of school till his leg begins to heal."

Knowing how fond the Simmons boys were of school, Margaret smiled. "I'm sure Chad'll . . ."

"Margaret!" Chase's voice boomed through the closed door, causing Margaret's eyes to widen. She swallowed, exchanging a worried look with Doc when the door was thrown open a second later and Chase entered, looking angrier than she had ever seen him.

"Margaret, I need to speak with you." Chase nodded at Doc, who, after taking one look at the menacing expression on Chase's face, was astute enough to excuse himself and move into the pharmacy.

Indignation sparked in Margaret's eyes at Chase's high-handedness. "How dare you barge in here like this? This is my place of employment, and I'll thank you to keep a civil tongue in your head."

A cold mask blanketed Chase's features. Striding forward, he grabbed onto her wrist, yanking her toward the door. "We're going home. We have things to discuss."

A tight knot of fear settled in Margaret's stomach. Chase was going to force the issue of their lovemaking. She knew she'd been foolish to try and withhold his marital rights. "Let go of me!" she cried, trying to pull her hand out of his grasp. "You're hurting me!"

A momentary look of regret passed over his face at her admission. "No more than you've hurt me." Disregarding her protestations, he dragged her from the building and into the street.

Margaret was mortified to discover that their actions were being observed by several of the shopkeepers who were just opening up for the day's business. Nodding at Esther, who stared at her with mouth agape, she felt her cheeks burn in humiliation. "Let go of me," she said through clenched teeth. "You're making a spectacle of yourself, as well as of me."

Ignoring her pleas, Chase continued to march down the main street of town, pulling his errant wife behind him. When they finally reached their house, he kicked open the gate, giving no thought to the hours he'd spent fixing it, or caring that it now hung lopsided, on only one hinge again.

Pulling open the screen door, he hauled Margaret up the stairs, past a startled Lupe who was just returning from bringing Phoebe her breakfast.

"Margarita, what is wrong?"

"Stay out of this, Lupe, and get back to work," Chase barked. "I'll get to you later."

Her eyes round with fright, the Mexican woman scurried the rest of the way down the stairs, taking refuge in the kitchen. Once inside, she crossed herself. *"Madre de Dios,"* she whispered. She had never seen the señor so upset. Folding her hands in supplication, she prayed that Margarita would be spared the terrible beating she feared the poor woman would receive at

311

her violent husband's hands.

Once inside the privacy of their room, Chase released his hold on Margaret, tossing her onto the bed, then bolted the door behind him to prevent her escape.

Trying to catch her breath after the vigorous walk she had just been forced to take, Margaret gulped in large amounts of air. Noting the way Chase stood in front of her, his arms folded across his chest, she knew this was about much more than his annoyance at being denied her bed. "Are you going to tell me what's wrong?" she shouted out, pushing herself off the bed to stand before him. If he was going to beat her, she wasn't going to take it lying down.

"Why have you tried to deceive me, Maggie?"

Disbelief touched her features. "Me, deceive you?" That was a twist. She'd been the one deceived. And here Chase was, trying to turn the tables on her. What could he possibly be talking about? Unless . . . She bit her lower lip. Unless he knew about her father. "I don't know what you're talking about."

Pulling the letter out of his pants pocket, he handed it to her. "I suppose you don't know anything about this?"

Her eyes widened. "Where did you get this?" She glanced over at the dresser, noting for the first time that the drawer was open and her clothing was askew.

"How long has Parker been here, Maggie? And why didn't you tell me?"

"Why? So you could arrest him? Keep him from me like you've kept him from me for the past eight years?"

"Is that what he told you? That I'm the reason he

hasn't been able to come home?"

"Well, isn't it?" She prayed he would deny it—prayed fervently that everything her father had told her wasn't true.

He shook his head. Parker was smart; he'd give the bastard credit for that. "Your father is a wanted man."

Accusation filled her voice. "That's the real reason you married me, isn't it? So you could get your hands on my father." Tears filled her eyes, but she blinked them away.

"That may have been the reason that I started to court you, but it isn't the reason I married you. I told you, I love you."

Her voice rose sharply. "You're a liar. You've lied about everything. Why don't you just admit it: You married me for revenge. You married me so you could get your hands on Jonathan Parker."

"Your father is a criminal; it's my job to bring him to justice."

"You hunted him like a dog, all because he stole a little money."

"Is that what Parker told you? That I've been hunting him because of the money he stole from the bank?"

A flicker of indecision entered her eyes. "Well, isn't it?"

Chase stepped foward, reaching for her hand, but she took a step back. "Maggie, your father is much more than just a bank robber; he's a murderer."

She reeled back as if struck. "No! I don't believe you. My father would never hurt anyone. He's kind, gentle. He could never kill another human being."

"He killed my parents, my fiancée. They were in the bank the morning of the robbery. He shot them down in cold blood. He wanted no witnesses to his crime."

"Liar!" she screamed, trying to slap him, to silence the awful things that he said about her father. But he was quicker, grabbing onto her arm.

"Listen to me, Maggie. Jack Parker has killed many people in the last eighteen years. Innocent people. My mother and father were God-fearing folk, they never harmed anyone. And Amy. Christ! She was only seventeen. Seventeen years old and she had her life snuffed out before she ever had a chance to live it."

Margaret shook her head in denial. "I'm sorry for your loss. I know you still grieve for your family . . . your fiancée. But my father wasn't responsible."

Noting her anguish, the tears streaming down her face, Chase's tone softened. "He was, darlin'. I saw him with my own eyes."

She dropped down on the bed, refusing to look at him. "Then you're mistaken," she whispered.

"I've been wrong about a great many things in my life, Maggie, but I'm not wrong about this. I approached the bank just in time to see your father fleeing out the door. The gun he held in his hand was still smoking. I'll never forget his face . . . not ever."

"And was it his face you saw when you made love to me? When you told me you loved me?"

"No," he shouted. "You have nothing to do with him. You're nothing like him."

She took a deep breath. "But I am. I'm his daughter, which is why I can't believe what you've told me. My father would never deceive me; he loves me."

"I love you, Maggie."

She looked up and brown eyes locked with silver.

"If you love me, then you'll let my father go. He's dying. He only has a short time to live."

Chase's lips twisted into a sardonic smile. "He told you he was dying and you believed him? You really are naive."

"I guess I am. I believed you, didn't I?"

"You're not to see him again. Do you understand? He's evil. I'm going to arrest him, bring him to justice."

Rising to stand, her voice was full of determination when she spoke. "I'll see my father, if and when I choose. And you won't stop me. I'll not be kept from him again." She turned away from the hurt she saw reflected in Chase's eyes.

"You would choose Parker over me? A murderer? A thief? Over your own husband—the man who loves you? The man you profess to love?"

She refused to look at him. "He's my father—my flesh and blood. I can't turn my back on him."

"But you can turn your back on me? Is that it?"

She turned to face him then. "You married me under false pretenses . . . lied to me . . . made love to me . . . all the while knowing that it was my father you really desired. I do not want a marriage based on deceit."

"Are you saying that you want a divorce?" He sucked in his breath, fearful of the answer.

She swallowed the lump rising in her throat. "I'm saying that you've used me cruelly—that you've hurt me more than you will ever know."

He reached for her, but she turned toward the window. "Maggie, I love you."

"I'm sorry."

"That's all you have to say?"

She nodded but didn't turn to see the anger, hurt, and confusion in Chase's eyes.

"In that case, I'll be moving out."

She winced at the sound of the bedroom door slamming behind her. Turning to find herself alone, she hugged herself, rocking back and forth, tears of anguish streaming down her face.

"Chase," she whispered, "I love you, too."

Chapter Twenty-Four

The days following Chase's departure were the loneliest Margaret had ever experienced. She had remained virtually secluded in her house. The thought of encountering Chase on the street, or hearing the snide remarks she was sure had circulated about their separation, had turned her into a coward. Even the promise of a meeting with her father could not dissipate the sorrow that had wrapped itself around her heart.

Standing over the cookstove, she watched the ribbons of steam evaporate into the air from the kettle of water she had put on to boil. If only her problems could disappear as easily, she thought, sighing, as she reached for the tin canister of tea leaves.

"Margarita, why won't you tell me what is wrong? You don't eat, you don't sleep, you never smile anymore. I am so worried for you." Lupe shook her head sadly as she stared at the blank expression on Margaret's face. She knew the young woman's sadness had been caused by Señor Gallagher's leaving, but she didn't know why the señor had left.

"I don't wish to talk about it," Margaret responded, her tone harsher than she had intended. Turning, she saw the hurt in the housekeeper's eyes and her expression, as well as her words, softened. "Please, just tell me if you've arranged another meeting with my father. I'm very anxious to speak with him." She wanted to tell him that he was right about Chase, that everything he had told her had been confirmed by Chase's own admission. Why did that knowledge still have the power to hurt her? Why couldn't she extinguish the feelings, the love, she felt for Chase?

"I ask Sandy, Margarita, but he tell me that Señor Parker cannot meet with you right now. I tell him that it is very important, but he say it can't be helped." Lupe shrugged. "I am sorry; I tried."

Fixing Lupe a cup of tea, Margaret handed it to her, saying, "I'm sorry, too, Lupe. I shouldn't have snapped like I did. My whole life seems to be coming apart at the seams, and I don't have the means to sew it back together." Slumping into the chair at the table, Margaret clutched herself tightly about the middle, staring down at the wooden planks of the kitchen floor.

"Everything will work out for the best, Margarita. You will see. One day the answers you seek will make themselves clear to you. You have only to look within to find them."

Later that night, as Margaret lay in her big empty bed, she thought of Lupe's words and tried to take comfort in them. How could she look into herself to find the answers? she wondered. Everything she

318

believed in—her marriage, Chase's love—was a lie. There was nothing left inside her but emptiness. No anger. No answers. No hope. Chase had taken it all.

Why had she been given this small glimpse of happiness, only to have it snatched cruelly away?

"Why?" she breathed softly into the darkness. But no answer came.

Pushing the swinging doors of the saloon wide open, Tom paused in the doorway, surveying the smoke-filled room. He frowned, his eyes narrowing as they fell upon the object of his search. Chase sat in the corner of the room in the company of the whore known as Lillie Mae, looking drunker than Tom had seen him in years.

When Wooley had come to fetch him at the mercantile a short while ago, explaining that Chase had worked himself into a rage the likes of which Wooley had never seen and was proceeding to drink himself into a stupor, Tom decided to see for himself what the matter was.

Observing Chase in his present condition, he was glad he had come, if not for Chase's sake, then surely for Margaret's. Shaking his head, he strode into the room, heading straight for the table that Chase occupied with the redheaded woman.

"What the hell do you think you're doing, Gallagher?" Tom asked when he approached.

Chase lifted his head, trying to focus on the familiar voice. Suddenly, he smiled a crooked grin, saying, "Is that you, Tom? Come sit down and join us. This is my friend, Lillie Mae." His speech was slurred, the words slow and thick as they poured from his mouth.

Tom stared at the red-haired woman menacingly and jerked his head, indicating that she should leave.

Not one to cross swords with the law or former law, as was the case this time, Lillie Mae Morton drank down the rest of her whiskey, leaned over the table, displaying two very lush mounds that were about to pop out of her low-cut red satin dress as she kissed Chase good-bye, and said in a throaty whisper, "I'll see you later, Chase, honey." With that, she sashayed out of the room, her well-rounded posterior the object of many admiring glances.

If Chase heard her farewell, or caught the anger in Tom's eyes, he didn't acknowledge it. He just sat and methodically poured another whiskey into his glass.

"You mind telling me what's going on, Chase? You've got Wooley fussin' like a broody hen, and Margaret must be sick with worry."

At the mention of Margaret's name, the cloud covering Chase's eyes lifted and he tossed the whiskey down with a vengeance. "It's not likely she gives a damn what I do," Chase replied, staring up at Tom. "We're no longer living together." His lips curled, reminding Tom of a rabid dog.

Pulling out the chair, Tom eased himself into it. "What the hell are you talking about? No longer living together? You're married for God's sake. You just can't stop living together."

"Tell my darlin' wife that."

Tom's eyes widened. "Margaret kicked you out?" The pained expression crossing Chase's face seemed to indicate that he'd hit the nail on the head. But why?

320

Tom wondered. Chase and Margaret had been getting along so well. Like two lovebirds, they'd become inseparable.

Chase heaved a sigh. "If you'll help me over to the jail and pour me some coffee, I'll tell you everything you need to know."

Nodding, Tom helped Chase to his feet.

A short time later, they entered the brick building where Tom deposited Chase in the swivel chair behind the desk while he poured two mugs of strong black coffee, silently thanking Wooley for his habit of always keeping a fresh pot brewing. Handing Chase a cup, he waited while the inebriated man took several large gulps of the hot liquid.

"Better?"

Chase nodded. "Thanks."

"Now, you going to tell me what this is all about? I find it hard to believe that Margaret would kick you out of the house. That doesn't sound like her at all."

"She didn't kick me out; I left." At Tom's shocked expression, he proceeded to tell him about Margaret's meeting with her father, who her father actually was, and how he had come to find the note in her drawer. "She deceived me, Tom. Deceived her own husband."

Tom rubbed the back of his neck, trying to ease the tension out. "Why in hell didn't you tell me about Parker? I could have been the one to bring him in; I could have spared you and Margaret all this misery. Shit! He had known all along that Chase harbored some deep, dark secret in his soul. Why in hell hadn't Chase confided in him?

Chase's features hardened as did his voice. "Parker's

321

mine. He always has been. And I'll not rest until I see that bastard as dead as my family."

"You told Margaret about him?"

"She doesn't believe me. He told her I was after him for the money that he stole from the bank in St. Louis. He's a clever bastard."

"Clever enough to fool Margaret, apparently."

Chase nodded, his lips thinning in disgust.

"You can't blame Margaret, Chase. She's as much a victim in all this as your parents and fiancée. Her father is using her."

A pain so intense filled Chase's eyes that Tom could almost feel it himself.

"But why can't she see through him? I love her. I've told her countless times."

Refilling the cups, Tom took a seat in front of the desk, placing his booted feet atop it. "Margaret was deeply hurt when her father left. She blamed her mother, never her father, for his leaving. As a matter of fact, we all did. No one in the entire town faulted Parker for his sudden disappearance. Margaret was left with an embittered, selfish woman who did her best to make Margaret's life a living hell. I should know; she convinced Margaret not to marry me."

"That doesn't condone Maggie going behind my back."

"Maybe not. But Parker's her father, despite the fact that he's a murderer, a bank robber, and a liar. Blood ties bind tight, Chase. You should know that better than anyone. Look how long you've been searching for your family's killer."

"I won't give it up, Tom. Not even if it means losing

Maggie. I've waited too long for my revenge."

Tom stared sadly at his friend. "Revenge makes a poor bedfellow."

"You're right. But it's the only one I've got at the moment."

Phoebe's lips tightened smugly as she noted the tautness around Margaret's mouth and the pained expression her daughter had been sporting the past week. Although Margaret hadn't told her, she knew Marshal Gallagher had moved out. The Reverend Dorsey had let it slip when he'd been by last Sunday to read the scriptures with her.

The marshal's leaving was inevitable. She had tried to tell Margaret that before she married him. Men were faithless dogs, always sniffing from one woman to the next, never content to remain with just one.

Didn't she know, Phoebe thought, an agonized expression adding more wrinkles to her brow. Her own dear husband had treated her in much the same way. And with her own housekeeper, no less. Isabel Diaz— the slut. It still sickened her to look upon Lupe and remember Jonathan's infidelity with Lupe's mother.

Of course, Isabel hadn't been the only one. There'd been others . . . lots of them. She'd been the injured party, but everyone pitied Jonathan for what they all believed were his wife's inconsiderations. Just because she didn't choose to rut like some mare in heat every time he got the inclination. Procreation was for the sole purpose of having children, not for pleasure. Hadn't her sainted mother drilled that into her from the time she had been old enough to receive callers?

Folding her arms over her ample bosom, she watched as Margaret efficiently smoothed out the linens on the bed. The child was a blessing to her in her old age, Phoebe thought. They didn't need that lawman interfering in their lives. His leaving was a fortunate occurrence as far as she was concerned. She and Margaret had each other and that was enough; it always would be.

Hoping that Margaret would choose to confide in her, Phoebe finally asked, "You look a little down-hearted, Margaret. Is there something wrong?"

Unwilling to meet her mother's eyes, Margaret fluffed the two goosedown pillows, pulling the counterpane up to cover the sheets. "Not really. I'm just a little tired."

"I hope you haven't been working too hard. That marshal's hardly worth the energy you've expended on him."

Margaret's head shot up, her eyes narrowing a fraction. She bit her lip to keep the angry retort that hovered about her lips from escaping. If Phoebe noticed Margaret's pique, she gave no indication and went on speaking without taking a breath.

"Reverend Dorsey was here to visit Sunday. We had a very interesting discussion."

Margaret sighed. She knew. Her mother knew Chase had left and was toying with her. "Really? How nice." Margaret's smile never reached her eyes as she turned to face her mother. "Your bed is all ready. Would you like me to help you into it?"

Phoebe shook her head. "I'll just sit here awhile

longer. The sun feels good and I get so tired of lying in that bed."

"Well, if you don't need anything else, I'll be about my business." She started for the door but halted in her tracks when she heard her mother say, "What business is that, Margaret? It's my understanding that your marshal isn't living here anymore—that he's taken up residence over at the hotel. Of course, I wouldn't be at all surprised to learn that he's been living at the brothel. Men like that always have a penchant for loose women."

Margaret felt the tears burn behind her lids, but she willed them not to spill. She wouldn't give her mother the satisfaction of seeing her cry. "I don't really think where Chase resides is any of your business, Mama."

Phoebe snorted. "He left you, didn't he? Just like your papa did. They all leave, Margaret. It's the lust in their loins; they've no love in their hearts for us poor, innocent women."

Suddenly, the anger that had been building for the past eight years burst forth from Margaret like an untapped artesian well. "Did you ever stop to think that maybe Papa left because of you, Mama? Because you drove him away with your vile tongue and vicious words?"

Phoebe clutched the ruffles at her throat, her eyes filling with tears. "No! It wasn't because of me. I loved your father."

"Maybe so, but you drove him away, nonetheless. You demanded too much; you always have. No one is perfect enough to live up to your expectations, Mama. Not even me."

"What are you talking about, you ungrateful child? I've given you a good home—taken care of you the best I know how."

"It is I who have taken care of you, Mama. You have done nothing but make my life miserable, just like you made Papa's miserable. You drove him away; don't drive me away, too."

"Your father was a faithless creature who had many women. He shamed me in front of the whole town." Phoebe's cheeks flushed bright red, her forehead perspired profusely.

Margaret wagged her head in denial. "My father is a good man. He loves me; he told me so. I don't believe a word of what you're saying. You've always tried to come between us—always tried to poison me against him. I won't listen to any more of your slanderous lies. I won't let you or Chase malign my father ever again. Not while I have a breath of life left within me." Yanking the door open, Margaret stalked out, slamming it behind her.

Phoebe stared at the door, wiping her eyes with the edge of her nightgown. How could Margaret be so cruel? How could she choose her father over her, after everything they had been through together?

Blowing her nose loudly into the handkerchief that she pulled from the sleeve of her nightgown, she forced herself under control, remembering back to the conversation she had just had with her daughter. Something Margaret had said intrigued her: *"I won't let you or Chase malign my father ever again."* Her brow wrinkled in confusion. What terrible things could the marshal have said about Jonathan? And why? she wondered.

Knowing that there was only one way to find out, though she dreaded the confrontation with all her heart, Phoebe withdrew a sheet of paper from the desk situated next to her chair.

If Marshal Gallagher had knowledge of Jonathan Parker, then she wanted to know about it. And as far as she could see, there was only one way. She proceeded to write a note to Chase Gallagher.

Chapter Twenty-Five

"Your daughter's getting a mite agitated, Parker. What if she tries to find this place on her own?" Sandy lit a cigarette, filling the dingy room with smoke. They'd been holed up in the hideout for months, and Sandy was beginning to doubt that this mysterious plan of Parker's was ever going to materialize.

Parker's lips thinned. He was getting damned tired of Sandy's questions. Didn't the fool know that he had everything planned down to the minutest detail? "Let me worry about Margaret. You just take care of those three idiots you hired. I want them out of the way as soon as possible."

The cowboy's brows lifted slightly. "You mean permanently?"

"There's no other way. They know too much. I'm sure I can rely on you to do your usual efficient job."

Sandy smiled smugly, grinding his cigarette beneath his boot heel. "Sure, boss. I've never disappointed you before have I? I'll take care of the Donaldson brothers."

"Good. Now, did you arrange the little diversion that we spoke of? It wouldn't do for Gallagher to stumble upon our plan before we're ready?"

"Yeah, I arranged it. But I don't see why we just can't kill him and get it over with. What the hell are you keeping him alive for?"

"Rest assured, I have my reasons. You just do your part and leave Gallagher to me. It's always good to have an ace in the hole."

Pulling his gun from the leather holster strapped on his hip, Sandy checked the load. "This is the only ace I need."

Sandy wasn't capable of seeing farther than the barrel of his gun, Parker thought disgustedly, which was why Sandy wasn't going to be around much longer himself.

Gallagher was the leverage he needed to keep Margaret cooperative. He wouldn't hesitate to use the love she felt for Gallagher if it became necessary. No one was indispensable. He only hoped it wouldn't be necessary to eliminate Margaret as well as her husband. She was really a sweet little thing and would be a comfort to him in his advancing years. Who knows, he might even form a fondness for her, though he doubted it.

Like the poets said, love was for fools and dreamers, which is why he never allowed time for the emotion. He was a practical man—a smart man—and he would let no one interfere in his quest to retrieve the gold. With enough money, a man could buy all the love he needed anyway.

"You ready to put your plan into action?" Sandy inquired.

329

Parker smiled confidently. "Ready, willing, and able."

"Why, Marshal, how nice to see you again." Like a water-deprived cactus, Laurette Appleton's gaze drank in the virile form of Chase Gallagher, then lit with pleasure. He was the handsomest man she'd seen in a long time and just the type she liked to take to her bed: big, strong, muscular. The kind of man that made a woman feel small and protected.

Chase turned to find the pretty milliner standing directly behind him and smiled in greeting. "What brings you to Fraser's Mercantile so early Monday morning, Miss Appleton?"

"Why the same as you, Marshal." She sidled up next to him, tilting her head to just the right angle so he was afforded the best view of her face. "I've come to fetch my mail." Her bow-shaped lips curved up into a smile.

Chase leaned against the counter which fronted the area sectioned off as the post office. Laurette was a very attractive woman, he thought. Unfortunately, she knew it.

Were all women shallow and dishonest creatures? he wondered. He thought of Maggie and sighed. Shallow . . . maybe not. But dishonest! She had that trait in spades.

Engrossed in their conversation, neither Chase nor Laurette saw the hostile glare directed at them from across the store. Betsy had just entered from the back room and was not at all happy to see the husband of her best friend engaged in conversation with that simpering Southern belle who considered herself to be the foremost authority on women's fashions. Not about to let Laurette Appleton get her hooks into Margaret's husband, she strode purposefully across the room, determined to rectify the situation immediately.

"Hello, Chase . . . Miss Appleton," Betsy said when she approached, trying to keep her smile friendly, though she felt like spitting nails. "Have you both come to check on your mail?" She leveled indignant blue eyes on Chase and thought she saw some color come into his cheeks. He should be embarrassed, she thought, parading around town with that two-bit floozy from the brothel and now this man-hungry creature.

"If you'd check my mailbox, Betsy, I'll be on my way," Chase said. He'd sent a telegram to the territorial marshal in New Mexico to see if he'd received any wanted posters on Sandy Loomis. If Loomis was a wanted man, he would arrest him and lock him up, and Parker would have one less member of his gang to aid him in his nefarious scheme.

Betsy turned to check the pigeonhole boxes on the back wall. Sorting through the letters in the box marked Gallagher, she turned back to face Chase, shaking her head. "There's two letters for Margaret but none for you, Chase."

Chase stiffened at the mention of Margaret's name. He hadn't failed to notice the accusation in Betsy's eyes and knew that Betsy blamed him for his and Maggie's marital woes. "Maggie seems to be receiving a lot of mail lately."

Ignoring the speculative gleam in Laurette's eyes, Betsy smiled smoothly, saying, "When people are loyal and kind, they attract a lot of attention. Not all of it's good and not all of it's welcome. They're like magnets;

331

both good and evil attach themselves and there's no way to pull them off without someone to help. Sometimes they're stuck in situations they have no control over."

Chase listened to Betsy's speech, then smiled. "You're a good friend, Betsy."

"I try to be and so should you."

"I'll try to remember that." Turning to Laurette, he tipped his hat. "Ladies." He walked out the door, a thoughtful look on his face.

"You and the marshal seem to be well-acquainted," Laurette remarked, her eyes following Chase's departure with a hunger she couldn't disguise.

"We are. My husband Tom is Chase's best friend and Margaret's mine."

"It was my understanding that the marshal and his wife are thinking of getting a divorce."

"Who told you that ridiculous lie?" Betsy asked. She wasn't about to confirm the malicious gossip that had been floating around town the past week.

"Nobody told me," Laurette replied. "I just heard rumors. You know how people love to talk."

"Chase and Margaret are very much in love with each other, so if you're smart, you'll dangle your hook in another direction. Perhaps you could cast it at Francis Brooks. I hear-tell he's looking for a wife."

Laurette's cheeks flushed crimson and her eyes sparked fire. "Really, Mrs. Fraser, your presumptions astound me! How dare you infer that I'm interested in the marshal? Why he's a married man, after all."

"That's right, he is. And you'd be doing yourself a favor to remember that fact."

"Well, I declare. I have never been so rudely maligned."

"Really? I find that extremely hard to believe."

Sputtering with indignation, Laurette spun on her heel, heading for the door. But before she could escape, Betsy's final barb stung her. "Your hats are as pretentious as you are, Miss Appleton. All frills and furbelows with no substance beneath them. Perhaps that's why you sell your wares so cheaply."

A loud gasp flew out of Laurette's mouth as she ran out of the door.

Betsy smiled widely, peering out the window to see Laurette hightailing it down the street like her corset was on fire. The milliner's humiliating departure filled her with satisfaction. It serves her right! Betsy thought. Margaret had enough problems at the moment. She didn't need a man-chasing Southern belle to complicate her life.

Engrossed in her observations, she didn't hear her husband approach until he was standing right behind her.

"You're pretty proud of yourself, aren't you," Tom remarked.

Betsy turned, expecting to find condemnation in her husband's eyes, surprised to find admiration instead. "Damned right, I am. That woman meant to get her hooks into Chase, and I wasn't about to let that happen."

Pulling his very pregnant wife into his arms, Tom kissed the top of her head. "I'm proud of you, though I fear Miss Appleton's wounds from that tongue lashing you gave her are going to take quite a while to heal."

"Women like her always bounce back. I'll bet you in the space of a week she'll be practicing her wiles on Francis Brooks again."

"That's one bet I won't take you up on. I'd be sure to lose."

Betsy smiled. "Smart man."

"Smart enough to marry you, honey." He kissed her sweetly on the lips.

"Oh, Tom," Betsy wailed, "we're so happy and things between Chase and Margaret are just awful."

"Chase and Margaret will work things out. You'll see. Chase is too smart to let Margaret slip through his fingers."

Tipping back her head to stare into the blue of Tom's eyes, Betsy saw the conviction there. "Do you really think so?"

"Chase may be many things, but he's no fool. He loves Margaret and she loves him. With a little help from their friends, they'll get back on track." He winked, giving her thick waist a squeeze.

"I love you, Tom Fraser."

He grinned. "I know."

"And do you also know that, at this moment, I find you utterly desirable?"

A sensuous light entered his eyes. "I think perhaps we should close up shop for a while. There's some business in the back room that needs taking care of."

A warm blush suffused Betsy's cheeks. "I'll lock the door; you pull down the shades," she said, hurrying toward the door.

"Careful you don't hurt yourself in your haste to be ravaged," Tom teased, noting how his wife's cheeks had suddenly turned bright red.

"You're terrible!"

"I am, aren't I?" he agreed, chuckling in amusement as he circled her waist. "Come on. I want to show you just how *terrible* I am."

Adjusting her shawl tight around her shoulders to ward off the chill of the September evening, Margaret turned the key in the lock of the pharmacy, rattling the knob to make certain it was firmly closed. She had just finished an exhausting day of work and was eager to get home and soak in a tub of hot water. Her back ached, her feet were swollen, and she'd fought the urge to vomit more times than she cared to remember.

Her pregnancy was making itself known in more ways than one. As Doc had predicted, the nausea hadn't ceased but had grown worse with each passing day. Her breasts were full and tender to the touch and her waistline was thickening, making her skirts and dresses extremely uncomfortable. Betsy had been right; she wouldn't be able to hide the fact that she was going to have a baby much longer.

Wrapped up in her disquieting thoughts, she turned toward the street a bit too quickly and lost her footing, colliding against a solid wall of male muscle. Two hands clenched her shoulders to keep her from falling, and when she gazed up to thank her rescuer, her heart jumped into her throat, freezing her expression of gratitude.

"Chase," she whispered, not realizing she had spoken his name aloud. The scent of bay rum surrounded her, rendering her light-headed.

"Maggie," he said, matter-of-factly, setting her from

335

him. "You should pay more attention to where you're going, lest you hurt yourself." For a moment, Chase let himself feast on the sight of her, noting how flushed her cheeks were, how her hair was once again pulled back in the severe style she had worn when he'd first met her, though it did little to detract from her loveliness. Nothing could. In fact, she was even more beautiful than the last time he had seen her.

"Thank you. I'm sorry I was so clumsy." She felt herself warm at the speculative gleam in his eyes as they traveled over her form in a provocative fashion. Her nipples hardened involuntarily.

"You've put on a few pounds," he remarked, his eyes settling on the fullness of her breasts.

She colored, fidgeting nervously with the edges of her shawl, hoping the thickness of her muslin skirt would conceal what she needed desperately to hide: her slightly swollen abdomen. "Have I?" She smiled to hide her discomfort. "I guess I've been eating too much of Lupe's food. She's prepared a lot of those Mexican dishes she's so fond of, lately." Margaret hoped Chase would be satisfied with her explanation. If he suspected she was pregnant, her life would become even more of a living hell than it already was.

Stepping forward, he cupped her elbow in a proprietary fashion. "I'll escort you home. It's getting dark. It wouldn't do for you to walk about unescorted."

The feel of his hand on her elbow sent a bolt of charged current through her entire body. She wanted to pull away—to run from the unwelcome desire that surfaced whenever Chase was near her, but she didn't. It would be fruitless to argue with him. Hadn't she learned that lesson once before? She nodded her compliance, allowing him to lead her down the sidewalk.

Their boot heels sounded loud to her ears as they tapped along the wooden planks. The walk home reminded her, all too vividly, of their first encounter. Then, the silence had been companionable; now it was strained. Then, the bloom of love was new in her breast, filling her with a joy unknown to her before; now it withered, like last summer's roses, a bitter memory of what might have been.

"How have things been at home? Is your mother still driving you to distraction?" Chase asked, breaking the silence. He wasn't about to tell Maggie about his recent visit with Phoebe. It had been illuminating, to say the least. Apparently Margaret's mother didn't hold Parker in such high esteem as her daughter did. Phoebe had been more than willing to reveal the darker side of his nature.

"Surprisingly, Mama's left me alone, of late. We haven't had a full conversation in weeks." Not since their abusive confrontation concerning Margaret's father, but Margaret wasn't about to admit that to Chase.

"And Lupe, is she still seeing that cowboy?" He watched her expression cloud with unease. "I'm only asking out of concern for Lupe. I've just found out that Loomis is a wanted man." Reaching into his coat pocket, he extracted the wanted poster that had just arrived from New Mexico and handed it to her.

Filled with disbelief and trepidation, Margaret unfolded it, her eyes widening as they scanned over the likeness of Sandy Loomis. She began to read: Wanted,

Dead or Alive, for the murder of Ben and Laura Johnson . . .

"This can't be true," she said.

"I'm afraid it is. I was going to show it to Lupe myself. Perhaps you'd like to tell her?"

She blanched. "I . . . I couldn't. It would hurt her too much." Poor Lupe. What would she do when she found out? She'd be devastated . . . heartbroken. Lupe was head over heels in love with Sandy Loomis.

"No matter," Chase replied, removing the poster from her fingers. "I plan to arrest Loomis as soon as I can locate him. She'll find out soon enough."

Before Margaret could respond, Chase eased open the gate in front of her house, saying, "Looks like we're here." He glanced around for the familiar form of Evelyn and felt keen disappointment when he didn't see the musk hog rounding the corner of the house. He'd missed the bothersome little creature. In fact, there were a great many things he had missed since moving out.

Annoyed at the direction his thoughts were heading, he sought to take his mind elsewhere. "Where's Evelyn? I expected her to greet us."

"What?" Margaret answered in a distracted fashion. "Oh, Evelyn. She's in the house, on the back porch. She hasn't been feeling her old self, lately. I think she's taken ill."

Chase frowned. "Have you had the vet out to look at her?"

Feeling her cheeks warm, Margaret shook her head. She'd been so wrapped up in her own misery, she hadn't spared a thought for her poor faithful companion.

"Mind if I take a look at her?"

Relief crossed her face. "Would you? I've been worried sick about her." Though she could see from the skeptical expression on Chase's face he didn't believe her for a second.

They walked to the rear of the house and entered the porch adjacent to the kitchen. Evelyn lay in her makeshift bed that Margaret had fashioned out of an old counterpane. She was listless; but when Chase bent down next to her, she made an effort to raise her head, bringing tears to Margaret's eyes.

"Easy girl," Chase crooned, running comforting hands over the pig's side and belly. Evelyn snorted in her familiar way, allowing him to continue with his examination. After a few more minutes of prodding and poking, Chase pushed himself to his feet and turned toward Margaret, grinning from ear to ear. "We're going to be grandparents, Maggie. Evelyn is pregnant."

"Pregnant!" Reflexively, Margaret's hands went to her abdomen, but she dropped them quickly, relieved to note that Chase hadn't noticed her response. "I wonder who the father is?"

"I expect he's been coming around at night while Evelyn is supposedly guarding the chickens. Isn't that right, girl?" he asked the pig.

Evelyn's mouth opened, and for a moment, Margaret thought she was actually smiling. Margaret started to giggle, which brought an instantaneous response from Chase who threw back his head and roared.

Their merriment continued for several more moments until their eyes locked and their smiles faded into something more serious that neither wanted to acknowledge.

"I'd best be going," Chase said, heading for the door. "I'm sure Evelyn will be fine. Nature has a way of taking care of these types of things."

"Yes, it does," Margaret responded, but she wasn't thinking about the hog. "Thank you for walking me home, Chase."

He tipped his hat, but didn't respond, slipping out the door and into the night.

Margaret watched him walk away and sighed, feeling a tremendous void deep within her breast. Would she and Chase always be at cross purposes? she wondered. Would they ever be able to close the chasm that had widened between them?

"Margarita? Is that you?"

Hearing Lupe's call from the kitchen brought Margaret back to the present. Sandy Loomis was a wanted man—a murderer! How could that be? He was her father's friend.

What did it all mean? she wondered. If Sandy Loomis was her father's friend, then maybe . . . Chase's accusations came back to haunt her.

She shook her head, unwilling to face the implications. No! It just couldn't be. It couldn't!

But she knew deep down in her heart that it could, and it terrified her.

Chapter Twenty-Six

"Lupe, wait!" Margaret shouted, staring helplessly as the poor, distraught woman ran out of the house. She hadn't meant to tell her about Sandy. But after spending a sleepless night wrestling with her conscience, Margaret had decided it was the only decent thing to do. She couldn't let Lupe find out about Sandy Loomis's sordid past from strangers.

Grabbing her shawl off the chair, Margaret wrapped it about her. She'd have to go after Lupe, try to explain, smooth things over, and comfort her.

Grateful at the knowledge that her mother had fallen asleep and wouldn't awaken for several hours, Margaret stepped onto the back porch and gave Evelyn a quick once-over. The hog was resting comfortably. With a promise to Evelyn to return shortly, Margaret rushed out the door, heading in the direction of the livery. If Lupe meant to confront Sandy Loomis then there was going to be trouble. And there was no way she was going to allow Lupe to face that trouble alone.

*　　*　　*

The first body came into view just as Chase and Wooley reached the rise overlooking the San Carlos River. Galloping toward the macabre sight, they reined in to find Skunk Donaldson suspended from a thick branch of a cottonwood tree, twisting like a grotesque human wind chime as the breeze zigzagged his body to and fro.

"It looks like Skunk's bit the bullet," Wooley said, shaking his head. "Guess there was some truth in that note you received, after all."

Chase frowned as he stared at the body, thinking back to the missive he'd received this morning. The note had been stuck under the front door of the jail, indicating that he would find a dead body if he rode toward the river. There were additional instructions on where two more bodies could be found. The map pointed to a deserted farm southeast of where they were now. Chase assumed that the murderer was referring to the remaining two Donaldson brothers.

"Looks like Parker's cutting his losses," Chase said, dismounting. "He was never one to share the wealth." His voice was thick with disgust. "The poor dumb bastard never had a chance. From the looks of the hole in his back, he was shot from behind."

"Loomis?"

Chase nodded. "That'd be my guess. Well, I guess the only decent thing to do is cut him down and bring him back to Purgatory. His horse is probably close by. Once we find the animal, we'll strap Skunk to his back. By the time we're through following this map, Donaldson's horse is going to bear a heavy burden."

Wooley spit. "It ain't likely the creature's goin' to be able to carry the other two. Bear's weight will break his back."

Removing his hat, Chase wiped his forehead with the back of his hand. It wasn't noon yet and the heat was already intense. The stench from the dead, decaying body of Skunk Donaldson was proving to be unbearable. Pulling his bandanna from around his neck, he tied it over his face, instructing Wooley to do the same.

"Skunk always did stink to high heaven," Wooley commented, shaking his head in disgust as he followed Chase's lead. "Why, even in death the man's revolting. I guess the grim reaper ain't too choosey who he picks."

"Enough talk, Wooley. We've got a long ride ahead of us. I don't want to be gone from town any longer than we have to."

"You expecting trouble?"

"Let's just say we're in the middle of a bizarre game . . . sort of like pawns on a chess board. Right now the score is Parker three, us nothing. But I'm about to even it up."

Wooley smiled. "We're fixin' to win, right?"

There was a lethal calmness in the gray eyes when Chase spoke, "That's right, Wooley; this time we win."

Phoebe wasn't sure what woke her. Maybe the persistent cackle of the hens as they scurried about the yard beneath her open window, or the cooling breeze that drifted in, fluttering the curtains. Whatever it was, she was wide awake now, and she'd heard something— something unfamiliar, like a scraping noise.

She knew it wasn't Margaret; Margaret always announced herself when she came home. And she'd caught sight of Lupe running across the yard hours earlier like the very devil was on her heels. No . . . it was something else.

Pushing herself into an upright position, she ambled down off the bed. She wasn't quite as helpless as she'd led others to believe. There'd been plenty of occasions when she had strolled about the house to admire her things when no one was about.

Trying to outsmart Margaret and Lupe had become a game to her. Sometimes, when she felt particularly daring, she would wait until Margaret had opened the front gate and was walking up the path, before she hurried up the stairs to get back into bed. It wouldn't do for Margaret to catch her. If Margaret thought she wasn't sick, she would leave her . . . leave just like Jonathan did.

Tying the sashes of her robe together, Phoebe eased open the door to her bedroom, peering down the hall. It was empty. No one was about on the second floor.

A door banged from below. She sucked in her breath. Someone was downstairs. Cautiously, she approached the staircase, grabbing onto the railing. With measured movements, she eased herself down the steps, her massive weight making the going slow. If someone was meaning to rob her, they'd be in for a big surprise, Phoebe thought. She could defend her home with the best of them.

Entering the house through the same door she had exited hours earlier, Margaret sighed wearily, tossing her shawl onto the kitchen chair. She'd been unsuccessful in finding Lupe. The woman wasn't at the livery, wasn't at her home, and Margaret had no idea where to look next. With too many possible destinations and no clue as to where Lupe might have gone, Margaret decided to come home and wait, hoping that the distraught housekeeper would calm down and return home to talk.

Knowing that her mother was probably awake and clamoring for some refreshment, Margaret loaded a tray with a glass of lemonade and three sugar cookies, hurrying up the stairs. If Mama's disposition had soured while she was gone, the food was sure to sweeten her up.

Reaching the landing, Margaret paused, noting that the door to her mother's room was ajar. That's odd, she thought, nudging it open with her foot, entering to find the room empty. Her brow wrinkled in puzzlement as she set the glass and cookies down on the dresser. Where could Mama have gone?

Crossing the hall to the bathroom, she knocked. Hearing no response, she peered inside; it was empty, as well. Fear for her mother's safety suddenly battered her calm.

"Mama," she called out, hurrying from room to room, only to find each one empty. Running down the steps, she rushed into the parlor. She knew her mother had a penchant for pretty things. Perhaps she'd gone in there to look over her possessions. She looked quickly around, but the parlor was empty, too. "Mama, where are you?" Margaret called to the empty room, becoming more concerned with each passing moment.

Hurrying back into the hallway, she turned toward

the rear of the house. The basement door was ajar. Panic rioted within her. If her mother had tried to descend the narrow basement steps by herself, she might have fallen and broken her leg.

Approaching the door, she ground to a halt at the sound of voices. There were two—male and female, and from the sounds of it, they were arguing. The high-pitched, female voice was definitely her mother's. But the other . . . She listened again. Jonathan Parker's cultured tones drifted up to send a shiver of fear down her spine.

"You should have stayed up in your room, Phoebe. You always were an interfering bitch."

Margaret gasped, covering her mouth as she moved closer to the door.

"You haven't changed a lick, Jonathan. Still a fancy dresser with morals no better than a tomcat. You might have fooled Margaret all those years, but you didn't fool me. I've always known you for what you are."

"Shut up, you cold bitch! I might have had to put up with your nasty barbs while we were married, but I don't have to any longer. Now get the hell out of my way. I've come a long way for this gold and neither you, nor that naive little daughter of yours is going to stop me."

"Gold," Margaret mouthed the word, unable to believe her ears. What gold was he speaking of?

"That gold doesn't belong to you, Jonathan Parker. Now leave it be and get out. I'll have the law on you if you don't."

A laugh so sinister that it made the hairs on Margaret's neck stand straight up on end floated up the staircase.

"Get out of my way, Phoebe, or by God I'll shoot you with this gun. I've already killed three people for this gold. Don't think I won't hesitate to shoot one more."

Tears filled Maggie's eyes as she clutched her chest to still the rapid beating of her heart. *My God! My God!* It was true. It was all true. Everything Chase and her mother had said about her father was true, and she hadn't believed them.

Wiping her face with the back of her hand, she turned, running quickly back up the stairs. There was a gun in the drawer by the bed. Chase had left it there for her when he'd gone to Yuma and she'd never removed it.

Bursting into her room, she rushed to the nightstand, ripping open the drawer. Thank God! The gun still rested within. Retrieving it, she clutched the cold metal to her breast. This would make her father think twice about threatening innocent people.

Descending the steps, she reached the bottom floor as the first shot was fired; it was followed by another and then another. "No!" she screamed, rushing toward the basement door, unmindful of the danger that awaited her.

When her eyes adjusted to the dimness of the poorly lit area, she caught sight of her mother's prone body lying in the dirt. "Mama!" she yelled, rushing forward, dropping the gun to kneel beside the still form.

Caught up in her grief, she didn't see her father, didn't hear him bend over to retrieve the gun she had dropped until he spoke.

"You're as foolish as your mother, Margaret. You have many of the same detestable traits as Phoebe did."

She turned her head to find him standing behind her.

Eyes that were full of pain and unrelenting hatred blazed at him. "I hate you! You killed her! Murderer! Murderer!" she screamed, over and over again.

"Shut up!" he ordered, advancing toward her, "or you'll end up as dead as your mother."

Margaret shook her head at the sight of the gun pointed at her heart. "To think I actually loved you—mourned you all those years." She pushed herself to her feet. "You're nothing but a thief and a murderer. Chase was right; he was right about everything."

"Fortunate for me that you didn't believe him."

"How could you kill all those people? Kill your own wife? My mother loved you in her own fashion. She lived for the day when you'd come back to her."

He shook his head. "Tsk . . . tsk . . . more's the pity for her. Phoebe was a bitch, right up to the end. She loved no one but herself, least of all me. You should know that, Margaret. I'm sure she made your life a living hell."

Guilt and grief suffused Margaret as the words she had so recently flung at her mother came back to haunt her. Tears welled up in her eyes as she glanced down at the still form of Phoebe Parker. "Mama, I'm sorry," she whispered.

"Not as sorry as you're going to be if you don't do exactly as I say."

Her head snapped up. "What kind of an animal would kill his own daughter?"

"Survival of the fittest, my dear. It's the unwritten law of the land. I've waited too long for this day. No one, including you, is going to stand in my way. Now pick up those flour sacks and start loading those gold coins into them. We've got a long ride ahead of us."

"And if I don't?"

"Then I'll kill you and your husband." He noted her hesitation and smiled. "I thought that would bring you around. You always were a noble one, Margaret."

Fear for Chase and her unborn child jolted Margaret into action. Kneeling by the open metal chest that rested only a few feet from where her mother lay, she began scooping the coins into the bags.

"I'll do as you say for now. But rest assured, you won't win. I'll kill you myself, if I have to."

Parker laughed. "You've got more spirit than your mother; I'll say that for you. Perhaps you and I will get along. After all, you're my flesh and blood. You may be more like me than you think."

Margaret's brown eyes lit with fire; her hands trembled with rage as she loaded the money into the bags. He would pay. Jonathan Parker would pay. If it was the last thing she did, she would see that he paid for the evil he had done. She would do it for Chase; she would do it for Mama. But most of all, she would do it for herself.

Chapter Twenty-Seven

Dusk was beginning to descend, turning the horizon into a palette of purple and pink as Chase and Wooley, trailed by two body-laden horses, rode wearily down the main street of town. The horror both men had witnessed weighed heavily on their minds as they reined their horses to a halt in front of the wooden building that housed the undertaker.

Dismounting, Chase looked over at Wooley and shook his head unable to keep the revulsion out of his voice when he spoke. "Let's get these bodies inside as quickly as possible, Wooley. I can't stand looking at them any longer." Though they were covered by blankets, Chase would never be able to erase the gruesome sight of Bear Donaldson's mutilated body. He'd been cut open, disemboweled like an animal who'd been hunted for sport, then left out in the open, easy prey for vultures and other birds of carrion.

"I'll take 'em in, Chase," Wooley offered, shuddering inwardly at the thought of the undertaker. Simon

350

Pettigrew gave him the creeps with his somber black suit and his long, white fingers that had touched many a dead body. "You go on along and see if you can find Margaret. I know she's been weighin' heavily on your mind."

"Thanks, Wooley. I'll head on over to Doc's; they should be finished with their patients by now. Then I'll walk Margaret home. See that no harm comes to her."

"After what I've seen today, I think you'd be right smart to do that. Margaret's not safe with that lunatic Loomis on the loose."

Wooley's words cut into Chase like a knife, slashing what was left of his composure. He'd thought of nothing else but Margaret's safety the entire way home, pushing Lucifer harder than he ought to in order to get home quickly. Patting the lathered, winded horse affectionately on the rump, he picked up the reins once again and headed in the direction of Doc Watson's, this time on foot.

Upon reaching the pharmacy, Chase secured his horse to the hitching post and entered to find Doc mopping up a puddle of purple liquid which smelled to Chase very much like laudanum.

"Hi, Doc. Margaret around? I need to speak with her right away." Chase waited for Doc to turn around and when he did was instantly alarmed by the concern reflected in the older man's eyes.

"I haven't seen Margaret all day, Chase. I've been worried sick about her. Usually, if she can't come in, she sends Lupe to tell me. But when I went to the Diaz's home to inquire, Isabel said that Lupe hadn't been home since early this morning."

351

"Did you check Margaret's house? Maybe she wasn't feeling well and fell asleep."

Rubbing his chin, Doc heaved a sigh. "I'm well aware of Margaret's condition, Chase. That was the first thing I thought of. I went to the house, but there was no answer."

Chase rocked back on his heels. "Margaret's condition?"

"The baby. I thought perhaps she'd taken ill. It's perfectly normal in her condition, but I . . ." Doc paused at the shocked expression on Chase's face. The man looked as if he'd just been knocked alongside the head with a piece of timber. "You knew Margaret was pregnant, didn't you, Chase? She told me it was to be a surprise."

Chase paled, his eyes widening to the size of two silver dollars. A surprise! It was a surprise all right. His heart suddenly filled with love. A baby!

His elation quickly turned to trepidation. "I've got to go, Doc. Maggie's in danger."

"Danger? From whom?"

A cold, hard mask congested Chase's features. "Her father's back, and I'm going to kill him if he's touched one hair on Maggie's head."

"Back? Jonathan Parker is back?" Doc's brow furrowed in confusion. "Why would he want to hurt Margaret? She's his daughter."

"I don't have time to explain, Doc," Chase replied, crossing to the door. "Wooley is down the street at the undertaker's. Go there. He'll explain everything."

At Doc's nod, Chase rushed out the door, running the short distance to the Parker residence.

*   *   *

The house was dark when he entered. Finding a kerosene lantern sitting on the table in the entry hall, he lit it. It took him only a moment to inspect the downstairs rooms of the house. As he suspected, they were empty. Heading up the stairs, he searched the bedrooms, finding each one deserted.

"Maggie," he shouted, descending the steps once again. Upon reaching the first floor, he took another quick look around and was about to head out the door when he noticed a shiny, gold object on the floor. Crossing to it, he picked up the gold coin, crushing it into his palm. "Parker!" he yelled.

Looking down the length of the hall, he sighted another coin and walked back to pick it up. It was then he noticed the basement door had been left open. Tingles of fear caressed his spine. Margaret always kept the door locked, fearing for her mother's safety.

Approaching cautiously, he held the kerosene lamp out in front of him as he descended into the cellar, thinking back to when he was a kid and all the spiders that lurked in the dark corners of the basement in his home back in St. Louis. The thought made him shudder, but not as much as the gruesome sight that greeted him when he reached the last step.

Phoebe Parker lay dead, a bullet hole engraved in her forehead, her eyes frozen wide-eyed in disbelief. Bile rose thickly in his throat. Unable to stomach the hideous sight a moment longer, he bent down, placing his fingers on her eyelids, pushing them closed.

No one deserved to die like this, even Phoebe, he

thought. Raw terror for Margaret's safety suddenly ripped through him like a hurricane-force wind. An anguished cry tore from his throat. "Maggie, where are you?"

At the moment, Margaret had no idea where she was. They'd been traveling south through open desert for miles. It was dark, and she was cold, the temperature having dropped considerably. But she pushed on, riding the horse her father had provided and not saying a word. She wouldn't give him an excuse to harm her—wouldn't give him the satisfaction he craved in wanting to kill Chase.

She would once again play the dutiful daughter. But not for long. Soon she would kill the man known as Gentleman Jack Parker. He wasn't her father; her father was dead. This monster, this murderer, was not the man she remembered, not the man her mother had given her heart to. He was a stranger—an imposter—and she would have no qualms about taking his life as he had taken her mother's.

"You've been awfully quiet, Margaret," Jack Parker said, turning his head to face his daughter, ignoring the hatred on her face. "We're almost there." He pointed to the mountain range up ahead. "That's where we're headed. There's a series of caves carved into that mountain. No one's going to find us, my dear. It's just going to be you and me from now on."

Her lips curled. "And what of your murderous friend, Sandy Loomis? Won't he be there to greet you with open arms?"

Jack's smile grew sinister, almost secretive. "Loomis will be there but not for long. We've no more use for him."

Margaret gasped, despite her resolve to remain impassive. "You're evil! You would double-cross your own partner?" She laughed sarcastically. "But why should that surprise me? You've turned on the rest of us. Why not Mr. Loomis?"

Jack's voice hardened ruthlessly. "Shut up! When I want your comments I'll ask for them. Remember, I can eliminate you just as easily as I eliminated your mother. Don't push me. Fatherly affection only goes so far." He rode ahead of her, lengthening the distance between them.

Margaret bit the inside of her cheek to keep from spewing forth all the vile things she wanted to say. Resting her hand on her abdomen, she caressed it tenderly, then stiffened her spine.

Bide your time, Margaret, she told herself. *Don't let the bastard get to you.* But it was hard! she thought, tasting the blood inside her mouth, feeling the tears drip from her eyes.

"Chase," she whispered into the darkness, taking comfort in the saying of his name, "I'm so sorry, so very sorry."

At the same time Margaret was making her trek across the desert, Chase was at the jail securing the guns and ammunition he would need to kill Parker and Loomis and bring Maggie back home.

Word of Phoebe's murder had spread like a fire

355

across the prairie, and many of the townfolk had gathered at the jail to offer their assistance. Tom had come, as Chase knew he would, and it wasn't going to be easy to convince his friend that his help wasn't needed. The angry expression on Tom's face told him that much.

"You're crazy, Chase, thinking you can go after Parker alone. I've brought my rifle . . ." Tom held up his Winchester. ". . . and I'm ready to ride."

Chase stared at Tom and then at Betsy, noting the fear that glittered in the depths of her eyes. He shook his head. "No, Tom, I'm going alone. This is my fight—my job. It's what I'm being paid to do. You've got Betsy and the baby to think about."

Tom's face reddened in anger. "You've got Margaret and a baby to think of, too. My God, you'll all be killed if you go it alone."

"I'm goin'," Wooley stated, as if the matter were closed, spitting a stream of tobacco juice into the spittoon. "I already told the marshal I was."

"Neither one of you is going and that's final," Chase reiterated, staring over Wooley and Tom's head to face Doc, Henry Pursall, and the rest who had gathered. "Nor any of the rest of you. Now get back to your business and let me take care of mine. I know what I'm doing."

His speech was greeted with a chorus of protests until Doc held up his hands for silence. "The marshal's right. We're all well-meaning individuals, but we've got no experience when it comes to hunting outlaws. We'd just be in the way."

Several of the men nodded, and the rest, recognizing

the wisdom of Doc's words, began to file out until all that was left was Doc, the Frasers, and Wooley.

"You may be right about the others, Doc, but Wooley and I have the experience," Tom argued. "We should be allowed to go."

Doc puffed thoughtfully on his pipe, then said, "Margaret's been like a daughter to me. No one wants her brought back safely more than I do; that's why I'm siding with Chase. He's got the most to lose—the best reasons to succeed, which is why he will."

Betsy had been silent up until now, but noting the stubborn set of her husband's jaw and realizing the truth of Doc's words, she grabbed on to Tom's arm. "I know this is going to sound selfish, Tom, but I'd never be able to go on if I lost both you and Margaret. Please let Chase do what he thinks is best." She stared at him imploringly. "I think the wisest thing the rest of us can do is pray that they both return home safely."

Tom sighed, rubbing the back of his neck. "I don't like it."

"You don't have to like it, Fraser, only go along with it," Chase said. "Give me three days. If I'm not back in three days' time, you and Wooley can form a posse and follow. Fair?" He stared at the two men, waiting for their response, and was relieved when both men nodded their consent.

"Good. Now get out of here and let me finish packing." He grabbed two holsters of cartridges and crisscrossed them over his chest. Grabbing his carbine, he headed toward the door.

"Be careful, Chase," Betsy said, clutching his arm. "Jonathan Parker is a madman."

Chase smiled sinisterly. His eyes, as silver and hard as the bullets he wore across his chest, were filled with determination.

"The Silver-Eyed Devil," Wooley whispered, not realizing he had spoken his thought aloud until he heard Chase's chuckle.

"That's right, Wooley. And I'm going to send Parker straight to hell."

Chapter Twenty-Eight

The rain had begun to fall shortly after Chase departed, making the going slow and Parker's trail difficult to follow. He had ridden hard during the night, stopping only once to give Lucifer a rest and to put on the oiled cloth poncho that shielded him from the dampness.

Now, gazing up at the sky, which was beginning to clear, he could see that there would be no need for the poncho today. The sun would be out and it would be hotter than Hades in no time. He pulled Lucifer to a halt and dismounted. Removing the outer garment, he rerolled it, strapping it onto the back of his saddle.

With his horse in tow, he walked on foot, searching the ground for any sign of tracks. The damp, sandy dirt might aid him in his search, for the horses' hooves would leave a deep impression.

Parker was heading south; the trail he had followed thus far indicated as much. And if he wasn't mistaken, he had a pretty good idea of where the bastard was going.

He observed the Rincon Mountains in the distance and smiled in satisfaction. It wasn't like Parker to be so predictable, but Chase would bet his last dollar that Parker was heading for the Colossal Cave, located southeast of Tucson.

The cave, known locally as the "Hole in the Wall," had been a frequent refuge for outlaws. Chase had worked on a case back in '84 when train robbers, relieving the Southern Pacific of over sixty thousand dollars, had hidden their stolen loot inside the cave. The posse he'd been riding with managed to track the outlaws to Wilcox, shooting three of the four dead on the spot, with the fourth surviving to stand trial.

His knowledge of the cave might just give him the edge he needed to surprise Parker. The slippery bastard wouldn't be expecting him to know about its whereabouts. And, unless he missed his guess, Loomis was probably already there, waiting with food. There would be plenty of water. Over the preceding years seeping water had hollowed out an underground river and tributaries.

Knowing Parker, the man would figure on waiting out the law. Then, once the coast was clear, he would make his escape with the gold intact.

Parker was clever, but not clever enough, Chase thought. This time he had misjudged the opposition and he would die for his mistake.

Several hours later, Chase reined in his horse at the base of the mountain and dismounted. Surveying the massive rock formation before him, he sighed, wiping his sweat-stained forehead with the back of his hand. It would be tough going on horseback. The treacherous trail was steep and slippery; it would be easier to traverse on foot, he decided, leading Lucifer behind him.

The trail climbed vertically, winding around the mountain like a corkscrew. Picking his way carefully over loose rocks and gravel, he inched his way up the incline.

Two hours later, after he had gone what he judged to be halfway, he stopped and removed his canteen from the saddle. Pouring a small amount of water into his cupped hand, he gave the horse a drink, then took a swallow himself. He was about to replace the canteen when a bright flash of color caught his eye. It came from behind a large granite boulder up ahead.

He withdrew his gun and silently approached, pulling up short at the sight of Sandy Loomis sprawled on his back, his gun still holstered, dead from a bullet wound to the head. Parker's trademark, he thought, shaking his head.

Worried that Margaret would face a similar fate if he didn't reach her soon, he left Loomis to the vultures and proceeded the rest of the way up the mountain.

Margaret shivered, rubbing her arms to warm herself against the dampness of the cave. They'd finally stopped to rest after traversing miles of twisting passageways and crystal-walled chambers. She was tired, hungry, and dirty. Her skirt was ripped in several places from the arduous climb they had made on foot, and she wasn't sure how much longer she could keep up the brave facade she had assumed.

Sandy Loomis's death had almost been her undoing. Though she hated Loomis for what he had done to Lupe, and for the part he had played in her father's scheme, he was just a dupe like the rest of them. He'd been used, then discarded, and she knew that her turn was coming.

"Get up, Margaret. We've got a little farther to go," her father ordered. He had just returned from surveying the next tunnel and apparently, from the pleased expression on his face, he liked what he saw.

"I thought you said we could rest awhile. I'm tired. I'm not used to all this physical activity." That part was true enough, though she really wanted to stall for time in the slim hope that Chase was following. She knew Chase's determination to see Jonathan Parker dead. And even if he didn't return for her, he would come to kill her father.

Parker snickered. "You're as easy to read as a newspaper, my dear. Your hope that Gallagher will come for you is clearly written for all to see. How touching." He shrugged. "I hope he does. That'll make my job of finding him that much easier. I've no intention of living the rest of my life looking over my shoulder like I've done for the past eighteen years."

Concern for Chase's life gnawed at her composure; she bit the inside of her cheek, balling her hands into fists, digging her nails into her palms, struggling to get herself under control. When she did, she lifted her chin, swallowed hard and boldly met his gaze, saying, "He won't come. You've fixed it so he wouldn't. What man would want a wife who had betrayed him?" It was a question she had asked herself over and over again on the journey here. And the answer she'd come up with

362

had always been the same: none.

Picking up the sacks of gold, Parker tossed them over his shoulder. "He might not come for you, my dear, but he'll come for me. I've not a doubt in my mind." He smiled confidently.

She rose to her feet, easing the tiredness out of her back with the palms of her hands. "Why did you kill his parents? His fiancée? Couldn't you have just stolen the money and let them be?"

He stared at her as if she'd lost her senses. "And leave them to identify me? You're such an innocent, child. I never leave loose ends. Gallagher is the only mistake that I've made in my illustrious career. But I soon aim to rectify that."

Following her father's lead, Margaret trailed behind, wondering what her father intended to do about the loose end he had just created: her. She shuddered at the thought of what he had done to her mother and Loomis. Was she to end up dead, just like the others?

And what of her baby? Tears clouded her eyes but she blinked them away. Perhaps if she told him . . . No! she told herself. She wouldn't give him another tool to use against Chase. If her father knew of the baby, he would use it to his advantage. And Chase. Thank God he didn't know. If he did, he might act with caution, not striking at the most advantageous time. No! It was best that neither of them knew.

As Chase approached the entrance to the cave, he halted, tying Lucifer to a creosote bush. "Wait here, boy; I'll be back soon," he instructed, rubbing the

363

horse's nose affectionately.

Peering into the dimly lit cave, a strong feeling of panic overwhelmed him. It was dark; he had only one candle. And where it was dark, there were spiders. He didn't doubt for a moment that the place was infested with scorpions. They were nocturnal creatures that loved dark places. And the damn things were as venomous and aggressive as rattlesnakes!

His forehead broke out in a sweat. He swallowed, edging his way inside. The dank, musty smell immediately assaulted his senses. His skin prickled; he rubbed vigorously at his arms and neck, trying to dispel the itchy feeling he always had at times like these.

Think of Margaret, he told himself, as he made his way deeper into the tunnel. Suddenly, something scurried across his boot; he jumped back and swallowed. Then he heard the squeaking noise and knew it was a rat. He breathed a sigh of relief. Rats were far preferable to spiders; rats, he could deal with.

He continued on for several more hours, ignoring the spiders that frequented the interior, ignoring the hunger that gnawed at his belly, ignoring the fear that tore through his gut each time he thought of Maggie being held captive by her lunatic father. He pushed himself; and with each step he took, he swore his revenge.

The candle had burned down halfway. If it went out before he could find them, he wasn't sure what he would do. There was no way he could search without light. There were too many passageways—too many places for Parker to hide. As it was, the candle wasn't very helpful in following their tracks, but it was all he had. He kept on.

Margaret and her father had finally reached their destination, and from what Margaret could ascertain, the plans for their arrival had been assiduously put into place long before their arrival.

The cave had widened out, creating a walled camp of sorts. Two narrow pallets were spread out on the dirt floor, most likely for her father and Loomis, she thought, her arrival being unexpected. There was a kerosene lantern, utensils for cooking, and a pot of coffee brewing. It seemed as if her father had thought of everything.

"All the comforts of home, heh, Margaret," Jonathan Parker said, pouring himself a cup of coffee. "One thing about Loomis, he knew how to make a decent cup of coffee."

Margaret swallowed her revulsion. "Too bad his efforts were rewarded so treacherously."

Parker chuckled. "All's well that ends well, I always say. Loomis is dead; we're alive, and we've got a fortune in gold to see us through."

Her eyes widened. "You plan to take me with you?" There was a note of incredulity in her voice.

"But, of course! I've decided that you will be a great comfort to me in my declining years. Every father wants his family close to his bosom."

"You're mad!" She could see her comment angered him, but she continued anyway. "I would never go with you. I hate you . . . despise you. I thought I had made that perfectly clear."

Seating himself on the cold ground, Parker leaned back against the wall of the cave, fingering the flour sack at his feet. Opening it, he fondled the coins like a lover would stroke his lady, rapture shining on his face as bright as the gold. When he spoke, his anger of moments ago was gone.

"You have little choice, my dear. You can either come with me and live in the lap of luxury, or I can leave you here for the rats to feast on. It matters little to me; it's your choice. But if I were you, I'd think carefully, Margaret. Life is life, no matter where you live it . . . and death is so final."

"How long do you intend to stay in this rat-infested hovel you've brought me to? Is this the kind of life I can look forward to? Hiding in caves? Running from the law?" She didn't have any intention of going with him, but he didn't need to know that.

He smiled smugly. "So, you're giving some thought to coming with me, heh? Smart girl. I always knew you were a survivor."

"You've given me little choice in the matter. I don't want to die."

Suddenly, the smug smile disappeared and his expression grew serious. "We could do all right together, you and I. I'm not such a bad sort, once you get to know me. After all, I'm still your father. No matter what else has happened, nothing can ever alter that fact. And you used to harbor a deep affection for me," he reminded her.

Searching her father's face, she could see the sincerity there. He believed what he told her. But then, he was mad. She had seen the madness in his eyes when he'd killed Sandy Loomis. She had felt his insanity when he spoke of her mother's death and how he had actually done her a favor.

She shook her head. Poor Mama. She probably was better off dead than living with a lunatic such as her father had become. Tears filled her eyes for the man that used to be. If she closed them, she could still imagine the kind, gentle face of the father she had loved. But when she opened them and gazed upon the man before her, she knew that man was dead.

"The affection I once felt for you died the moment you pulled the trigger and killed my mother. For that, I will never forgive you."

"Tsk, tsk, Margaret, such disrespect coming from my own daughter. What's a father to do?"

She didn't dignify the question with a response, but approached the pallet, lying down on top of it. She would sleep—rest her mind, her body—and when she awoke, perhaps she would find that this had all been a bad dream, a nightmare. If only it were true, she thought. If only it were true.

Margaret didn't know how long she had been sleeping, but when she awakened, she could see, by the lantern that had been left burning, that her father slept soundly beside her. The gun he wore was still strapped on his hip, and she wondered if she would be able to retrieve it without waking him.

Deciding that she had to try, though the effort might cost her her life, she pushed herself to her knees. Leaning over his inert form, she held her breath, letting her fingers inch toward the handle of the gun. She let out a scream when his hand came up to grab her wrist in a viselike grip.

"I wouldn't do that if I were you."

She swallowed at the burning hatred she saw in his eyes and lunged for the gun with her other hand, attempting to pull it free.

"You little bitch!" he yelled, slapping her across the face with such force she was propelled backward. "You're just like your mother and you're going to end up as dead." He pulled the gun from his holster, aiming it at her head.

When Margaret heard the gun click, she screamed again.

Chase heard Margaret's scream and rushed toward it, fear knotting his belly with every step he took. Arriving to find Parker holding a gun against her head, an intense rage overwhelmed him, filling him with deadly determination.

"Drop it, Parker, or you're a dead man."

Margaret looked up, tears of relief rushing to her eyes. "Chase!" She knew he would come; deep, down in her heart she knew.

"Gallagher!" The older man's eyes widened, admiration evident in their depths as he turned to face his opponent. "So we finally meet."

"Drop the gun," Chase repeated, his voice as deadly as his weapon.

Parker smiled. "It seems we're at an impasse. You could kill me. But then, I could very easily pull this trigger and kill your wife."

Margaret gasped, looking from her father to Chase, whose face was perfectly impassive, telling her nothing.

"I didn't come for Margaret, I came for you, Parker. And if you think I'm bluffing, go ahead and pull the trigger. I owe you big, Parker. Nothing you can do or say is going to change my mind."

Chase's words pricked Margaret's flesh like a thousand needles. If he had taken a knife and stabbed it into her heart, she wouldn't have suffered any less. He hadn't come for her; he didn't want her. But how could she blame him? She had deceived him—chosen her father over him.

Chase's eyes were glacial and filled with confidence when she looked into them, in direct contrast to her father's, which were filled with indecisiveness.

"How do I know what you're telling me is the truth?" Parker asked. "After all, you married her."

Chase's laugh was cynical. "To get to you, Parker. Margaret knows that, don't you, Maggie?" He leveled his gaze on her, keeping the gun pointed at Parker's back.

"Chase is telling the truth. He only married me for revenge. He doesn't love me." Her voice was filled with resignation when she spoke.

Margaret's words stabbed into his gut like a double-edged blade, but Chase couldn't dispute what she said—what she believed. Her life was at stake, and he would say whatever he had to, to save it.

Slowly, Parker's arm came down and he lowered the gun, dropping it to the floor. "You win, Gallagher. But let me remind you that you're a United States marshal whose duty it is to uphold the law. You can't murder me in cold blood. You have to take me back to stand trial."

Chase instructed Margaret to pick up the gun and bring it over to him. Once she had done so and was safely standing behind him, he smiled sinisterly at

Parker, removing the silver badge from his chest and tossing it at Parker's feet.

"I resign, Parker. Now that I'm no longer empowered to uphold the law, I don't see anything standing in my way of filling you full of lead."

Parker's face paled, beads of perspiration dotted his upper lip and brow.

"Please, Chase," Margaret implored, coming to stand beside him. "Don't kill him. He's not worth it. Let him rot in prison; that'll be a worse punishment for someone like him."

"Still defending him, Maggie? I thought by now you'd see him for what he is?"

"I do see him for what he is. He murdered my mother in cold blood and Sandy Loomis, too. But I don't want his blood on your hands. That would make you no better than him."

Parker saw the hesitation on Chase's face and made the most of it. Lunging forward, he tackled Chase about the waist, catching him off guard, knocking the gun from his hands. He reached for the other gun that Chase had secured in the waistband of his trousers and felt a moment of elation when his fingers touched the cold metal.

Seeing what her father was about, Margaret screamed, "No!" Looking frantically about for some sort of weapon, she spotted a large rock near the campfire and grabbed it. With as much strength as she could muster, she brought it crashing down upon her father's head just as he pulled the trigger. The bullet glanced harmlessly off the wall of the cave, and Jonathan Parker slumped into a lifeless heap upon the ground.

Staring at her father's body, the blood that oozed from his scalp, Margaret's eyes filled with tears. "Is he dead?"

Chase pushed himself to his feet, dusting off his breeches. Hunkering down next to Parker, he felt for the pulse at the base of his throat. It still throbbed. Figures, he thought, the bastard had nine lives. "He's alive."

"Oh, thank God. I don't think I could have lived with myself if I had killed him. I thought I wanted him dead, but I realize now that it would have served no purpose."

Chase stared at her in disbelief. "No purpose? The bastard would have killed us both. I should have shot him when I had the chance. Maybe I should do it now and get it over with." He bent over to pick up his gun.

"Please, Chase," Margaret pleaded, grabbing onto his arm. "There's been so much killing, so much bloodshed. Please, don't add to it."

His eyes traveled over her tear-ravaged face and his gut twitched. She'd been through hell and survived. "All right," he agreed, grudgingly. "We'll bring him back to Tucson to stand trial—I wouldn't trust myself if he were locked up in my jail—and then, you and I are going to get a few things straightened out."

Chapter Twenty-Nine

Rocking back and forth on the front porch swing, Margaret stared out into space, seeing nothing, but thinking volumes about what the last week had wrought.

Their return to Purgatory had been met with joyous celebration. The town had turned out to welcome them upon their arrival, as if they were heroes returning from the war.

Jonathan Parker had been deposited with the sheriff in Tucson. She never thought of him as her father anymore; he was just Jonathan Parker, the outlaw to her now. Her mother had been buried in the town cemetery. Mr. Pettigrew had waited for her return before committing Phoebe Parker's body to the ground. It had taken every ounce of Margaret's strength to attend the brief ceremony, for she had no wish to honor her mother, feeling that both her parents had betrayed her in life and there was no need to honor them in death.

She had shrouded herself in bitterness and grief,

allowing no one to get close to her, especially Chase, though he had tried. They'd had a bitter confrontation upon their return. His idea of "straightening things out" had been to demand that she become his wife once again and forget "all her nonsense" about his loving her out of revenge. Her thoughts rolled back to the night of their arrival.

Chase had brought her home, dropping his saddle-bags and bedroll by the door, as if the matter of his living in her house had all but been settled by his rescue of her. She had looked at him as if he were out of his mind and had said things that now, she wished she hadn't.

"What do you think you're doing? You can't stay here. What would people think?" she had told him.

"Not stay here? Are you addled? I'm your husband. It's my right to stay here. I've let you have your own way up until now, Maggie, but I'm enforcing my marital rights."

"You've got no rights. You lost them when you married me for revenge."

"Are you still singing that old tune? I told you, I love you. I married you because I love you."

She shook her head. "I heard what you told my father back in the cave. I'm not stupid, Chase."

He grabbed onto her shoulders then, shaking her as if she were a rag doll. "I said what I had to, to save your life, you fool. Are you so filled with doubt and self-pity that you can't see clearly?"

"Well, you saved it, and I thank you. Now, I'll thank you to leave. We're through . . . finished. There's nothing else between us."

"If you think that, then you really are addled.

Aren't you forgetting that there's something very much between us?" He placed his hand gently on her abdomen. "That baby you're carrying is mine."

Accusation filled her eyes. "So you know? I thought as much. It's the only reason you want me. Why don't you admit it."

"I've heard-tell that women who are pregnant sometimes lose their wits, but I never thought it would happen to you."

"Get out! And don't come back. I never want to see you again." The wounded look on his face had hurt her as deeply as she had hurt him.

"I'll go and give you time to get these crazy notions out of your head. But don't wait too long, darlin'. I'm not a patient man, as I've told you once before."

Thinking of Chase's angry departure brought tears to her eyes. He had told her that he loved her, wanted her to be his wife. But she knew differently. He had made his feelings clear in the cave and no amount of denial could alter those facts. Besides, she thought sadly, he was only being nice because of the baby. No one wanted her for herself. Her father, whom she loved, had used her cruelly; her mother, whom she devoted most of her life to, had never wanted her; and Chase . . . He only wanted her for revenge.

Absorbed in her self-pity, Margaret didn't hear her caller approach until he cleared his throat.

"Beggin' your pardon, Miss Margaret, but I was wonderin' if we could talk."

Wooley stood before her, hat in hand, his hair slicked back, his beard neatly groomed, as if he were paying her court. She smiled. "Sit down, Wooley. Would you care for something to drink? Some iced tea perhaps?"

"No ma'am, but thanks anyway. I won't be takin' up much of your time. I just had a few things to get off of my chest. Things that have been wearin' on me."

Margaret's eyes widened. In all the years she had known Wooley Burnett, he had never come to her for counsel. Something terrible must have happened between him and Concita for him to seek out her advice. Leaning over, she patted his arm. "I'll do whatever I can to help. You know that, Wooley."

The old man blushed. "'Taint about me that I've come, Miss Margaret. It's Chase." He saw her stiffen and swallowed. "He's in a bad way, Miss Margaret. He's been drinking himself silly every night. He don't sleep; he don't eat." Wooley shook his head. "I don't mind telling you, I fear for his health."

Heaving a sigh, Margaret replied, "I'm sure the marshal will get over whatever is bothering him, Wooley. It's kind of you to care, but sometimes folks just need time to sort things out."

"Is that what you're doing? Sorting things out? 'Cause if it is, I sure wish you'd hurry it up. The marshal loves you, Miss Margaret. He mopes around like a lovesick animal. It ain't right you causin' him this much misery. Not after all he done for you."

A guilty blush stole over her cheeks. "I've already told Chase how grateful I am that he saved my life and spared my father's. What more does he want?"

"He wants you, Miss Margaret. He wants to see you."

She shook her head. "That's not possible."

"But it's been near a week since you've been back, and you haven't even allowed him to visit. He says every time he comes to the house, you pretend you aren't home. That ain't right, Miss Margaret."

"It might not be right, but that's the way it's got to be. I've suffered a great loss; I need time to come to grips with things."

Wooley stood, scratching his beard thoughtfully. "'Pears to me that you might come to grips but lose the most important thing to hang onto."

Before Margaret had a chance to reply, a familiar female voice called out to her from the road. "Yoohoo! Margaret!"

Margaret stared in dismay as Betsy pushed open the gate. Good Lord! How much more chastisement could she take in one day? She wasn't foolish enough to think Betsy was paying a social call.

"I'll be takin' my leave now, Miss Margaret," Wooley stated, stepping down off the porch.

"Thank you for coming, Wooley. You're a good friend to both Chase and me."

He didn't reply, but when he was shoulder to shoulder with Betsy Fraser on the walk, he shook his head and whispered, "Hope you have more luck than I did. That woman's stubborner than a jackass crossin' a river. And that's a fact."

Betsy smiled, patting the older man's arm. "I'll do my best."

"See that you do. Marshal's been making my life miserable. I'm at my wit's end." He stalked off.

Approaching the porch, Betsy took in Margaret's gaunt appearance—her wan complexion—and was filled with renewed determination. Wooley was right. Margaret was stubborn, but so was she. This visit was going to prove very interesting.

"Good morning, Margaret. I thought I'd drop by

and see how you were faring. You haven't been by the store lately."

"I've been busy. You know . . . canning . . . gardening."

"Hasn't Lupe been by to help?"

"I'm afraid Lupe's given notice. She's taken a job out at the Bar H; she's working in the cookhouse."

Betsy smiled knowingly. "I've seen her a time or two with Charlie, the foreman of the Bar H. It looks as if she's recovered from her infatuation with that Loomis character."

"Yes. We had a long talk, and Lupe confided that she was relieved their affair was over with. Apparently, Mr. Loomis was possessive, and, as we know, prone to violence. He hit her a few times."

Betsy gasped, saying, "No!" Then, "But why did she quit? Was it because of Chase?" She searched Margaret's face and saw the color that crept into it.

"I hardly think that would matter now. He doesn't live here anymore. Remember?"

"Which is precisely the reason I'm here."

Margaret sighed, holding up her hand. "Please, don't lecture me, Betsy. Wooley has already done that."

"I'm not going to lecture you, Margaret, merely fill you in on some facts. The first being that Chase is madly in love with you, and you're just too blind to see it."

"Betsy," Margaret cautioned.

"The second is that Laurette Appleton has been sniffing around the jail the last few days. She's heard about the trouble between you and Chase, and she's not wasting a moment to try and lure him away from you."

377

The thought of Laurette Appleton and Chase together brought a stab of pain to her breast. *"Men have their needs, Margarita. If they don't find what they're looking for at home, they go elsewhere."* Lupe's words flooded back to drown her composure.

"I can see by your expression that news of Laurette Appleton's intentions have made an impression."

"I won't deny that I love Chase. But it's over between us. Don't you see? I betrayed his love, just as he betrayed mine. It would never work."

Pushing herself to her feet, Betsy shook her head. "My mama always says if you want something bad enough, go after it. Seems like good advice to me."

Long after her friend had departed and the sun was beginning to melt into the horizon, Margaret still sat on the porch swing, digesting everything Wooley and Betsy had told her. But it wasn't until the next day that she made up her mind to do something about it.

Margaret looked up as the kitchen door banged open, surprise then apprehension lighting her features at the sight of Chase strolling casually into the room. He was dressed much the same as the first time she had seen him. His coal black coat hugged his broad shoulders, the black vest accentuating his muscular chest. A lump formed in her throat, making it difficult to swallow.

"Good morning, Maggie," he said. He didn't toss his hat onto the chair as was his usual habit, but merely clutched it in his hands, staring gravely at her.

"Hello, Chase. What brings you here?" Her heart beat wildly in her breast. She hadn't been this close to him in days. The scent of bay rum tickled her senses; her palms began to sweat.

"I've come to say good-bye."

Her mouth dropped open, and her eyes widened in disbelief. "Good-bye?" she repeated stupidly, barely above a whisper.

"I've resigned my position here as United States marshal. I'm leaving as soon as I get my gear together."

"But why?" Her cheeks colored at his irate expression. "I mean, I thought you liked being marshal."

"It's time for me to move on, darlin'. There's nothing here for me now. I just wanted to come by and say good-bye—wish you well. I've asked Doc to write and let me know when the baby comes. I'd like to send money from time to time."

She swallowed the lump in her throat, nodding mutely.

"Well, I've come to say what I had to say, so I guess I'll be leaving. It's been . . ." He searched for the right words to say, then smiled. ". . . a pleasure, darlin'. Take care." Leaning over, he placed a chaste kiss on her cheek and spun on his heel, walking out the door.

Stunned, Margaret slumped into the kitchen chair. Chase was leaving. She'd never see him again. Tears filled her eyes and began to pour forth like an undamned river. Soon her handkerchief was soaked. She knelt her head on the table, sobbing piteously into her arms. Chase was leaving. . . . Chase was leaving. . . . The words became litany, pounding through her head, over and over, over and over, until she couldn't stand it anymore.

"No!" she screamed, pushing herself out of the chair. He couldn't leave; she loved him. She had to tell him.

Grabbing her shawl off the rack by the door, she gave the briefest of glances to Evelyn, who was nestled snugly in her bed with her new litter of piglets. "I'll be back," she promised the musk hog.

As if the wind were at her heels, she fairly flew across the street, heading in the direction of the hotel. When she reached it, she was relieved to see that Chase's horse was still tied to the hitching post out front. He hadn't left yet.

Ignoring the shocked expression on Bert Hobson's face as he stared at her from behind the counter, she brushed past, heading for the stairs. She ground to a halt when she realized that she had no idea which room Chase occupied and retraced her steps.

"Good morning, Mr. Hobson. If you'd be so kind, I'd like to know the room number of Marshal Gallagher."

The bald man's pate flushed red. "He's leaving, Margaret. He's already settled his account."

She held out her hand. "The number please and the extra room key."

His Adam's apple bobbed nervously. "But, Margaret, he's not alone. He's got a visitor."

Pure, unadulterated jealousy poured through Margaret's veins. She said nothing, but continued holding out her hand expectantly.

Knowing a determined woman when he saw one, Bert reached behind him and pulled a brass key from the box marked number six. "Here you go."

She muttered her thanks, and as quickly as her feet would carry her, climbed the stairs to the second floor. Once there, she paused to ascertain which room was number six. She'd never had an occasion to visit the second floor before, though she distinctly remembered that the whore Lillie Mae certainly had.

More determined than ever, she marched to the door and inserted the key into the lock. The sight that greeted her eyes when she threw open the door made her blood boil: Lillie Mae was draped around Chase's neck like a tie; she was pressing her painted lips to his, and he didn't look like he minded in the least.

"Get out," she ordered the startled woman. "Get out this instant or I will tear every one of those dyed hairs out of your head."

Lillie Mae's face whitened as she stared from Margaret, back to Chase, then back to Margaret again. "Who are you?"

"I'm Mrs. Gallagher, the marshal's wife."

The whore's mouth rounded, as did her eyes.

Chase's expression was almost as surprised. When he'd finally recovered enough to speak, he said, "You'd best leave, Lillie Mae. Thanks for coming by to say good-bye." He escorted the garishly dressed woman to the door, then turned hard gray eyes on Margaret. "What the hell do you think you're doing coming in here like that? It's a bit late to play the outraged wife, don't you think?"

Undaunted by Chase's anger, Margaret strolled casually to the bed, noting the half-packed saddlebags. She frowned. "Mr. Hobson said that you've already settled your account."

His eyebrow arched. "So? I told you I was leaving. Why does that surprise you?"

She fingered the folds of her skirt nervously. "I . . . I . . . I don't want you to leave."

"What?" He ran impatient fingers through his hair.

"Maggie, you've made it perfectly clear on more than one occasion that my presence in your life isn't wanted. What are you saying?"

"I'm saying that I love you—that I don't want you to leave."

Chase's chest tightened. He took a deep breath to stem the erratic beating of his heart. "Just like that? You don't want me to leave, so I should change all my plans?" He shook his head. "Uh, uh, darlin'. Your moods and whims are as variable as the weather. What if you should decide a week from now, a month from now, that you no longer want me around? I'm sorry, Maggie. I've made up my mind. I'm leaving."

"I deserve your anger, maybe even your hatred, for what I've put you through, but please don't punish me any longer, Chase." Her eyes filled with tears. "I love you. I don't want to live without you."

He fought the urge to take her in his arms. She had hurt him once already; he couldn't let her tear him apart again. "I'm sorry, darlin'. I love you, too, but I can't stay."

Spotting Chase's revolver by the side of the bed, she rushed over to it and picked it up, leveling it at his chest. "You're not leaving! Do you hear me, Chase Gallagher? I don't care what I have to do to keep you here, but I'm not letting you walk out that door."

Chase grinned, folding his arms over his chest. Standing there holding his gun, Margaret reminded him of an untamed she-cat. Her hair had come loose from her bun, flowing about her shoulders like a wild mane. And she definitely had claws. Her confrontation with Lillie Mae proved that. "Just how do you propose to keep me here?" he asked.

She waved the gun at him in a threatening gesture, but all she got for a response was a loud guffaw that made her bristle. "Start taking off your clothes. And be quick about it. I don't like to be kept waiting."

"And if I don't?"

She lowered the gun, pointing it at his crotch. "Then I guess I'll just have to shoot. If you're not going to make love to me, then you sure as hell aren't going to do it with anyone else."

"I've never been forced to strip at gunpoint before."

She smiled. "I guess there's a first time for everything."

"I guess there is," he agreed, removing his jacket.

When he had taken off his vest, shirt and tie, she said, "Now the pants."

A moment later, he was standing stark naked before her. She drew a deep breath at the wondrous sight. His male member jutted forth stiff and proud, ready and waiting for her command. "Now lie down on the bed."

His right eyebrow cocked at a sharp angle. "Are you meaning to rape me?"

Licking her lips, she transferred the gun to her left hand, and with her right, nimbly began undoing the buttons of her dress. "I doubt seriously if one could call it rape. After all—" she stared meaningfully at his member—"it's not as if you aren't interested."

Resting his head back against the headboard, Chase watched intently as Margaret stripped out of the remaining pieces of her clothing. She had set the gun down, though it wouldn't have been necessary for her to use force; he had no intention of resisting.

Completely naked, she stood before him proudly, allowing him to feast his eyes on the banquet that awaited him. Her breasts were fuller, making his fingers itch with want of her; her slightly rounded stomach proclaimed his child—their child—growing within her. He had never beheld such a beautiful sight and it awed him. Holding out his hand, his voice thick with emotion, he said, "Come to me. Make love with me. Be my wife."

Margaret's eyes lit with happiness. Rushing to the bed, she threw herself on top of Chase's naked body. "I love you, Chase. I love you with all my heart." She showered kisses over his face.

His grin was wicked as he patted her behind. "Darlin', as much as I want you to love me with all your heart, right now, I need you to love me with some of the other, more accessible, parts of your anatomy."

She smiled seductively, and then she did.